PRAISE FOR LIZ TALLEY

"Talley packs her latest southern romantic drama with a satisfying plot and appealing characters . . . The prose is powerful in its understatedness, adding to the appeal of this alluring story."

—*Publishers Weekly*

"Relevant and moving . . . Talley does an excellent job of making her flawed characters vastly more gray than black and white . . . which creates a story of unrequited loves, redeemed."

—*Library Journal*

"Talley masters making the reader feel hopeful in this second-chance romance . . . You have to read this slow-burning, heart-twisting story yourself."

—*USA Today*

"This author blends the past and present effortlessly, while incorporating heartbreaking emotions guaranteed to make you ugly cry. Highly recommended."

—*Harlequin Junkie*

"Liz Talley has written a love story between a mother and daughter that captured me completely. By turns tender and astringent, sexy and funny, heart wrenching and uplifting, *Room to Breathe* is an escapist and winning story that will carry you away with an imperfect pair of protagonists who just might remind you of someone you know. A delight."

—Barbara O'Neal, author of *When We Believed in Mermaids*

"There is no pleasure more fulfilling than not being able to turn off the light until you've read one more page, one more chapter, one more large hunk of an addictive novel. Liz Talley delivers. Her dialogue is crisp and smart, her characters are vivid and real, her stories are unputdownable. I discovered her with the book *The Sweetest September* when, in the very first pages, I was asking myself, How's she going to get out of this one? And of course I was sleep deprived finding out. Her latest, *Come Home to Me*, which I was privileged to read in advance, is another triumph, a story of a woman's hard-won victory over a past trauma, of love, of forgiveness, of becoming whole. Laughter and tears spring from the pages—this book should be in every beach bag this summer."

—Robyn Carr, *New York Times* bestselling author

"Liz Talley's characters stay with the reader long after the last page is turned. Complex, emotional stories written in a warm, intelligent voice, her books will warm readers' hearts."

—Kristan Higgins, *New York Times* bestselling author

"Every book by Liz Talley promises heart, heat, and hope, plus a gloriously happy ever after—and she delivers."

—Mariah Stewart, *New York Times* and *USA Today* bestselling author

"Count on Liz Talley's smart, authentic storytelling to wrap you in southern comfort while she tugs at your heart."

—Jamie Beck, author of *If You Must Know*

THE
WEDDING
WAR

OTHER TITLES BY LIZ TALLEY

Bayou Bridge

Waters Run Deep

Under the Autumn Sky

The Road to Bayou Bridge

Oak Stand

Vegas Two-Step

The Way to Texas

A Little Texas

A Taste of Texas

A Touch of Scarlet

Novellas and Anthologies

The Nerd Who Loved Me

"Hotter in Atlanta" (short story)

Cowboys for Christmas with Kim Law and Terri Osburn

A Wrong Bed Christmas with Kimberly Van Meter

THE
WEDDING
WAR

Liz Talley

Published by Montlake, Seattle

www.apub.com

Amazon, the Amazon logo, and Montlake are trademarks of Amazon.com, Inc., or its affiliates.

ISBN-13: 9781542009744
ISBN-10: 154200974X

Cover design by David Drummond

Printed in the United States of America

For the friends who have come in all seasons of my life. Whether we are now in touch or not, you each gave a piece of yourself to me and made my life better for it. I'm so grateful for the beauty of friendship.

PROLOGUE

Once upon a time . . . in the summer of 1985

"Code Hot Pink" was the only thing the person on the other end of the phone said before the line went dead.

Tennyson O'Rourke stared at the harvest-gold handset before hanging it back on the cradle. With five O'Rourke kids in the house, she was lucky she was able to get the message at all. Her sister Bronte had been on the phone for hours with her boyfriend, talking about which girls at the high school were cool and which ones were sluts. If Tennyson heard another "gag me," she was going to literally, well, gag.

Code Hot Pink meant one thing—she *had* to rendezvous.

Tennyson pulled on her jellies and tried to get her unruly sandy-blonde hair into a scrunchie. Luckily, she'd already brushed her teeth and done her chores.

"Hey, that's my scrunchie, you little brat," Bronte screeched from the hallway, hands fisted at her sides as she came through the living room, heading for Tennyson. Tennyson yelped, flung open the front door, and took off through their front yard. Bronte stood framed in the doorway, her face a mask of rage. "And stop using my nail polish, cretin."

"Bye, Bronte," Tennyson called back in a singsong voice, knowing she'd have to stay out until their mother got home. Tennyson's mom was getting her classroom ready for the new school year, and the O'Rourke children were on their own until dinnertime.

She sped around to the backyard, jetting through a split in the chain-link fence toward the grassy area cut by a concrete ditch. They weren't supposed to play near the culvert when it had been raining because once a little boy had tried to swim in it, and rushing waters had swept him away. Tennyson's mom had taken a JELL-O salad to his wake, but that was before Tennyson was old enough to remember good. She just remembered her mother crying and the way the green JELL-O had pieces of peach in it.

The culvert separated her very middle-class neighborhood of Broadmoor from her best friend Melanie Brevard's upscale one. Most days the girls got together in their meeting spot—a cooler area beneath the shroud of a willow tree—but their summer days of running wild were about to be curtailed by the dreaded first day of fifth grade.

But that was tomorrow.

Today they had a Code Hot Pink to deal with.

When Tennyson arrived at the meeting place, she found Melanie sitting on the broken lawn chair they'd found on the side of the road. In her lap, she held a cardboard box.

"Hey," Tennyson said, pulling up the other chair they'd redesigned by bending the legs so it was flat to the ground. She plonked into it. "So what's the emergency?"

Melanie looked funny. Like she'd seen something scary. She grudgingly lifted the box she'd been holding like it was a bomb or something. "I thought we'd gotten in the stickers we ordered. I wanted to take them with me tomorrow."

"Don't remind me about tomorrow. I wish you didn't have to go to St. Ignatius. It'll be weird going to school without you. Who will calm me down when I see bees?" Tennyson said, taking the box from Melanie.

She was *so* allergic to bees.

On Tuesday, they would start the fifth grade . . . at different schools. Melanie's parents were making her go to private school because someone had found a condom in the boys' bathroom at Glenbrook Elementary. Tennyson wasn't sure exactly what that was, but she'd overheard her mother telling their neighbor about it, and the way her mother had whispered the word made her think it had something to do with s-e-x.

"I don't want to go to St. Ignatius, either. Penny loafers and blazers are my worst nightmare."

Tennyson turned the box over. "So if this isn't our stickers, what is it? There's no name on it."

"I don't know what it is. I mean, I do, but I don't." Melanie sounded like she wanted to cry. What could be that bad?

Tennyson traced the Brevard address with a finger. Her fingernails were painted carnation pink. She'd "borrowed" the polish from Bronte. Her sister pretty much hated her and had told her repeatedly, "Keep your grubby hands off my shit." Tennyson would have told their mother about Bronte using cuss words, but she knew no one liked a snitch. Melanie was lucky when it came to sisters. Her sister, Hillary, wasn't mean as a snake like Bronte. Sometimes, Hillary played salon with Tennyson and Melanie, doing their nails and hair.

But Bronte was a bitch.

Tennyson opened the flaps of the box, shaking it so the contents fell out into her hand. When she caught what was in the box, she blinked a few times. She rotated the object, taking in every inch, her eyes widening with each second. Then she quickly put it back into the box, closing the flaps emphatically. "Whose *is* this?"

Melanie's lip trembled. "I don't know. What is it? I mean, is it, um, really bad?"

"It's stuff we're not supposed to mess with."

Tennyson knew what it was. Having two older brothers had taught her a lot, and usually she liked knowing things that Melanie didn't. Her best friend was what Tennyson's mother liked to call "sheltered." Melanie didn't get to listen to rock and roll. Her parents made her listen to Bach and Beethoven. She also had to play the violin, which Melanie hated. Tennyson didn't think she would mind playing the violin or the piano. Her grandmother had wanted to buy their family a piano so she and Bronte could learn something useful in life, but Tennyson's mother had said they didn't have room in the house. Not even for an upright.

"What do I do with it?" Melanie asked, looking at the box like it was a snake, then looking up at Tennyson with eyes that pleaded for help.

Thing was, Tennyson wasn't sure what to do with the box. She wasn't going to take it back home with her, that was for sure. There was no privacy at her house. Melanie should probably take it back and put it where she'd found it. Then try to forget about it. Or they could toss the box into the culvert right in front of them. But someone else might find it. And the Brevard's address was on it. "I don't know . . . yet. Let me think."

Melanie set the box away from them.

Usually a Code Hot Pink wasn't so . . . serious. Once, Melanie had burned off her bangs with Hillary's curling iron. Another time, Tennyson had stepped on a nail and had to get a tetanus shot. Oh, and then there was the time Shaun Angelo had found the note they'd passed in math class. But this was . . . serious serious.

"You know what? Let's lie out. I want to get some more sun before we start school. That will give us time to think about what to do with"— Tennyson looked over at the box—"that."

"I guess so," Melanie said. They both flipped their T-shirts up and tucked them through their necklines so they looked like Daisy Duke. Then Melanie carefully rolled up her shorts.

They pulled the chairs out into the sun and sweated in the dry heat for ten minutes, neither saying a thing. Finally, Tennyson pulled her shirt from where she'd tucked it between her nonexistent breasts and sat up. "Did I get any sun on my stomach?"

Melanie squinted. "Um, I think so?"

Tennyson frowned down at her red belly poking out over her cut-off jean shorts. She'd probably made the stupid freckles on her cheeks worse. She hated her complexion and had tried all kinds of ways to get rid of what her daddy called her cute "sprinkles," but nothing worked. Her only chance was God working a miracle, so she whispered a prayer each night along with ten Hail Marys. Her mother had once told her that she had said ten Hail Marys every day when she wanted to have children. It worked, 'cause her mother had had five of them.

Melanie had darker skin because her mother was Japanese and her father had Indian in him. Not the kind from a different country, but the kind that lived here once upon a time in Louisiana. Melanie had straight, brown hair, skin that was smooth and honey brown, and a birthmark on her thigh in the shape of California. Her daddy was a surgeon, and she had her own bedroom with a canopy bed, a bathroom she didn't have to share, and a housekeeper named Martha, who made them peanut butter–banana sandwiches while she watched *As the World Turns* on the television in the kitchen. Yeah, the Brevards had a television in their *kitchen*.

Melanie was lucky she was so rich, but Tennyson's friend didn't even seem to care that she had been blessed with a boom box, two pairs of Tretorns, and a membership at the country club. And tennis lessons. God, Tennyson would die to have tennis lessons just so she could wear one of those cute white skirts.

"So did you figure out what to do?" Melanie asked, casting a glance over at the box.

"Is anyone at your house?"

"Mother invited some students in Hillary's new class over for a 'get to know you' event. She's even letting them order Domino's Pizza. She wants Hilly to be popular and stuff." Melanie flipped her own shirt down. They'd been trying to get tans for the past few weeks so they would look awesome for school. At Tennyson's school, fifth grade was in the new wing with the sixth graders. She didn't want to look like a baby around the sixth-grade boys.

Tennyson's stomach growled at the thought of delivery pizza, but before they snuck a few slices, they had to do something with the box. "Good. That means Martha will be distracted."

"Why?"

"I think we have to see exactly what that is before we decide what to do. It may be no big deal, but . . ." Tennyson looked over at the box, wishing Melanie hadn't brought it to their spot.

"I think we need some magic," Melanie whispered, following Tennyson's line of vision before reaching down and lifting up the cheap silver chain Tennyson had brought back from Silver Dollar City.

Tennyson's pappy and nanny had taken Tennyson and her four siblings to Branson last summer. They'd been gone for only five days, but it had been the best five days of Tennyson's life. They'd eaten hamburgers at a diner counter, taken a tour of stalagmites, and watched some dude blow glass into a vase. She'd strained at the bit to ride the big roller coaster zigging by as they left the saloon where the dancers shook big, ruffled skirts and stole her pappy's ball cap, but after the first exhilarating ride, she'd thrown up on her nanny's new Keds. Nanny had said no more rides for Tennyson, so instead she'd haunted the gift shops looking for the exact right gift to bring back to Louisiana.

She'd found the split-heart best-friends necklaces in the General Store, and now she and Melanie wore them every day.

"Best friends forever," Tennyson said, lifting her own pendant and fitting it with Melanie's.

Melanie sighed like that would fix everything. Her friend was funny. She really believed there was magic between them. That was probably because Tennyson had been able to superglue the Madame Alexander doll together so that Melanie's mom didn't find out they'd broken her. They weren't supposed to play with those dolls because they were collectibles. Not that Tennyson played with dolls anymore.

No duh.

Tennyson wished she had something collectible. Her mother had plates from different states mounted on the wall in their cramped kitchen, but that was it. Melanie's house was not only filled with expensive art but had wall-to-wall carpet and a crystal chandelier in the dining room. Not to mention a game room with an intercom and an Atari console Melanie's dad had bought them against her mother's wishes.

All Tennyson had was a blow-up pool and Scrabble.

Melanie stood up and stared at the bushes around the dusty culvert that contained a Big Gulp cup someone had tossed into the depths. "I don't want summer to be over. I don't want to go to stupid St. Ignatius. I'm scared, Teeny."

"It'll be okay. You can still come hang out with me after school."

Melanie shook her head. "Mother says I'll have to have a tutor because I'm academically behind. I'll never get to see you."

"We can talk on the phone. We can figure anything out." Tennyson slung an arm around her best friend's shoulders and gave her a squeeze.

"Pinkie swear?" Melanie asked, her voice trembly again like she might cry. She lifted and crooked her little finger.

"Pinkie swear," Tennyson said, linking her littlest finger with her friend's. A pinkie swear wasn't a light thing between her and Melanie. When they pinkie swore, it happened.

Melanie picked up the box, her expression still troubled. Tennyson moved beside her, and together they walked toward the worn path that led to Melanie's three-story house. Right as they climbed the incline to the other side, Tennyson looked back. She wasn't sad that summer was over, because she was ready to wear her new Izod polo and the grosgrain ribbon her mother had bought her in lieu of a belt. She was ready for fall . . . she just wished Melanie were going back to Glenbrook with her.

But no big deal. They'd always be friends. Nothing was going to break them apart.

Best friends 4ever.

CHAPTER ONE

Spring 2020

"If Tennyson Whatever Her Name Is Now thinks I'm hosting a gradu-ation party with her, she's lost her mind," Melanie said, folding her son's athletic socks into neat stacks on the matelassé spread covering the king-size bed. The abandoned iPad with the email from her daughter about the "fabulous" grad party had been tossed aside.

Her husband poked his head out of the closet. "She's gone back to O'Rourke. Besides, *we're* not doing the party. Just attending."

Melanie rolled her eyes.

"Come on, Mel, you know we have to play nice. It's for the kids. For Emma."

"I'm not sure anything is worth having to deal with Tennyson," Melanie huffed, looking for the mate to the Under Armour sock that had a hole in the heel. Dang dog. Poppy loved to steal the socks Noah left in the game room and chew on them. She'd asked her son not to leave his dirty socks on the floor, but Noah wasn't good at listening these days. Most everyone around her wasn't good at listening. "And *kids* is the right word. That's exactly what they are. Emma actually said something about how it might make sense for her and Andrew to move in together while she was in med school. *To save money.*"

Kit came out adjusting his tie. "She's not wrong. I don't have a problem with that."

"Them living together?" Melanie looked at him like he'd agreed to a three-way with their seventy-two-year-old oversexed next-door neighbor, Coco Festervan. She knew Coco was probably up for it. There were rumors for good reason.

"Well, it makes sense financially," Kit said, wrapping the navy tie he always wore to make deals around his neck.

Melanie dropped the T-shirt she was about to fold. "You're seriously advocating our *daughter* live with a man before marriage?"

She knew she sounded like a Puritan because times had changed and people lived together all the time, but how in all that was holy was she going to tell her mother that Emma was moving in with her boyfriend? That little nugget would go over like a dog turd in the punch bowl. Anne Fumiyo Brevard, Melanie's mother, was the president of her book club, the secretary of her Bible study, and the chairperson of the South Shreveport Garden Society Tour of the Greens. Which meant she didn't cotton to loose morals even if they saved a person money. There was a right way, and that was Anne's way.

"Hon, Emma's twenty-two years old and about to be twenty-three. She's a grown-up."

Melanie shoved the basket away and set her hands on her hips. "She's not a grown-up. Not if *we* still pay her bills."

A ball of aggravation curled tight in her gut. Kit always took their kids' side, leaving her to be the heavy-handed parent. Ol' Melanie, permanent stick-in-the-mud. He gave the kids too much free rein to do what they thought was best. That was not parenting. That was taking the easy (and more popular) way out.

"Can we shelve this argument? You know I have a big day today. Meeting with Hal is always nerve-racking. That old bastard doesn't let go of the purse strings easily. I need this to go through so I can retire before I'm dead."

"You know that's not true. You could retire today."

He gave her an alligator grin. "My kind of retirement will be expensive."

Melanie sank onto the bed and tried to calm herself. Emma was set to graduate next week from the University of Arkansas, where she'd excelled in her studies (and, if Snapchat was to be believed, keg stands) and now was heading back home to attend medical school at LSU in Shreveport. But while she was in Arkansas, Emma had managed to fall in love with the one person Melanie would have wanted her to steer clear of.

Melanie hadn't realized that Tennyson's son, Andrew Abernathy, had gone to the University of Arkansas—she'd lost track of Tennyson's whereabouts years ago. Of course, U of A was Tennyson's father's alma mater, but the woman had been living on the East Coast. Or so she'd heard. Anyway, it was surprising her son would eschew a plethora of blue-blooded schools to go to Arkansas. Even more surprising was that Emma had sat next to him in microbiology. Two weeks later the two sophomores met at Marley's for pizza. Two weeks after that, Emma took Andrew to Chi Omega's spring semiformal. And then, the two were as inseparable as Melly and Teeny had once been.

When it came to incalculable odds, Melanie would have rather had the bad luck to lose her leg in a shark attack than have her daughter date her mortal enemy's son.

God had a sense of humor.

Obviously.

Melanie hadn't actually seen Tennyson since running into her when Bronte got married fifteen years ago. Even then they'd stared at one another and disappeared to the opposite sides of East Ridge Country Club. This past year, when Kit and Melanie went to parents' weekend, Tennyson went to Saint Croix. When they'd traipsed up to Fayetteville to see the LSU Tigers take on the Hogs, Tennyson had skipped the game and gone skiing in Park City. Tennyson had taken Emma and Andrew to Jackson Hole right after Christmas that past December, and Melanie had seen pictures of her once-upon-a-time best friend, but she hadn't had to actually face her.

But that would change next week when they went to graduation. Emma and Andrew had planned a big party for after the ceremony. Tennyson would be there.

"Wish me luck," Kit said, emerging from the bathroom looking as handsome as ever, even if his eyes were slightly squinty and his hairline a bit thinned. Time had been gracious to Kit Layton, that was for certain. He still turned heads when he entered a room, his blue eyes vibrant against the craggy, tan face, his lean physique commanding, his teeth bright when he flashed a smile.

"You don't need luck," she said, allowing her lips to curve as she slid her gaze over her husband in his best suit. Still such a babe.

"You always say that," he said with a chuckle.

"Because I believe it. You're good at what you do."

Thanks to her father gifting her money and the acreage right off the Red River before he died and Kit's innate talent for developing property into profitable ventures, the company she and Kit had started when they'd first married was flourishing. Early on, Melanie had worked elbow to elbow with her husband to build their property-development company. With her degree in accounting and Kit's marketing acumen, they'd given birth to some of the most successful housing developments in South Shreveport. The venture Kit was currently working on encompassed a development based on their favorite beach-vacation community, harkening back to days of old when neighbors met in a common area and activities promoted tight-knit relationships. Instead of going for the pastels-and-beach vibe, Kit had envisioned something more native to northwest Louisiana, focusing on natural flora and fauna with hints of rustica, like a "farmers' market colliding with an upscale state park."

Right as Kit turned to say something to her, his phone rang. His mouth twitched into something pleasing as he clicked the button. "Hey, Char, I'm about to leave now. You pick up the boards from the printers? They do them right this time?"

Melanie watched as his face reflected his approval at what the other person was saying on the line. Charlotte Mullins was his administrative right-hand woman, who he'd hired last year when his longtime assistant had retired to New Mexico to be closer to her grandchildren. Charlotte was the cousin of one of Melanie's Junior League friends and had moved to Shreveport to start her life over after a bitter divorce. With a degree from Wharton's business school and a desire to not be part of corporate America with its impossible demands on time and energy, Charlotte had agreed to work for Kit part time. That part-time job had morphed into a full-time pseudo partnership, with Kit agreeing to a hefty bonus for her if this deal went through.

Melanie liked Charlotte. Or at least she had at first.

Charlotte was thirty-two with long, dark hair and fit legs that came from daily tennis. Pair that with her crackling energy and sexy Carly Simon vibe, and the younger woman made Melanie feel like two-week-old cheese—once desired but now avoided when rooting in the refrigerator. It didn't help that at times Kit seemed to anticipate Charlotte's company more than he did that of his own wife. Melanie quickly grew tired of hearing about how smart the woman was, how men hit on her when they were out to lunch, and how Char had hiked some mountain in Colorado. Blah, blah, blah.

So she was young, fit, and pretty? Whoop-de-freakin'-do.

"Yeah, Heritage Woods is going to blow their minds. I can't see how Hal wouldn't want a piece of this. You did good, Char. After we seal this deal, we'll have dinner and toast your brilliance."

Melanie turned away from Kit and rolled her eyes so hard she had a moment of dizziness.

Kit pocketed his phone. "That was Char. We're good to go."

"Her name is *Charlotte*," Melanie said, trying not to sound testy but failing. Use the person's given name, for heaven's sake.

Her husband made a frowny face. "I know. Anyway, I'm out of here. I'll call you once I know something. Do you want to join me and Charlotte after the presentation? I'll spring for the good champagne."

"Noah has a baseball game. It's on your calendar."

Kit slid his wallet and keys into his pocket. "Oh, yeah. Of course. I'll try to make the game before it's over."

"I know he'll appreciate seeing you in the stands."

When Noah first started playing his freshman year, he'd been an incredible pitcher with a curve and slider that fooled the batter almost every time, but then he'd injured his shoulder in football the next year and hadn't been able to pitch that spring. So far, his junior year had been rocky with him sitting the bench a lot and not making the travel team. Kit had gone from being involved in the dads' booster club to barely mentioning the sport he'd once thought his son would excel in. Noah had asked to quit the team. Melanie responded with hiring a pitching coach and getting him better physical therapy for his shoulder. She didn't raise quitters. Even if every game now felt like watching an execution—starting with hope, ending in a solemn ride home.

Kit disappeared out the bedroom door, and Melanie picked up the piles of laundry she'd stacked on their bed.

She walked toward her daughter's room, now lifeless since Emma had taken all her favorite things with her when she went to college. Periodic summer and Christmas breaks brought the room back to its former state of disaster, but those times were like a summer storm— quick, brutal, and gone before a mom could blink. She placed the sweater her daughter had left behind on the shelf in her closet and then headed to Noah's room to put away his raggedy socks.

When she opened the door, she registered two things—Noah was still home, and Noah thought the door was locked.

"Mom! Oh my God!" he shrieked, jackknifing up and covering himself with a towel. "You're supposed to knock!"

Melanie ripped her eyes from her son and focused on the baseball print she'd had matted and framed for him last year. "I-I didn't know you were here. I thought you'd left. And why—"

"Get out," he yelled.

"Noah, it's natural—"

"Please, Mom. Please," he pleaded.

Melanie tossed the stack of clean laundry onto his cluttered desk and pretty much ran from the room. She closed the door a bit too loudly and then leaned against it. She heard her son utter a word he was not allowed to use in the house, but she figured after having someone walk in on a masturbation session, she would let his use of the mother of all curse words slide.

Why was he still home? It was eight thirty, and school had started a half hour ago.

Then it hit her. He had an appointment with the optometrist to get fitted for his new contacts. She'd forgotten they'd agreed he would check into school afterward.

"For goodness' sake, lock the door next time," she called through the closed door.

Still a little shaky from what she'd glimpsed, Melanie made her way downstairs, where Poppy met her with a wagging tail and one of the Aquatalia boots she'd just purchased. Poppy looked so pleased with herself as she dropped the mangled suede bootie at Melanie's feet. Her "wanna play" face was in place.

"Poppy, no," Melanie groaned, stooping to pick up the boot she'd just taken from the Nordstrom box last week. She'd had her eye on the boots all winter but refused to pay full price. When they'd gone on sale for 33 percent off, she'd snagged them, knowing they'd be perfect for next fall.

Or not.

She examined the damp boot, noting Poppy had gnawed on the heel. She glanced around and spied the right boot in the center of the living room. Poppy had chewed a big hunk off that one.

"Son of a b," Melanie muttered under her breath, wanting to reach out and smack the good-natured retriever. Poppy was still like an overgrown puppy, given to her kids five Christmases ago only because she could think of no other gifts for them. They'd been thrilled with Poppy—there had been tears and a precious video that went semiviral. Noah and Emma had vowed to walk her and bathe her and love her . . . and that had lasted about a week. After that, Poppy had become yet another one of Melanie's responsibilities. A cute responsibility, but another to-do on her list.

"Bad dog," Melanie said, picking up the boot and making a mean face. "Bad Poppy."

Poppy's happy puppy face disappeared as she hunched down, shamed.

And that made Melanie feel bad because Poppy didn't know her new chew toy was a pair of expensive boots Melanie had yet to wear. And the dog hadn't opened the closet and walked in. No, Kit had left the closet door ajar, giving the dog entrance into the forbidden cavern of a thousand smells. Poppy had already chewed up one of Kit's driving moccasins and a scarf that Kit's mother had given her. No real loss on that one, though. His mother had atrocious taste.

"Let's go outside, Poppy," she said, walking toward the mudroom that led out into their fenced backyard. The dog cheered up and bounced toward the screened porch where her doggy door allowed her entrance into a realm where squirrels begged to be chased and neighboring dogs were prepared to chat . . . loudly.

Melanie walked into the kitchen and frowned at the mess Kit had made at the coffee maker, drips of creamer and rogue sugar crystals. The man had never been much for cleaning up after himself . . . or ensuring he shut the closet door fully, something Melanie had reminded him to do every day for the past month. She reminded people of stuff all the time. *Pick up your shoes. Don't forget to pay your fees. Rinse the toothpaste from the sink. Don't forget your father's birthday.*

And if she forgot, her kids and husband always said, "Why didn't you remind me?"

Like she was in charge of everyone's life and decisions.

She tired of being the person she was. People called on her to be on every committee, saying, "You're so organized, Melanie. You can get so much done." She went from meeting to meeting, chairing this and that. But no one ever asked her to brunch. Or to a girlfriend weekend. Or to go shopping . . . unless it was for supplies for Chatman House or the battered women's shelter.

If she said no more often to committees, she might be invited to drink mimosas at the club. If she stopped being the responsible one, maybe she would be more fun. Spontaneous women wanted fun people to be their "ride or die." She wasn't sure what that meant—she'd seen a meme on Instagram—but it had to be better than doing spreadsheets for the PTSA budget.

Darn it. She wanted to be in someone's squad.

Melanie wiped up the mess at the coffee bar, then set the juice glass and coffee mug in the sink for Louisa. Her housekeeper of fifteen years would be there later that day, likely with some banana bread for Noah because he'd mentioned not having any in a long time. Louisa spoiled Noah more than anyone.

Melanie turned as her son dashed by the kitchen, hooking his backpack with two fingers and heading toward the garage without as much as a glance at her. He was a missile locked on to a target.

"Hey, don't you need breakfast?" she asked.

"I'll get a protein shake," he called, not looking back.

She followed him. "What about your lunch?"

His neck was as pink as her favorite lipstick. "I'm not hungry, Mom."

The garage door rose, and her son stood and waited, his back to her. He wasn't going to face her. His parting words had said as much. She lamely offered, "I'm happy to fix you a sandwich."

He shook his head and ducked under the aluminum garage door sliding up. "Bye."

"You know it's natural, Noah. You have to look at me eventually," she called, clutching her soft cardigan across her breasts as she moved to the edge of the garage.

Noah climbed into his truck, tossing the backpack into the passenger seat. "But not today."

He closed the door and fired up the truck, shifting immediately into reverse. The sound of the dual exhaust he'd had put in with his Christmas money never failed to unnerve her. Sounded like a motorcycle gang. Melanie gave a half wave as Noah backed a bit too recklessly down their driveway.

"Great," she said to herself, catching Coco out of the corner of her eye. The older woman was gardening, wearing shorty shorts, a skimpy tank, and kitten heels. Good Lord.

"Hey, Melanie," Coco called, giving her a wave.

"Morning, Coco," she returned before picking up a magnolia leaf the size of a saucer that had skidded into her garage and depositing it in the trash can. "Have a good day."

Not waiting for a response, Melanie closed the garage just as Poppy started a high-pitched barking frenzy that signaled a threat in the backyard. Likely just a mama cardinal bringing breakfast to its babies in the *Ligustrum* on the corner of the house. Poppy alerted them to all intruders, big or small. As Melanie passed the catchall desk in the mudroom, she heard a ding.

Kit had forgotten his iPad, and he'd be upset because he preferred using it over his laptop when he was on the move.

Melanie craned her neck and saw the text was from Charlotte.

Room 342. Key is at the front desk. Can't wait.

What the—

"Mother. Effer." Melanie picked up the iPad, not exactly repeating the word her son had used earlier but totally thinking the real version in her head.

Was Kit cheating on her with Charlotte?

CHAPTER TWO

Tennyson O'Rourke set the glass of somewhat decent cabernet on the glass-top table beside her and tried not to scream. Another bump sounded from the back of her house. She may be on her third glass of wine, but she wasn't hearing things.

Someone was in the house she'd moved into only a week ago.

More specifically, someone was in her bedroom.

Slowly she reached for the cell phone she'd tucked beneath her thigh and dialed 911, praying that whoever was in her room would stay there long enough for the police to arrive.

Tennyson wasn't ready to die . . . especially looking the way she currently looked.

For one thing, she'd slapped a charcoal mask on her face minutes ago. Then there was too much gray lining the part of her too-shaggy mane. Those hairs of doom would be dealt with the next day. If she managed to live long enough. And finally, she wore an old T-shirt of Andrew's, one she'd tugged on to unpack the rest of the boxes, that was now stained with the red wine she'd spilled when she opened the bottle. Oh, and her lululemon leggings were torn at the knee, thanks to a rogue fence at the park. She was a mess.

Tennyson watched *CSI*. She knew they took crime scene photos that the detectives tacked on the wall and then later passed around to the jury. So she could *not* die looking like this.

Could not.

"911. Where's your emergency?" said a very professional-sounding woman.

"There's someone in my house," she whispered, glancing desperately toward the back of the house.

"Ma'am, you're going to have to speak up. I can't hear you," the 911 operator said.

"I said there's someone in my house," she said in a whisper-yell.

"Someone's in your home?"

"Yes. Send the police. Please."

"Okay, ma'am. Are you calling from a landline or a mobile phone?"

"My cell phone," she said, trying to concentrate on the woman's words. Fear squeezed her so hard she could hardly think.

"Okay, I'm pinging it now. Please confirm the address."

What was the house number? "Uh, I just moved in, but it's on Fairlane Boulevard. I can't remember the number."

"In Briarcliff Estates?"

"That's it."

"Okay, ma'am, I'm sending help. Is there a way you can safely exit the premises?"

"There's a set of French doors off the kitchen, but I'm afraid he will see me." Someone else could be outside in a getaway car. With a gun.

"Okay, ma'am, stay with me. Are you armed?"

Armed? Tennyson darted her gaze around the small sitting area off the kitchen. She didn't own a firearm, and the butcher block with her new knives was still in the box on the kitchen cabinet. What could she use as a weapon? On the table to her right lay the nail file she'd used earlier, her wine, and a copy of *Us Weekly*. The nail file might work. Or she could smash the goblet and use the glass in some way? Or the lamp. She could throw the lamp and try to run. Her eyes landed on the nearly empty bottle of wine.

"Ma'am, are you still there?"

A crash and thump sounded in her bedroom.

"Oh God. I hear him. He's in my bedroom." She pressed a hand to her mouth and thought about what she should do. "Uh, I don't have a weapon. Um, there's a wine bottle on my coffee table."

Had she locked the windows in her bedroom when she'd closed them earlier? She thought she had. Earlier that afternoon, she'd opened them to air out the stuffy house. She'd been sick with a cold for the first few days after moving in and finally felt well enough to unpack the boxes she'd shoved against the wall. Was that how he'd gotten in? Oh God, what if there was more than one person?

Another muffled thump made her heart leap.

"Ma'am, I have an officer en route. Is there a secure place you can go? Perhaps a place to conceal yourself?" the 911 operator asked. The woman's voice was so professional. So calm.

Tennyson's hands shook so hard she thought she might drop the phone. A place to hide? Something inside her told her to stay as quiet and still as possible, but perhaps hiding would be best. There was a closet to her left, but it had shelves. The couch sat flush against the wall, but her grandmother's refurbished armchair might be big enough to crouch behind.

"Should I hide?" she whispered, keeping her eyes trained on the hallway just beyond the kitchen. Her Louis Vuitton bag sat agape on the marble counter. Surely the burglar would go for her wallet and the cash she'd taken out at the bank earlier that day. Unless he wasn't after money.

What if . . .

"If there is a safer place for you, please go there. An officer should be there in two to three minutes."

"Okay," Tennyson said, easing off the couch and moving as silently as she could toward the chair that had been delivered from the upholstery shop three days before. She could still smell the fabric dye. Her body ran hot and cold, and the panting breaths she took sounded loud in her ears. Her galloping heart thumped so hard against her chest she was certain whoever had broken into her house could hear it.

"When the officer arrives, I need you to make sure he can access the property."

"What?" she asked as she sank into a crouch behind the chair.

"You have to let him inside, ma'am."

"Okay. Can you tell him to come around back? I mean, that's where I am, and I'm afraid to walk to the front. It's a big house, and I don't know how to work all the locks and stuff yet."

If the intruder came into the hearth room and saw her, she would grab the wine bottle and throw it at him and then bolt for the French doors that led out onto her patio. The dead bolt was probably turned, so she would have to be fast. And she wasn't very fast. She'd always been picked last in gym class . . . even if her toe touch was to die for. Or, well, it used to be before she got freaking old.

She sat with the phone glued to her ear, reminding herself to breathe and stay calm. Finally, flashing lights glanced off the freshly painted wall.

Thank God.

She strained to hear any further noises from her room but heard nothing more.

A shadow fell across the floor, and she reared back only to realize it came from the French doors. The door made a sound as the officer tried the knob. It was locked.

Just as Tennyson was about to move to twist the bolt so the officer could get inside, the door exploded, smashing against the wall with a huge crash.

She screamed as a uniformed officer with a gun drawn moved into the room. He held the weapon out in front of him like they did in the movies. He had dark hair and wore a black belt with all kinds of equipment. He said, "Clear," into a microphone on his chest.

He turned to look at her, a question in his blue eyes. Tennyson shouldn't have noticed how hot he was, but she wasn't dead yet, so she totally noticed.

She knew his questioning look meant he wanted to know where he should search. She pointed past the kitchen into the recesses that led to the bedroom, sitting room, office, and powder room.

He nodded and jerked his head toward the now open doorway.

She kept her hand on her mouth and moved behind him into the dark yawn of the night. The officer moved past the gleaming counter where her purse sat and crouched behind the counter. His gun remained trained on the empty space. Tennyson clutched the doorframe above the splintered wood of the jamb, too afraid to let the police officer out of her sight.

"This is the Shreveport Police. I need you to come out with your hands completely visible," the man commanded.

Silence met his demand.

"If you do not come out with your hands visible, you will not like what comes next," the man said. "Let's do this the easy way."

Tennyson watched with eyes wide as the man stood. He said a string of numbers and words into his microphone thing and then nodded when someone on the other end said some more numbers and something that sounded like "Proceed with caution."

She yelped as someone tapped her.

Spinning around, she prepared to fight, but another officer stood there, her weapon drawn. Behind her was another policeman. The woman officer pulled Tennyson outside as she entered the house.

Tennyson stood, arms wrapped around her waist, though it wasn't cold. She shook so hard she thought she might rattle. This was why she should have gone against her stupid inclinations and stayed in New York. She knew she made bad gut decisions. Always wanting to believe things would be as good as they were in her head before realizing that those decisions could . . . uh . . . land her in a casket. Moving back to Shreveport had been a mistake. Yeah, her boy would be here, but there were too many memories . . . and secrets . . . and Kit and Melanie.

Just as she had that thought, she heard a bark of laughter, and then the female police officer holstered her gun and said something into the mic on her uniform. Something that sounded like dispatch contacting animal control.

"What is it?" Tennyson said, drawing the attention of the officer.

"Ma'am, there's not an intruder. Well, unless you count a raccoon as a burglar."

"A raccoon?" Tennyson repeated. She stepped back in the house and stood surveying the opening to the back of the house with suspicion. It hadn't sounded like a raccoon. Did they make that much noise? Oh God. What had it broken? Stephen's ashes were on the shelf along with her priceless collection of lacquered makeup boxes. And where had she left the Tiffany candlesticks her grandmother had given her? Damn it.

The female officer cracked a smile. "Seems like you have a new pet."

"I don't . . . wait, it's a *raccoon* in my bedroom?"

The good-looking police officer came out and shook his head. "I shut the door. Did someone call animal control?"

"Shut the door?" Tennyson asked, shouldering her way toward Tall, Dark, and Hot. "What about my things? It broke something. I have some expensive pieces in there. Can't you go in and roust the thing out of there? Chase him back through the window or something?"

The officer whose name badge read J. Rhett turned bright-blue eyes on her. Bright-blue eyes that looked almost startling against his tanned skin. His gaze then dropped slightly to take her in, and she wished like hell she wasn't wearing the stained T-shirt and no bra. "Ma'am, did you leave the window open?"

All three police officers were now looking at her like she'd committed the crime. "Well, I aired the house out. I thought I had closed and locked all of them, but I must have missed one. A friend called, and I sat down with my wine and . . ."

She could see in their eyes exactly what they thought of her—a stupid, rich blonde wasting their time. They'd be wrong on two accounts, though. Not that she would let anyone know her IQ was over 140, and she was pretty much mousy brown under her blonde hair dye. God forbid. People expected things of smart people, and blondes had more fun. And she'd given it the old college try on the fun.

"We're out of here, Joe," the woman said, raising her hand in a half-salute wave thing. "Gotta get that hit-and-run report on the captain's desk."

"Joseph," the man uttered under his breath before returning the "later" wave.

"Thank you," Tennyson remembered to call out as they disappeared through the French doors.

Joseph Rhett, hot cop that he was, didn't seem to be pleased to be left with her.

"What's on your face?" he asked, securing his weapon.

Tennyson lifted her hand and encountered the goopy charcoal mask that was half-dried and half-gummy. She'd forgotten about the stupid mask. "Uh, a purifying mask. It's charcoal."

He looked at her again, and damn her, she couldn't help but tuck a strand of hair behind her ear. *Disaster* wasn't even the word for what she looked like. "You probably need to call someone to repair the lock on the door."

Tennyson looked at the door. "*You* broke my door."

"Well, I thought you were in danger."

There was that. If a dangerous criminal had been in the house, would she be upset over the splintered wood? Probably not. But it wasn't a burglar, and *she* was the person who'd left the damned window open. Wasn't like she could blame the SPD when she'd caused the issue.

A crash came from her bedroom.

"Damn it," she said, starting toward the bedroom. Officer Rhett caught her by her elbow. She turned. "I don't want that thing to tear up my bedroom."

"Raccoons are known to carry rabies and distemper."

"Did it look like it was sick?"

He blinked. "I don't know."

"Well, I can't have it tearing up my stuff." She pulled her arm away and stalked toward her bedroom. She didn't want to face a rabid raccoon, but she also wanted to sell some of the stuff the creature was likely rummaging through. The Colorado house was still on the market moldering even after she'd lowered the price, and the apartment in Manhattan was still without a lease. She'd paid cash for the Shreveport house, but it had wiped out one of her savings accounts. If she could sell some of the couture she never wore anymore, she could use that to pay the decorator's bill.

Nothing wrong with upcycling. It helped the environment. And she wasn't going to wear last year's styles.

She threw open the door and damned if the raccoon wasn't lying in the middle of her bed like a freaking sultan. It had rifled through her trash, leaving tissues and a tampon wrapper on the floor, and knocked over a goblet she'd left on the bedside table. The crystal pieces lay strewn on the wool rug she'd brought from the mountain house. The lamp had fallen, and the curtains she'd had custom made framed the six-inch crack the little bastard had somehow managed to climb through.

Tennyson, with an eye on the raccoon, who sat regarding her curiously, stomped to the window and raised it higher. She then moved toward the end of the bed, far enough away from the raccoon that she could dart toward the open doorway if it came at her, but close enough to command the little beast's attention. Throwing out her arm toward the window, she said, "Out."

The raccoon rolled into a Jabba the Hutt pose and twitched its nose.

"Out. Get out," she yelled at it.

"How much wine have you had, anyway?" Officer Rhett asked from the doorway.

Tennyson glanced back at him. The man had his hand on the gun, ready at any moment to fire if needed. Well, that was somewhat comforting. Just in case Rocky did, in fact, have rabies.

"Enough to not be afraid of a stupid raccoon," she said.

The raccoon followed instructions the way most men followed instructions, which is to say, it sat there and did nothing.

"Ugh, why doesn't it move? Isn't it scared of us?" she asked.

"I don't know. I'm not a raccoon expert."

She waved her hands, and the raccoon leaped up and moved toward her pile of down pillows. "Shoo!"

Then the animal turned and came toward her.

Tennyson bolted, sliding behind Officer Rhett. She pressed against his back, peeking around to see the raccoon lumbering off the bed. She also noticed how firm the hot cop felt beneath her fingers. Oh, and he smelled yummy—like fabric softener and something manly.

Who did his laundry?

"Stop," Officer Rhett said, trying to pull away from her, but Tennyson had a death grip on his waist.

The raccoon leaped to the sill and climbed out the window. The little bastard didn't even look back as a farewell gesture.

Tennyson released her hands. "Oh, thank God. Go close the window."

Officer Rhett turned. "You do it. It's your house."

"But you're the cop."

"Police officer."

She made a face. "Are you scared of a raccoon?"

"No." But he looked a bit like he was. His hand was still on the butt of the gun. She felt him stiffen his spine before striding to the window and slamming it down with a bang. The glass panes actually rattled.

The doorbell rang.

"That's probably animal control," she said, hurrying back toward the front of her house, leaving Officer Rhett behind.

Ten minutes later, animal control was gone with no raccoon in their animal trap, and Officer Rhett had finagled her broken French door into a reasonably secure position. She'd found a toolbox—a cute pink one she'd bought at Home Depot the only time she'd ever been to Home Depot—that had enough tools for him to make the door somewhat functional.

"You need to call someone tomorrow to fix this. Do you have someone?" he asked. He'd spent a good five minutes cleaning up the debris. Tennyson wasn't sure if that was supposed to be done by a police officer, but she appreciated that the man was conscientious. And smelled like an invitation for a big-person playdate. She kept noticing things like the way his pants fit him (nicely), the way his jaw clenched while he was working (chiseled), and the way he talked to himself under his breath (sort of adorable).

"Do I have someone?" she repeated.

"Like a boyfriend? Or a neighbor?"

"Are you asking if I have a boyfriend?"

He looked at her like she was nuts. "Only if he can fix this. I know a guy and can leave you his number. Let me go out to my unit and grab my card in case you need his information."

Officer Rhett went to his police car and returned seconds later with his card. Joseph C. Rhett. There were other things on there like his badge number and his rank and yada yada. She flipped it over and bingo—his cell phone number was scrawled across the back.

Why that thrilled her, she hadn't a clue.

"Again, ma'am, I'm sorry about your door, but I'm glad you're safe. Remember to check your windows and make sure they're *all* locked. This is a safe neighborhood, but you still need to take precautions."

"Yes, Officer," she said.

"If you have any other trouble, call us. We are here to protect and serve."

Tennyson nodded and walked him to the door. "I'll be sure to call if I need you."

Her words sounded flirty, and Officer Rhett's expression looked puzzled. Okay, so her flirting skills were rusty and—

Tennyson caught her reflection in the mirror she'd hung in the foyer a few days ago.

Holy hell. She looked like death warmed up in the microwave. Clumps of hair falling (and not in a sexy, cute way), the mask dried in patches, her lips drawn tight and pale, and her boobs not as perky as they were in her expensive padded bra. Total mess.

"Have a good night, ma'am," Officer Rhett said.

Then he walked down her front walkway, looking clean-cut and unruffled . . . and very much not interested in Tennyson.

Her flirting skills may be rusty, but her interest-level radar worked just fine. And this man was not interested. And for some reason that really hurt. Because Tennyson used to be able to seduce even the most stalwart of men. She'd even had a hard-nosed general groveling and begging to kiss the toe of her black stiletto boots. Of course, that was back when she was into that sort of thing.

But this Shreveport patrol cop?

Nada.

"Damn it," she said, closing the front door and ignoring the lock just because it suited her to disobey. She needed to get her shit together because this version of herself was unacceptable.

If she was going to live in Shreveport, she needed to do it right.

Tennyson O'Rourke was back home, and she wasn't going to be ignored.

CHAPTER THREE

Melanie plopped her wine down on the table, though she was tempted to throw it against the wall of the perfectly nice restaurant her daughter had chosen to deliver the most shocking, horrible, ridiculous news of her life. "No. I'm sorry, you aren't doing this. It's preposterous."

Emma's mouth flatlined. "Marrying Andrew is *not* preposterous. We're doing this with or without your support. I don't need your permission." She then turned to Andrew, who looked about as comfortable as a woman in stirrups. Maybe more uncomfortable.

"Now, let's all calm down," Kit said, pressing his hands against the air between them.

"Daddy, I knew she'd react this way. I told you she would, but it doesn't matter. If y'all don't want to pay for the wedding, Andrew's mom said she will."

"Wait, you already knew about this, Christopher Douglas Layton?" Melanie said. She was on the verge of losing total control, something she never did. But her daughter had told Kit she was engaged before she told her own mother, and that hurt. Of course, Emma had likely already told her father because she knew how to play her daddy like a

Steinway. Then the last part of her daughter's statement hit her. "Wait, Tennyson knows, too? You told her before *me*?"

"We told her a few hours ago. Jesus, Mom, why is everything such a competition with you?" Emma said, rolling the blue eyes she'd inherited from her father.

Her possibly lying, flirting-with-cheating father.

Okay, so Kit hadn't already tilted over into adultery. Or at least he'd proclaimed he hadn't, but Melanie knew without hesitation that if Charlotte could, she would have her tanned, toned legs wrapped around Kit Layton before anyone could blink. The younger woman was definitely laying the groundwork for more than a professional partnership with Melanie's husband. Not that Kit would admit as much when she'd confronted him with the text about the hotel room.

He'd claimed it was the meeting room, a pseudo suite/meeting space within the hotel because the other conference rooms were booked, and Hal had insisted on the meeting being at the Hilton. Melanie had, of course, looked up the meeting space availability online and had drawn no firm conclusions on that claim. She'd hemmed and hawed over calling the Hilton, but her husband had been forthcoming about Charlotte and her . . . well, flattering attentions. She had to trust that he was being true. Even though what he'd confessed after she confronted him was just as soul-crushing—he'd admitted to being somewhat tempted to pick up what Charlotte was laying down.

After that little bombshell, she'd booked an appointment with a therapist for the following week. They could fix this lull—or what had Kit called it? Yes, *dissatisfaction* in their marriage. If there was one thing Melanie knew, it was that she could fix almost anything. They'd weathered a lot in their marriage, and Kit being bored with her or having a midlife crisis was just one more thing they would laugh about when they celebrated their golden wedding anniversary over cake and champagne at the club.

But she hadn't expected her daughter to announce that she was getting married in August.

August!

And Emma had already booked the church and reception space for the wedding—the same church where she and Kit had been married years before. Bad memories slammed into her. What should have been a wonderful day had been ruined by the woman who would soon be Emma's mother-in-law.

Holy cow, she couldn't believe this.

"Your mother didn't mean it that way, sweetheart," Kit said. His glance her way was quelling because he knew she *had* meant it that way.

Tennyson shouldn't have been the first person told about Melanie's daughter's wedding. No. It absolutely should have been Emma's own mother who'd heard it first. The thought that she hadn't been was . . . Melanie blinked away the sudden prickling of tears.

Andrew looked down at his phone. "Uh, my mom is running late. Traffic."

"Wait. She's coming? Here? To dinner tonight?" Melanie managed without sounding as alarmed as she felt. Hurt was forgotten as something ugly wound its way into her gut. She didn't want to see Tennyson, and she danged sure didn't want to be connected to her by her daughter's marriage. God, they'd have to spend holidays together. Oh, and plan a wedding.

Why was this happening?

Okay, so she knew she would see Tennyson at some point this weekend. That was why she'd gotten a pedicure and her roots touched up along with a special intensive conditioner applied to make her dark helmet of hair shine beneath the light. She'd carefully chosen clothes that disguised her slight belly and bird legs. She'd even paid a ridiculous sum for eyelash extensions. If her mother found out she'd done something so preposterous, Anne would scoff. Maintaining one's appearance wasn't to be left to obvious deceit. A woman ate well, exercised, and always, always moisturized. If the time came for touch-ups, a woman went to the best surgeon in Dallas so no one would know. End. Stop. Fake eyelashes and hair extensions were for strippers. And don't even contemplate a tattoo unless one was preparing to be a cocktail waitress or a homeless person with a crack addiction. Melanie was almost certain those were the exact words her mother had used.

"Uh, yeah, she's coming." Andrew looked at Emma with alarm in his eyes. "That's why we're seated at a table for six. She's not bringing anyone, though. She and my stepdad just got divorced six months ago. Besides, I thought you knew each other."

Like the back of her hand.

But that had been once upon a time. Before they hated each other. Before college. Before Kit. And before the wedding catastrophe that had ruined the Brevard family. It was something she'd buried, that her whole family had put behind them. Emma and Noah didn't know about what had happened that night or the aftereffects, and she'd hoped to keep it that way. The past was better left . . . in the past.

But that might not be possible now.

"We do know each other," Melanie said, trying to get control of her spinning emotions. She'd thought she had years before Emma got engaged, but the gleaming two-karat ring on her daughter's left hand declared that belief null and void. And now her daughter wanted a hurry-up ceremony so she and Andrew could play house during the most difficult and demanding year of her life—year one of medical school. Nothing made sense to Melanie about this plan.

"We're merely surprised. That's what your mother means." Kit gave his daughter a comforting smile.

"Yes, we're *surprised*. You said you didn't want to be in a relationship while you were in medical school because it wouldn't be fair to the other person, and now you want to get married. That's, like, a major relationship, honey." Melanie lowered her voice and spoke with slower modulation. The way her mother had always demanded. "Are you sure you've both thought this through?"

Andrew nodded. "We have, and we think this makes more sense than being six hours apart. Larson Hart has a branch in Shreveport, and they granted me a transfer. Besides, I can help pay the bills while she's in school. Oh, and make sure she gets food, rest, and support during that tough first year. We're young, but we know we're meant to be together."

He made it sound so reasonable.

"But this seems so fast," Melanie said, trying to sound lighter . . . and likely failing.

"I know it does," Andrew continued, looking contrite. "I'm sorry I didn't come to you both first. Emma found the ring in my sock drawer, and, well, it—"

"I screwed it up," Emma interrupted, her irritation fading when she looked at Andrew. Damned if the child's eyes didn't shine with absolute adoration when she looked up at the boy who had obviously stolen her heart.

"But I tried to redeem myself," Andrew said, and the way he quirked his mouth looked so much like his mother. For a moment, something squeezed in Melanie's chest.

"Yeah, he said, 'Put it back, and pretend you didn't see it.'" Emma smiled, reaching for his hand. The diamond sparkled as if it, too, was in on the whole convincing-the-parents campaign. "So I did. The next day, I awoke to ten dozen roses surrounding me and a latte with the cutest little heart. We went on a picnic, and then that night under the stars at a rooftop restaurant in Bentonville, Andrew took my hand and led me to the dance floor. The band played my favorite Ed Sheeran song, and he got down on one knee and asked me to be his forever and always."

The two were staring into each other's eyes, a sheen of tears glistening as Andrew lifted her daughter's hand to his lips and brushed her knuckles with a kiss.

Melanie felt tears prick at her own eyes. The couple before her looked about as much in love as two people could. It was almost eye-roll worthy, but so sincere she wouldn't dare. As upset as she was that her baby wanted to get married at twenty-two to the son of the woman who betrayed her, she was also pleased to see the affection between the two. She wanted love for her daughter. The kind she'd found with Kit. The kind she still hoped knit them together.

Emma swallowed back her tears. "And then all of a sudden all our friends were there with champagne. It was just magical. I wish you could have been there."

"Yeah, I'm sorry about that," Andrew said, ripping his gaze from Emma and looking at her and Kit. "I should have asked. I know that. But . . ."

Kit shrugged. "It's okay. I would have said yes because you two are perfect for one another. We're happy for you."

Melanie nodded, though she wasn't so sure *happy* was the right word for how she felt. More like *resigned* because unless she wanted to alienate her daughter forever while at the same time looking like sour grapes, she would have to make the best of the situation.

At that moment, she heard someone shout, "Ma'am, ma'am?"

Kit craned his head. "Well, she's here."

Coming toward them in a tight, no doubt designer dress with her boobs spilling out was the person Melanie had vowed to hate until her last breath. Tennyson sashayed when she walked, wearing giant Dolce & Gabbana sunglasses like a celebrity. Her heels were high, her hair coiled perfectly, and her lipstick was piranha red. From a large bag slung over her shoulder, a ridiculous little puppy peeked out, giving a yipping bark as the man dressed in a white jacket and bow tie scurried toward them.

"Ma'am, we don't allow dogs in here," the maître d' said, his finger raised.

Tennyson stopped and pivoted.

"This dog is my emotional support dog. I'm entitled to have my animal with me as long as it is properly restrained. Check titles two and three of the Americans with Disabilities Act. Are you going to deny me my legal rights, sir?" Tennyson asked, sliding her glasses down her nose and glaring at him.

The pup yipped again, doing its emotional support thing, one supposed.

"Uh, no, ma'am, it's just this is a—"

"I'm not stupid. I know it's a restaurant, and my service animal will remain in this bag. Do you have a problem with that?" Tennyson looked around and said very loudly, "Does anyone in here have a problem with my *legal* service animal?"

Several diners shook their heads. The maître d' closed his mouth and then bowed his head. "My apologies, ma'am."

Tennyson nodded like a queen dismissing her subject and then proceeded toward the table. "Oh, and get me a vodka martini, will you? Make it a double."

Melanie stifled the insane impulse to laugh. Tennyson was like a Hollywood caricature come to life. Lord.

Her former friend halted at the table and looked them over. "What a sad little party. Where's the happy tears and champagne? We *are* celebrating, aren't we?"

Kit smiled, rose, and kissed her cheek. "Ah, Tennyson, you always bring the party, don't you?"

Tennyson gave Kit a sly smile. "Something you haven't forgotten, have you?"

She then bent to smack a kiss on the cheek of her son, leaving behind a smudge of red, before wrapping Emma in a hug. Looking over at Melanie, her lips twitched. "I'd hug you, but I don't know what weapon you're carrying in your, wait, is that a Brighton bag?"

Melanie didn't want to bristle, but Tennyson hadn't changed one dang lick. Always pushing, always sliding her digs in . . . or rather out-and-out tossing them like hand grenades.

"Hello, Teen—uh, Tennyson," she said, stumbling past her old nickname for Tennyson because she wasn't ready to let Emma know just exactly who this woman used to be to her. Instead, she found her calm, vowing to ignore Tennyson's barbs.

"It's been a while. You look good for your age," Tennyson said, sliding into the empty chair beside her son. She sat her bag with the little Yorkie on the extra chair. "This precious angel is Prada, my new baby-kins. Isn't she adorable? You are so adorable, sweet baby girl."

"When did you get a dog?" Andrew said, looking at the little puppy whimpering and lifting a paw in the most adorable way.

"This morning," Tennyson said, pulling off a piece of bread from the basket and offering it to the puppy.

"But you said it was a service dog," Andrew said, frowning at his mother.

Tennyson waved a hand toward the front of the restaurant. "But he doesn't have to know that she isn't. I mean, last week, I had a raccoon get into the house. I thought it was a burglar at first, and that got me to thinking about being alone in that big ol' house. So when I saw Prada, I knew she would keep me company. Totally an emotional support animal."

"You think that dog can handle a burglar?" Kit asked. He slid a look over to Melanie, humor glinting in his eyes.

Tennyson slid her glasses off and set them beside her water glass. "Of course not. But she *will* bark. That might dissuade intruders."

"Only if she can sound like a rottweiler," Kit said.

Tennyson shot Kit a withering look before folding her hands and looking at Andrew and Emma. "Now, you two, what have we decided? Still set on mid-August?"

"It's a suicide mission," Melanie said, twisting her napkin into a noose. "We can't possibly get everything done in that amount of time. What about Christmas? That at least gives us—"

"Mom, we've booked the church, and we are committed to August." Emma may have rolled her eyes a little.

Melanie excelled at reading a crowd, and if she wanted to have any control of this wedding, she needed to assert herself quickly. Otherwise, Tennyson would have this whole next three months off the rails with crazy antics and wild ideas. Oh, and wasting a crap ton of money. "How about your father and I host a small engagement party in June? I think we can pull that together fairly quickly."

"Uh, well, we hadn't really thought about it. But that would be cool, I guess?" Emma looked at Andrew.

He nodded. "Yeah, that would be good."

Kit glanced quizzically at Melanie. She gave him a confident smile. "I'll get the list together and let you check it. I'm thinking something intimate with a nice champagne toast. We can announce the wedding date and location."

Tennyson accepted the martini from the waiter. "That sounds so . . . well, there's no other way to say it, so what is always done. But I suppose a tasteful, small engagement party would be a good idea. Emma and Andrew should be moved into their new place by that time."

"New place?" Melanie tried to modulate her tone and volume but failed. Just how much planning had her daughter done without her?

"Tennyson is letting us live in her carriage house for the first year. It will save us money. Actually, we will pay her rent, but then turn around and use what we paid her as a down payment on a house next year. Isn't that brilliant?" Emma beamed at her soon-to-be mother-in-law.

"Wait, Tennyson has a place in *Shreveport*?" Melanie's voice rose to almost panic stage.

"Emma didn't tell you?" Tennyson said, her smile almost evil. "Yes, Melly, I'm finally returning home. Perfect timing since my boy is moving there, too. And now I can help these two out as they start their life together."

Kit raised his eyebrows. "That's incredibly generous of you, Tennyson."

"I've always been generous, Kit," Tennyson purred.

Melanie shot her a look. "You have, haven't you? Rumors prevail."

Tennyson's gaze might have been Chinese throwing stars. "Since Melly and Kit are doing the engagement party, I'll host the wedding shower."

"I'm sure there will be several showers," Melanie said, signaling the waiter so she could get another glass of chardonnay. *Tennyson had moved to Shreveport.* She needed a freaking bottle. "I know Mother's garden club will want to do something. Oh, and you know your friends will want to host something, Emma. We need to get a calendar."

Tennyson lifted the sleeping puppy from her bag. The little thing wore a tiny diaper. Melanie blinked once. Twice. "Is that dog wearing a diaper?"

Tennyson rooted around inside her large Louis Vuitton bag, setting sunglasses cases and lipsticks on the table. "Yes. I learned that trick from the Kardashians."

Well, that explained everything.

"Here," Tennyson huffed, setting a slim-wrapped package on the table and pushing it toward Emma. "I found this today."

Emma lifted the gift and unwrapped it. "*Wedding Bible?*"

"By Sarah Haywood. She's a fantastic wedding planner, but probably not able to do your wedding. It's too short notice. Still, I called David Tutera and Kevin Lee, but, again, too short notice. So anyone worth anything is booked. I made a few calls to Dallas, but at this point, I think we're going to have to use Marc Mallow. He's local but tolerable. He did the Murrays' wedding, which was written about in *Southern Society* magazine. Three months is not much time, but I promised him twenty percent more than his normal fee. He's a money-hungry little beast, so he's in. But this book will give you some things to be thinking about. We have a meeting with him in three weeks, but in the meantime, you can send him your preferences. Will that work?"

Melanie knew her mouth had dropped open, but so did Emma's.

Emma snapped her mouth closed. "Oh my God, he said he'd do it?"

Tennyson patted the now groggy pup and set it back within the depths of her purse, nestling it into an expensive-looking scarf. "Yes, so does that work for you?"

"Absolutely," Emma said, grinning at Andrew. "I loved the lighted trees he did for Ainsley Polk's wedding. Oh, and the flowers were amazing. I already have a list of some ideas. I'm thinking lavender and cream for the color scheme. Perhaps a bit of spring green as an accent."

So much for getting a leg up on this wedding thing. Melanie closed her mouth and glanced over at Kit, who now had a furrow between his pretty blue eyes. She knew why. Dollar signs were dancing across his vision. Marc Mallow did every society wedding in North Louisiana . . . if he wished to do it. The man was as flighty and fickle as any she knew. And she really didn't know him. She knew his mother owned the floral shop Marc always used. Don't even suggest another florist, or he'd walk away. She knew this because one of her friends had suggested using her own friend who was a florist to do the arrangements, and Marc got up and left. That being said, Marc *was* the best in the area.

The waiter appeared. "Are we ready to order?"

"Another drink," Tennyson said, draining the last of her double martini.

"Right away, ma'am," the waiter said, disappearing with a slight bow.

Tennyson looked up and smiled. "I do love a man who does what I ask."

Emma's delighted laughter was a cheese grater against Melanie's nerves. If she could figure out a way to leave without looking as if she were in retreat, she would do it, but at this point any slinking about, even for self-preservation, would be acknowledged by her former friend with a twinkle of triumph in her eyes. So Melanie would have to sit and suffer.

She'd come up with something to counter Tennyson's initial move. Her nemesis had gotten a heads-up on the engagement and used that to her advantage by buying the planner, booking Marc Mallow, and offering to do the shower.

But the game was on. And just like last time she faced Tennyson, Melanie didn't plan on losing.

CHAPTER FOUR

Two weeks later

Tennyson stood in the threshold of her open French doors and surveyed the area around the pool with a critical eye. She needed to get the cedar-and-stone structure sheltering the enormous hearth restained and get new furniture in place. She'd already called an outdoor-design expert in Dallas, who would arrive for a consultation Wednesday. The pro would then hire the gardening team to redesign the landscaping in time for the wedding shower. For that event, clear tents would cover the entire pool area in case a pop-up thunderstorm made an appearance, and she'd made sure there would be large fans and air conditioners to cool the late June evening. Marc Mallow was handling the catering and decorating for the wedding shower of the decade.

"Mom, where should we put these boxes that were left in the carriage house?" Andrew asked, poking his head out from the two-story "garage" apartment that sat to the left of her property. Advertised as a mother-in-law apartment, the small bungalow-type structure was a perfect space for Emma and Andrew to live in their first year.

"What boxes specifically?" she called back, scooping up Prada, who had just piddled on the expensive Turkish rug in her dining room. The puppy didn't seem to understand the difference between wool and grass. She should probably invest in a puppy training book and a few vats of carpet cleaner.

"I don't know. Not yours. They must have been forgotten by the previous owner or something. Can I put them in your garage until they can pick them up? It's tight quarters, and we don't have room. Emma has a lot of stuff."

"*I* have a lot of stuff? You mean *you* have a lot of stuff. Like this Peloton bike you don't even use," Emma called out, sounding so much like Melanie that Tennyson winced. Still, their teasing banter made her smile, especially when she heard a delighted squeal and knew her boy was probably lovingly harassing his fiancée. Oh, to be young and in love.

She'd been that once upon a time. A few times, to be exact. Hadn't worked for her. She'd accepted that she wasn't meant to be in a relationship. She liked her freedom, hopping over to Milan if she wanted, taking a month in the mountains, dating men who knew good champagne from the cheap stuff. She was a butterfly made to flit.

So why in the hell was she *here*?

She didn't really understand her own inclinations sometimes.

Seeing Melanie a few weeks ago had been surreal. Even more so was seeing Kit and remembering what it was like to be the one to sit beside him. He'd been the one guy she'd never gotten over. Well, that wasn't altogether true. She had gotten over him. Still, there was a part of herself that held on to that torn-apart piece of first love. The girl who still lived inside her remembered the boy who'd teased her about her wild hair and bubble butt (that he proclaimed to worship). Kit had been her first for many things—first boyfriend, first love, first sexual partner—and she'd been unable to uncurl her fingers and let go of that romanticized first love.

As much as she hated to admit it—she wasn't good at letting go.

Kit had broken her heart. That he'd done so with Melanie, the one person she'd thought she could always depend on, had made it somehow ten times more devastating.

Of course, there was much neither Kit nor Melanie knew about that first year after high school, the year she stretched out her fingers and brushed them against a dream that was too big to hold on to, the year she'd tossed something away . . . and paid the price.

Those were the days she didn't like to remember.

Those were days she tried to forget.

Andrew appeared before her, his face flushed and happy, a reminder of the good things she'd done, the best being him. "Hey, we're going out for pizza. You wanna come with?"

Tennyson should go with them—it was Memorial Day weekend, and everyone seemed to be happy celebrating the launch of summer. Since she'd moved back to Shreveport, she hadn't gone out much, electing to stock up at Whole Foods on salads and fresh fruit. She'd hired a personal trainer who worked out of a small studio, and so far she'd managed to shed nine pounds of booze and macaroons she'd put on after the divorce. Pizza with Andrew and his soon-to-be wife sounded amazingly good. There was so much to enjoy about their enthusiasm and high spirits. And pizza *was* her favorite cheat food.

When Andrew had told her he was dating a girl who had grown up in Shreveport, Tennyson had been shocked. Not many high school graduates from the area made their way up to Fayetteville to her father's alma mater. When she'd found out the girl Andrew was nuts about was the daughter of Kit and Melanie Layton, her knees had literally buckled. For months she'd heard about Emma this and Emma that, and had seen multiple pictures of them at parties, but never guessed the pretty brunette was the daughter of her former boyfriend and former best friend. Once she knew, she could see both Kit's and Melanie's resemblance in the young woman.

Melanie had given Emma high cheekbones and Kit had bequeathed those brilliant baby blues and rangy physique. But Emma's mannerisms were handed down by Anne Brevard herself. That lift of the chin, the hard dismissal when she was displeased, and the pure elegance in her movement. No wonder Andrew was putty in Emma's hands.

Her son was tall, dark, and serious with a quick smile and kind words. He'd always been a little awkward, a bit dorky, as if perpetually awaiting adulthood. Andrew was everything Tennyson wasn't—easygoing but resolved, kind to a fault, and always willing to retreat to high ground rather than scrabble about in the trenches.

But she had learned that staying low and getting her hands dirty netted results. It was a skill that served her well, something she might need to get through the next few months as she reestablished herself in a town she never loved.

After all, Shreveport wasn't an endgame. Her mother and father had moved to a retirement community in Texas, where her brother Heathcliff and his wife, Wendy, lived, and her sister Bronte lived right outside Natchitoches on a cotton farm. Her other two siblings—Shelley and Blake—were almost ten years older than Tennyson and lived in California and Arizona, respectively. So she had no real reason to come back where she'd started other than Andrew and whatever itchy, weird vibe had made her search out real estate in Shreveport.

Perhaps it was the divorce that had done it. She thought after she and husband number three split she'd go back to NYC and pick up where she'd left off—shopping, tennis, and lunching. Maybe serve on a few committees, get Fashion Week passes, a place in the Hamptons—all the gal-pal glamorousness of her past life, but she found most of her friends in their midforties were now living in Connecticut or focusing on making partner at their firm. They didn't want to go to pop-up restaurants in the Village or warehouse parties in the Meatpacking District. Not to mention, when Tennyson really examined what she wanted, it wasn't the busy streets and flashing lights. So one night she started looking at houses in her old hometown, which were ridiculously cheap compared to the Upper East Side. The memories came back, and she began to wonder what it would be like to go home . . . to return and buy a big house in the best neighborhood. To live the life she'd always wanted as a child.

"Mom? Pizza?" Andrew called.

"You two go ahead. I still have to shower and make a few calls. And Prada needs a walk."

Emma emerged from the carriage house, brushing her hands on the long-sleeved top she wore over her bikini. A pair of athletic shorts covered the bottoms, and her brightly painted toes in the flip-flops made Tennyson feel a million years old. She hadn't worn a ponytail in a good ten years.

"You ready?" Emma said to Andrew, who wore just as young and slouchy a uniform with his frat shirt and lululemon shorts. Running shoes graced his feet.

"Mom, can we bring you back anything?" Andrew asked. Always courteous, that boy.

"Nope. I'll have a salad. Have to get ready for this wedding."

"Mrs. O'Rourke, um, Tennyson, you know you look incredible, and besides, as much as I love the idea of a big wedding, I don't know if we should . . . uh, go crazy with it. We have only a few months before the date, and we're worried things could get too big. Maybe simple would be best," Emma said, looking at Andrew as if she was waiting for him to agree.

Tennyson tilted her head. "So you want me to cancel Marc Mallow?"

"No, I just . . . well, I don't want my parents to get stressed. My mom can be—"

"Easily overwhelmed? I remember. Don't worry. It will be fine. Have the wedding you want, sugar," Tennyson said.

Emma's shoulders sank in visible relief. "Okay. You're right. It's our only one."

Exactly. Or maybe. But at any rate, this was her only child's wedding, and *simple* wasn't anything close to what Tennyson wanted for the nuptials, which was why she'd essentially begged Marc Mallow to be the coordinator for the event. She was thinking more along the lines of stunning. Something fabulous to set Shreveport on its ear. And it would start with the wedding shower. Melanie could host her tasteful, small gathering to announce the engagement, but Tennyson was going to blow that engagement party out of the water with her spectacular bridal shower.

Like, literally.

She'd already told the backyard specialist she wanted to do something with the pool. And fireworks to end the night.

Yes, the wedding shower she hosted would set the city abuzz. She'd already determined the theme would be a Tour of Italy to accompany the honeymoon to Italy she'd be gifting the happy couple as a surprise. Tennyson knew it was over the top, but big deal. The Colorado house would sell soon, and the Manhattan apartment already had several people interested in leasing. Her monthly stipend of thirty thousand could sustain her if she was careful. So this would be a mind-blowing wedding because that's how much her only child meant to her. He deserved the best she could give him. That was how she paid her debt. That and the checks each month. To an outsider, it likely made no sense, but to Tennyson it did. It made the only sense she could make of the mistake she'd made.

After Kit had broken things off with her for good, Tennyson had been messed up, making one bad decision right after the other. Those years of living recklessly landed her pregnant with Andrew at twenty-three years old. Andrew's father had been a small-time director who was—surprise!—married. Rolfe had thought he was going places, but instead he overdosed on cocaine. But before he croaked, he'd made it plain that he wanted nothing to do with the baby if she kept it. Tennyson hadn't loved Rolfe, but she *had* expected him to help her in some way . . . not selfishly die. Instead the man who'd financed Rolfe's attempt at an off-Broadway show had stepped in. Stephen Abernathy was the gentlest, kindest person Tennyson had ever known. He wanted a child more than anything and had more money than the ocean had fish, so she'd married him and given him happiness until pancreatic cancer had taken him when Andrew was four years old. Stephen had given Andrew his name and his fortune, leaving Tennyson enough to live comfortably for the rest of her life, too.

"We're off," Andrew said, laughing as Emma hopped on his back. Her overgrown puppy of a son then galloped toward his monstrous F-250 with Emma squealing the entire way.

"Damn, they're too young." Tennyson sighed, even though she'd proclaimed they weren't only weeks before. Mostly because she could see that Melanie thought their children were out of their minds to wed at such an age. Tennyson agreed. Those two needed time to season, but she wasn't going to agree with Melanie. Besides, plenty of people, including her own parents, had married right out of high school, and they were still together. Sometimes it was best to grow up together.

Maybe that was why Melanie and Kit were still together. They had married right after college, a day Tennyson would never forget. She'd been living in SoHo, recovering from Rolfe's overdose and the shock of finding out she was pregnant when she got the invitation. She'd stared at the cream vellum in utter disbelief. For one, she had no clue Kit and Melanie had gotten engaged. For another, she couldn't believe their effing audacity. Pain had crushed her, and she'd stayed in bed for two days, eating ice cream, crying, and watching old movies featuring women who'd been cast aside getting their revenge.

Then she'd booked her flight to Shreveport for the wedding weekend. They'd sent the invite . . . and she was damned well going to show up.

Andrew tooted the horn as he backed down the driveway, and it jarred her from her thoughts about the past. She gave a wave, and nearly an hour later, she sprawled on the couch, her legs freshly shaved, sipping from a nearly half-empty bottle of her favorite wine. Andrew had texted that they'd run into friends and would be home later than expected. Not that he owed her any notice.

She'd skipped eating the salad, and the wine was already giving her that mellowness she craved. Maybe she drank too much each night, but damn it, ever since she'd divorced her third husband, she'd been lonely.

Not that she would admit it.

By the time the bottle was empty, she was utterly bored. Prada was snoring softly on the cushion beside her, not even bothering to be company to her.

She should have gone with Emma and Andrew. Or called a few old friends who she swore she was going to stay in touch with but hadn't because she'd never planned to return here. Not that any of her old crew had reached out to her since she'd returned. Hell, they might not even know she was back in town. Melanie hadn't, and that had been fun.

Tennyson rose, not waking the pup, and walked out back, where the pool shimmered in the dawning starlight. She wore a gorgeous silk caftan that fluttered around her ankles in the soft twilight breeze. Her hair had been colored, highlighted, and cut into a flattering shag that softened her pointy chin. Her painted toes dug into the blue slate as she walked around to the in-ground spa, dipping one foot in. She could slip the caftan off and slide into the water in just her Agent Provocateur bra and thong.

Or not. The lingerie was expensive, and no need to have the shock treatment Andrew had dumped in earlier damage the delicate lace and silk.

So she kept walking to the far side of the yard, admiring the oleander that would soon bloom. It would be perfect later in June for the shower. Invitations would go out on Monday. God, people were going to be so surprised by the personalized hand-lettered invites.

Something to her left caught her eye. On the side of the pergola covering the outdoor seating area was a large black duffel bag. Her heart sprang into her chest. Just days ago a suspicious backpack had been discovered in the stairwell of the Caddo Parish courthouse. Turned out a student left it, but the city had been cautious, deploying a bomb squad just in case. No doubt this was merely a bag left by one of the workers who'd come that morning to change out the pool pump.

But what if it wasn't something left by a worker?

What if it was something more dastardly . . . something danger-ous . . . something that should be checked by a good-looking officer of the law?

She laughed because she was a little drunk and a lot lonely.

Turning, she hurried back into the house, looking for her purse. Inside was her Chanel lipstick with the slight shimmer. Not totally trashy, but just enough to make her lips vibrant with desire. That was how the saleswoman had put it, and that silly thought made her laugh again. Then she pulled out the card she'd slid into the pocket of her wallet.

Officer Joseph C. Rhett. Hot Cop himself.

Ten minutes later, she fluffed her hair and pulled the door open. She may or may not have spritzed herself with her favorite Tom Ford scent.

Okay, she totally had.

"Officer Rhett, thank you for coming so quickly," she said, sum-moning her best victim voice, perfected when she'd played Lois Lane in an off-off-Broadway mash-up called *Superman Saves the Dame*. Of course she'd been nude the entire play, so that could have had some-thing to do with the vulnerability factor.

He blinked at her slightly overplaying her role. "Sure. It's my job."

"Of course it is. Come in, and I'll take you around back where I found the suspicious package." Prada toddled toward her, yawning with a yip. The pup went right to the door, and Tennyson's heart soared with hope that Prada finally understood she was to do her business outside.

"What's that?" Officer Rhett asked, stooping and extending his hand. Prada smelled his hand, and then, very ladylike, gave him a simple swipe of her tongue before squatting on the oriental runner and peeing.

"That's my attack dog . . . one who seems to think the carpet is grass."

Officer Rhett stood. "Attack dog, huh?"

Tennyson shrugged, scooped Prada from where she now stood, obviously empty of bodily fluids, and gestured to the back. "This way."

"Is it a package? Or a bag? You said *bag* on the phone." He stepped inside, his big body brushing slightly against her shoulder. He smelled good. Warm and woodsy. Like a real man would smell, not a well-manicured businessman with $500 loafers. This man was a Wolverine boots kinda guy. And she only knew about those because a guy in high school used to wear them.

"It's a . . . bag. I think."

Officer Rhett looked at her with suspicion. Maybe all cops looked at people with suspicion. "Let me take a look before I call for backup this time."

He made her sound silly. She wasn't silly. She was opportunistic. And lonely. And maybe slightly horny. Hey, it had been a long time, and Officer Joe looked mighty fine in his uniform. "Just come through here."

She led him through the living area, out the solarium, and through the French doors that led to her back patio. She'd bought the house because of the outdoor area. The blue-gray slate stretched out to a gorgeous leveled pool with a large brick wall from which water cascaded. Beyond was the outdoor pergola with the stone hearth and small pool house. The slate also extended to the carriage/mother-in-law house, which was a minireplica of her house. On the other side was a once-lush garden that needed some TLC, but would be breathtaking once her landscape artist got ahold of it.

Officer Rhett looked around at the splendor, and she didn't miss the appreciation in his eyes. He turned to her and arched a dark brow . . . which was sexy. Totally sexy.

"Over there." She pointed, kissing Prada on the head and earning a doggy kiss in return.

When he turned toward the area by the pump, she quickly tugged her breasts upward in the lace bra and intentionally allowed the caftan ties at her throat to come undone. Prada seemed to understand and immediately started chewing the ties, widening the gap even more. This dog was finally being useful beyond mere cuteness.

Officer Rhett approached the bag, shining a light he'd pulled from his heavy-looking utility belt. "Did you have any workmen out recently? Someone who might have left this?"

Tennyson made a thinking face. "Hmm . . . well, oh, you know, the pool company came out to service the pump." She pretended to look embarrassed. She was almost 99 percent certain the pool company had left their bag behind and hadn't missed it yet. But she wasn't telling him that.

Officer Rhett walked over to the bag and lifted it. Parting the sides, he nodded. "Just a tool bag."

"Oh, thank goodness," Tennyson said, moving closer. "I guess I got nervous after that whole deal with the courthouse last week."

"You thought this was a bomb?" he asked, his voice laced with disbelief.

"Well, I mean, I didn't know." Tennyson gave him a guilty smile.

The man shook his head. "Is there a reason someone would leave a bomb at your house?"

He made it sound like someone might have a legitimate reason to do so. Sure, she could be a pain in the ass, but no one had tried to kill her. Yet.

"I'm sorry. It just made me nervous, and then I remembered you'd given me that card and . . ." She held a hand up and shrugged.

"It's fine. That's what I'm here for—to protect and—"

"Serve?" she finished.

Officer Rhett narrowed his eyes. "Did you call me out here for some other reason, Mrs. . . . what's your last name again?"

"You can call me Tennyson. Can I call you Joseph?" She smiled and stepped back so he could pass. Prada stopped chewing and watched him as he walked by.

Joseph made an annoyed face, but she didn't miss that he also noted her parted caftan, which did a great job of showcasing the valley between her breasts. "Sure. Whatever works for you."

Following him back to the house, Tennyson fluffed her hair and pinched her cheeks. Like a nutcase. She had no clue why she was attracted to this cop. She needed to get a grip. "Officer Rhett, I mean Joe, can I offer you a drink for your trouble? I have beer, vodka, and wine."

"It's Joseph. Not Joe. And you realize I'm on duty at present, right?"

She felt sort of dumb now. "I'm sorry. Of course you are. I'm just very appreciative of you. You know, having to come save me twice over the last few weeks. I'm going to have to vote yes to fund police raises."

"I don't think . . ." Joseph stopped inside the house and turned to her. "Never mind. Thanks. I could use a raise."

And then he smiled.

Hot damn, the man had a great smile. "Uh, a bottled water then?"

He stood for a moment, looking at her. "You look a lot different than you did the last time I was here. That mask thing must really work."

Tennyson had no idea how it happened, but it happened—she blushed. "Oh well, if you pay enough you can repair anything."

It was the wrong thing to say because his smile disappeared. "That's what they say. I'll see myself out, but you probably need to lock up after I leave. You've checked all the windows, correct? We don't want random raccoons, squirrels, or a curious burglar to come inside."

"I don't want specific ones," she quipped.

He made a confused face.

"You said *random* . . . uh, it was just a joke," she said, wondering if he even had a sense of humor. It wasn't a requirement, though she usually preferred a man who had one.

Tennyson led the way to the front door, strangely disappointed. She wasn't sure what she expected to happen between her and Officer Rhett. She wanted to see him again but didn't know how to ask him point-blank—she had never asked a man out before. Never had to. And though his gaze had held a flicker of interest, she wasn't sure he was into her enough to accept a clumsy invitation to dinner or coffee. He was a man doing his job. That was all. "I have a security system I need to get activated, but I checked the windows after Rocky ransacked my bedroom, and they are all secure. Plus I have Prada now. She's got a ferocious bark."

Joseph snorted.

"Well, I'm sorry about the whole bag thing. I guess I . . . I just thought it would be best to call you and make sure. Now that I'm divorced, I'm here alone." Of course not totally alone anymore since Andrew and Emma were a stone's throw away, but he didn't have to know that.

Joseph paused at the door and turned to her. "I'll stop in sometime and check on you. I patrol this area frequently, and I don't live too far away, either. You have my card if you need me."

Tennyson bit her lip, playing a bit ingenue before saying, "That would be nice, Joseph."

He paused a full five seconds and studied her. She could feel something change. Or perhaps she wanted to feel that way, as if he saw something worthwhile in her.

"Okay, then, have a good night, ma'am," he said with a curt nod.

"Tennyson," she reminded him.

"Tennyson," he said, his mouth curving slightly. "Take care."

CHAPTER FIVE

Two weeks later

Melanie counted the crystal one final time. Seven rows of ten. Seventy glistening champagne flutes ready to toast her daughter with the Veuve Clicquot currently chilling in the extra refrigerator. Kit had picked the boxes of bubbly up from the Bottle Shoppe earlier in the day and brought them home, his one concession to helping with the party. Maureen Godfrey had delivered the layer cake earlier. The ballet-pink cake with the scalloped fondant sat atop the buffet on the crystal pedestal that Melanie had received as a gift for her own wedding. All that was left was for the caterers to arrive.

Where *were* they?

She glanced at her watch and straightened the monogrammed napkins she'd ordered for rush delivery for the third time. The caterers were now thirty minutes behind schedule. Dang it.

"Oh my goodness, Mom," Emma said, stepping into the dining room and looking around. "It smells like a funeral parlor in here."

Melanie managed to smile despite the tension she felt. "I'm not sure if that was what I was going for. I just wanted lots of pretty flowers."

She turned and surveyed the dining area and formal living room. Her friend was a florist and had shown up with soft violet hydrangeas, white roses, and other delicate blossoms that spilled from crystal vases. White linens had been pressed and freshly polished silver trays sat side by side on the antique buffet. Soft instrumental music spilled from the speakers Kit had paid a small fortune to have installed last year. The overall mood was elegant and highbrow, something that would rival whatever Tennyson would do for the couple at the end of the month. Overdoing the party was petty. She knew this, but that didn't stop her from maxing out Kit's credit card to impress people with her hostess skills. Melanie looked at the perfection of a cake, and her stomach growled.

She'd been doing Weight Watchers ever since she'd found out 1) there was going to be a wedding at the end of August no matter how much she wished there wasn't, 2) Tennyson looked ten years younger and thirty pounds lighter than she did, and 3) Charlotte had been invited to the engagement party. Melanie now knew being "hangry" was a real thing. Like a really real thing that made her want to kill Charlotte and eat a whole sleeve of the Girl Scout Thin Mints she'd hidden in the freezer from Kit and Noah.

But she wouldn't because she was in control. And Charlotte wasn't the problem in her marriage, according to the therapist.

I am in control.

That was the mantra the therapist had suggested she use when she felt her world unraveling. So far it hadn't worked because words don't repair ruts in the front yard or help her get into the Spanx that no longer fit. How did Spanx not fit, anyway? She currently wore the top part of a pair of control-top pantyhose with the legs cut off.

Melanie and Kit had gone to the therapist last week. The woman had given them a profile to complete, things Melanie wouldn't tell her doctor of many years much less a veritable stranger, but she'd tried to be as honest as she could. That seemed to be the therapist's buzzword—*honesty*. During their first session, the woman had used it twenty-three times. Melanie had started counting when she saw where things were headed. Kit didn't seem to have a problem being honest. He was like the golden retriever of therapy, eagerly oversharing and fetching anything the therapist tossed his way. Even about their sex life.

Melanie had nearly died when the therapist asked how often they were intimate.

And then she'd felt guilty when she realized it was actually a lot less than she thought.

She knew she needed to work on being more open to having sex, but she was so darned tired. At the end of the day she felt anything but sexy. The thought of wearing a thong and having the energy to be playful or "into it" seemed as desirable as having to scrub around the toilet. When she and Kit did have sex, it was very vanilla, and she made the appropriate sounds and said the things she knew he liked to hear, all the while wondering if she had mailed the check for Noah's summer camp or if she had called the vet to order Poppy more special dog food. Kit seemed to know this, and when he asked, "Are you sure you want to?" she always brightly said, "Of course I do," but she knew he knew she really didn't. It was the game they played every time he rubbed her shoulders.

So she'd started staying up late to finish up the dishes or pay bills in order to avoid him.

How horrible was that?

"Mom?" Emma asked, snapping her fingers in front of Melanie's face.

"What?"

Emma laughed. "Where'd ya go?"

You do not want to know.

"Sorry. I'm distracted. Goodness, it's going to be a busy summer for us all."

"Mom, you really don't have to stress about the wedding. Tennyson has volunteered to help, and we have a wedding planner who can take some of the burden off." Emma looked so sincere. And she looked so pretty in her simple Lilly Pulitzer dress and neutral platform sandals. Her brown hair fell straight, the caramel highlights catching in the soft lighting. Such a lovely girl to be saying such a horrible thing to her mother. Let Tennyson help? Only if Melanie were half-dead. As God as her witness, at the very least, this wedding would be tasteful and elegant.

"It will be exactly how you want it, but you have to indulge me a little. I'm not sure your brother will ever get married. His hygiene is going to have to improve, and he'll have to convince a girl to tie the knot before he takes off his shoes," Melanie said.

"True. He's pretty disgusting." Emma walked around the table and stood, staring at the white roses. "I can't believe we're doing this. Married. Wow."

Hope burgeoned inside Melanie. "You know you don't have to get married right now. I mean, you could live together. I don't think it will cause a stir."

She didn't want her daughter living with Andrew, but it would be better than marrying Tennyson's son. Taking vows was a major commitment . . . and the marriage brought Tennyson with it. Her daughter shacking up sounded better than a legal union.

Emma's dreamy expression faded. "I don't care if it does. I *want* to marry Andrew. I've wanted to marry him since our third date, when I knew he was the one. We're adults and ready to make this commitment now . . . not when the rest of the world thinks we're old enough."

Something in her daughter's words caused a niggle of . . . something. There was something more there. Was Andrew pushing this? Or did Emma think it would bind him to her at a time that would be difficult for her? The first year of med school was no joke. Emma would be snowed under with work and study. Maybe she was afraid

Andrew would lose interest and find other pastures. "I know you believe that, sweetheart, but he's the first guy you've ever been serious about. Sometimes you have to kiss a lot of frogs, you know?"

Melanie knew it was the wrong thing to say the minute the words left her lips. Emma's expression narrowed. "So you're saying your first love can't be your only love? Because you've always said Daddy was your first love."

Mic drop.

"Yes, but I dated other guys before your father."

"Yeah, and I did, too. I mean, no one super official, but that doesn't mean I don't have some experience. You're acting like I just met Andrew. We've been dating for two and a half years. We're committed to each other and in love, so please stop trying to talk me out of marrying him." Her gaze hardened, and Melanie was reminded of how incredibly stubborn her child could be.

"I'm sorry. I'm worried about you overloading yourself."

Emma exhaled heavily. "You're *always* worried. So why would me waiting to get married change anything about that?"

"What's all this fussing on a day when my beautiful granddaughter is announcing her good fortune?" Anne Brevard asked, gliding into the room, her hands outstretched toward Emma. One thing she could say about her mother—she loved her grandchildren and rarely found fault with them.

"Gee Ma," Emma said, her face changing from irritation to pleasure. "You look so pretty."

Melanie's mother preened and gave her granddaughter's hands a squeeze. "Thank you, and you look lovely as well. Are you ready for your big night?"

"I'm excited. It's going to be a bit of a whirlwind, but I feel like I have to do this now. I was just saying as much to Mother," Emma said, glancing over at Melanie with an emphatic look.

"I understand. Your grandfather and I married when he was in his last year of medical college. We were so young, but we were very determined." Her mother dropped Emma's hands and turned to Melanie. "Daughter, you look nice. Very much like a mother of the bride."

What did that mean?

Melanie glanced down at the dress she'd found at Nordstrom. Okay, yes, it was a bit staid, but it camouflaged her rounded belly—stupid premenopause and chocolate chip cookie dough—and covered her appropriately from neck to knee. And it had been on sale. Melanie hated paying full price, so she'd snapped it up when it fit her without gaping or looking like a furniture cover. It was a size 12, something she knew her mother would disapprove of. Anne had always managed to stay in single-digit sizes and had been very vocal on the subject. The woman definitely had standards, and that was the issue sometimes. "Thank you, Mother."

Her mother surveyed the dining room and living area. "I see you went with Vendela roses? I've always found them a bit fussy, but they do like to show out."

Melanie had no clue what kind of roses they were. She couldn't care less as long as they lasted through the party.

Her mother turned, her features settling into something Melanie knew well. Disapproval. "Is there something I can lend a hand with? I arrived early in case you needed some assistance."

Melanie shook her head. "No. I have it all under control. Is Hillary coming tonight?"

She had called her sister earlier in the week, and Hillary had sounded stronger. She'd said that she would come to the party if at all possible. Melanie's spirits had been lifted just thinking about Hillary getting out of the house and trying to join the land of the living. She stayed in far too much.

Her mother's expression shuttered. "Your sister doesn't enjoy social events, and today wasn't a good day for her. She sends her best wishes, of course."

Of course.

Melanie's older sister lived with Anne in a tasteful town house in the middle of the Spring Lake subdivision. Hillary had once owned a successful salon in Baton Rouge, parlaying her skills as a stylist into a lucrative business, but after their father's death and her divorce a year after, her struggle with both anorexia and bulimia—two diseases Hillary had thought she'd beaten back in college—had come roaring back. Eventually Hillary had moved in with her mother and seemed to have given herself over to the diseases, hiding herself even more, selling the salon her business partner had kept afloat for years. The constant binge and purge had taken its toll on her body, and in the past months, Hillary looked worse than she ever had, dwindling down to a mere eighty-eight pounds, making people wince when they looked into her now-hollow eyes.

Her sister's refusal to get help, and her mother's dismissal of the subject, broke Melanie's heart. She felt tears prick at her eyes, something that happened all too often these days when she thought about her sister.

But she didn't have that luxury at the moment, nor did she want to examine too closely the feelings she had about her mother and how Anne had contributed to Hillary's lack of mental well-being. Her mother had spent a lifetime making passive-aggressive comments about Hillary's adolescent chubbiness, sending her to "healthy living" camps each summer and buying oversize clothing to hide her "little rolls that no one wanted to see."

The doorbell rang.

"That must be the caterer. Finally," Melanie said, hurrying to the side door. Standing on the doorstep were several workers dressed in black chef jackets emblazoned with Gloria Jay's. "Come on in. I thought you had gotten lost. You were supposed to be here forty minutes ago."

"Sorry, ma'am," one of the women, sporting a nose ring, no less, said. Anne would probably say something to the woman. "There was a tanker turned over on I-49 that had traffic at a standstill."

"Oh well, that makes sense. Come in, and I'll show you where I want everything placed."

Ten minutes later, the caterers had put the heavy hors d'oeuvres in chafing dishes, sending the delectable smells of shrimp and grits, smoked oysters, and spicy jambalaya to compete with the scent of the "fussy" roses. Two staff members filled silver trays with bite-size smoked Gouda and crawfish toast points and mini-Natchitoches meat pies. The cuisine of Louisiana would be on display for Emma and Andrew's guests this evening.

Kit emerged from upstairs, looking like a seasoned model for a fancy country-club brochure. He wore an open-throat linen shirt, navy sports coat, natty trousers, and leather driving moccasins. His hair was swept back from his high forehead, and those crinkly blue eyes looked prepared to charm. He dropped a surprise kiss onto her mother's cheek, earning a light slap.

"Such a rogue. How do you manage him still, daughter?" Anne asked, her laughter like wind chimes, light and delightful. The diminutive Japanese woman adored being noticed by the opposite sex, especially one as nice looking as Kit. Her mother was, after all, a woman who enjoyed attention, negative or positive.

"I don't. Kit manages himself." Truer words had never been spoken.

"Andrew and his mother are here," Emma said, trotting out the front door, a smile blooming on her face.

"Great," Melanie deadpanned, straightening the napkins for the fourth time and eyeing the spot where the silver cake knife needed to go.

"Behave," Kit said, dropping the same kiss he'd just given her mother onto her cheek. "Tennyson is Tennyson. She hasn't changed."

"Yeah, she has. She's got money now, and from what I understand, she has a lot of it. She makes sure everyone knows it, too."

"Mel, you said you'd try," Kit breathed, his words a sigh. He knew how she felt about Tennyson, but that didn't mean he felt the same way. It wasn't his family she'd ruined, and she knew by the tone of his voice when they talked about high school that he still had a small place of affection for his old love. It incensed her, but she never pursued it because she knew she, too, had a place that still longed for what once was. She trampled that feeling any time it came up with the image of Tennyson in that black dress on the night of their wedding. "I'm going to fix myself a scotch. You want a drink?"

"No, I need to keep my wits about me," she said as her husband walked out.

Her mother appeared at Melanie's elbow, and they both watched from the dining room window as Emma hugged Tennyson and then kissed Andrew. "She's like a bitch cat."

Melanie glanced at her mother. "Tennyson?"

Her mother's steely gaze said everything she felt. "She looks fluffy and harmless, but her claws sink deep. And she's not afraid to bite, is she?"

Anne would never forgive Tennyson for what she'd done that night. People in Shreveport still used the debacle as a cautionary tale for brides who were tempted to invite an ex-girlfriend or -boyfriend to their wedding as a token of goodwill. A lot of vodka and a tiny spark of anger couldn't be dampened by a cheerful piece of wedding cake and a fun flirtation with a cute groomsman. No, that kind of angry wrecking ball of emotion plowed through good intention, destroying any wedded bliss in its path.

"And she'll be part of Emma's family now," Melanie whispered, feeling hopeless.

"But not ours. She'll never be part of ours, and I refuse to accept her as anything other than the trash she is." Anne's voice had grown frosty enough to freeze the windowpane they stood in front of.

"You should steer clear of Tennyson tonight, Mother," Melanie said, giving her mother a firm look. "I'll repeat Kit's advice—this is about Emma and Andrew, not us. Em doesn't know that Tennyson broke our family, and I want that knowledge to stay in the past where it belongs. The Brevards have to own our own mistakes. Tennyson didn't cause what happened. She just lit the match. So let's *try*. For Emma's sake. Okay?"

Those were the words Kit had used on her earlier. *Let's try to ignore Tennyson.* But she knew that ignoring anyone like Tennyson was akin to tearing a winning lottery ticket in half. Nothing easy about actually doing it.

Her mother looked at her, defiance and perhaps hate shimmering from her eyes. "I will *try*."

Melanie started to quote Yoda but realized her mother would have no clue what she spoke of. *Star Wars* wasn't something Anne Brevard would deem suitable entertainment. Instead Melanie walked to the buffet and looked for the cake knife, praying it wasn't tarnished and could be set out as is. She didn't have time to clean it properly.

"Hello, darlings," Tennyson trilled from the open doorway, pausing for a moment in a vogue-like manner that suggested everyone look at her.

It worked.

Melanie and Anne turned to survey their guest. Kit walked in from the kitchen carrying a highball glass, his blue eyes on the woman standing in the doorway with leg pointed and hand on hip to showcase her figure.

Tennyson smiled brilliantly, sliding her sunglasses from her nose and folding them. Then she clacked into the house in impossibly high heels, a dress she'd obviously poured herself into, and an expensive-looking bag from which that stupid dog peeked out. Tennyson's blonde hair had been swept up into something suitable for prom, diamond earrings dangled, and the large emerald on her finger couldn't be real, but probably was because only Tennyson would choose something so obnoxious.

Melanie sucked in a deep breath and set the cake knife she'd just pulled from the depths of her buffet beside the cake. "Hello, Tennyson. Welcome to our home."

Tennyson looked around, her eyes critical as she took in the space. Melanie had redecorated the public rooms in the fall. She'd had muted silver curtains custom made and painted the walls a dove-wing gray. Glossy, white trim, a slate hearth, and creamy velvet Chesterfield sofas sat facing each other with flax basket-weave armchairs anchoring the end facing the fireplace. Soothing slate, ecru, and white dominated the traditional space, which flirted with a hint of modern farmhouse because watching *Fixer Upper* did that to a person. In fact, Melanie had nixed the shiplap at the last minute. Punches of dusky blue and teal livened the space, and a huge crystal chandelier watched over the muted Turkish rug. The space was tasteful and fashionable enough to be featured in a local magazine.

Melanie was quite proud of it, but looking at it through Tennyson's eyes, she could see that it was safe, boring, and exactly like a dozen others she'd seen in magazines. When she'd walked into Sherwin-Williams wearing lululemon (bought on sale, of course), carrying a Louis Vuitton bag (anniversary gift), and driving a Lexus (because, yes, they are awesome), the clerk had probably pulled the South Shreveport Basic Bitch color palette.

"Well, it's very . . . you, Mel," Tennyson said.

Melanie tried to smile, but she really wanted to slap Tennyson, which was not "trying." So instead she summoned her best hostess voice. "Thank you. They featured it in *SB Magazine* this past January."

"Oh well, a nice feather in your cap for sure," Tennyson said, patting the dog, who wore a bow the same persimmon as Tennyson's dress.

Why had she said that? Ugh. She sounded so insecure.

"Uh, the puppy? Are you . . ." Melanie arched her brows and looked at Prada. The dog's pink tongue curled adorably as she panted all over the expensive leather.

"She's my service animal and will stay in my purse," Tennyson said, a challenge glittering in her eyes. Melanie didn't want to deal with this again, even though she knew the dog *was not* her service animal. Instead, she nodded.

But why in the heck had Tennyson brought the stupid dog? Of course, Melanie knew why. It was one more way to draw attention to herself. People would coo over the little fluff ball, and Tennyson would look . . . something. Trendy? An animal lover? Any logical, sensible person would look askance at someone who brought a puppy to a party, but that was Tennyson. She always did the unexpected. That was her MO and had been for as long as Melanie had known her.

At that moment, Andrew and Emma breezed in, and Melanie got caught up in last-minute preparations. Thirty minutes later, guests began arriving, glasses clinked as toasts abounded, and the loud buzz of conversation distracted Melanie from her defensiveness around Tennyson. Everyone seemed to be having a great time, even her normally stoic mother, who sat on the sofa and held court over a few of her invited friends. The waitstaff circulated with Pimm's Cups and mint juleps, which everyone seemed to enjoy. Laughter rang out, and after another thirty minutes, Melanie had forgotten Tennyson was even there.

Until Poppy got out.

Melanie wasn't sure exactly how it happened. She had put Poppy in the crate in the laundry room. They never shut the kennel door because Poppy liked to lay her head over the lip of the crate so she wasn't fully inside. If Melanie hadn't let the dog have her way, what happened next wouldn't have occurred.

Melanie supposed someone had been looking for the lavatory and bumbled into the wrong room. The headstrong retriever wasn't nose blind and took advantage of the situation by escaping out the open door. Poppy was somewhat obedient, except when it came to shoes, socks, and food. And, man, did Poppy love to beg for food. The delectable smells in the living and dining rooms had likely been too much to ignore, and Melanie caught sight of the fluffy, sneaky dog slinking in and weaving through the crowd toward the fragrant chafing dishes. She'd been in the middle of a conversation with Janie Thackery over the trends in bridesmaids dresses and failed to catch Kit's attention so he could head Poppy off.

Of course, Kit was oblivious to her piercing stare. Her husband was locked in a conversation with their banker, and standing next to him, glowing with a healthy tan and wearing a size 4 black dress that accentuated her utter skinniness was Charlotte. The woman kept darting admiring glances at Kit and touching his arm as if *she* were his partner in life and not business. Her weird high-pitched laughter had been abusing Melanie's ear all evening.

"Kit's got the perfect plan for that. He always does." *Yeeeheee, tee hee, haaahaaahaaa.*

"You should see this guy try to kill a wasp." *Yeeeheee, tee hee, haaahaaahaaa.*

"A foot-long hot dog on a stick. That's exactly what Kit said when we went to the Rangers game." *Yeeeheee, tee hee, haaahaaahaaa.*

Please. It was nauseating.

Melanie and Kit used to have that psychic-connection thing where they could read each other's mind, but that was a big ol' fail at present because Kit hadn't glanced her way in a while.

"Excuse me a minute, Janie. I have to attend to something," Melanie said, setting her wineglass on the edge of the buffet. She slid past Janie, who had literally stopped midsentence and still had her mouth open. Poppy was skirting the table, and several people were smiling indulgently because Poppy was pretty darn cute. Of course they didn't know what Melanie knew. Poppy was an expert counter surfer, and she'd just hit the Big Kahuna with the rows of delectable, meaty wondrousness spread before her.

Melanie caught Poppy's collar just as she was about to go paws up on the table.

"Oh no, you don't, missy," Melanie said, tossing a smile to John Reeves and Ed Deemer, who were scarfing down Natchitoches meat pies like they were Skittles.

"Woo, she nearly got her some," Ed joked.

"She'd give you a run for your money on hitting this spread, Ed," Melanie said, teasing their across-the-street neighbor, tugging Poppy's collar, and looking around desperately for Kit. Instead Tennyson appeared.

"So who's that heifer trying to climb Kit?" Tennyson asked, not reading the situation with the dog at all.

"What?"

"The woman trying to mount your husband in the living room," Tennyson said, her eyes finding Kit over by the piano. Charlotte had her hand on his arm and was smiling up at him. Melanie gritted her teeth.

"Oh, that's his new business partner. Her name is Charlotte. She's Heather Frommeyer's cousin."

Tennyson's eyes widened. "Really? Does she know he's married?"

Aggravation reared its head inside her. It wasn't like Melanie didn't know exactly what Charlotte was doing, but to have Tennyson, the best friend who had betrayed her, who had tossed their friendship into the flames, who had shown back up in town looking thinner, younger, and wealthier than Melanie ever hoped to look at nearing fifty years of age say such a thing made it worse. "Don't worry about it."

Tennyson looked down at her, where she crouched, holding on to Poppy. "Oh, I'm not worried about it. But maybe *you* should be."

At that moment, Prada decided to make like a jack-in-the-box and pop from the depths of Tennyson's bag. The dog gave a little yip, and

Poppy turned like a serial killer sensing a nubile blonde tripping over a felled log.

Melanie opened her mouth to warn Tennyson, but it was too late.

In Poppy's defense, Prada looked a lot like the squirrel that had been terrorizing her in the backyard all spring. Same color, same size, same big brown eyes. At that moment, Melanie had the most ridiculous thing pop into her head—that Ray Stevens song. The one where the squirrel went berserk in the First Self-Righteous Church. Both Melanie and Tennyson had loved that silly song when they were kids, but that was neither here nor there because what Poppy did next was . . . well, it was epic.

Prada chirped again when she caught sight of the big, fluffy retriever, perhaps in delight. Who really knew? It didn't matter, because Poppy didn't take anything about Prada as a delight.

Nope.

Her friendly, lovable family pet went into protect-and-kill mode, ripping from Melanie's grasp and jumping on Tennyson. Tennyson wasn't prepared, and she stumbled into Ed, who dropped the glass of bourbon he'd been drinking. Ed hit the buffet hard. Tennyson yelped as Poppy's nails hooked her bodice, making the straps on her dress pop, and, well, at that point everyone got the chance to view the "works of art" created by no doubt one of Manhattan's best breast guys.

Tennyson's purse slipped from her arm, the puppy tumbled out, and Poppy went for the Yorkie with all the pent-up aggression she'd been harboring toward the squirrel. Meanwhile when Ed slammed into the buffet, it caused Melanie's wineglass to spill all over Janie, who had followed Melanie to the table still expounding on the bridesmaid dresses she'd seen in *Southern Living* magazine. Janie had already told Melanie she'd just bought the dress she wore at Neiman's and paid full price (sucker), so Melanie wasn't surprised to hear Janie gasp. "My dress! Oh my God, it's ruined."

Prada wasn't stupid. She knew a determined, fluffy golden retriever when she saw one, so she jetted between Janie's legs. Janie grabbed the lace runner, pulling it and the tiered cake off the buffet. Prada turned for a microsecond toward the smashed cake and no doubt the delicious scent of buttercream before realizing cake didn't matter when death was breathing down her neck. She took off again, and then Poppy collided with the horrified Janie. Melanie's friend went down like a sack of stone, missing the Yorkie and landing right on the ruined cake. Janie's landing provided enough of a roadblock that Melanie was able to catch Poppy by the collar. Prada took off toward the kitchen with a panicked *erp, erp, erp* sound that could peel the wallpaper from the walls.

Everyone had stopped chatting and moved to observe the aftermath in the dining room . . . which was pretty spectacular with exposed breasts, a middle-aged woman squirming in frosting, and a dog scrabbling against the hardwood. The scent of buttercream and bourbon would forever be imprinted on Melanie's brain, as would the color Tennyson turned before she tugged up the bodice of her dress.

"Stop it," Melanie demanded of Poppy, who had taken to lunging repeatedly and chuffing toward the direction of the kitchen.

Luckily Kit showed up—about time—and grabbed Poppy, dragging her through the living room toward the laundry room.

Melanie straightened and then rushed over to Janie, who was in the process of shaking frosting from her hands. "Oh, Janie, I'm so sorry. Are you okay?"

Janie tried to rise but slipped and fell back. Her face was pale, and at that moment she looked older and frailer than her sixty-some-odd years dictated. Melanie reached down and took her elbow. "Here, let me help you."

Ed thankfully scrambled over and helped her get Janie off the floor. As the older woman rose, Melanie tried to discreetly brush away the clumps of cake while simultaneously shooting her daughter a look that said *distract*.

Emma had been staring slack jawed but snapped to it when she caught Melanie's imperative gaze. "Okay, everyone, come on in here and let me tell you about how Andrew proposed. Y'all won't believe how romantic it all was."

Like lemmings, the crowd of their friends and family turned and followed her daughter back to the living room, leaving Melanie with Ed, Janie, and Tennyson. Melanie noticed her mother hadn't been a spectator. The woman had taken her seriously about staying away from Tennyson. Speaking of which, Tennyson had pulled herself together and clacked into the kitchen, probably looking for the now-silent dog.

"Oh my. I can't believe this," Janie said, wiping her hands down her sides, smearing her pink dress with white icing. A clump of cake fell with a splat onto her shoe.

"I'm so sorry, Janie. Are you okay? Not hurt?"

Ed helped steady Janie. "Yeah, you okay?"

"Well, my pride is hurt. That's for certain. But all my parts seem to be working. The dress"—she glanced down at her ruined dress—"well, it's pretty much destroyed. Did anyone happen to get it on video? I'm dying to go viral and embarrass my grandchildren."

"Oh, Janie, you have way too good of a sense of humor about this," Melanie said, giving her a rueful smile. Everything was such a mess, and Janie could have seriously been hurt. "Please don't sue me."

Janie swiped a finger through the frosting on her lapel and sucked it into her mouth. "The cake is good, and, honey, I wouldn't sue you. You have a wedding to pay for."

Melanie managed a rueful smile. "Come on, let's go to my bathroom and get you cleaned up. You're smaller than I am, but surely I can find something I can't fit into any longer for you to change into. I'll pay for the dress, of course."

Kit appeared again, handed Ed a fresh bourbon, and gave Janie an apologetic look. "Don't worry, Janie. Poppy is put away, and she will get no dog treats for at least a month."

"Oh, it's not her fault. She was doing what dogs do," Janie said, following Melanie through the kitchen, where Prada cowered under the bar at the end of the kitchen island. "I mean, look at that poor puppy. Where did she come from, anyway?"

Melanie stifled the sudden anger.

This was Tennyson's fault. Service animal, her ass!

Who did something like bring a puppy to an event . . . outside of some brainless Hollywood celebrity? And Melanie knew very well that Tennyson was anything but dumb. She was, however, good at playing parts. Tennyson may not have wanted to expose herself in front of everyone, but she sure had wanted the attention.

Wish granted, bitch.

Five minutes later, after having found Janie a dress that pretty much swamped her petite figure, Melanie slid out of the bedroom to address the mess in the dining room. She was met with apologetic smiles and a couple of pats from friends and family. Emma and Andrew had done an admirable job of distracting everyone from the disaster. When Melanie finally rounded the corner into the dining room, she found Charlotte and her neighbor Coco, a most unlikely duo, cleaning up the cake and spilled bourbon. Thankfully, neither of the glasses had shattered and sent splinters of glass careening.

"Such a shame because it really was a pretty cake," Coco said. The woman wore a miniskirt and stilettos, but her blouse fully covered her enhanced breasts. Small wonder.

"Thank you, ladies," Melanie said, giving Coco's arm a squeeze. She was surprised to find her older neighbor's arms were pretty well defined. More so than her own. Which was kind of sad since Coco was a good twenty-five years older than Melanie. God, she needed to start working out.

"You're welcome. I'm always happy to help. Goodness, I'm like family to Kit, anyway," Charlotte said, wiping up the last of the frosting and tossing it in the white kitchen trash bag. Kit came into the dining room with more towels and a bottle of kitchen cleaner. He handed it to Charlotte wordlessly.

"Teeny's dog peed in the kitchen," he said, matter of factly.

"Where *is* that woman?" Melanie asked, looking around for Tennyson.

"It's okay, Mel," Kit said, pressing his hands toward her in the manner she hated. She despised when he tried to tell her how to think and feel. Like he was the voice of reason.

"It's *not* okay. It's our children's celebration. This is not the occasion for a dog in a purse, for heaven's sake. She should know better."

"You just said the important words—it's our children's celebration. Let it go. No one was hurt, and who needs cake, anyway?" he said, trying to smile and lighten the mood.

"I never eat cake," Charlotte said, drawing the bag's ties together.

"Of course you don't," Melanie said, turning on her heel so she didn't say or do something she regretted. She needed a moment. She needed a drink. Or Xanax. She wondered if she had any left from the root canal. Or was that some other drug they'd given her to relax? Whatever. She felt tight as a snare drum.

She moved through the kitchen, where the staff had gathered to replenish hors d'oeuvres, and then snuck onto the small back patio that seemed to have no real purpose since it wasn't attached to the larger one. One of her friends had suggested it was specifically for a kitchen garden, so she, with the help of Hillary, had dutifully installed oregano, mint, and basil in containers. No one came out here, so it was the perfect place for her to escape when she needed something more than a glass of wine.

Lifting the ceramic frog Noah and Emma had given her for Mother's Day ten years ago, she fished out the Ziploc bag containing her contraband pack of smokes and a lighter. She tapped one out, stuck it in her mouth, lit it, and sucked in the sweet nicotine that would soothe her jagged nerves.

"I'll have one of those," Tennyson said from the darkness, startling her.

"You can go to hell," Melanie said, shoving the plastic bag back up the frog's ass.

Tennyson's smile split the darkness. "You first."

CHAPTER SIX

Tennyson had been hiding from Melanie's wrath on the small screened porch right off the kitchen. She'd first gone to the powder room to pin her straps, then she'd come back and scooped up her troublesome puppy on the way out. She had every intention of returning to clean up the piddle Prada had delivered to Melanie's kitchen rug, but over the past week she'd learned Prada often did her business back to back. When she'd picked up the terrified puppy, Prada had clamored up her bodice, making the torn dress sag again. Thankfully, it did not pull it down to give her boobs an encore performance. The pup had immediately tried to hide beneath Tennyson's chin, which turned her irritation at the dog to sympathy. Poor Prada. Golden retrievers were usually friendly, but then again, Tennyson had seen *Cujo*.

Eventually, Prada calmed and struggled to be free of Tennyson's grasp. Independent little cuss. Tennyson set her on the brick pavers and opened the screened door. Prada waddled out and proceeded to take a dump on the pristine lawn. Great. Something else Tennyson would have to clean up. Seemed almost prophetic. Things had gone to shit fast.

Tennyson sank onto an abandoned gardening stool in the corner so she could keep an eye on Prada. She'd seen an article about small dogs being scooped up by owls and coyotes, so she never left the puppy alone. She was so focused on watching the hunched-over dog, she nearly screamed when the back door opened.

In the full moon, she could see it was Melanie, who looked super stressed.

Tennyson knew she should say something to alert the woman, but she didn't feel like dealing with the fussing she'd get over the buttercream, bourbon, and dog pee all over Melanie's floor. Mel would probably suck in a breath, square her shoulders, and go back to deal with things the way she always had. Her former friend was the queen of dealing.

But then Mel did something that made Tennyson raise her eyebrows. Or kind of raise them. She'd had Botox on Thursday.

Mrs. Goody Two-shoes pulled a baggie from beneath a frog statue and filched a ciggie.

When she and Melanie had been juniors in high school, they'd taken up smoking. They figured it would make them look cooler to smoke while they drank their Miller Lite ponies out in the Ferriers' field. It was tradition after every Friday night football game to drive out and circle their cars and trucks around a bonfire. So one Monday, Tennyson bought a pack of cigarettes from an obscure grocery store owned by a small Chinese man who spoke little English and didn't realize she was underage. She and Melanie practiced all week so they wouldn't cough or struggle to light the cigarettes. Tennyson didn't really like smoking that much, but surprisingly Melanie was brilliant at smoking and looking cool doing it. From then on, Mel liked a cig when she drank.

"I'll have one of those," Tennyson said, standing and walking over.

"You can go to hell," Melanie said with a glower after shoving the baggie back up the frog's ass.

"You first," Tennyson said, latching on to the old joke they had made after watching James Bond movies on TBS when they were girls. Melanie had made fun of how there was always a funny line delivered before 007 offed the villain. Ah, silly jokes between friends. How they came back to you when you least expected them.

Melanie's lips twitched, and she didn't protest when Tennyson pulled the baggie out, tapped out a lung dart, and lit it.

Tennyson took a drag and exhaled the smoke. "That was a real shit show."

"Yeah, thank you so much for bringing your dog to the engagement party. I didn't know they offered so much emotional support. Can I borrow her?" Melanie drawled, heavy on the sarcasm. Then she jabbed a finger at where Prada still hunched on her lawn. "And you're cleaning that up, too."

"She's been constipated for days."

"Try changing her food. It helped with Poppy," Melanie said.

"I *am* sorry for what happened. I shouldn't have brought her." Tennyson knew this was true. Thing was, she'd sort of fallen in love with the little dog. Never before had she wanted a pet. Growing up in a large family, she'd been surrounded by too many animals. As the youngest child, the walking and feeding always seemed to fall to her. After a while, she got tired of manning the pooper-scooper and cleaning the litter box. It had put her off animals, and since she'd traveled so much over the past fifteen or so years, she hadn't wanted to feel tied down. But she had forgotten how nice it was to have their weight on her lap or the snuggly goodness of their affection. Prada's little doggy kisses and adorable excitement at seeing her when she entered the room had done a lot to lessen Tennyson's irritation over the ruined rug in her living room.

Prada was at least a partial cure for her loneliness.

Of course, she wasn't really lonely. She didn't miss her ex-husband much. Robert had been gone on business a lot, anyway. Once Andrew had graduated and taken himself off to the University of Arkansas, she'd had plenty of luncheons and other engagements to fill her time when her husband was traveling (and doing his secretary). She visited Andrew in Fayetteville, gamely trying to hike with him and enjoy the wonders of nature. *Try* was the key word. She didn't get the obsession he had with kayaking the Buffalo River or scaling cliffs at the various state parks. So when Emma came along and was more interested in shopping and lunching, she marked herself lucky to gain an ally against mosquitos and ugly hiking boots. Her life had felt very full. But then after the divorce was final, and she was truly alone and newly single in Manhattan, she'd felt like an imposter trying to reclaim a life she wasn't sure she wanted anymore.

So maybe that was why she was here—a place where she had once felt very real. Once upon a time she'd belonged here. Once upon a time she'd been young, confident, and ready to take the world by storm. Tennyson had been a girl who had dreams, goals, and a safe place to rest her head each night. Maybe she wanted that part of herself back, the one that believed she still had something to give the world. Just what that was she wasn't certain, but she was willing to figure it out as she went.

Or maybe deep down beneath the expensive breast implants and Botox, she wanted to fix what was really broken. The one mistake she hadn't been able to fix, cover up, or atone for.

She'd broken a promise and hurt Melanie. In the moment, she hadn't cared. Maybe she still didn't. Or did. She wasn't sure about anything when it came to her old friend.

Melanie didn't speak. Instead she sucked on the cancer stick and blew out hazy clouds against the brilliance of the night sky.

"Did you hear me?" Tennyson asked.

"I did. I don't know whether to say okay or just gripe some more because that feels better."

Tennyson laughed because she didn't know what else to do. Things were definitely awkward between them, but that was to be expected. After all, Melanie had stolen Kit, and then Tennyson had gotten a little drunk at their stupid wedding and lit a fire that had burned their friendship to the ground. Afterward, there weren't even embers. Just ashes.

"Why are you laughing? None of this is funny," Melanie said.

Tennyson knew Melanie wasn't talking about the disaster of the cake and dogs. She meant the whole engagement thing. She'd sensed Melanie's displeasure when they'd met for the graduation dinner. She wasn't sure if it was because Andrew and Emma were so young or if it was because they would now be attached to one another forever . . . or however long the marriage lasted. Tennyson had learned to doubt "till death do you part."

But Melanie's anger wasn't fair to Emma and Andrew. After all, their children didn't know about what had happened between her and Melanie. Or at least *she* hadn't told them. When Tennyson had discovered Emma was Kit and Melanie's daughter, she'd been very careful to say they'd once been friends but had lost touch as people did before the internet and smartphones. She didn't say it was intentional, of course.

Perhaps the truth would have been better, but she didn't want to malign Melanie to her daughter. How was she supposed to tell Emma that Melanie had stolen Kit and that she'd been so angry about it that she had told a secret she'd promised not to tell . . . to everyone.

It was her circus, but she wasn't feeding that monkey.

On a not so emotional level, Tennyson understood what had happened between Melanie and Kit when they went off to college together. Disassociation was an acting technique she'd often applied to study the actions and emotions of characters. Applying that, she knew the following:

Fact one: Kit was Kit—wholly gorgeous with charm and an aw-shucks attitude that drew people like hummingbirds to a hibiscus.

Fact two: Melanie had always had a thing for Kit. Tennyson had always known this and couldn't fault her friend because Kit was easy to love, and half the teen girls in three parishes had the hots for him.

Fact three: Tennyson had broken up with Kit and left Shreveport. She'd chosen her potential career over love.

Fact four: Kit and Melanie had been lonely. And drunk. And . . . well, she knew what happened when one mixed loneliness and alcohol.

The only thing was—Tennyson had truly believed she was special to Kit and that he would choose her over Melanie every day of the week.

She'd been wrong. In her newly turned nineteen-year-old head, she believed she could leave Shreveport, catch her star, and bring a still-besotted-with-her Kit to NYC. Once he arrived, he'd propose to her with a giant diamond, and they would go on to live their most fabulous lives, basking in her fame and success. Made total sense back then. But the truth was nineteen-year-old girls could never imagine their life going any other way than what they'd envisioned. They could never foresee double lines on a pregnancy test or hearing no from every casting agent from Broadway to community theatre in Jersey. They couldn't imagine not getting the happily ever after they thought they deserved.

All those dumb inspirational posters had sold them a load of crap. Except the "hang in there" one with the kitten. That one was totally worth the $5.99 she'd spent at Spencer's.

When Tennyson had come home for fall break after having spent all summer and fall in Manhattan, everything had been fine. She, Kit, and Melanie fell into what they'd always been, with Kit doting on her and Melanie being their third wheel. But when she'd come home for Christmas, she'd known something was wrong. Her boyfriend and her best friend looked guilty. Correction: Melanie looked guilty. Finally, drunk on Zima at a New Year's Eve party, Melanie had admitted that she and Kit had (gasp!) kissed after the fall party. She was sorry. Tears ensued. Tennyson may have slapped her best friend, and in turn, Melanie had begged Tennyson to forgive her and promised it would never happen again. Kit seemed to be unaware that Tennyson knew he'd made a mistake with Melanie. His kisses were just as sweet, but Tennyson knew deep down things were changing, and she was afraid.

When she was in Manhattan, her old life was far away, but when she was home, she wasn't ready to let Kit go. She did everything she could to bind Kit to her, even going all the way with him, something he'd been begging her for since they'd started dating in high school. It had been beautiful, just what she'd imagined even though she'd promised she wouldn't have sex until she was married. She'd signed that pledge and worn the purity ring her daddy had given her when she'd turned sixteen. Of course, she'd upheld that vow until that night . . . unless oral counted. The lines were blurry on if going down on one another was really sex.

But after they'd done the deed, Kit broke up with her. Oh, he did it in a gentle, "it's not you, it's me" manner. Essentially, he felt they didn't need to wait on each other and needed the freedom to pursue their own lives. Yeah. He was sorry, but it was time they move on. Tennyson hadn't expected it to hurt so much, but it had. And, like, he couldn't have done that before they'd spent the entire break together having sex that violated her purity vow?

When she went back to NYC after the holidays, she made a new vow to herself—she was done with old things. Kit had been right about one thing—time to move on. She started accepting party invites, tried some things she shouldn't, and ended up in bed with a few guys she should have never slept with. She tried like hell to forget who she'd been and find a new Tennyson, one who was modern, sophisticated, and never going back to Shreveport.

Yet now here she was, looking at Melanie, accepting that her only child would be marrying her ex–best friend's daughter. Thirty years ago both women would have been ecstatic to know their offspring would marry. Today, not so much.

"I know it's not funny or ideal, but our two kids are in love, Melly," she said, finally responding to Melanie's statement.

"Don't call me Melly. You don't get to call me that anymore. After what you did to me—to my family—you don't get to act like we're friends. We're not. And never will be." Melanie dropped the cigarette and ground it out with her sensible kitten heel. Then she stooped, picked up the butt, and shoved it under a potted plant.

Tennyson bit her lip because, again, that was so Melanie. Of course she hid anything bad she did. That was her way. Always toeing the line. Always the status quo. Never going after what she really wanted.

Except that one time. When she went after Kit. And got him.

"Fine." Tennyson took a drag, not really liking the way the tar burned her lungs but not willing to smoke less than what Melanie had. "I will call you *Melanie*, or would you rather me call you Mrs. Layton?"

The look Melanie shot her was withering. "I don't care. Just clean up your dog's mess."

Then the woman who she'd thought would always be her bestie spun on her heel and went back to her friends and family, leaving Tennyson to finish her smoke and somehow clean up dog shit without a scoop, shovel, or paper towel. Such was the story of her life.

An hour later when Tennyson pulled away from the Laytons' perfectly tasteful house, she desperately needed a drink. She'd endured the remainder of the party, talking to Coco, who was about as interesting a person as Tennyson had ever met. Coco had been a Rockette back in the day and married an investment banker who'd come home to manage his family's estate. She spoke three languages and owned a Picasso. She also hinted that she was into swinging, which was admirable for a septuagenarian. No one else approached Tennyson, but she received a lot of guarded looks. Especially from Anne Brevard, Melanie's mother. The tiny Japanese woman had watched her all night, her gaze obsidian chips of sheer hate.

Well, ol' Annie had good cause, she supposed.

Tennyson had never liked Melanie's mother—she was cold, critical, and used her money to buy advantage for her daughters, but what Tennyson had done to her and to Mel's family had been wrong. Still, it wasn't like Anne hadn't deserved what she'd gotten. She had. But it shouldn't have been done out of revenge or spite.

When she pulled into her driveway, she was surprised to find a Toyota 4Runner sitting in the drive. Perhaps one of Emma's or Andrew's friends? The kids would probably be home much later. She overheard them planning to go out and have drinks after the party.

She passed the darkened car, weaving her cute red Mercedes coupe into the garage, immediately closing the garage door before she climbed out of her locked car. Living in the city had made her cautious. Not to mention the raccoon break-in from a month ago had revived the doubt of living in a house alone. Prada popped her head out of Tennyson's bag as if to say *we're here?* The little dog gave a yippy yawn and pawed the side of the bag.

"Okay, out you come," she said, lifting the puppy once the garage door settled against the slab and climbing out. When she entered the house, she deactivated the alarm and set Prada on the floor, hoping the dog wouldn't do her business before she had a chance to take her outside.

Just as she set her purse on the counter, the doorbell rang.

She shouldn't be as nervous as she felt. Perhaps it was because the whole night had been unsettling. When she'd dressed to kill earlier, she'd been determined to take the high road, play the charming mother of the groom, and work the room as only she could do when her mind was right. And things had been good until she saw Kit with Charlotte, and her "cheating" antennae rose a few inches. Then once she'd shown her boobs to the room and watched the cake crash to the floor, she'd gone into survival mode.

Clacking to the door, she peeped through the hole, very aware that if a murderer were on the other side, he'd shoot through the door and kill her. Common ploy in action films. Use the peephole advantage.

But on the other side of the door stood Officer Rhett.

Tennyson fluffed her hair and opened the door. "Officer Rhett."

"Hi, Mrs. . . . uh. Or is it Miss?" he asked, his face so serious. She wondered how a man could always look so grave. And then she remembered the one time he'd smiled. It was almost orgasmic. And now Officer Yummy stood on her front porch, wearing his uniform very well.

"It's Tennyson, remember?" she said, opening the door wider. Prada toddled toward them. "To what do I owe the pleasure?"

He looked discomfited. "I'm off duty."

She looked out at his car. "So I see."

"I thought I would check on you. I told you I would. Remember?"

Something sweet bloomed inside her as she realized his "I'll check on you" was the same ploy she'd used when she called him about the "dangerous" black bag the pool guy had left behind. Hot Cop had wanted to see her.

"Oh, well, that's awfully nice of you. Would you like to come in? I just got home. Maybe you could check for rabid raccoons?" She smiled to show she was joking. She'd been keeping her windows firmly locked.

"I don't have . . . I mean, I was just stopping by . . ." He seemed unsure how to play the fact he'd come by. She liked his uncertainty. It was endearing. And somehow hotter.

"Since you're off duty, how about a drink? A beer?"

He narrowed his eyes as if he were considering what that would mean. "That's not necessary."

"I know it's not necessary, dutiful public servant. Still, you've been so patient with me. Surely, I owe you something," she said, stepping back, knowing full well her words were suggestive and liking the way that made her feel.

"I guess a drink wouldn't hurt," he said, stepping inside.

She tried not to huff him because that might scare him. Instead she let her gaze wander over the body brushing against her own. Joseph was a big guy, all muscle, but not absurdly so. Just in the way that made women wonder what his uniform shirt hid from view. Okay, and maybe the pants, too. His hair was too short. She bet it curled a little when it was longer, making him look softer, more approachable. That was probably why he kept it short. His pretty eyes were wary and his jaw somewhat scruffy. Uniform shirt tucked tight into pants that could have been tighter. Lord, he'd make a fine-ass motorcycle cop. She'd keep that fantasy in her head because it was a good one.

"So beer? I also have vodka and can whip up a mean vodka tonic," she said, sauntering toward the kitchen.

She felt his eyes on her and allowed her hips to sway a bit more than natural. She was very glad she'd worn the Marchesa Notte dress that fit her perfectly now that she had lost a few extra pounds.

"A bottled water would be fine. What happened to your dress?" he asked when she reached the kitchen and opened the fridge. She grabbed a Perrier, wishing he'd gone for something stronger. The man could use a little loosening up. The man could use a lot of loosening up. And maybe she was just the woman to do it.

"Oh, well, a bit of a catastrophe at my son's engagement party," she said, glancing down to make sure the safety pin was keeping everything in place. Her almost DD breasts were doing a great job of holding the dress up by themselves. She felt Officer Rhett's eyes on her girls, too.

He jerked his gaze to hers when she looked at him.

"You have a son who's old enough to get married?" he asked.

"I had him when I was twelve, so . . . ," she joked.

His forehead crinkled almost adorably.

She handed him the Perrier, and he looked at it like she'd just handed him a tampon. "I'm joking. He's twenty-three. I had him when I was young, but not twelve. You don't like Perrier?"

"Never had it."

"I have tap water. Totally paid the bill this month."

Officer Rhett smiled, and she felt it in her girl parts. Jesus, the man had some power in that smile. It turned him into a total panty-dropper. He opened his sparkling water, and Tennyson busied herself pouring a vodka on the rocks. Who needed tonic? Extra calories.

"I'm fine, and I'm just saying that you look much too young to have a child getting married," he said, raising the bottle and taking a long draft.

His throat muscles working to swallow were even sexy. Damn, she'd never found a guy drinking mineral water so hot. Of course, she wasn't sure she'd ever been with a guy who requested water when she offered booze. "Flattery will get you everywhere, Officer Rhett."

"You can call me Joseph," he said, setting the bottle on the marble and looking at her with amusement.

"Not Joe?"

He shook his head. "That's what my mom called me."

No further explanation.

"Okay, then, Joseph, would you mind stepping onto the patio? I need to let Prada out to do her business before I put her in her kennel for the night." She indicated with a nod of her head the double French doors.

He walked to the door, unlatched it, and slid it open. Tennyson scooped up Prada, who was sitting at her feet staring up adoringly, and went out into the night. Summer had arrived, bringing a hefty dose of humidity that made her hair curl. She hadn't missed the frizziness that Louisiana brought to her hairstyles, that was for damned sure. But she liked the soft nights with the still darkness and quiet streets. So peaceful.

"Getting warm," he commented as she clacked over to the grass and set Prada down. The full moon cast an oyster glow over the oasis of the backyard. The landscape design firm had already begun work, bringing in large potted plants and pulling out scraggly azaleas and replacing them with lush knockout roses. A partially built retaining wall leveled the yard into neat sections that with the addition of slate steps would make all areas accessible during the shower she would throw for Emma and Andrew at the end of June. She had three weeks to get everything done. Three weeks to make Melanie's party look like chump change.

Somehow that was comforting.

She needed to beat Melanie at this wedding thing.

"It *is* getting warm. I forgot how quickly the heat's turned on in Louisiana," she responded to Joseph.

He stood framed against the pot lights of her patio. His face was shrouded in the darkness, but his hunky form was starkly outlined. "Where did you live before moving here?"

"I'm actually *from* here. Grew up about a mile that way in Broadmoor. Had a nice view of all the big houses in South Highlands."

"Really." It was a statement, not a question.

"Yeah, I sort of lost my accent. When I graduated high school, I moved to NYC and never really looked back. I still have a place in Manhattan. Another in Winter Park, Colorado. I've lived in Paris for a year, Rio for six months, and a small island off the coast of Maine. Now I'm back here. Go figure."

Joseph shoved his free hand into his pocket, sipped his beverage, and eyed her. "Why?"

"Why Shreveport?" Loaded question. "My son just moved here. His fiancée, soon to be wife, is attending medical school. She's from here, and Andrew has always romanticized the South. He used to spend a few weeks every summer here with my parents, climbing trees, catching crawdads, and generally running hog wild. He longed for this place, weirdly enough. Honestly, I believe Emma being from Shreveport was half the initial attraction to her. He latched on."

"Huh."

Joseph wasn't much for conversation. He reminded her of her father—a man of few words. She waited while Prada waddled back and looked up expectantly. The damned dog wanted to be carried around like a princess. Tennyson sighed and stooped down, picking up the pup. When she did, a strap popped loose. "Crap."

"What?"

"My dress is . . ." She tugged the spaghetti strap, ripping it from the dress. It could damned well be a strapless dress now. The other strap hung uselessly. She left it for later, afraid the ripping sound on the other side had done irreparable damage. "There."

"Are you tearing your clothes off? Do I need to remind you I have an obligation to protect the public from indecency?" he asked, his voice holding humor.

She turned around. "Are you making a joke, Officer Rhett?"

He shrugged. "I have a sense of humor."

"Where do you hide it? That uniform looks tight," she said, adding a flirt to her voice because why the hell not? She hadn't been with a man in so long she'd forgotten how they tasted, felt beneath her fingers, or did weird things like leave the toilet seat up. No, she wouldn't mind taking a spin on Joseph Rhett at all.

She walked past him and noted his cheeks looked slightly flushed, but his eyes looked hungry.

Good.

She waited at the door, and as he stepped through, he said, "I didn't say *I* need protection, did I?"

He dropped his eyes to where the dress strap hung loose. Then the good officer reached out and gave it a tug before slipping back into the house. She closed the door, her body suddenly warm, her breathing slightly off-kilter.

Joseph Rhett was definitely a pro at playing the seduction game. Thing was, Tennyson *loved* playing that game. Even more so, she loved winning that game. Because in this particular game there really wouldn't be a loser. Not if she could actually get that man where she wanted him.

Under her.

She clacked off, and with a quick kiss near the bow on Prada's head, she shoved her pup into the fancy kennel in the laundry room. She'd considered letting the pup sleep with her, but then had a nightmare in which she rolled over on the dog and killed it. So kennel for Prada. She switched on the noise-canceling machine sitting on the granite counter and closed the door.

Joseph stood behind her, and she bumped into him. He reached out to steady her, causing little darts of pleasure to shimmy up her spine. She almost leaned back into him. Instead, she bent slightly as if she were listening for the little dog's whimpers and intentionally brushed her ass against his fly.

She felt his shock before straightening and walking back into the kitchen. "Can I get you something else, Officer . . . I mean, Joseph?"

By his expression she knew she was playing with fire, and it felt good to feel like the old Tennyson, the one who knew how to control her world and make decisions that were, if not smart, hers alone. But that wasn't true. The decisions made *were* hers. Perhaps her discontent was more about feeling like she was floating with no true anchor. She'd come back to Shreveport and had done nothing more but move in and watch Netflix for days. Of course, the wedding would occupy a lot of her time over the summer, but what next?

Joseph set his nearly empty bottle on the counter and moved toward her.

Anticipation hummed in her belly.

Please. Please. Please.

He drew close enough for her to see his pores, for her to smell the piney, masculine, yummy scent that was his alone, for her to hear his breathing, which was a little uneven. Leaning toward her, very close, he said, "Better not. I have to drive home. Maybe next time."

Joseph moved past her toward the front door. Momentary disappointment blanketed her, but then he turned and gave her a half smile that was so sexy, she almost squeezed her legs together. His gaze moved down, taking her in. "If you need me, you have my number."

She glanced involuntarily at the cute corkboard mounted above the built-in desk in the kitchen. Officer Joseph Rhett's card was pinned right in the center. "I *do* have your number, Joseph."

He opened the door and stepped onto the threshold. "Good night, Tennyson. Don't forget to lock the door behind me. Appreciate the hospitality."

Tennyson stuck a hand on her hip and tilted her head. "Oh, sugar, it was just a drink. Next time maybe I'll let you frisk me."

His expression before shutting the door was almost wolfish. Right before he closed it all the way, he opened it and tapped the lock. "Don't forget."

Then he closed the door. She walked over and turned the dead bolt, resisting the urge to part the curtains in the dining room to watch Joseph walk away.

Well, the man had the "protect" part down.

Now what about the serve?

Perhaps she would get the chance to find out. Tennyson was fairly certain a warning shot had crossed her bow, the ref was standing in center court holding the ball, and the horses were in the chute thingy. Along with all the other euphemisms for "it's about to be on" she could think of.

She smiled and strolled toward her bedroom, switching off lights and kicking off the Louboutins that had been killing her feet all night.

As she went, she hummed Carly Simon's "Anticipation."

CHAPTER SEVEN

Melanie slid off her shoes and set them on the shelf in her massive closet. She'd worn the nude kitten heels for the engagement party and those went on one of the two neutral-shoes shelves. She looked down at her dress and noted a bit of dried frosting on the sheath. Sighing, she unzipped it, slid it off her body, and placed it in the dry-cleaning hamper. She caught sight of herself in the mirror affixed to the back of the closet door and made a face. The tight control top of the pantyhose pressed into her flesh, making a significant muffin top, and her knees looked saggy beneath the bottom elastic band. Her bra was serviceable, not even close to a sexy scrap of lace, and she was almost certain her neck was starting to sag into turkey territory.

And, God, was she tired. She could see it in her face and the circles under her eyes. The way she looked, it was . . . middle-aged.

Just a month ago she'd turned forty-six years old, but most days she didn't feel that old. Sometimes when she was required to tell someone her age, she was surprised when she remembered exactly how old she was. The big five-oh was coming at her, and that seemed . . . wrong. She couldn't be nearly fifty years old because that was, well, old. But now she was officially the mother of the bride. Before too long, she could be a grandmother.

A *grandmother*.

Melanie had always said she would grow old gracefully and wouldn't be one of those women who desperately plied their face with cream and stalked plastic surgeons. She wouldn't need a lift or tuck because she wasn't the vain type, but staring at herself in the mirror, and thinking about a new phase of her life coming at her like a 747 coming in hot, she wondered if she needed to set up a consultation with a plastic surgeon. Her boobs weren't pointing at her feet yet, and her behind wasn't totally saggy, but if she didn't start working out soon, she may be heading in that direction. She didn't want to be a fluffy, middle-aged, tired woman.

Then she thought about Charlotte and the way she was stealthily worming her way into Kit's life, and that not only made her feel old but also discouraged.

Growling at her reflection, she jerked the stupid control top down, waddled out of it, and kicked it off. It flew like a flesh-colored jellyfish and nailed Kit right in the face as he came into the closet.

"What the fu—"

"Sorry," Melanie said, covering her breasts with her arms and sucking in her stomach, something she never did with Kit. Why did she feel that compunction now? She'd never been ashamed of her body, and Kit had always loved the flare of her hips, her soft breasts, and dainty feet. Or so he proclaimed when he was sexing her up.

Kit tossed the makeshift girdle back to her. "What are those, anyway?"

"Shape wear. It helps things stay in place," she said.

He started unbuttoning his shirt. "I like when things don't stay in place. Come on over here, and I'll show you how much."

Melanie wanted to slide the bra straps down her arms, unhook the clasp digging into her back, and do exactly what her husband suggested, but she no doubt had the imprint of the waistband around her midsection, and her hair smelled like étouffée. She hadn't had a shower since that morning, and she knew she'd done her fair share of sweating as she readied the house for the event. "Uh, that sounds good, but maybe tomorrow night? Or the morning?"

He jerked his head up, his gaze showing both irritation and disappointment. "Sure."

Kit turned his back, and she knew she'd made a mistake. Who cared if she was bone tired and possibly smelled like an advertisement for the Louisiana seafood industry? Her still-sexy husband was flirting with her and wanted her. "I mean, it's just that I need a shower."

"Don't worry about it," he said, sliding out of his pants and folding them carelessly over a hanger. Melanie's fingers itched to match the seams and rehang the pants.

"I don't want you to think I don't want you. I do."

"Mel, it's fine," he said, shrugging out of his shirt. "I'm tired, anyway."

But she could tell it wasn't fine, and she felt guilty. But at the same time she was aggravated. Didn't he know *she* was exhausted? She'd spent all day getting everything ready for the party, and then for the past hour, she'd seen guests out and made sure everything was turned off and put away. She still had a big stack of silver that she and Louisa would have to tackle in the morning when the housekeeper arrived. And they had an appointment with the wedding planner in the afternoon, something that was sure to drive her to drink. And Kit was miffed because she didn't drop her panties and climb aboard?

I bet Charlotte would.

Her snarky inner voice made her even angrier. Why should she have to feel like she had to have sex with her husband in order to prevent him from picking up what Charlotte was laying down? She shouldn't. Not when she was this dang tired.

"I'm tired, too," she said, sliding past him.

Once upon a time, he would have looped a hand around her waist, pressed her up against the wall, and persuaded her to not be tired in a most delicious way. She'd squeal and laugh . . . and then quickly sigh. Kit knew she liked to be dominated in the bedroom—slightly aggressive seduction was her favorite game, probably because she'd grown up reading 1880s historical romances with dashing sea captains who practiced their wiles on windblown virgins. She had a weird penchant to want to be persuaded. Or maybe it was because she was in charge of so much, constantly having to handle every situation in their family that made her want to surrender control and let someone else slide into the driver's seat.

But now Kit seemed content to let her pass without a second thought.

"Are you going to bed?" he called after her.

"I just said I was tired," she said.

He padded out of the closet in his underwear, looking not middle-aged at all, damn him. "How about that cake-astrophe, huh? What a shit show."

The same words Tennyson had used.

"It would have been avoided if Tennyson had not brought her dog. How much attention does one person need? She only totes that dog around so people will look at her."

"People would look at her anyway," Kit said, pulling his toothbrush out of the holder and running water over it.

"What does that mean?" Melanie asked, pausing at the door, stomach still sucked in, arms still wrapped around her breasts.

"You know," Kit said, catching her gaze in the mirror, looking slightly caught.

"You mean Tennyson's still pretty."

"I mean, yeah. She's always been attractive and, you know, had a good body. Plus she displays it."

Something about his words hurt. They always did when it came to Tennyson. Mostly because Kit had chosen Tennyson first. Back when they were in high school, Kit had shown up their sophomore year, an athletic, tanned sixteen-year-old with thick, blond hair, an alarmingly sexual smile, and eyes that made every girl sigh. By that time, she and Tennyson were back in school together, Tennyson having gotten a scholarship to the private college-prep school Melanie attended. Kit's first day had sent the female population on drool alert and the male population on butt-hurt alert. Tennyson had taken one look at Kit and actually uttered *mine*.

And he had been . . . for a while.

Melanie had always taken a back seat to Tennyson, but it hadn't bothered her because she was nothing like the temperamental, high-strung, creative beauty who was her best friend. On the contrary, Melanie was steadfast, reliable, and unremarkably pretty with a clear complexion, rich brown hair, and high cheekbones. Her pleasing countenance, compact figure, and unassuming manner was the kind that grew on a person rather than bowling them over. Melanie had no desire to be like Tennyson because she was comfy in her own skin. And in the end the tortoise had won the race, hadn't she?

Kit trailed her into the bedroom with a leonine grace she'd always admired. He moved with fluid movement that drew the eye as he lifted a magazine from the bedside table and tossed back the covers. In the process, he upended the decorative pillows onto the floor. Melanie bit her tongue instead of pointing out the bench at the end of the bed that had been placed there for such a purpose. Instead she pulled a nightgown from her chest of drawers and jerked it over her head, unfastening the bra beneath. She saw Kit watching her do this and knew he wondered why she was hiding herself. Melanie really didn't have an answer. All she knew was she didn't want to be naked in front of him. Perhaps it was because of his words about Tennyson. Or maybe it was the image of Charlotte looking at him with something just short of possession in her eyes. Or maybe it was because she felt old and flabby.

"She's always been stunning. I haven't forgotten that," Melanie said, picking up her laptop and heading toward the bedroom door.

"I thought you were tired?"

"I remembered that I promised Emma I would look at the wedding software she wants to buy. I don't want to disturb you with the tapping."

He took off his shirt and tossed it on the floor. She tried to ignore that, too. Then he slid on his reading glasses, looking quite delicious as he opened his magazine. "You can work here. I'm going to read for a bit."

So neither one of them were really that tired.

And still . . .

Kit looked up and lowered his glasses. "Why software?"

Melanie shrugged. "Supposedly you need software. It's what the wedding planner will use to keep tabs on everything."

"Then shouldn't the planner buy the software?"

"Kit, I don't really know."

"Just how much is this going to cost us?" he asked.

Melanie felt her stomach tilt south. She'd been dreading this conversation. Not because she wanted to blow their retirement on Emma's wedding, but because the preliminary research she'd done on weddings over the last few weeks had essentially inferred that no wedding was done on a budget under twenty-five thousand. Kit was very good about giving his children the things they wanted, but even he would stroke out over what she estimated this wedding might cost, even if it were done as something "simple" as her daughter requested. The thing was, Emma had no clue what things actually cost. Melanie had discovered this when she took Emma shopping for prom dresses. Conclusion—her firstborn had champagne tastes. Simple didn't mean cheap. "I'm not sure. Don't worry. Emma says she wants something simple and elegant."

Kit sighed and looked back down at his magazine, effectively dismissing her.

Melanie padded into the living room and then the kitchen, avoiding the still damp patch created by Tennyson's puppy. She turned on the kitchen light and nearly screamed when she saw Noah sitting at the kitchen island eating a bowl of cereal.

"Oh my goodness."

"Hey, Mom," he said, crunching away.

"I thought you were at Matt's."

"I *was* at Matt's, but it was boring, so I came home."

"Oh, well, I wish you would have texted. Your father has a gun, you know."

Noah raised his eyebrows. "How was the deal?"

"Your sister's party was nice. I wish you would have come, especially now that I know your prior obligation was something 'boring.'"

"Mom, I had to be at the kickball tournament. I'm the best one on the team." Noah then tilted the bowl, drank the milk, and poured another big bowl of something that would rot his teeth out if given the chance. It was the one thing she bought him that was absolute crap for his diet. A mother had to choose her battles.

"So humble, too," she said, fishing a delicate china cup from the cabinet and starting the fire under the kettle.

"Why is Emma getting married so fast? Just seems weird, you know?"

At last someone who agreed with her. She'd spent all night expecting someone to remark on how young Emma was to be getting married, but no one had said diddly. And here was her voice of reason—a man-child who smelled his dirty socks before putting them on and existed solely on peanut butter cups and Cap'n Crunch.

"She's in love," Melanie said, reaching for the chamomile tea and scooping some into the tea ball.

Noah rolled his eyes. "I'm never getting married. Don't need no chick telling me every move to make."

"Use correct grammar, please," she said. Then she realized she sounded exactly like her own mother and wanted to snatch the words back. This was likely the longest conversation she'd had with her son in two months, and she had to go all Japanese mother on him.

"I don't need no *female* telling me what to do," he amended with a smart-ass grin.

Melanie chuckled. "You already have one telling you what to do."

"Touché," he said, slurping up the cereal, swiping at the milk dribbling down his chin with his bare hand. Melanie stopped herself from going to the paper towel holder and tearing off a sheet. If Noah wanted milky hands, he could dang well have them.

"Emma told me about Mrs. Janie falling in the cake. I bet that was dope."

Melanie looked up. "It was actually dangerous."

Noah didn't seem to care. He shrugged. "She said Andrew's mom brought her dog in a purse. I met that woman at graduation. She's totally bougie. And drama."

And again, someone who saw exactly what she did. Of course, what Noah didn't know was that Tennyson had always been that way. He also didn't know that half of it was an act because Tennyson was afraid people might see the real person beneath the carefully manicured surface. Beneath was the girl she'd grown up with, the one who wore brand-name clothes she'd scored at the secondhand store, the one who stood outside the country club fence and looked inside, the one who never learned to drive in high school because she didn't want to get the hand-me-down Pinto. But Melanie didn't say that. She settled for, "Yeah, Tennyson is a piece of work, all right."

"Does this mean she's going to be, like, coming to Christmas and stuff?" He looked horrified.

Melanie rather felt like that herself. It wasn't like once the wedding was over, Tennyson would be out of her life. The woman had moved to Shreveport. Why exactly, Melanie wasn't certain. And now Emma and Andrew would be living in her backyard. Holidays would be on them before she could blink. She tried to envision Tennyson at Thanksgiving or sitting next to her during the Christmas Eve candlelight service singing "Silent Night." Then there was the thought of grandchildren.

Dear Lord, one day they would be grandmothers, fighting to be the first to hold the little bundle of joy.

Hell on earth.

That's what her life was turning into. She was getting old and fat, her husband had a side piece at the ready, her daughter was getting married, and she was getting Tennyson as an in-law. *Kill me now.*

"Uh, not necessarily," she said, hoping her words would be true.

"Cool. She makes me nervous or something." He got up and set the bowl down too hard in the sink. The clank made Melanie wince. "I'm going to bed."

Melanie reached for him and wrapped him in a hug. The child tolerated it for .002 seconds before moving away. "Good night, buddy."

"Yeah, about that. How about not calling me your buddy." At her crestfallen look, Noah stopped. "At least not around other people."

Melanie smiled. "I can do that. But you'll always be my buddy. After all, you're the only other person who thinks this wedding is crazy."

Noah nodded. "I'm not so dumb, am I?"

"Never thought you were, Noah," she said, fighting at the guilt that once again appeared to grab her by the throat and shake her. Why did her child feel stupid or inadequate? She'd felt that way much of her life and had tried so hard to make sure her children never felt as if they were not enough. Still, sometimes the things that came from her mouth, the way she pushed and managed, steered her toward that parenting style that had crippled her when she was herself a child . . . the same critical pushiness that had turned her sister, Hillary, into a virtual shadow of herself.

"Night, Mom," Noah said.

"Night, bud—" She caught herself in time. "Good night, Noah."

Her son left, the kettle chirruped, and she poured a cup of tea while opening her email and looking for the link her daughter had sent. Melanie had pointed out that her future mother-in-law had bought her a planner, but Emma had had a friend who'd worked for an event planner one summer and insisted it was the best way to keep everything organized. And then there was something about a vision board. Emma had already started amassing a color palette and font samples on a digital vision board. Melanie had asked to see it beforehand, but Emma had been vague about it, saying she wanted to unveil it at the meeting with Marc Mallow.

Putting on an engagement party in three weeks' time wasn't much harder than planning PTSA teacher appreciation or a baby shower for Millicent Hyde's last daughter. Hire a caterer, pick up champagne, and arrange some flowers. Presto chango. No problemo.

But a wedding in less than three months was daunting if not out-and-out harrowing. One of the ladies in her book club had a daughter who'd gotten married last fall, and the event had dominated every aspect of the entire year. From haggling over event space to family histrionics over seating to something called a house party, Esme Roemer had just about gone nuts. And she'd had almost eighteen months to plan the wedding. How in all that was holy was Melanie going to pull this off?

Of course, Tennyson had volunteered to help split the cost of the wedding, but that would come with a huge, huge price tag because there were strings all over that offer. Not strings. Straps. Big, strangling straps that would cut off her airway. Because Tennyson would want her hands all over the wedding. She'd be weighing in on everything from calligraphers to wedding bands. Melanie knew this because they'd had their high school graduation party together. Melanie's suggestion of a casual beach bash was quickly overridden in favor of Tennyson's vision—a southern lawn party.

They'd wore linen and seersucker with fancy hats and made bets on the Kentucky Derby. After a horse had to be put down on the track, Melanie had cried for a good twenty minutes and then drank too many mint juleps. And then she'd gotten totally smashed and thrown up in the pool. Her mother had been livid and had ordered everyone out of the backyard, even the white-gloved waitstaff Tennyson had talked Melanie into spending her graduation money on. Melanie could still remember the smell of sour bourbon and the way they'd brought a curtain out on the track to prevent people from seeing them put down the poor horse. So, yeah, she'd partnered with Tennyson for an event before and learned the hard way that some people had no compunction about steamrolling the other. Yeah, Melanie had been a doormat long ago, but she'd long since learned how to be a steel blockade when it came to people smacking her down.

Except your mother. And your family. And every person who asks you to serve as a chairperson.

She thumped that little gnat of truth out of the way and smiled as her messenger dinged.

You up, jellybean?

Hillary.
Couldn't sleep. You know how it is after a party. Wiped out, but a million things going through my mind. Or maybe her being up was more about the fact that her husband wanted to have sex, and she didn't

want to. Because she wasn't slim enough or sexy enough or in the mood enough. Maybe she needed to go to the doctor and get some testosterone or estrogen or whatever made a woman want to roll in the hay . . . or rather four hundred thread count sheets. Or maybe she just needed to lose the extra premenopause pounds. One of her friends had gone on a diet, lost fifteen pounds, and said afterward she'd had more sex in one month than she'd had in two years. Maybe Melanie needed to up her commitment to weight loss for more than just looking good in a dress.

I remember, but it's been a while. Mom told me about the cake and the dog. Bummer.

That was an understatement.

Tennyson.

That's all she would need to type—her sister totally understood. Hillary had been in town when all the crap with Tennyson had gone down, and, of course, she'd been there for the wedding.

Hillary sent a funny GIF of a diva Hollywood star walking into a room, dropping her fur coat, and taking her gloves off one finger at a time. It was so much like Tennyson, Melanie laughed.

Bingo.

Melanie smiled as she typed the next response. God, she missed her sister so much. Over the past year, their time together got smaller and smaller. Hillary didn't like company, and she was an excellent liar—all people who struggle with eating disorders are. They lie to themselves, and they lie to others. Hillary pretended she was getting better, but Melanie knew she wasn't. She'd tried to intervene, but both her mother and Hillary had erected barriers. At one point, Melanie had threatened to call the authorities and report her mother for essentially letting Hillary kill herself, but her sister had threatened to move back to Baton Rouge. Melanie had relented when her sister promised to go back to the outpatient therapy program, but that had lasted only a few months.

I missed you. Especially tonight. Emma looked so pretty. Can you believe she's getting married?

Little bubbles appeared as her sister typed. And then they stopped. Melanie waited a full two minutes, but Hillary didn't respond.

You there?

Nothing for another minute.

Alarm curled around her heart and sneaked up into her throat, clogging it. Her sister's health issues were sometimes scary, and she'd had a few episodes that had necessitated a trip to the ER. The prognosis wasn't great because Hillary's organs had starved for too long, but so far her sister was managing. She had good, consistent care and counseling that helped her deal with her diseases. Still, at times, Melanie felt fear tear through her at the thought of losing her sister. She wasn't sure if she could survive being left behind with their mother.

From the very beginning, Hillary had been the anomaly in the driven, acerbic, somewhat disillusioned Brevard family. Her mother liked to say Hillary was born without a single sound. Even after the nurse had smacked her behind in an effort to issue a cry, the newborn hadn't made a peep. She'd merely opened her blue eyes and peered around as if she were surprised she even existed. As a baby, her sister was placid and content, and as a child, she was friendly and kind. But when she became a teen, it became obvious Hillary was too tender to withstand the onslaught of ugly in the world, including the pressure exerted by an exacting, ambitious mother. Plump, pleasant, and oddly charming, Hillary seemed too good for the world she lived in. Her sister had done what any survivalist would do: she'd tried to assimilate. Which meant Hillary had tried to be what she was supposed to be.

Of course, Melanie had never noticed how Hillary had lost the weight she had during her junior year of high school . . . until her biology teacher did a unit on mental health that included eating disorders.

Like a baseball winging in from right field, the realization had clonked her on the head. As a sixteen-year-old kid who had her own crap to deal with—mainly crushing pressure from her parents regarding her grades and being totally besotted with her best friend's boyfriend—Melanie found she was ill equipped to address her sister's binge-and-purge cycle. Even when she presented evidence of the harmful behavior to her parents, she was brushed off or set aside. Her parents didn't want to dig beneath the foundation to look for the creepy-crawlies hiding beneath their suddenly popular and pretty eldest daughter. Instead they'd shifted their attention to Melanie's faults, making her wish she'd kept her damned mouth shut.

Sorry. Had to go to the bathroom. I'm beat and off to bed.

Melanie gave an audible sigh at her sister's words. Hill was okay. She paused before typing. You feeling okay?

I'm fine.

It was what her sister always said. But then Melanie realized it was what she always said, too. Hadn't she just said as much to her husband when he'd asked if she was okay? But how did one say she was scared her world was about to fall apart when she was *supposed* to say she was fine?

Maybe that's what Hillary had always understood—you didn't tell the truth. You hid it because then everyone would leave you the hell alone.

Love you, Hilly Billy.

You too, Melly Bean.

CHAPTER EIGHT

Tennyson wore the dress she'd worn to her first husband's funeral to meet with the wedding planner. The navy St. John knit dress was classic, expensive, and easy to recognize. From what Tennyson knew about Marc Mallow, she understood he enjoyed a certain level of je ne sais quoi in a person . . . mostly because she read his Twitter feed last night, and that was part of his bio. She also knew that while the man professed to be obsessed with undefined elements, he very much would appreciate the very tangible quality of her dress.

Tennyson was prepared to like the diminutive man who seemed to be a cross of Martin Short's character on *Father of the Bride* and the discerning Tim Gunn of *Project Runway*. That being said she knew he'd hailed from Sarepta, Louisiana, a virtual speck on the map, and had earned his way to being prima donna of Shreveport's wedding scene only because the man knew how to play the game . . . and could get picky mamas and pouting brides on the same page in order to produce a wedding that everyone talked about for at least a good three days after the bride rode away in the carriage, limo, bicycle, or hot-air balloon. Whichever she chose.

And, really, he was the best they could get at this late juncture.

Tennyson parked her car and stepped carefully onto the rocky driveway. She'd worn a pair of neutral Stuart Weitzman heels because they were stylish enough to suit her and classic enough to match the dress.

Marc's office sat in a picturesque garden behind his mother's successful floral shop. He'd had a lovely, large gazebo constructed, which served as the entrance to his building. On Marc's Facebook page he'd professed the unusual office was in order to aesthetically blend into the beauty of the roses and fragrant climbing jasmine beneath the spread arms of the mossed oaks. That, and he loved the gazebo scene from *The Sound of Music*. Whimsical garden statues and blown glass à la Chihuly studded the landscape, making the overall effect a mishmash that was more *The Hobbit* meets *Alice in Wonderland*.

"Charming," Tennyson said, coming up behind Melanie and Emma, who both stood staring at a nude statuary of Pan in which certain parts had been overexaggerated.

"Are we sure we want this man to do the wedding?" Melanie asked, shooting a side-eye at her daughter.

Emma rolled her eyes. "Mom, you have been to the weddings he's done. They are always suited to the couple and their vision. It's what I want."

Tennyson ran her gaze over Melanie. Whereas Tennyson had chosen to put her boring but stylish foot forward, Melanie had gone with middle-aged matron for her look. She wore black pants that did nothing to flatter her figure because they were too big, a top that was better suited for someone who was seventy-five and owned six cats, and hair that was so severely cut she looked somehow sad. Girlfriend needed a makeover in the worst way. Melly looked more and more like her hard-assed mama than Tennyson would have ever thought she could.

Melanie turned to her. "Seriously, are you sure about this, Tee—"

"Yes, and I thought we agreed to call each other by our *given* names." Tennyson walked past Melanie, not quite pissy, but close. Okay, fine.

She was a bit miffed that Melanie had acted like a total jackass the night before with her cold "you don't have the right to call me Melly" thing. And no one called her Teeny anymore anyway. That girl was *so* gone.

"What was that all about?" Emma inquired behind her.

"Nothing. Never mind," Melanie said, sounding perturbed.

Tennyson pressed the buzzer, and the door swept open as if someone had been lying in wait, biding his time before sinking his well-manicured nails into a defenseless bride. It was off-putting to say the least, and Tennyson almost fell back into Emma.

"Darlings," the man cooed, spreading his arms wide, his teeth perfectly white against his tanned skin. He stepped back, holding the door. "Come in, come in."

Marc Mallow was three inches shorter than Tennyson, and likely a good twenty pounds lighter. Whipcord thin with a dramatic sweep of silver hair draped strategically over his high forehead, Marc wore tailored monochromatic clothes that looked as if he might break out into some weird Bob Fosse choreography at any moment. His glasses were square and his grooming impeccable. Shiny red Gucci loafers were his lone statement piece.

Tennyson extended her hand. "I'm Tennyson."

Marc actually lifted her hand to his lips and bestowed a very light kiss atop the back of her hand, which was kind of gross but also sort of courtly. "A pleasure, my dear. You could very well be the bride, you know. So young and a true beauty."

He knew who was paying the extra 20 percent, no doubt.

"Ah, this is what I missed about the South. You're such a gentleman, but *this* is our blushing bride," Tennyson said, turning and extending her hand toward Emma. She caught Melanie's eye roll and almost laughed.

"My dear, you are indeed a radiant beauty. I will have such fun planning an exquisite, memorable day for you and your intended." Marc enfolded a surprised Emma into his embrace.

Emma gave a nervous laugh. "Thank you. I'm so excited you agreed to help us on such short notice."

"Oh, darling, someone is going to pay me very well for that, don't you worry," he said with a chuckle. He released Emma and moved past to Melanie. "And here is our mama. I can see she will put up with none of my shenanigans, as well she should not."

Melanie stared at Marc as if he'd sprung a pair of horns from his well-coiffed head before giving him a nod. "Indeed, and I take that job seriously."

This caused Marc to titter. "Oh, well, I *will* have to behave. These managing mamas are like mountain goats—a hardy bunch who pack a wallop and never go down."

Melanie's mouth may have twitched. Or perhaps it was gas. Either way, she managed a strained smile. "I don't think anyone has ever compared me to a goat. This should be fun."

Marc clapped his hands and stepped back, indicating a well-appointed area with a velvet Victorian settee, two tapestry armchairs, and a delicate coffee table filled with various large binders and a lone orchid as a reminder they sat within a garden. "Shall we?"

"We shall," Tennyson murmured, sliding in and taking an armchair.

Emma sat on the edge of the couch, looking somewhat nervous. Melanie settled herself next to her daughter while Marc took the other armchair. He picked up a small bell, rang it, and then settled back into the chair, folding his hands across his compact stomach.

A door behind him opened, and an incredibly large woman carrying a tea tray emerged. She was a good six feet tall, wide-shouldered, with a buzz cut. She had a small hoop ring in her nose and a wide smile.

"Thank you, Donna." Marc crossed his legs and waited as she settled the tea service on the small table to his left. "This is Donna, my assistant."

They murmured polite hellos to the blonde giantess, who gave an adorable bob of her head along with a curtsy. "Nice to meet you, folks.

I've brought tea, scones, and clotted cream as his majesty expects. Is there anything else, milord?"

Marc made a face and muttered something about ungrateful heifers.

Donna winked at them. "He truly loves me."

Marc made another sour face and a shooing motion. "Get back to the salt mines before I fire you."

Donna grinned, dropped a kiss atop Marc's head, and saluted. "As you wish."

She disappeared quickly for a large woman, and Marc shook his head. "My apologies. The woman is incorrigible, but magnificent at her job. I would fire her for her insolence, but then I couldn't reach the vases on the top shelf of my storage, so . . ." He gave a shrug.

Tennyson laughed. "I think I love Donna."

Marc sighed and passed around the small box with assorted teas. "Everyone does."

After the tea was poured and scones sent around, Marc leaned forward and looked at Emma. "So, my dear, tell me *why* you want to marry this man."

Tennyson thought it a stretch to call her boy a man, but she let that go because the why seemed rather important at the moment.

Emma tried to swallow the last of her scone but sort of choked. She lifted her tea and looked desperately at her mother as if she expected Melanie to answer. Tennyson's once upon a time friend had been taking all this oddness in stride but didn't seem eager to help her daughter out. Melanie likely also wanted to know the answer to *why*.

"Um, because I love him," Emma finally managed after a large sip of Earl Grey.

"Well, yes, but loving someone is not a requirement for marriage, is it? One can be in love and never marry. Why do you want to don a fancy dress, spend your parents' hard-earned money, and say vows in front of people who quibbled over whether to buy you the toaster or the crystal on your registry?"

"I . . . well, I *want* to marry him. I mean, we want to make that commitment to each other because we know we belong together. We knew from almost the beginning. It was like we were meant to be."

Melanie glanced briefly at Tennyson and looked away.

Marc made a moue of his mouth and nodded. "Just so, just so."

Melanie uncrossed her legs and leaned forward in her "I'm about to take charge" posture. "Mr. Mallow, I'm sure you have other things to do this afternoon, so let's not waste time. My daughter is marrying, and you are the person who has agreed to make that happen. We are putting our money and trust in you, so this is more about the hows and not the whys."

Marc tsk-tsked. "My mama goat. You don't waste time. I like that. Yes, yes, let's get down to it."

Emma pulled her MacBook Air from the depths of the large tote she'd brought with her. "I have my vision board."

Marc arched a brow. "These brides and their damned Pinterest. I do believe the internet would put me out of business if it could. Let me see, dear."

He took the opened computer and looked it over, making little noises as he clicked and scrolled. "Lavender and absinthe. Very southern. Perhaps flaxen seersucker mixed in with the linens, even a bit of wisteria in the bouquet. Yes, yes, I like the raw linen for the table, leveled floating candles, maybe even some country ceramic vases for a more grounded feel." He looked up at Emma and narrowed his eyes.

Her soon-to-be daughter-in-law fidgeted slightly. An uncomfortable silence sat like a fart in a PTA meeting. Finally, Marc sat the computer down and folded his hands.

"The colors are lovely, and I'm seeing a bit of nostalgia tied to this wedding. Ties to the past of who you are, who your mamas were. I think this overall feel is very fitting since your mothers were once best friends, yes?" He spread his hands, a diamond pinkie ring winking at them.

So the bastard knew about her and Melanie. Of course he did. He would have a line into the Shreveport gossip circuit, of course.

Tennyson glanced over at Melanie, and damned if it didn't look like she had swallowed a bullfrog. Seemed their time of keeping their past from their children was over. Wasn't like it could go on much longer, anyway. Emma and Andrew were bound to discover the truth.

"Well, uh," Emma said, looking from Tennyson back to her mother with suspicion. The child hadn't graduated magna cum laude for nothing. It was as if the moment was wound tight, a clock with tension ticking at every second hand. "What's he talking about? Like, you were best friends?"

Tennyson pressed her lips together and shrugged.

"Mama?" Emma's voice sounded like a reprimand.

"She's Teeny," Melanie managed through lips drawn tight as a bowstring.

"Wait, Andrew's mom is Teeny? *That* Teeny?"

Melanie looked away.

"The Teeny who put the hole in Gee Ma's china hutch and talked you into painting the castle on your wall? The one who broke the Madame Alexander bride doll and sold your grandmother's funeral urn in a garage sale? That Teeny?" Emma darted a wide-eyed look over to her with the question since Melanie wasn't answering.

Tennyson stayed quiet.

Finally, Melanie made an annoyed face. "Yes. She would be *that* Teeny."

"You said Teeny was *dead*," Emma said, her expression changing into one of horror.

"To me she was," Melanie said, brushing a piece of lint off her ugly pants.

Tennyson couldn't stop the stab of pain at Melanie's words. Melly had told her children that her former best friend was dead? How could she lie that way? How could she even think it?

"Well, surprise, everyone! I'm not dead," Tennyson said, trying to lighten the mood, even though Melanie looked about as bitchy as she ever had. And she'd never been bitchy. Quite the opposite. She'd been the one to give her money to the Red Cross and sit with the unpopular kids at lunch upon occasion. *Bitch* and Melanie didn't go together. Or they hadn't. She still didn't know this new Melanie.

Marc had been watching with fascination and more than a bit of glee. Perhaps he'd planned the entire thing because why not elicit more emotion than they already had going? There was fun in that drama.

Tennyson held up a finger. "In my defense, I did not know Gammy Mui was in that vase."

"Oh, please, it wasn't a vase." Melanie rolled her eyes. "I told you that we could sell everything in the closet *but* the urn. I even put a sticky note on it so you wouldn't forget. But you took it anyway. You made enough for the Six Flags tickets. Too bad I couldn't go because I was punished for four months."

"Jesus, let it go, Melly."

"*You* let it go. You sold my dead grandmother," Melanie said, the low heel of her ugly shoe clonking the tiled floor. "And you're the one who always causes problems. You're the definition of wreaking havoc in every circumstance. Take last night. I have to buy Janie a new dress, and we wasted perfectly good cake because someone had to have her dog there."

"She's an emo—"

"Don't give me that crap, Teeny. That dog isn't anything of the sort. You use that animal for attention. What emotional support do you need? Doesn't the booze work anymore?" Melanie said.

Tennyson felt like Melanie had lobbed a knife at her head. "Fuck you, Melly."

"I see you still use your words, Teeny." Melanie sniffed and turned her head.

"Oh my God, what is happening here?" Emma asked, her gaze going from her mother back to Tennyson. Her eyes were as big as the gerbera daisies gathered in the Royal Doulton china vase on the table, and she looked like she might cry.

Marc even looked a bit shocked, but then he clapped his hands. "Now, now, ladies, weddings are an emotional ev—"

"This has nothing to do with the wedding, and everything to do with Tennyson getting her way. As always," Melanie cut him off, delivering her best frigid stare. Déjà vu slammed into Tennyson because the woman looked just like her mother. Brrr.

"Oh, give me a break. You say that shit to make you feel better about what you did to me in the first place. Come to think of it, this has everything to do with a wedding. This bullshit has sat between us for too many years. If our children are going to have a prayer's chance in hell of surviving the next two months, we need to clear the air between us." Tennyson sat her teacup on the table and wished like hell Marc Mallow offered more than stupid tea. She could use a shot of vodka right now. Two shots. Or three.

"I don't have to do anything. You caused all of this. You. Not me," Melanie said.

"Mom, I don't know what's going on, but you're acting totally crazy. We're so behind on everything already, and Mr. Mallow has agreed to help us. Can't we just put whatever this is aside for the next forty minutes of this appointment so we can make a few decisions?" Emma asked, pleading evident in her voice.

Melanie turned the color of the drapes—a wholesome pink—as if she had just realized she'd lost it in front of everyone. Her expression softened. "Yes, of course. I'm sorry about losing my composure. It's a rarity, I assure you, Mr. Mallow."

"It's Marc, and as I said earlier, weddings bring forth many, many emotions."

Melanie didn't apologize to Tennyson. She didn't even look her way.

So this was how they were going to play it—tit for tat? Seemed about right because that was how Melanie had always been. Passive-aggressive should be her middle name. That she had even lost her temper in front of Marc and her daughter, allowing herself to grow angry enough to even say "crap" was in itself a small victory for Tennyson. Not to mention, Melanie hated it when Tennyson used any affectation, so Tennyson's playing it blasé earlier had likely driven Melanie right off the edge.

Good.

Melanie didn't get to be any more comfortable than she was about this impending marriage. Tennyson adored Emma—it was hard not to—but she didn't have to love that her son was marrying into Melanie's screwed-up family, did she?

After all, Melanie had turned into her own worst nightmare—her mother.

And she'd told her children that Tennyson was dead.

Jesus.

"Yes, we're sorry, Marc. Emma is right. We're here for a wedding," Tennyson said.

Emma gave a tremulous smile. "So let's get started on the plans. I booked the church for August thirtieth and the Remington Hotel rooftop for the reception. It will be hot, but I like the idea of dancing on the rooftop. All the lights up there are so pretty, and it's just fun."

Marc rolled up his sleeves and pulled out a notepad. "We can do some cooler fans outside. Not a problem. Ladies, let's hammer out the major decisions. I need to know number of people, budget, and things like band or DJ so I can do inquiries tomorrow morning. We're on a time crunch, so once we decide and book, we stick."

"Whatever Emma and Andrew want, we can make happen," Tennyson said, crossing her legs and picking up the album marked for floral arrangements.

"And what they want is something *simple*," Melanie said.

"Don't worry, Melanie. I can help you and Kit pay for the wedding. No need to set a tight budget."

Melanie's mouth went flat as a frog's. "This isn't about money, it's about being reasonable. And tasteful."

Irritation flared inside Tennyson. Reasonable? Now that really could be Melanie's middle name. How many times had Melanie asked her to be reasonable? Ten? Twenty? A thousand times? She was fairly certain the last time that word had flown from her mouth had been when Melanie and Kit had told her that last summer that they were "together now." Tennyson had pitched a hissy fit, and Melanie had grabbed her by the shoulders and said, "Come on, Teeny. Don't be like this. Be reasonable. You don't want him, but you don't want anyone else to have him. That's not fair to Kit."

To which Tennyson had said, "I don't mind someone else having him. Just not *you*."

Melanie had released her shoulders and cried.

But her former BFF hadn't given Kit up. Nope. Instead she'd married him.

So saying Tennyson should be reasonable wasn't something she wanted to hear because she didn't want to be reasonable. Not for Andrew's wedding. Not for Melanie or Kit's pocketbook. Not for anyone in the world. Because reasonable was boring as hell. And trite. And commonplace. And *not* the way Tennyson O'Rourke rolled.

As for taste, Melanie had a lot of nerve when she herself dressed like a bag lady.

"How about you decide what's reasonable, Melly, and I'll add the ridiculous to it so this wedding can be something perfect rather than just *tasteful*." She said that last word as if she were spitting out a cockroach. Then she turned to Emma. "Does that work for you, Em?"

Emma blinked once, twice, and finally said, "Uh, thank you, Tennyson."

"Darling, *you* can call me Teeny."

CHAPTER NINE

"I hate her. Like truly hate her," Melanie said to Kit as they pushed into their favorite Mexican place. They'd just gone to the Remington Hotel to pay the balance on the deposit Emma had put down on the hotel. Her mother was out doing the preliminary scout for wedding dresses with Emma, and they would join them for dinner. Melanie wasn't looking forward to dining with her mother, but when Emma had suggested they meet up to go over the finalized plans to that point and hadn't invited Tennyson, Melanie had agreed. Kit would also be joining them because he'd been downtown in a meeting with Hal, who was signing the legal papers giving him the money for the new subdivision.

"You don't. Not really," Kit said, a smile flirting with the corners of his mouth.

"No. I do. She implied we couldn't afford to pay for our daughter's wedding just because I said we should be reasonable. I was so embarrassed in front of Marc. Not to mention, Emma had that look in her eye. You know, like she doubted we could do this . . . and that she trusted Tennyson could."

"If Tennyson wants to pay for some of the wedding, let her. I'm not going to lie—I'm not really looking forward to the total waste associated with weddings. You know how I feel about them. We witnessed first-hand how they can tilt into disaster faster than a fart in a whirlwind."

"Our wedding was fine until the end." She approached the hostess stand. The older woman behind the stand arched a brow in the universal *how many?* inquiry. "Four, please."

"Better make it six. Charlotte's coming and bringing her friend Brendan."

Melanie gritted her teeth and tried not to frown. "Sorry. Six."

The hostess nodded, gathered the menus, and proceeded to the large metal table at the front of the eatery. All that without a single word.

"Juan will be your waiter," she said, finally finding her voice.

"I'll take a margarita," Melanie said, throwing her diet out the window. She needed a drink if she had to dine with her mother and Charlotte. And Brendan. Whoever the hell he was. She could hope it was a boyfriend who would screw Charlotte seven ways to Sunday so she would stop looking at Kit like she'd like to dine upon him. Three cheers for Brendan being a stud in the sheets.

"Um, I'm the *hostess*," the woman said without a smile, disappearing before Melanie could respond.

"Well, she was rude," Melanie said, pulling out a chair next to Kit and sitting.

"But not a waiter," Kit replied.

"Can you never take my side?"

He looked up. "I didn't know there were sides."

"Didn't you?" Melanie said, lifting her gaze from the cheese- and sour cream–laden dishes pictured on her menu to her husband's face. "You never agree with me. You always discount what I say. Like with Tennyson. Or the kids. Or even the stupid hostess. I'm just asking if you are ever on my side?"

"Mel, of course I am. I'm your husband."

"Let's hope Charlotte remembers that. And why is she coming to dinner, anyway? Who invited her?" Melanie sounded grumpy but didn't care. Everyone was pleased in life but her. Everyone got the benefit of the doubt from Kit but her. With her, he constantly pointed out how crazy she sounded, placating her, reminding her how "blessed" they were, like she had to take everyone's crap because she drove a Lexus and had two healthy children.

What-effing-ever.

"Char was there when you called to see if I wanted to meet you. She said something along the lines of loving Caliente and not having eaten here in a while. So I said she was welcome to join us, and she said maybe. I was being polite. I mean, that's okay, right? Charlotte *is* merely a friend, and I think if you could become friends with her, you'd see that your fear that I would cheat with her is unfounded."

"You admitted to wanting to sleep with her."

"I did not. I admitted to being attracted to and flattered by her. Those are two different things. The therapist said as much. Remember, we have to trust each other and know we have the other's best intentions at heart."

Melanie blinked away the sudden tears. Yeah, therapy was fun. Because the therapist also made her female intuition about Charlotte sound like someone going off her rocker. Melanie wasn't crazy. Even Tennyson had seen the way Charlotte overstepped when it came to Kit. But her husband hadn't cheated, and he was right—everyone is flattered by the attention of an attractive person. "Fine."

She looked up to Emma pushing into the restaurant with her mother on her heels.

"Mom!" Emma said, weaving around diners who'd paused mid-chimichanga to watch her progress. "I found it! I found the dress!"

Melanie set the menu down. "I thought you were just scouting to see which shops you wanted to visit. You said you weren't trying anything on." Her heart clenched at the thought of Emma committing to a dress without her even seeing it.

"I didn't try it on. Because it's not in Shreveport. It's in Dallas. Tennyson found the one I liked online at Stanley Korshak. It's so pretty and perfect." Emma sank onto the booth seat with a swoony sigh.

Melanie looked up at her mother, who was slightly out of breath. "I thought . . . what's going on?"

Anne Brevard made a displeased face. "I don't agree with Tennyson being the person to decide your dress."

Emma laughed. "She's not. But you have to agree that it's beautiful. We have an appointment in four days. We'll have to pay more for alterations because usually that takes three months, but they have my size, so hopefully there won't be too much to do. Even Gee Ma has to admit that what we looked at today just wasn't right for me. I mean, there were so many mermaid dresses and fluffy princess ones with tacky crystal belts. Even the lace looked cheap."

Melanie leveled a knowing look at Kit, who had started to look pale.

Juan chose that moment to show up. "Hello, mis amigos. Can I get you a drink?"

"I'll have the two-for-one margarita," Melanie said, quick as spit.

Her mother looked disapproving as she lowered herself onto the chair opposite Melanie, but not before inspecting the cleanliness of the utensils. "I'll see your wine list."

Juan's engaging grin didn't disappear as he said, "All we have is red or white."

"I beg your pardon?"

Juan grinned even bigger. "We don't have a wine list. Just a house red and a house white. And tequila. We always have tequila, Grandmother."

"Water with lemon, please," Anne said, with a lift of her chin. Disapproval of Juan's boldness glittered in her dark eyes. "Bottled water, please, as I do not care for tap."

"Gotcha," he said. "And you, sir?"

"I think I'm going to need the tequila flight," Kit said, tapping the table.

Juan laughed. "You have your hands full with these beauties, yes?"

Emma ordered water and some tableside guacamole, Juan went off to gather the libations, and Melanie's mother folded her hands on the Formica and looked at Emma. "You cannot deny your mother the privilege of helping you select your gown. That does not belong to Tennyson, no matter how helpful she intends to be."

Emma made a face. "I'm not. Mom is totally included. And you, too, Gee Ma."

"Well, thanks for that," Melanie said, feeling a bit of relief. Her mother sticking up for her was always a small pleasure because it felt so rare.

Emma sighed. "All I'm saying is that this is an incredible opportunity. It's an exclusive salon, and it's hard to get an appointment. Tennyson knows the owners or something, and they're doing her this favor. We got an appointment on Tuesday. Marc agreed to move the cake tasting to the day after in order to accommodate us."

"I have to take Poppy to the vet on Tuesday, and your brother has his first summer league game," Melanie said, withdrawing her phone and tapping on the calendar.

"The appointment is for one o'clock. You can move the vet appointment and probably still make it back in time for Noah's game, not that he's going to even play. Please, Mom. Stanley Korshak. You know we will find the perfect dress there."

Melanie didn't want to go to Dallas, but she *did* want to have that special experience with her daughter. Hey, she watched *Say Yes to the Dress* and knew how sweet that moment was when a mom saw her daughter in the perfect dress. She'd dreamed about seeing Emma in her bridal gown since she first changed the child's diaper. Of course, it felt surreal that it was happening in four days. However, she wasn't going to miss her daughter donning frothy white dresses, pirouetting and swishing in the lace, tulle, and seed pearls even if it felt too fast and was orchestrated by Tennyson. "Okay, I'll move Poppy's appointment."

"Good. Tennyson said we can do brunch in Dallas and go to the salon from there. She hired a car to take us. This is going to be so fun. I mean, it's silly, but I'm so excited. Do you want to go, Gee Ma?"

Melanie looked at her mother. She knew that Anne would rather be caught in her underwear at the outlet mall than go anywhere with Tennyson. Her mother gave a rare smile and reached over, patting Emma on the arm. "I will wait to see you in your gown. I will cherish the surprise of seeing you the same way your groom will."

Her mother was brilliant at negotiating conflict . . . or rather avoiding it. Anne's refusal to go anywhere with Tennyson required a good reason, otherwise she'd have to explain why she disliked Tennyson, and that meant rattling the skeletons in the closet. This was what had made Anne such a good attorney. She was the ultimate spin doctor.

"Okay, then. Mom, you, me, and Tennyson will go. I'm so excited," Emma said, her face portraying exactly that. Her cheeks were flushed, her eyes sparkling, and in that moment, Melanie didn't think she'd ever seen a prettier girl.

Melanie knew her emotions about the trip were evident when Emma's expression shifted to concern. "I know you and Tennyson aren't exactly friends anymore, but maybe this will be good. After all, our two families are going to be spending a lot of time together. And whatever your past, surely you can try to be reasonable about . . . uh, being together? Find some middle ground?"

"Sure. I can be reasonable, remember? Finding your dress will be . . . fun." Melanie managed to not choke over the word. After the meeting with the wedding planner, the thought of picking out a wedding dress with Tennyson made her feel itchy. But she would try because Emma deserved as much. And her daughter was correct—she'd have to find some middle ground. Or at the very least, learn to ignore Tennyson.

"Thank you, Mom. And who knows? Maybe you can find your way to being friends again," Emma said over the top of the menu she'd opened. She gave Melanie a big smile, one that might have been a little sassy.

"Fat chance," Kit whispered toward her as he bent to retrieve his napkin. When he lifted his head, he was distracted by two stilettos and a pencil skirt. "Char, you made it. We were just about to order."

"Hello, everyone," Charlotte said, obviously having moved through the restaurant like a viper approaching prey. Or maybe that was how it always felt—like she was stalking them, ready to strike at any moment and swallow Kit whole.

Melanie's mother looked up and frowned, offering no greeting. Emma said a polite hello, and Melanie tried to smile. "Hello, Charlotte. Where's your . . . uh, friend?"

She made a confused face. "Friend?"

"Brendan?"

"Oh, yeah, he couldn't come after all," she said with a wave of her hand.

Melanie would place a hundred-dollar bill on the bet that Brendan had never been invited. "Well, we're glad you could join us."

Liar.

Charlotte pulled out a chair and sank onto it. "I am, too. I never get to spend much time with Kit's family. I see him almost every day, of course, but it's nice to spend time away from the grind. We've been so busy on this new development, I've lost five pounds from the stress. Guess that means I can have extra chips and salsa."

Really? She lost five pounds from stress? If that were true, Melanie should be a veritable waif. Didn't stress make you eat? Like whole sleeves of Oreos and tubs of ice cream?

Guess everyone dealt with stress differently.

"Well, don't worry. We'll be getting away from the grind in Destin. You can drink piña coladas and chill at the pool when we're not in sessions," Kit said, handing Charlotte a menu.

Melanie went hot and then cold in a matter of seconds. Destin? What?

"Wait, when are you going to Destin?" Emma asked, dropping the menu and looking at her father.

"In two weeks. It's the Sky Com Conference for NARED. It's on our family calendar. Char and I will be gone for four days. We're actually presenting a program on climate adaptations for new developments." Kit looked pleased. He loved to present his knowledge to his colleagues; thus, he put in to host workshops every year. Last year it had been in Las Vegas. Melanie hadn't gone because Noah had his wisdom teeth out that week.

She vaguely remembered Kit mentioning it, but then all this wedding stuff happened, and she'd forgotten all about it. Melanie wasn't concerned about Kit going to the conference—he went almost every year. She'd even gone with him a few times, calling it a getaway from the stress of being a SAHM. Nope, the conference wasn't the problem at all.

It was the five-pounds-lighter, hungry-for-another-woman's-husband hussy who sat next to him nibbling a chip who was the problem.

"I just bought two new bikinis on sale at Dillard's. I *will* find time to hit the beach," Charlotte said, tossing a smile at them all before picking up her menu and scanning the offerings.

Melanie looked over at Kit. The man had to know her concerns. They'd been discussing ad nauseam their relationship and Melanie's concern that Kit secretly desired to dump his sane, stable life and pursue something less . . . confining. *Being honest* was the therapist's constant decree, and Kit hadn't held back on admitting he was flattered by the attention the younger women bestowed on him and troubled by Melanie's refusal of him, particularly in the bedroom. His words, not hers. So why hadn't he thought to mention that he was plopping himself down in the land of temptation in two weeks' time? With a younger woman who seemed to have set her cap for him? Wouldn't that have been flipping honest? Wouldn't that have been worth addressing with their marriage counselor?

"I guess I forgot about this conference. The wedding has seemed to dominate the conversations lately. I can go with you. I haven't been to the beach in years," Melanie said, sliding a look to her mother, who she could feel tightening with suspicion. If anyone had cause to safeguard against potential scandal, it was her mother.

"When is the conference again?" Emma asked, her brow furrowed.

Kit pulled out his phone. "June twenty-fifth through the thirtieth."

"The shower Tennyson is hosting for me is on the twenty-eighth," Emma said.

"Well, pumpkin, I can't be there. I'm sorry. This has been on my calendar for eight months. Our presentation is on the morning of the twenty-ninth. No way can I be in both places, and as much as I love celebrating these nuptials, I have to pay for them. So . . . I have to mind my career. Lots of big names roll into this conference." Kit spread his hands out in an apologetic manner. "But your mom will be there."

Melanie couldn't believe what was happening. Her husband was going off to the beach with Miss Hot Pants, and she was stuck with Tennyson and her Tour of Italy shower? At that moment all she could think about was the bridal-shower scene from the movie *Bridesmaids* where Kristen Wiig's character punched the giant cookie and tried to empty the giant chocolate fountain. Because Melanie felt really close to losing it herself. Just punching whatever came her way.

Maybe it would be Charlotte.

She'd really love to punch Charlotte.

"Mom? You have to come to my shower. You're my mom," Emma said, doing that hurt-puppy look that wasn't totally pathetic but was still very effective.

"Of course I'll be there. Wouldn't miss it for the world."

Emma smiled and went back to deciding on her dinner, but her mother caught her eye. Anne's mouth was a hard line, and as she slid her glance to Charlotte, Melanie knew exactly what her mother was conveying—a snake is in your henhouse.

The snake in question set her hand lightly on Kit's forearm. "Have you had the margaritas here? Should I get the mango or the traditional? You always know the perfect thing to order."

Kit literally preened. "I know my way around tequila. Now this one"—he leaned over and pointed to something on her menu—"is a top-shelf reposado. I had it in Cabo once, but this one is a good añejo tequila. It's been aged longer than the reposado. But in margaritas it doesn't matter because the quality of the tequila is masked by the citrus fruit."

"See? How do you just know this stuff?" Charlotte marveled.

Melanie wanted to gag. Like, literally gag at the ridiculousness in front of her. But the thing was, she didn't know how to deal with it. She could be direct and ask Charlotte why she was constantly hitting on her husband, but Charlotte was clever and never did anything overt— just light touches and adoration. Melanie could come off looking like a jealous shrew and perhaps a bit crazy. Or she could play dirty with Charlotte, going toe to toe with the seduction and flirtation, but the thing was, she didn't know how. She and Kit had grown together over the years with a steadfastness that was true, solid, and deep. She'd never had to use her wiles or trickery to make him fall in love with her. She'd never learned to flirt.

But she couldn't let this go on.

"You know what? I'll come to Destin with you on Wednesday night and leave Friday morning . . . as long as everything is good here. Tennyson is hosting this shower, and all I have to do is show up. It will be nice to sink my toes into the sand. You two can work, and I'll play. You said swimsuits were on sale at Dillard's?" Melanie directed the question to Charlotte, who looked . . . perturbed.

Good.

Kit was hers. She'd taken him from one conniving woman, and she could damned sure keep him from another. If Charlotte wanted to play this game, Melanie was ready. She might not be a size 4 who lost weight when stressed and never ate cake (and climbed effing mountains in her spare time), but she was the mother of Kit's children, the keeper of the fires, and the person with a prenup that would require Mr. Christopher Layton to give up a substantial amount of money if he jumped ship.

And Kit liked money.

"Oh, yeah, they do have them on sale, and I'm sure they have one-pieces in your size," Charlotte said with a smile.

Melanie curled her fist.

Emma tilted her head and looked at Charlotte. "Um, my mom wears regular sizes. They have her size everywhere."

"I didn't mean anything like that. I just remember that she prefers one-pieces. She wore one to the Fourth of July party last year, so I was just confirming that they have a lot of different sizes on sale. You know, so she could find one. I didn't mean it as an insult, Melanie."

Right.

"That's fine. Let's order." Melanie lifted a hand and waved to Juan, who was setting their drinks on his tray.

"But first, drinks," Kit said, looking tired. And perhaps very aware of what just went down. Perhaps he was even seeing what happened when a man left the door open a crack. Because Charlotte had barreled through. Now he had to decide if he would fish or cut bait.

"We definitely need drinks," Melanie said, feeling very much like a knife was swinging her way.

CHAPTER TEN

Tennyson watched as Emma walked from the dressing room toward the raised platform with the triple mirrors, wearing the Cristina Ottaviano gown she'd found online and fallen in love with.

The simple white gown wasn't "the" dress, but it was very beautiful nonetheless.

Emma glowed as she lifted the detachable back drape, twirling slightly. "What do you think? I like that it's so simple without any embellishment. Besides, the train comes off for the reception."

Melanie sucked in a breath, reached for the box of Kleenex to Tennyson's left, and pretty much dissolved into a ball of emotion. Her former friend would be little help in this endeavor. Every gown she'd seen on Emma's Pinterest page, which they perused on the drive over from Shreveport, had been *perfect* for Emma. Tennyson was a bit more discerning on what would suit her son's bride. Emma needed something that wasn't so plain and unembellished.

"It's a lovely gown, and I agree with you on the simplicity. The style suits your figure. But since we're here, why not try on a few others. Becky?" Tennyson shot a look at the stylist who hovered on the perimeter, allowing the bride her spotlight.

The stylist nodded, and Tennyson could see that Becky understood Emma needed to try on something more . . . her. "We have a Serge Jevaguine trunk show coming in a week, but the gowns are already here. The dresses are, well, they're wonderful and inspired by the ballet. Are you opposed to trying shades other than white?"

Emma looked to her mother.

"Well, I think she prefers a white or ivory, but she can try whatever she wants," Melanie managed with a sniffle. Her eyes were red rimmed, which just matched the terrible patterned shirt she was wearing with a pair of very nontrendy capri pants. Melanie truly needed some fashion guidance. If the woman didn't hate her so much, Tennyson would be willing to take her to the women's department and help a bitch out. But she doubted Melanie would appreciate the opportunity.

"I have one I think will be lovely on her. Let's try it and see what you think, Emma," Becky said before disappearing into the depths of Stanley Korshak.

Emma studied herself in the mirror. "I mean, I really love this one. It's so elegant and refined. But I don't know. Is it too . . . severe for me?"

Tennyson stood and walked to her future daughter-in-law, eyeing the elegant fabric. Cristina Ottaviano was an excellent designer, but Emma had glimpsed exactly what Tennyson had seen plainly—the dress was too old for her with a sophistication that wasn't Emma at all.

Becky came back with a fluffy ball gown. She saw Emma's forehead crease. "I didn't really want something so . . . big."

The stylist grinned as she hooked the dress on the stand, unzipping the protective bag. "I understand, but I think it's important to try a few styles. You look lovely in the trumpet gown, but I have a hunch this might suit you better. Note the cascading pale-pink silk-and-pearl flowers on the bodice, which spill down elegantly over the sheer organza. Your bosom is tastefully covered, but there's some sexy sheerness, and then there is the skirt—multiple layers of the softest tulle. The back is the most magnificent one I've seen in a while. Enormous attention to detail in this dress that is youthful, elegant, and, well, one of my favorites."

Emma eyed the gown and nodded. "Okay. I'll try it."

Off the two went, leaving Tennyson alone with Melanie. They hadn't said much to each other all day, instead directing their conversation to Emma. It had been an awkward ride over, and Tennyson had several times over the course of the three-hour ride in the limo and the rushed luncheon at her favorite sushi restaurant thought she should have stayed at home. But she needed a mother-of-the-groom dress that didn't make it look like she was sixty-five years old. And, Lord help her, but Melanie probably needed one, too.

Melanie had always had a tendency toward dressing conservatively. Mostly because her mother liked all things covered, so Melanie had followed that directive. Yet the sheer bad taste the woman had been displaying lately, in an effort to cover up the weight she'd gained or whatever, made Tennyson too nervous to leave her to decide one of the most important elements of the wedding—Emma's dress.

Nope.

"Have you already found your dress for the wedding?" Tennyson asked after a good three tense minutes of silence, hoping Melanie hadn't already bought a MeeMaw dress to wear with her favorite clodhoppers.

"Uh, I will probably pick up something at Dillard's. I was hoping to lose a few pounds before . . . why am I even telling you this? I'm fine." She wiped a finger beneath each lower lash and looked grumpy as a codfish.

"I'm going to look for mine while we're here. The store carries a great selection of designers. You might be able to find something special," Tennyson said, trying to be diplomatic. She was tired of Melanie's anger. Okay, yeah, Tennyson deserved a lot of it, but wasn't Melanie tired of being hostile? How much longer was she going to be a blazing bitch?

"I saw the price tags on the dresses when we came in. Two thousand dollars for a simple sundress? No thank you." Melanie pulled out her phone and tapped on the screen.

"But it's your daughter's wedding. You're not really going to wear an ugly dress off the sales rack from somewhere in Shreveport, are you?"

Melanie looked up at her. "Who *are* you anymore? What's wrong with a dress from Dillard's? You used to think Dillard's was great, remember?"

Tennyson stared down at her. "I'm exactly who I want to be."

"And that's someone who does . . . what exactly? Flits around with no purpose? Have you even had a job? Or was your career merely marrying wealthy men and spending their money? Or maybe it's marathon champagne drinking?" She glanced pointedly over at the empty flute on the table next to the seating area.

"I *like* champagne."

"I think everyone knows *that*. Not to mention you're a walking advertisement for plastic surgery. Oh, and particularly good at making everyone else feel cheap and . . . fat. If that was your goal for coming back to Shreveport—to show everyone how rich and tacky you are—mission accomplished."

Tennyson laughed, even though deep inside Melanie's words were a pair of brass knuckles delivered to her gut. *Ouch.* "Jealous much, Mel?"

"Of you?" Melanie asked, doing her best Anne Brevard impression, chin high, eyes cold. "Hardly."

"But you are. I can see that as plain as a billboard. But I can also see you love being a martyr, don't you? You probably get a hard-on from everyone in the PTA saying 'Melanie can do it. She's so good at doing all the things,' and I bet secretly you enjoy bowing and scraping to your kids, setting out the perfectly cut watermelon in pretty glass bowls, planting herbs you'll never use, hiding your smoking habit so everyone will think you're the perfect wife and mother. But, God, Melly, you're so *boring*."

Melanie's cheeks suffused with color. "And you're a blow-up, plastic wannabe who likes to flaunt money. But then again, that's what the nouveau riche do. Bless your heart, you just don't know any better, do you?"

Okay, gloves off. "At least I get laid. I bet you haven't given Kit a blow job since the Obama administration."

Melanie's whole face turned red. "But I bet *you'd* like to, wouldn't you?"

"Oh, sugar, been there, done that," Tennyson said.

Melanie's face showed the emotional blow she'd dealt, but there was nothing more to be said because at that moment Emma and Becky came into the room.

Both she and Melanie turned, their eyes widening when they saw the full effect of Emma in the confection that was the bridal gown. They knew this dress was the one because the sheer pleasure, the absolute delight was written all over Emma's face. Becky looked fairly pleased herself. If she would have blown on her knuckles and brushed them onto her silk-clad shoulder, she would have deserved the boast.

The gown was perfect and fit Emma like it had been made for her.

Emma stepped onto the platform and met their eyes in the mirror. "Well?"

Melanie sat down on the overstuffed chair a bit too hard, and when Tennyson turned and caught sight of her old friend's face, she felt something inside her soften. Even though she was still super pissed at Melanie for her rude-ass comments, she understood what this moment meant to her. Emma looked breathtaking in the gown.

"It's . . . uh, it's . . . I'm sorry. I just . . ." Melanie waved a hand in front of her face.

Emma smiled, shaking her head. "Mom, don't cry."

"I can't help it. You look perfect," Melanie said, sniffling and probably getting snot all over everything. Tennyson reached over, grabbed another tissue, and gave it to her. Then she pulled about five more and handed those to her, too.

And she took one for herself.

"This one is exquisite on Emma, as you can see," Becky said, coming around to the back of the dress and fluffing it, though it didn't need it. The layered tulle lay perfectly, looking a bit like a ballet skirt with a barely perceptible uneven hemline that rose slightly in the front. The delicate pink blossoms were soft, flowery kisses trailing down the bodice, spilling onto the skirt. "Will you wear a veil?"

Emma turned and studied herself in the mirror. "I thought I would, but now I'm thinking something with flowers that mimic the bodice or perhaps something jeweled. Not a tiara, but perhaps a hair comb? I'm not sure."

"Let me call Lisa and have her bring a few of our headpieces. We have some lovely new Maria Elena combs that might look nice. We can always add a simple veil to a peineta, which I think will look very nice." Becky disappeared again, leaving them alone.

"I heard you arguing, you know," Emma said, turning toward them.

Tennyson slid a glance over to Melanie. Had she heard her talk about Kit and a blow job?

"Um, you heard what we said?" Tennyson asked.

"Not the words. Just the anger in your tone," Emma said. Melanie's daughter looked so disappointed in them. But she also looked confused. It was obvious she was still in the dark about what had broken her and Melanie's friendship.

"Em, your mother and I have some things between us that . . . aren't easy," Tennyson said.

"So I gathered. After the meeting with Marc and the weirdness in the car on the way over, I concluded that whatever it is between you—and my grandmother because I'm not blind to that either—is big enough to make everyone feel uncomfortable. But here's the thing—what are y'all going to do about it? Because we can't go on with my mom snipping at you about the dog, and you can't keep making Mom feel bad because she's . . . I don't know . . . a mom."

"What does that mean?" Melanie said, her body stiffening and her weepy mother-of-the-bride reaction disappearing.

Emma stroked the tulle and trailed her hands over the intricate flowers on the dress, avoiding her mother's gaze. "You know what it means, Mom. You go to Cheapcuts to get your hair cut and colored. You wear clothes that don't fit or flatter your figure. You wear horrible shoes. And you excuse it all by claiming practicality or saying you don't have time. But the fact is, you just don't try anymore."

Melanie's mouth dropped open, and she looked truly . . . hurt.

Emma was spot-on, but something about her saying so in front of Tennyson, especially after knowing they weren't friends any longer, was damned bold. And that bothered Tennyson. "Emma, I don't think—"

Her son's fiancée whirled around and looked at her. "And *you*, a lot of what my mom says about you is true, too. You're so . . . so much, Tennyson. Besides, you drink too much. Two vodka martinis at lunch and two champagnes since we've been here."

Tennyson crossed her arms. "If you're inferring I have a drinking problem, you're wrong. I can go without booze. And really, it's not your place to say anything to me about what I do and don't do. And what you just said to your mother is not very well done of you."

"Maybe not, but you still drink too much. I share the garbage cans with you, and I know. Besides, I'm about to be part of your family, so maybe someone has to say what needs to be said here."

"Emma," Melanie said, her voice a warning shot fired as she struggled to her feet. "That's enough. Tennyson brought you over here, did all this for you, and you're going to be rude? No, ma'am."

Emma laughed. "Well, that was easy. You just stuck up for each other after tearing each other down only minutes ago."

Tennyson frowned. "If you think you're going to play games with me and your mother, think again. You weren't meant to overhear us. Besides, what passed between us years ago won't be something to disrupt this wedding."

Emma arched an eyebrow. "Oh, really? Because every time we have gotten together for anything since Andrew and I announced we were engaged, you two have been uncivil and uncontrollable."

"We have not," Melanie said, her expression growing more and more perturbed.

Tennyson felt the same way. She didn't need some knock-kneed twentysomething telling her how to behave. They hadn't done anything too wrong. Okay, there had been a smashed cake, a near dogfight, and some choice words tossed about, but no harm had befallen either of their children. In fact, considering she and Melanie were pretty much enemies, they'd done fairly well. "Melanie's right. We have not."

Emma rolled her eyes. "You two need to figure out how you're going to survive because in two months, Andrew and I are going to be promising forever to each other. And forever is a long time . . . Teeny . . . and Melly."

"Okay, ladies," Becky said, breezing back into the salon with a tall, thin woman who carried a case and looked pretty much like a runway model. "Here's Lisa with some of our finest pieces."

Emma stepped off the platform and turned to Becky. "Before we go much further, I would like to see the Caroline Castigliano 'En Fleur' dress. It has pockets."

Becky looked confused. "But, this dress . . ."

Emma held up a hand. "I love this one, but I want to be certain."

Becky shrugged. "Let me go pull it."

Tennyson stepped in front of Becky. "No. Wait. Emma, the one you're wearing is perfect. I mean, I have never seen a dress be more you than that one, and I can tell you love it. When you came in, it was like magic."

Melanie nodded. "She's right. The one you're wearing is the one. Emma, it's perfect. It was your dress the moment you put it on."

Emma gave them another smile. "So you both are once again agreeing? This is the dress?"

Tennyson and Melanie looked at each other. No one liked to be manipulated by a twenty-two-year-old who thought she was smarter than them combined. Melanie ripped her gaze away.

"Yes. We agree. The one you're wearing is the most beautiful thing I've ever seen on you. I can't imagine another dress, even one with pockets, overshadowing the sheer beauty and rightness of this dress," Melanie said.

Emma's grin was triumphant.

"We've been played." Tennyson sucked in a deep breath and then flounced back to her seat, wishing she'd seen through Emma's machinations earlier.

"Sorry," Emma said, her grin not disappearing. "I just needed to make sure the last time you agreed wasn't an aberration. Try to do that more. Now, let's see what works for my hair. I'm thinking a low gathering of my hair into . . . well, let me show you."

Emma pulled out her phone, ignoring both Melanie and Tennyson as she showed Becky and Lisa something no doubt on a Pinterest board. After a few minutes of checking her email and scanning Facebook, Tennyson rose. "I'm going to look for a dress for myself."

Melanie set the phone she was using to take pictures of Emma in the dress on the table and nodded.

"You want to come look, too?" Tennyson asked.

She could tell that Melanie wanted to go with her. Melanie had never been good at waiting. By nature she liked to move and have purpose. "I don't know. Emma may need me."

"Em?" Tennyson called to the girl still tapping, scrolling, and mulling over a myriad of hairstyles. "Can you narrow it down to two or three possibilities while your mother and I take a look at the cocktail dresses?"

"Sure," Emma said with a wave of her hand.

Tennyson looked at Melanie. "Come on. I saw a royal-blue Lanvin that might work for you."

Melanie exhaled, dropping her phone into her purse. "Okay. Fine."

Fifteen minutes later Tennyson had Melanie inside the dressing room with six different options to try, the silk Lanvin with the sheer cape one of the final selections. Melanie came out wearing a Carolina Herrera tulle dress in a flattering shade of watermelon. It was strapless and sexy. And it looked good on Melanie.

"That one is nice," Tennyson said, hanging a bright-red Akris Punto jersey dress back on the hanger. "Good color on you."

"I don't know. It shows a lot of skin," Melanie said, tugging the bodice up.

"You have good skin. You always have. Go out by the pool and let the sun kiss your shoulders. They'll be perfect."

"I don't have a pool."

Tennyson almost said *come use mine* before she caught herself. Besides, even if she'd blundered into that invitation, Melanie wouldn't be caught dead poolside at Tennyson's house. "It might not be a good mother-of-the-bride dress, but it would be perfect for the bridal shower. In fact, it looks very romantic and Italian. You might get laid in that dress, Mel."

Melanie made a moue in the mirror, tilting her head, trying to decide if she liked it enough. "Teeny . . . I mean, Tennyson, don't be ridiculous."

But Tennyson had caught the old nickname and the knowledge that, for a few seconds, Melanie had forgotten she was supposed to hate Tennyson.

"I'm just saying. It might be worth the price tag." Tennyson disappeared into the dressing room, taking a short, sequined, retrofete wrap dress that was appropriately called "unicorn." The fun vibe might work for the shower, especially if she paired it with platform sandals and wore her hair swept up with large chandelier earrings.

"Well, it *is* on sale, and it's sort of timeless," Melanie said.

"As all Carolina Herrera dresses are," Tennyson called back, shrugging into the dress. She liked that it dipped to frame her décolletage. Maybe she could talk Officer Rhett, a.k.a. Hot Cop, into coming by and peeling the dress off her. She smiled at herself in the mirror.

They'd been texting and Snapchatting each other, and gradually those Snapchats had gotten a bit . . . well, titillating. She'd never realized a gal could practice foreplay with her phone. Of course, flirting with sexting was one thing, but actually going there . . . well, she wanted to do that, too.

Definitely.

Next, she pulled on a David Koma one-shoulder dress in a bright green. There were tiny round reflective mirrors sewn in swaths that swirled around the dress. It was a statement dress, sophisticated but somewhat daring, and it looked nice against her sun-kissed skin. Because some people had a pool and used it.

Tennyson walked out of the dressing room. "What do you think?"

Melanie was still clad in the strapless dress, swirling and most likely talking herself out of buying it. She turned and looked at Tennyson. "That looks incredible on you. Fits you perfectly, and while it's sexy, it doesn't look like you're about to go clubbing."

"So you're saying the unicorn sequin was too young for me?" Tennyson asked, heavy on the sarcasm, as she tried to tug up the zipper.

"Here," Melanie said, spinning her around and shoving her hair out of the way. She zipped the dress and then stepped back, narrowing her eyes. "You might want to take it up under the arms. It gapes slightly here . . . and here."

Melanie had reached under her arms and pinched the fabric together. Nostalgia hit Tennyson so hard she nearly stumbled. They'd done this countless times, slipping into dressing rooms, chatting about boys, and trying on things they shouldn't or couldn't buy. She'd zipped Melanie up hundreds of times, seen her bare-assed naked, and knew she couldn't wear peplums or too many ruffles. So this situation was almost too familiar, and something about remembering how they had both once been silly girls who loved each other and made sure each bought the exact right dress for the occasion made her wish she hadn't been the hotheaded, foul-tempered jealous bitch she'd been back in college. Because if she'd just accepted that Melanie and Kit were together, then maybe they wouldn't be so damned far away from each other.

But the Tennyson of the past hadn't realized the waves she created would still be rippling around her. Of course, she also hadn't known her son would go to her father's alma mater, sit beside a pretty brunette, and fall in love with Melanie and Kit's daughter.

But that was the way of life, right? A gal had to live with the decisions she'd made—both good and bad—and try, try to find some peace.

Yet she wasn't sure it would ever be possible after what she'd done at Melanie and Kit's wedding reception. But as her mother loved to say, "If wishes were fishes, we'd all be throwing nets."

"So what do you think? I had an off-the-shoulder swing dress I was going to wear for the shower, but I like the vibe of this one," Tennyson said, dashing away her regrets. Because regrets were always there. They were in the faint lines she tried like hell to erase on her face, in the memories that refused to leave her alone, in the check she wrote every month.

"I like this one. I wouldn't think that color would do well on you, but it's nice. And it doesn't look like you're a teenager," Melanie said.

"Gee, thanks."

"You know, you're prettier when you don't try so hard, Tennyson."

"And you're prettier when you stop trying to hide yourself." Tennyson looked at Melanie in the mirror. "Get the Carolina Herrera. You look good in it."

Melanie's eyes brightened. "You think so? I'm going out of town with Kit, and a new dress might be nice."

"When?"

"At the end of next week. Right before the shower. Kit has a conference in Destin, and I'm going down for a few days," Melanie said, looking at her in the reflection of the mirror. "You don't need help with the shower, do you?"

Melanie's expression was sincere, the way it had always been. If someone needed help with something, from cleaning her room and making spirit goody bags to volunteering as the designated driver, Melanie had always been willing to pitch in and help. But then Tennyson could see in Melanie's face that she'd forgotten they weren't friends and were instead enemies because she frowned, shook her head, and stepped away.

"I'm paying Marc Mallow enough that everything should be taken care of. But it's nice of you to ask. I want Emma and Andrew to enjoy being showered with gifts and well wishes. They're our kids."

For a moment their eyes met in the reflection of the mirror. Melanie looked like she wanted to say something. Now was the time for Tennyson to apologize. To say she shouldn't have done what she did. She opened her mouth, but something shifted in Melanie's eyes. Something hard returned, and the moment was over.

Melanie turned away. "They'll have other wedding showers. My book club and a few of the moms from the PTA are doing a Rock Around the Clock shower."

"I know. Marc told me that one of her friends called about the bachelorette party, and he had a brilliant idea." Tennyson tapped the fastener on the nape of her neck. "Would you?"

Wordlessly, Melanie reached out and unzipped her, retreating to her own dressing room as if she'd slipped up too much and now had to gather herself and mount her normal defensiveness.

This was what they had come to—two former friends who could never find their way back to one another. Because of a man. Because of ego. Because one of them had destroyed what they'd been with words that should have never seen the light of day.

It was something Tennyson couldn't change.

No matter how much she wished she could.

CHAPTER ELEVEN

Melanie sat out in the driveway of her mother's house, checking the time on her phone and tapping on the steering wheel. Her mother's gardener was pulling out the scraggly snapdragons that should have gone weeks ago and replacing them with jolly red begonias. The June sun had gotten warm quickly, reminding her she needed to pick up some sunscreen before she headed to the beach in a few days. She didn't need to go to the bridal shower looking like a lobster.

Not to mention she'd found no swimsuits on sale in her size. Which meant she'd paid full price for the stupid one-piece she'd be taking to the beach. Of course, she didn't feel too guilty because she hadn't had a new swimsuit in five years, and the elastic was shot in her old one, anyway. Her credit card bill would be astronomical this month since she'd bought the Carolina Herrera dress on the Dallas trip, but damn it, she deserved a few nice things. No use in the money she and Kit had being hoarded away for her kids to squander.

She tooted her horn.

Where was Hillary? They had to be at Marc Mallow's office at two. He'd squeezed the cake tasting in between two other appointments and made it clear he appreciated promptness.

Finally, the door opened, and her sister emerged. She wore a long, loose dress, and her hair had been curled. Hillary's thin body made Melanie wince every time she saw her sister.

She noted Hillary didn't have her purse and came around to the driver's side. Melanie rolled down the window, knowing what was coming. "Hey, what's wrong?"

Hillary looked around as if she'd stumbled outside naked and photographers lurked in the bushes. "Uh, why don't you go on ahead without me? I'm just not feeling very festive today, and I don't want to ruin the whole cake-tasting thing."

Disappointment thunked in Melanie's stomach. Her sister wasn't coming with her. "I don't understand. I thought you wanted to do this with me and Emma? Is it because we're tasting cake?"

"No," Hillary said with a wave of her spidery hand. In the afternoon light, her sister's gauntness seemed more pronounced. Her once luxurious hair was wispy frizz, her bones so prominent it hurt to think about how she rested upon them, and her once bright-blue eyes had sunken into dullness. Hillary had become a ghastly shadow of herself. It made Melanie's heart squeeze so hard that tears threatened. "I want to go, but I just . . . I can't, Melly bean. I know you don't understand, but . . ."

Hillary seemed to not be able to find the words.

And Melanie didn't have the words to make her sister feel better about her inability to show up. "It's fine."

But it wasn't. It was just something Melanie said because being angry that her sister couldn't put anyone else in front of her fears or being furious that Hillary was so powerless against her diseases wasn't going to change anything. Her frustrations would serve only to drive her sister further away from her, and at present she felt as disconnected as she had ever been from her.

"I'm sorry, Mel. I am. I love you and Emma, and I thought I could go, but I . . . just can't."

Melanie swallowed down the gigantic lump in her throat, unshed tears still threatening. She'd been excited to have Hillary involved in some way, another buffer against Tennyson's steamroller of "fabulous" ideas. She'd thought Hillary would be able to help her with the wedding, allowing them to connect, make memories, build something strong enough to ground her sister in wanting to get better. She knew it was stupid to think that, but she so wanted her old sister back. "I understand. I wish you could come today. But you'll be at the shower next weekend, right? It's at Tennyson's house and . . . you know."

Hillary nodded. "I know. Not going to be easy, but if I remember Tennyson, I'm sure there will be lots going on, so it won't feel like you're entering the enemy's camp."

"I better go," Melanie said, glancing at the clock radio. "I'm going to be late as it is."

"I'm sorry," Hillary said, shading her eyes.

Melanie needed to talk to her mother about getting Hillary a complete health workup and ensure she was still going to her therapy appointments. Hillary had become an expert at hiding her "sins." Melanie glanced at her sister's knuckles for signs she'd been purging. From her angle she couldn't tell.

"You're okay, right?" Melanie asked as she put the car into reverse. "I mean, you're still talking to Dr. Beth."

Hillary's expression shifted into one Melanie was familiar with. "Yes. Stop worrying. I'm just dealing with some anxiety, but I'm working through it. I should be fine by next weekend. I'll be at the shower. Now go before Tennyson orders a monstrosity of a cake with edible sequins and live doves."

Melanie managed a laugh as Hillary walked up the driveway. She gave a small wave as she shifted into drive, but Hillary was already closing the door.

Something that felt like guilt, grief, and ickiness waffled around in her gut. Something didn't feel right with Hillary, and she wasn't sure their mother was paying close enough attention. Another to-do item on her list. Talking with her mother about Hillary was never fun and always sucked the joy out of her life. Perhaps it could wait until she got back from the beach. Maybe Hillary would be looking better by the time the shower rolled around.

Fifteen minutes later, Melanie let herself into Marc's odd little gazebo office.

"Where have you been?" Emma asked, looking up from a portfolio no doubt filled with wedding cake prices.

"I went to pick up your aunt Hilly, but she had a headache." And so now she was lying for her sister. Great.

"Oh, well, I wanted her to come, but it's fine," Emma said, giving a half smile and shrug.

Marc wore white linen pants, a pale-blue button-down that was about as trim as a person could get a shirt without being indecent, a hot-pink bow tie, and a boater's hat. He looked ridiculous but somehow also right. Tennyson sat with Andrew on the Victorian settee, looking sleek in a silk romper. Her son was in his characteristic T-shirt, gym shorts, and tennis shoes. Andrew's shaggy hair needed a trim, but he looked every inch the southern frat boy he seemed to have become.

Tennyson's forehead crinkled. "Is Hilly okay? You look worried."

Melanie pulled on a fake smile. "She's fine. Now where are we on cakes?"

"We're just about to start tasting. You haven't missed a thing, darling," Marc said, sweeping his hand à la Vanna White over to the table holding samples of cake. "Donna!"

The tall woman emerged from the inner sanctum. "You rang, my lord?"

148

Marc gave her a flat look. "This is your show, Donna. I'm letting you take the reins."

Donna winked at Emma. "Usually I'm pulling the damn cart. Calm your buns, Marshmallow."

Marc affected an eye roll and overly dramatic sigh. "You can't get good help these days."

Donna ignored him, smiling broadly. Her short hair had been dyed purple, and the nose ring glinted in the sunlight streaming through the windows with the stained-glass transoms. "Okay, folks, let's gather round because today we will be choosing the bakery that will create Emma and Andrew's wedding cake, and we'll do that by taste and flavorings. Before we begin sampling, do either of you have firm preferences?"

"Honestly, I've always liked the regular wedding-cake flavor," Emma said, eyeing the varied samples on the table. "Just that almond-flavored one. I don't need anything crazy like they have on *Cake Wars*."

Andrew shrugged. "I want whatever she wants. I just came because there would be cake."

"Good answer," Donna said with a grin.

"Wait, so, like, the groom cake is always something fun, right?" Andrew asked.

Donna shrugged. "It can be. I've seen college football stadiums, duck blinds, and monster trucks incorporated into the groom's cake, but we've also done some tasteful cakes that were simple and more focused on flavor and presentation."

"Oh." Andrew looked at Emma. "What do you want?"

"Well, he's starting this marriage off right, isn't he?" Marc said from his seated position in a nearby armchair. The tapestried fabric had been threaded with gold lamé. Marc's throne.

"I want you to have what you want, Andrew," Emma said.

"I like the outdoors. Hiking, rafting, and all that, so how about a cake that reflects the area where we met, the things we love to do. Remember that hike at Devil's Den? We could do a river with little plastic boats? That sound good?" He looked at Emma for affirmation.

Emma smiled. "Sure."

He looked back at Donna, and behind him Emma shook her head and mouthed *no*. Donna's mouth twitched, and even Tennyson looked amused. Tennyson loved over the top, but Melanie was nearly certain she wouldn't embrace little plastic boats. Or would she?

"So instead of being literal, how about we take a subtle approach, a cake that on the surface looks more elegant but utilizes elements that represent your love of nature?"

"That sounds cool," Andrew said.

"Great. Let's move on to the tasting for the bride's cake. Represented here are three different bakeries. We have Gloria Jay's, We Take the Cake, and Evelyn's. These are the vendors we prefer because they are reliable, accommodating, and have the best cake quality. Ladies and gentleman, grab your forks."

They all picked up their forks and started on the first piece. Melanie had been dieting for weeks, and she was nearly certain what she was putting in her mouth was better than sex, a clean house, and a shirtless Chris Pine combined.

Donna pointed to the pale layer cake they were sampling. "This is a white vanilla bean with almond frosting. It's the most traditional of the cakes we'll be tasting."

"It's delicious," Melanie said, scooping up the last of her piece and licking the fork, even though it was inappropriate. Her mother would have had kittens if she'd seen.

"Eh, it's kind of boring, though," Tennyson said, setting hers down.

Of course Tennyson would say that. Of course.

"It's not boring. It's traditional," Melanie said, knowing that she was playing with fire but not caring. Her sister not coming for the tasting

150

had frustrated her, and she didn't feel like putting up with more of Tennyson's crap today. The woman had already forced her into paying too much for a dress in Dallas by making her feel self-conscious about her wardrobe. Tennyson wasn't going to bully Emma into a cake just because she didn't like traditional.

Donna nodded. "Nothing wrong with a classic choice for cake. Okay, the next piece is strawberry with a berry puree and a fondant icing. It's a versatile cake, but you will also have to consider strawberries are a common allergy."

"Better," Tennyson said, referring to the cake.

"But it's true lots of people are allergic to strawberries. I know of two people offhand," Melanie said.

Tennyson had the audacity to roll her eyes. Something ugly erupted inside Melanie. But she flattened her mouth and turned to Emma. "What do you think, sweetie?"

Emma made a thinking face. "I like it, but strawberry has never been my favorite."

Donna seemed to make a mental note and moved on. "Next is a white-chocolate raspberry."

"Not a fan of white chocolate," Emma said, taking a small bite before setting the cake down. "Not what I want."

Melanie thought it was pretty dang good, but she'd been going without her daily Snickers minibars for four weeks now. She'd probably think a Twinkie cake would work well. She polished off that sample piece, too.

"This next cake is unusual in that it pairs both vanilla bean and dark chocolate. There is a rosemary blackberry compote in the vanilla, while the dark chocolate has layers of an espresso mousse. It has a nuttiness without having nuts, and it's definitely a different feel for a wedding cake. It's one of the more expensive cakes, but worth every dime because the guests will be raving." Donna nodded for them to taste.

Tennyson immediately brightened. "Now this is good. I love that it's not as sweet and has great texture."

Melanie wanted to roll her eyes. She would bet a thousand dollars that Tennyson O'Rourke had never baked a cake in her life. She'd probably heard these things said on the Food Network, and when Donna said *unusual* and *expensive*, she'd latched on to it because those were Tennyson's requirements for everything. "I don't know. Rosemary is a strong flavor."

"But not in this cake. There is only an essence," Donna said.

Melanie took a bite and had to admit it was good. But she still liked the traditional white better. It was so versatile as a cake, and besides, everyone liked vanilla.

"The next sample is a pink champagne wedding cake made with Chambord, featuring a passion-fruit compote. The texture is light, very summery, and one of my favorites in taste and appearance." Donna tapped the plate with the light-pink confection.

"Ooh, I like this one," Emma said, taking one bite. Then another. Her eyes lit up.

"It's really nice," Tennyson said, nodding.

They moved on to a lemon cake with lemon-curd filling, a praline cake with salted-caramel filling, and finally a vanilla lavender cake with blackberry compote and brown sugar buttercream frosting.

"This last one is a bit more intense and flavorful. It, too, is on the expensive end of the wedding cakes offered, but with berries and fresh flowers, it can be a stunning choice." Donna pressed both hands onto the table and looked at Marc with a quirked eyebrow.

Marc moved over to the table. "These are the samples Donna selected. So what are our thoughts?"

Emma tapped her fork on the plate she was holding. "I've tasted a lot of good ones, but I really love the blackberries in this one."

Tennyson nodded. "Pretty spectacular."

Melanie shrugged. "I still like the first one. Almond buttercream is classic."

"And boring," Tennyson added.

Melanie narrowed her eyes. "What do you even know about cake?"

"Plenty. I've worked with caterers for decades, and I've sat at some of the best chef tables in the highest-starred restaurants in the world," Tennyson said, her eyes sparking with fight. "Why do you always go for the most basic choice?"

"Because sometimes basic is basic for a reason. People like regular ol' wedding cake. That's why wedding cake is, duh, an actual flavor. God, you have a piece of cake in Paris somewhere and suddenly you're a cake expert? Whatever."

Tennyson sucked in a breath and started mouthing numbers. She was counting to ten.

Andrew and Emma slid alarmed looks at each other, glances that seemed to say *do something*.

"Some of us didn't settle for Shreveport and a vanilla life, Melanie," Tennyson said when she reached the number six.

Before Melanie knew what she was doing, she scooped up the remaining cake on her plate and hurled it at Tennyson. The blackberry lavender cake hit her former BFF right between the eyes.

Emma gasped, her mouth dropping open.

Tennyson drew back and blinked, like she couldn't believe she'd been hit with cake.

Melanie couldn't believe what she'd done, either. She looked down at her offending hand like she had no clue how it had automatically launched a piece of cake at Tennyson's head.

Tennyson reached up and swiped the cake from her forehead. Then she gave a toothy smile that wasn't actually a smile at all. "I'm guessing this means you are strongly against the blackberry cake?"

Melanie watched as Tennyson rounded the table, picked up the white-chocolate raspberry cake Emma had abandoned, and smashed it right into her face. "So try this one."

"Oh my God, what is happening here?" Emma shrieked, grabbing Andrew's arm. Her future husband looked shell-shocked. Marc and Donna looked like they had no clue what to do, either.

Tennyson stood next to her, looking a bit taken aback at herself. The woman had cake crumbs scattering the fabric stretched across her breasts and blackberry jam smeared on her forehead. She also looked ridiculous, angry, and somehow delighted by what she'd done. Melanie licked her lips, swiping the icing from her cheek. "I actually like this one better. Thanks, Teeny."

Tennyson cocked her head, and then laughter burbled up. "Maybe you should try the praline again." She picked up a hunk of that cake and shoved it into Melanie's open mouth, making more of a mess. Tennyson dramatically licked her fingers while giggling.

That made Melanie start laughing. "It's good. It's really good."

Marc had been frozen in place, his mouth opening and closing like a beached catfish gasping for air. Donna actually looked amused. She seemed like the kind of gal who could handle almost anything.

"What is wrong with y'all?" Emma said, stomping over to them. "You're acting like children."

Melanie would have said something, but she was too busy laughing. Tennyson was, too. She had no clue why they were laughing. What they'd done had been awful and, yes, childish. But even as she realized how totally inappropriately they'd both behaved, she also recognized how good it had felt to nail Tennyson right between the eyes with that piece of cake. Melanie had never, ever misbehaved like a maniac in front of either of her children, but maybe she should have. Because this felt cathartic.

"Stop laughing," Emma said, trying valiantly to wipe up the icing and cake that had gotten all over the table. "Mr. Mallow, I'm so sorry. I don't know what is going on. They've gone . . . crazy!"

Andrew gave an embarrassed chuckle. "It's okay, Em. Just a little cake. We can clean that up easy."

"Don't take their side," she snapped at him. "This is important. We're trying to choose our cake here, and these two are turning this into a circus all because they have some kind of grudge."

Emma glared at them, and Melanie stopped laughing.

Andrew curved a hand around her neck. "Come on, babe. It's important, but our guests are going to eat cake whether it's lavender honeycomb or something from a grocery store."

Emma turned to him. "Are you serious? It's our cake, our *wedding* cake. I don't even know what is happening here. These two need an intervention."

Tennyson stopped laughing and grabbed a napkin from the stack on the table. She handed one to Melanie. "We got a little carried away. Sorry. Things have been tense, and this was us just letting off a little steam."

"I told you we should have just gone to Vegas." Emma started toward the door, her eyes crackling and sheened with tears.

"Oh, stop," Melanie said to her daughter's back side. "We can still pick the cake and proceed. Don't be dramatic."

Emma turned. "Don't be dramatic. Dramatic? I don't know what's gotten into you. You're acting like someone I don't even know, Mom. You just started a cake fight because someone didn't agree with you. That's . . . insane!"

Marc clapped his hands. "Ladies, ladies. Let's have some tea and talk through this."

"Tea? Don't you have something stronger? Because I think we could all use a drink," Tennyson said, wiping the remainder of the cake and jam from her face.

Marc nodded. "Donna, can you fetch the brandy to go with the tea?"

The person who looked the most delighted with all that had transpired was Marc's assistant. Her eyes danced with delight. "Are you sure you just don't want me to get the bikinis and baby oil and let them have a go at each other? We could charge admission and make a fortune."

"Donna," Marc said, with a warning in his voice.

"Brandy it is," she said, leaving the table and disappearing into the back.

Marc ushered them toward the seating area. Melanie grabbed a wad of napkins and scrubbed at her face. She could still taste the sweetness on her lips, and hey, maybe the butter in the frosting might help with the bags under her eyes. The expensive cream she'd bought wasn't doing a bit of good.

"I'm not one to fuss, but my job is to keep the bride happy. Our bride doesn't look happy," Marc said, looking at Emma, who had sat with her arms crossed, angry tears still glinting in her eyes. Andrew had sat next to her, but he'd wisely stopped trying to console her.

Melanie set the wadded napkins on the coffee table and crossed her legs. "What cake have you decided on, honey?"

"So you're really going to pretend that this didn't just happen?" Emma asked, her blue eyes flashing with annoyance.

"No, but we tasted all the cakes. Which one?" Melanie insisted, because she couldn't undo what she had done. And that was what they were here for. Cake.

Emma looked at Marc. "The last one. Blackberry." Then she looked back at Melanie. "And?"

"And what?"

"You aren't going to address your behavior?" Emma said, looking more like Melanie's mother than she ever had.

Melanie shrugged. "I don't have to answer to you. I'm a grown-up."

Tennyson's lips twitched, but she remained silent.

"*That's* your answer?" Emma turned from her and shook her head in what looked like disgust.

Donna came in and plonked down the tea tray a bit too hard. Marc winced, grabbed the brandy bottle, poured a decent amount into two cups, and handed one to Tennyson and one to Melanie. He seemed to think it over before pouring himself a double shot and tossing it back. Emma and Andrew seemed to be on their own.

Tennyson took the brandy and sipped it, making a face. Melanie picked hers up and tossed it back the way Marc had. It burned like a mother, but she needed the warmth and calm it might bring her. She'd never done anything this spontaneous. Or, well, she hadn't since she was friends with Tennyson. *This* was what that woman drove her to—misbehaving.

"Damn, girl," Tennyson said in admiration, eyeing her.

Emma poured a steaming cup of water and dropped a tea bag in. Silence reigned for a good minute before Melanie's daughter folded her hands and cleared her throat. "You need to tell me and Andrew what is going on between you. We can't continue planning the wedding with this disagreement still sitting between you. It's too much stress, and we need to put . . . whatever it is behind us. *Both* of you are going to be our family."

At that moment regret slammed into Melanie. Her daughter was right—the tension between her and Tennyson wasn't fair to either of their children. Still, how did she tell Emma the truth about her own family? For so long she'd protected Emma and Noah from the truth because she wanted the image of her father to be pristine. She hadn't told any mistruths—her father had been smart, talented, handsome, and so full of kindness. So, no, Melanie hadn't misrepresented the man who had given her rides on his shoulders and helped her build a play-house in the backyard, but she hadn't told the whole truth, either. Like her mother, she'd wanted the scandal to stay where it belonged—in the past.

But she had to say something, give her daughter some reason why she and Tennyson were at odds.

After another period of silence, Emma narrowed her eyes. "Well?"

"Fine. We fought over a guy," Tennyson said.

Both Emma and Andrew turned to her, their eyebrows raised. Emma blinked. "This is over a *guy*?"

"Mom, please tell me you and Em's mom didn't throw away your friendship over some random dude," Andrew said, sounding very mature and millennial. Guys weren't worth it. Dime a dozen. Girl power. And all that jazz.

Melanie squeezed her eyes shut and then opened them. "It wasn't just a random dude. It was Kit."

CHAPTER TWELVE

Andrew kissed an emotional Emma on the forehead and jogged toward Tennyson's car. He tapped on the driver's side window, ensuring she couldn't put it in reverse and get the hell out of Dodge.

"I'm riding with you," he shouted through the glass.

"I'm fine," Tennyson said with a wave. She didn't want him to ride home with her, because she needed some time to decompress after what had happened inside Marc's office. The whole afternoon was a colossal fail, not to mention she had frosting in her hair and her face was sticky from the blackberry compote. The only silver lining was that Emma had chosen a cake and marked the design she wanted for the wedding cake, which had been the whole reason for the appointment, so maybe it wasn't a colossal fail. Just a messy . . . mess.

Andrew had already jogged around her car. She pressed unlock so he could climb inside.

He closed the door, his knees nearly up to his chin. He moved the seat back as far as it would go and then looked at her. "Well, that was a real shit show."

Tennyson lifted a shoulder. "It all had to come out sooner or later."

"Why didn't you tell us earlier?"

When he and Emma had first started dating, she'd almost casually said, *I used to date your father and be BFFs with your mom*, but hadn't because it felt awkward to lead with something like that. She'd figured she'd hold off because it was likely Emma and Andrew would date a few months and then go their separate ways, as seemed to be Andrew's MO with most girls. But then this one stuck, and it seemed harder and harder to blurt out the background she had with Emma's parents. She'd gone with "We used to know each other" and left it at that. She figured one day she'd find a segue into a conversation about what had really happened between her and Emma's parents, but it never came. Or, if she were going to be truthful, she had avoided talking about the past because she worried that if Emma knew the truth, she would hate Tennyson as much as Melanie did.

Of course, Emma still didn't know what Tennyson had done at the wedding. Melanie was kind enough to refer to their behavior as "bad reactionary choices" and leave it at that.

"I don't know, Andrew. It's hard to talk about," she said, passing Emma and Melanie as they got into Melanie's Lexus. They seemed to be in a spirited conversation. No doubt the same one she and Andrew were having but with more emotion. Having a son had spared her theatrics . . . except her own, of course.

"Why is it hard to talk about? Your past with Em's parents would have been nice to know. Could have saved us a lot of awkward moments."

Tennyson turned. "You want to know why? 'Cause Kit broke my heart."

"But you said *you* broke up with him."

She pulled out onto Line Avenue, nearly sideswiping a Tahoe. Andrew grabbed the seat and made a sound, but she ignored it. "I did."

"So how were you heartbroken?"

Tennyson sucked in a breath. "Jared's your best friend, right? Well, imagine if you had to break up with Emma, and he started dating her.

Then he proposed. Then they got engaged and sent you an invitation to the wedding."

"I wouldn't break up with Emma. Why did you 'have to' break up?" He seemed very smug for someone who didn't really know how hard life was. What did her son know about struggling? About being invisible in the world? About having to cash in a savings bond to buy a prom dress or taking out huge college loans or eating Ramen noodles just so a gal could afford to chase her dream?

Her son had never known suffering. Andrew wore his white pretty-boy image like most—denying he had it, guilty for it having served him so well, but not willing to hand back that monthly check he received from his father's estate in order to stand on his own two feet. Hey, she didn't blame him, but he couldn't understand who she used to be and how her successes had depended solely on her ability to hustle, sacrifice, and constantly search for opportunity.

"I had a scholarship, a very tiny one, to the New York Academy and a job working as an assistant for a director who did summer theatre the June after I graduated high school. Sounds crazy, but I thought the world was very big. I decided I couldn't continue to be the Tennyson I had always been. I was starting over and needed room to come into my own. I loved Kit, and truly thought we would probably get back together. He was a marketing major and wanted to work in advertising. We'd always joked that he would come up to NYC and we'd live there together. We agreed to break up because we both needed to experience the worlds we were about to enter. You have to understand that there was no Skype or Snapchat. The only way to communicate was with letters and long-distance phone calls that made for an astronomical phone bill. It was a different world, and very tough to maintain a relationship if you weren't in the same area."

Andrew nodded. "Yeah, I guess I can see that. I can't imagine that world, but it seems logical."

"When I came home for the holidays that first year, we hung out and picked up where we left off. Things were normal, until they weren't. Kit and Melanie went to school together, and they gravitated toward one another. I suppose things just happened between them."

What she didn't say was that she had blamed Melanie and not Kit. From the very first glimpse of Kit, Melanie had fallen helplessly in love. She could still remember the exact moment they'd both laid eyes on the hot new sophomore. Melanie's parents had just bought her the cutest convertible Volkswagen Cabriolet, and since Tennyson lived around the corner, Melanie picked her up for school each morning. That morning, they'd decided to ride with the top down, singing Madonna and essentially being cool as shit because that was what you thought you were when you were fifteen years old. They'd been two sophomore girls channeling their inner rock stars, sexy, sassy, and about to get rained on. Tennyson had laughed when Melanie flipped out about not being able to get the top up as thunderclouds gathered overhead. Luckily, someone from the strip mall they'd pulled into had helped them. But it had made them late for school.

They'd just walked in, brushing the raindrops from their hairsprayed bangs, when Principal Addison opened his office door and led a well-dressed lady out into the main office. Trailing behind her was the most gorgeous guy Tennyson had ever seen.

Like every movie with a hot guy walking onto the scene, the world seemed to fade away, and "fine guy" music began to play in her head. She would have sworn real life slowed as Kit brushed back his too-long bleached hair and then shoved his hands into the back pockets of his acid-washed Levi's. He wore high-top sneakers, a pair of Oakley sunglasses perched on his head, and a JanSport navy backpack slung over one shoulder. In other words, he was super, mega fine with a cherry on top. And the smile around his sexy lips when he noticed the girls told her he knew it.

Tennyson later swore that her heart skipped a beat when she saw him, and she knew Melanie felt the same way because when she looked over at her best friend, she thought about reaching out and pushing her chin up to close her mouth. Melanie hadn't drooled, but if she had, Tennyson would have understood why.

"Mine."

Tennyson hadn't meant to say that word out loud, but it seemed imperative to call dibs on the gorgeous new student. She wanted it known because every girl who had a pulse would be interested in the new guy.

"Oh, here are some of our students. Both these young ladies are in the same grade as Christopher," Mr. Addison said.

"Kit," the boy said.

"Oh yes. Kit. Girls, come over here and meet our newest Falcon. This is Kit Layton and his mother. They moved to Shreveport last week," Mr. Addison said, motioning them forward.

They took the check-in slips from Mrs. Anita and walked over. Tennyson tried to act like she wasn't that interested, perhaps even bothered by having to greet a new student when geometry was waiting for her, but Melanie had been atypically animated, gushing about how happy everyone would be to have a new classmate. She'd really poured it on thick, and Kit looked slightly taken aback at her enthusiasm. Usually, Melanie was quieter, more willing to let Tennyson take the lead, but not this time. She was a positively chatty Cathy, with dimpled little smiles and a flirty laugh.

"I'm Tennyson," she said after Melanie ran out of steam.

Kit's mother smiled. "Like the poet?"

"My mother's an English teacher. She did this whole thing," she said, with a little exasperation tempered with an embarrassed smile. "My brother's name is Heathcliff. At least he can shorten it to Heath. Tenny doesn't really work as well."

"Oh, is your mother a teacher here?" Mrs. Layton asked.

163

"No, ma'am. She teaches public school. I'm here for the theatre program. It's excellent." She didn't add that it was on scholarship because there was no way her public-servant parents could afford tuition at Eastwood Prep with their salaries and five kids to feed. She tried to forget that she was a charity case at the private school.

"Kit does theatre. Or he did before he started playing sports."

Kit shrugged. "I like hitting home runs better than I like wearing stage makeup."

Mr. Addison nodded. "I played some ball in my day, too."

"Well, I must be getting back to the house. I have furniture coming," Mrs. Layton said, glancing out at the bright autumn day.

"Will one of you walk Kit to second period? He's in Mr. Leopold's world history class."

Melanie's shoulders sank a little. "Tennyson has that class next. It's nice meeting you, Kit. I hope we'll, you know, see each other again. I mean, we will because it's a small school, but you know what I mean." She then turned the color of the strawberry bubble gum she loved to chew.

"Yeah. Cool." Kit turned to Tennyson. "Guess you're my tour guide."

Tennyson lifted a shoulder and affected nonchalance. "I'm going that way."

Even back then she understood that guys liked a challenge. Before she turned toward the office door, where Melanie was standing looking a bit miffed she didn't get to do the honors, she saw exactly what she wanted to see in Kit's eyes—interest.

By the end of November, she'd kissed Kit after two football games and let him get to second base at Leeann Shelby's house party. At Christmas, he asked her to go out with him, and with their relationship official, Melanie had stifled her infatuation and slid into acceptance that Kit wouldn't be hers. But even as she and Kit dated for two more years, Tennyson was keenly aware that Melanie had a thing for Kit. She caught it in her friend's eyes sometimes, in the way she leaned toward Kit and laughed too hard at his lame jokes.

So when they broke up and Tennyson went to New York, she'd wondered if her best friend might be tempted, but she'd thought Kit wasn't remotely interested in Melanie as anything other than a friend.

Tennyson had been wrong about that.

Because after only six months post-breakup, Melanie got what she'd always wanted since the day that new Falcon had walked into both their lives—Melanie got the hot guy.

Her son turned down the radio and looked over at her. "If you loved Kit, why did you let him go? I mean, yeah, I get the distance thing, but you pretty much gave Melanie and Kit permission. You're the one who let him go."

Tennyson had been so caught up in remembering how hot Melanie had been for Kit that she'd forgotten she was driving. She'd almost blown through a red light. Slamming on her brakes, she skidded into the intersection. Quickly, she shifted into reverse and backed up. "Sorry. Um, but you know, Kit and Melanie didn't need my permission. Obviously."

"This is just all so bizarre. I can't believe you and Em's mom can't bury the hatchet. I mean, it was twentysomething years ago, and it's obvious you're not into Kit anymore. So why can't you put what happened behind you? Everyone has crap between them. Even good friends, but you don't act like assholes forever."

"You mean most people don't throw cake at each other?" Tennyson joked.

"Only assholes."

"Well, call me what you want, but you'll soon learn that often emotions can't be controlled. When something hard like this sits between two people, things bubble over. So in a few years, once you've faced things you can do nothing about, after you've survived heartache, tears, and loss, you give me a call, and then we'll talk about who's an asshole."

Andrew gave her a sharp look. "So you're saying you had a good reason to ruin this afternoon? You're justified because things didn't go your way all those years ago? Sorry, Mom, you and Melanie don't get a pass. You're both literally ruining some precious memories because you can't get your crap together. You're like the people who talk about how tough they've had it, how they walked to school barefoot, up hills and shit. And you're mad at me because I drive the truck you bought me. I can't help that I haven't had my heart broken. That doesn't give you and Melanie the right to punish everyone else for your 'feelings.'"

Tennyson wanted to tell her son to go fly a kite, but she knew some of what he said was true. Neither he nor Emma deserved to shoulder the crap she and Melanie had between them. Part of her wanted to ask Melanie to dinner, to just say all the things she'd been wanting to say for years, but she wasn't sure Melanie would agree to it, and, if she were truthful, she wasn't ready to be that vulnerable. "I'm sorry, Andrew. I truly am. I will try my best to take the high road. I'm not always good at that, but I don't want either you or Emma to feel like what is between the two moms will wreck the wedding."

"Thanks," he said, checking his seat belt when she floored the gas and shot through the green light. "So what about this guy you're messing around with?"

"What guy?"

"I know how you are when you've got a new guy."

Tennyson didn't want anyone to know she was flirting with something that may or may not be a good idea. Officer Joseph C. Rhett hadn't been by in a few weeks, even though she'd suggested he stop by when he had some free time. Sometimes he called her, and they talked for hours about inane things. She knew he was interested. He knew she wanted him in her bed. They had been skirting around something more, but she wasn't ready to put a name to what that something was. "He's just a friend."

Andrew snorted. "Is that what you call them these days?"

"I'm serious. We haven't slept together or anything. We haven't even gone on a date. We're friends." She swung into her neighborhood, giving a wave to a woman in a jogging bra and running shorts who probably didn't realize what she looked like from the back side, but, hey, you do you, girlfriend. Girl power.

"That's cool. Who is he?"

"Hot cop."

Her son laughed. "Hot Cop? That's what you call him?"

"No, that's what he is."

"*You* are dating a cop?"

"He likes to be called a police officer or a law enforcement officer, but yeah." She smiled when she thought of Joseph with his tight pants and panty-dropping smile. There were nice benefits to a guy in uniform . . . one with handcuffs and the knowledge of where people hid weapons and drugs on their body.

"That's so not your type. I'm surprised." Andrew gave her a smile. He didn't like her to be mad at him. He was a good boy that way.

"Well, I've been married three times to my type, and I'm going to say that maybe 'not my type' would be a good thing." She smiled as she pulled into the driveway, and the man himself was sitting there like she'd summoned him. But he was in his patrol car, which meant he was still on duty.

Dang it.

"Is this him?"

"Yeah, I'll introduce you. Please remember that we're just friends. For now."

Andrew laughed. "Yeah, but I saw how you smiled when we pulled into the drive. I bet friends won't last for long."

Tennyson pushed the garage-door opener. "It won't if he's lucky."

CHAPTER THIRTEEN

A week later . . .

The image of Kit and Charlotte sitting together on the patio sucker punched Melanie when she entered the hotel's outdoor restaurant and bar. Charlotte sat close to Kit, a fruity drink in front of her, shoulders bare and freshly tanned by the Florida sun. Kit perched on the stool, relaxed, his linen trousers adorably rumpled, dark glasses covering his pretty eyes, looking every inch the confident, sexy older man he was. The glittering green waters of the gulf coast framed them, making them look like a couple in a travel brochure. *Come relax and reconnect with your love.*

Except they weren't lovers.

Or maybe they were.

Melanie wasn't so sure anymore. Kit had seemed pleased his wife had come with him to Destin, but once they'd arrived, he'd disappeared into the wave of friends he'd cultivated over the years, Charlotte at his side looking very much sure she belonged there with him. Melanie had been left to see the bellhop up to the room and frantically text Kit to see where he was.

Answer: in the bar with a group of developers.

And, yeah, Charlotte had been right beside him, sipping a white wine and telling amusing anecdotes about the armadillos causing problems on the property they were clearing.

When Melanie had joined them, everyone had been friendly and said hello before going back to their builder lingo and past stories of funny things Bob or Edna had done back when the conference was in Vegas or Reno. Melanie had sipped her complimentary wine and tried to look interested in the conversation. But she was an outsider now, not knowing anyone but a handful of people, not understanding new building codes or materials. Eventually, she'd wandered over to the wives' table and made a few new friends who were also bored by their husbands talking shop and more interested in the hot pool boy who someone had flirted with earlier.

Melanie had never felt so lonely.

And that feeling was back as she wound her way through the busy dining room toward the outside deck where her husband sat with Charlotte.

After the therapy session a few days before, she'd been determined to reconnect with her husband and repair the widening divide between them.

"Why don't you trust me anymore, Mel?" Kit had asked at their last appointment. He'd set his hands on his knees and looked at Melanie as if he couldn't understand any of her fears. To Kit, things were cut and dried. He didn't wade into levels of emotion. He either did, or he didn't. Black or white. Hot or cold.

"I *do* trust you, Kit. I don't trust Charlotte," Melanie said, her voice sounding accusing to her own ears.

The therapist's office was sterile, the white walls punctuated with bright, modern art. Melanie supposed it looked like a therapist's office should—a blank palette to splash one's emotion upon. Or maybe the woman liked the balance of the ambitious art against nothingness.

Dr. Adele Marler tucked her severely cut dark bob behind both ears and leaned forward. "And why don't you trust Charlotte, Melanie? Be specific and honest so that Kit can understand your feelings."

Honesty. Ugh. Did people really want honesty? Not always. Take Melanie when she tried on the sale swimsuits at Dillard's a few days ago. Her daughter had been a little too honest about the cellulite on the back of her thighs. It made her not want to go to Destin. It made her not want to fight for her marriage. It made her want to pull on a muumuu and hide from the world.

Which was crazy because she was happy. Or had been until Tennyson moved back to Shreveport, her daughter announced she was marrying Andrew, and she had to tell her daughter about her past. Not the whole truth. Thankfully, Tennyson had seemed to understand that their children didn't need to know about Albert Brevard and the big secret thing.

And really, did Melanie even hate Tennyson anymore?

She wasn't sure.

"Melanie," the therapist said, using her soothing "I understand all the feelings" voice.

"Sorry. Because Charlotte flirts with Kit constantly. In front of me." Was that honest enough?

"Come on, Mel. That's just how Char is. She's a friendly person." Kit sounded defensive, which was not being open and compassionate—more buzzwords for the therapist.

Dr. Marler turned to Kit. "How do you tell the difference between 'friendly' and 'flirting'?"

Yeah. Answer that, Einstein.

"Guys just know. Charlotte is my business partner, and we spend a lot of time together. That requires a sort of intimacy, but it doesn't mean I'm going to have sex with her." Kit leaned back and crossed his arms a bit petulantly.

"At our last appointment you admitted that you liked when Charlotte gives you attention. You also said you often notice how attractive she is, and that you've had thoughts about what it might be like to be in a sexual relationship with her."

"Duh, I'm a guy," he said. Like that explained everything.

"And what does that mean specifically?" Dr. Marler asked. The therapist looked so sincere and interested. Well, hell, Melanie was interested, too. What *did* that mean?

Kit leaned forward. "It's simple biology. Guys notice physical appearance. That shouldn't be a surprise to anyone who has a rudimentary knowledge of science. But just because a guy notices a woman's assets doesn't mean he's going to put his hands all over them. As for liking attention, well, show me someone who doesn't like someone noticing his sense of humor or how he looks. Everyone likes attention. If I'm honest, Charlotte makes me feel good about myself. She looks up to me, like I can do stuff."

"And Melanie doesn't?" Dr. Marler asked.

Kit turned to look at her. "Mel, you know I love you. I mean, you and I have been through a lot, but you're hard to . . ." He sighed.

"To love?" she finished for him, her heart feeling like it was breaking into a bajillion pieces. Was that what had always been wrong with her? She was hard to love?

"No," Kit said, reaching over and patting her knee. "You're easy to love. But you're hard to feel competent around. You don't need me, and you don't seem to have time for me. It makes me feel . . . useless. And, yeah, Charlotte makes me feel brilliant, funny, and still attractive. She comments on my shirts, my stories, and my Twitter feed. She's interested in me as a person."

Melanie opened her mouth and then closed it. She wanted to say that she was interested in him, too, but she knew she hadn't been interested in him in a while. Not really. Oh, she loved him. Still enjoyed conversations with him upon occasion. They shared a bed, the shampoo, and two children, but sometimes he felt more like a roommate than her husband. And the worst thing was she wasn't dissatisfied with the way things were. "I'm sorry if I make you feel that way."

"I'm not asking for an apology, and I know you don't mean to ignore me. I suppose that after a while, when your wife's not excited to see you or interested in sex anymore, you just start . . . I don't know. I'm not sure what I'm even trying to say. I guess what I'm saying is that if Melanie was more into me, I wouldn't be tempted."

He made it sound like it was all her fault. How was his wanting to screw Charlotte her fault? What kind of man convinced himself it was normal to "think" about cheating on his vows merely because his wife didn't fawn over him 24-7? "Okay, yes, I have been struggling with some issues, and it's made me not so . . . attentive. That doesn't mean I don't love you or want you. I mean, sorry your ego is that fragile, but my sister is ill, our daughter is getting married, I'm overcommitted, and maybe I'm going through the start of menopause or something. I have zero energy, and I don't feel like myself. So, yeah, I'm having trouble wanting to do you every night. You act like that's the only thing you're interested in doing with me anyway. Do I have to fuck you every night just so you know I love you?"

Yeah, she said *that* word. And she didn't care that she had. They were being *honest*. That was what the therapist demanded, and so she was peeling away the polite veneer, the good-girl persona she'd been taught to use in all situations. Because that felt *honest*.

Kit's eyes grew big, and then his mouth flatlined. "Come on, Mel. This isn't about sex."

"Isn't it? Because that's probably what Charlotte's offering. That and what comes next. Let me fill you in on how this works, Kit. Charlotte is younger and probably doesn't have much in her 401(k). And you're older and have a lot in your bank account, retirement, et cetera, et cetera. Charlotte's not stupid. She knows what you're worth, and she knows her best years are slowly slipping away. Tick, tick, tick. She doesn't want to drive a Toyota. She wants a Mercedes, designer clothes, and vacations in Fiji, but she can't do that on her part-time assistant salary. But she *can* do that as the next Mrs. Christopher Layton, so she laughs at all your jokes, embraces the opportunity to touch you, and makes you feel like you're the greatest man alive because that's what her hormones and bank account are telling her to do. Because if she really wanted to do it all herself, she would have utilized that fancy business degree and stayed in Boston," Melanie said, standing up and striding toward the window that overlooked downtown Shreveport. The therapist's office was close to Kit's because that was what was convenient for him. He didn't care Melanie had to drive all the way downtown for the appointment because *she didn't work.*

"Okay, let's slow down here," the therapist said.

"So you think a woman can only want me because of what's in my wallet?" Kit asked, his voice quiet and somehow defeated. That tone caused Melanie's surging anger to abate. Her words had been spiteful and not altogether true. Kit had way more to offer a woman than a healthy bank account. He was a great conversationalist, never stingy in bed, and could even sew a button back on a shirt. Not to mention all the obvious things like his sense of humor, attractiveness, and kindness.

"No, that's not true." She sighed and pushed a hand through her hair, wishing she'd washed it that morning. "Look, I'm angry and scared. That makes me defensive. You know my past makes me act that way. Everything that happened with my dad paired with the fact Tennyson is back in town, and it's as if the black hole of bad in my life has reopened and is slowly swallowing me up."

The therapist was wisely silent, watching them with eyes that were intense.

"Mel, I know things are unsettled, but all that with your father is in the past," Kit said, rising and moving toward her.

Melanie snapped her head around. "He killed himself because of what Tennyson did. And now she's back, acting like she didn't . . ." She covered her face with her hands because she'd tried not to let Tennyson and the past tear at her, but there were times it all came back. And those memories still hurt. Even if she'd started not hating Tennyson as much. Even if she liked the way Tennyson pushed her buttons. For some reason, when she was with Tennyson, she felt stronger. Which was crazy cakes because the woman had betrayed her and ruined her life.

Kit braced her shoulders with his hands. "Mel, you can't make yourself crazy with all this, and your father's death wasn't because of Tennyson. He had his own issues, and it feels easier to blame her. Your father didn't handle the whole thing very well. He did what you're not doing—he ran from his mistakes and let them define him. You're a fighter, Mel. Come on, honey, let's fight for our marriage, huh?"

And then his arms came around her, like a favorite Wubbie Blanket enveloping her and giving her the peace she so craved. She wanted to cry everything out. If she could release everything, then it would be easier. But those tears didn't come, the emotions she needed to feel for her husband stayed barred behind the terrible defenses she'd erected against the hurt the world constantly gave her. Still, his arms around her gave a comfort she craved.

He released her, dropped a kiss on her forehead, and led her back to the white leather couch so they could further discuss her fears of abandonment and the alarming thought she wasn't enough for him. They also talked about her concern about the Destin trip. When they left the therapist's office, they were both better. Much better.

So why had Kit reverted back to a man who was oblivious to his wife the moment they arrived in Florida? Why was Kit allowing Charlotte to press herself beside him, making inside jokes that intentionally snubbed his wife?

When Melanie got to the table where Charlotte and Kit were seated, they were in such deep discussion that at first they didn't notice her.

"Hey," she said, sitting down.

"Oh, Melanie, hey," Charlotte said, tossing her a smile. "Did you have a nice day on the beach?"

Melanie pulled a napkin into her lap and flagged a waiter. She wore the dress she'd bought in Dallas. When she'd left the room, carefully patting her somewhat sunburned nose with a mattifying powder and painting her lips with the berry lipstick she'd gotten as a sample from the Neiman Marcus Chanel counter, she'd felt a prettier version of herself. But looking at Charlotte in her strapless white pantsuit with several gold chains casually looping her neck, she felt overdressed and trying too hard. "I did. Took a walk and picked up three sand dollars. You remember how hard we searched for sand dollars the year after that hurricane, Kit?"

He smiled. "We found one, and it was broken."

"The kids were so disappointed. It was definitely the golden goose that trip," Melanie said, congratulating herself on steering the conversation toward the warm familial glow of beach trips past.

Charlotte sipped her wine. "It must be weird to have all that behind you. Your children are grown, and I suppose that feels like starting a new life, huh? Almost like a blank slate for you both."

What the hell did that mean?

Kit nodded. "We still have one more year with Noah, but then he'll be off to college. And my daughter's getting married? Makes me feel a million years old."

"You're not old. You're in your prime. Look at you," Charlotte said, allowing her gaze to do just that. Heifer.

"Aren't I the lucky woman?" Melanie said.

The waitress showed up at that very second. "Can I get you a drink?"

"I'll have a mojito," Melanie said. No one else requested another drink, so the waitress vamoosed toward the bar.

"I love mojitos," Charlotte said, leaning back in her chair. "But they just have so much sugar. My figure can't handle it."

Score one for Team Whore.

Melanie curled her hand into a fist. God, she wanted to hit Charlotte. Like a hard throat punch that would lay her out and have her rolling around the sandy deck clasping her throat, eyes bugging.

"So I made dinner reservations for eight o'clock. That gives us time to have a few drinks and then change," Kit said.

Melanie's stomach growled as she glanced at her Apple watch. She wished she hadn't skipped lunch in favor of more rays. It was only 5:45 p.m., and she could cheerfully eat her own arm.

"That's perfect," Charlotte said, placing her hand on Kit's forearm. She looked up and smiled at Melanie. "I have a darling dress I just bought that I've been dying to wear. Tonight will be perfect. Because we're celebrating your nomination for treasurer."

"Really? You were nominated for treasurer?" Melanie asked, looking over at Kit and frowning at Charlotte's hand on his arm.

Kit seemed to get the hint and moved his arm. "Yeah, the nominating committee slated me on the ballot. Crazy, huh?"

"It's not crazy," Charlotte said, lifting her glass his way. "He's totally worthy."

Melanie looked over at Kit and tried to communicate all she felt. "He is. Very much worth it." *And he's mine, whore.*

The waitress set her drink down and asked if they wanted anything else. Kit ordered another bourbon, and Melanie longed to order something to eat, but there was no way in hell she was going to eat in front of Miss Size 4. So she sipped her drink, enjoying the sweet tartness and the way the liquor slid warm down her throat. Around them people conversed, but Kit looked content to play with a toothpick and enjoy the sea breeze on his face. Charlotte seemed aware that Melanie wanted to do her bodily harm. The smile flirting at her lips said that she liked making Melanie uncomfortable.

By the time Melanie sucked the last of her drink down, she felt loose and not so intimidated. She thumbed the big diamond Kit had bought her on their fifteenth wedding anniversary so that the dying light of the day caught it. It was nearly three karats and cost more than Charlotte's car. As she spun it, holding her hand up slightly the way Emma had been doing every twenty-two-point-five seconds, she smiled. Perhaps a bit goadingly.

Because she knew Charlotte was very aware of her unspoken message.

"Another drink?" the waitress asked, coming by after picking up a check at a nearby table.

"Absolutely," Melanie said, making a bit of a racket as she slurped down the last sip and handed the empty glass to—she squinted at her name tag—Sharla.

Kit's eyes widened. "Careful, honey. You'll be tipsy."

"If I remember correctly, you always liked me tipsy," she said with a sly smile.

Her husband looked pleased with that flirtation. Another score for Team Wife.

Suck it, Team Whore.

"And I'll have a water with lemon," Charlotte said, almost primly.

Well, well. Who was the boring one now?

Those words of Tennyson's came back to her. *Melly, you're so boring.* She didn't used to be. Tennyson had always made sure of that. She used to like herself when she was Tennyson's friend because the trouble they found together was always so freeing. And somehow life was much simpler because of it. Imagine that. Her life had felt simpler because she'd had a friend who didn't let her settle, who wouldn't let her be sensible, who wouldn't let her buy an ugly dress. For a few minutes in the dressing room at Stanley Korshak, Melanie had remembered the girl she used to be. She pretty much had to because Tennyson had finally huffed over all her pussyfooting about the cost of the dress and told Melanie that if she didn't buy the damned dress, Tennyson would do it for her.

And then the whole cake thing. For a few seconds of frosting-smeared joy, she'd loved being the person who would hurl cake across a table.

Melanie plucked the delicate tulle overlay of the dress.

What would Tennyson do?

WWTD?

She damned sure wouldn't let Charlotte one-up her.

Melanie leaned over to the older gentleman at the table next to them. "Excuse me. Can I bum one of your cigarettes?"

The man smiled. "Sure."

He tapped out a cigarette and handed it to her. Then he pulled out his lighter and, with a questioning hook of his brow, asked if she needed a light. She nodded, stuck the cigarette between her lips, and cupped her hand so the flame wouldn't be extinguished by the sea breeze.

She took a deep drag and exhaled with a sigh. "Thanks."

When she turned back to Kit and Charlotte, they were staring at her like she'd just sacrificed an infant and had quenched her thirst with its blood. "What?"

"You don't smoke," Kit said, his eyebrows almost touching his receding hairline.

Melanie smiled, a very Tennyson-esque smile. "Yeah, I do. Sometimes."

"Who *are* you?" Kit laughed.

So she said the words her ex–best friend but current enemy had uttered a week ago. "I'm exactly who I want to be."

CHAPTER FOURTEEN

Tennyson had twenty hours to get everything in place for the Tour of Italy shower the next day, but at present she could only think about the man who now stood in her kitchen wearing a pair of athletic shorts, a tight T-shirt (tucked in, of course), and a pair of running shoes. In other words, Officer Joseph Rhett looked absolutely delicious. He held a gas station disposable cup of coffee and sipped it thoughtfully as she made waffles. Which was to say she put a frozen waffle into the toaster and pressed the button.

"You really eat that stuff? I thought you shopped at Whole Foods." Joseph eyed the toaster.

"I don't eat it for breakfast. This is a protein waffle, and I'll spread peanut butter on it as an after-workout snack. I did two sessions today, and I'm starving."

He didn't say anything. Just watched her as she fetched the lower-fat peanut butter and cut up the strawberries to place on top.

She'd just gotten home from her barre class, all sweaty and tired from doing two classes in a row, when Joseph pulled in behind her, upholding his promise to stop by and check on her. He'd looked plenty appreciative of the way she looked in her shorts and racerback Lycra, so she'd invited him in to look around and make sure the house was safe. He thought that was funny. Then she almost asked him to shower with her and do her back.

And her front.

Tennyson smiled at that thought. She wondered what he would say if she asked him to wash her back in the shower. And then roll around on her clean sheets.

She hoped the good officer was down for that.

"Can I get you one? Have you had lunch yet?" she asked.

"No. I'm good. I had a big breakfast this morning."

"So you're fueled and ready to go. That's good." Tennyson fetched the popped waffle and slathered peanut butter on it. Her stomach growled at the delicious smell of the vanilla waffle colliding with roasted peanuts. Even the sweet homegrown strawberries she'd bought at the farmers' market tickled her nose with the smell of summer. "So tell me more about yourself. All we've talked about is TV and popular culture when we're on the phone. You a Shreveport boy? Where'd you go to school? Have you ever been married? Want to shower with me later? Do you have kids?"

Joseph laughed, and she damned near had an orgasm.

Shit, the man was so abnormally good looking. She imagined women of all ages trying to get a speeding ticket or praying that he asked them to step from the car so he could run his delicious hands all over their bodies as a sort of hot-cop silver lining to a ticket.

"I like how you ask questions," he said, setting his coffee down and rounding the kitchen island.

Tennyson stayed stock-still, leaning against the counter, a flirtatious smile hovering as she picked up a waffle and took a bite. "Mmm."

Joseph set a hand on either side of her, leaning in close. "I grew up in Arcadia, about an hour east of here. I went to Louisiana Tech and majored in business. I'm divorced. I would love to, and I have two kids."

His eyes were starbursts of blue, his jaw like a piece of granite. Joseph had thick eyebrows that a girl would have to pluck, a tiny mole on his earlobe, and a mouth that looked absolutely capable of sin. She would put that mouth to good use. Since he seemed up for it.

"How old are your kids?" she asked, taking another bite, even though she really longed to lick his neck.

He sucked in a deep breath, his gaze lowering to her mouth. "Five and eight. Both girls."

Tennyson set the waffle on the edge of the counter and looped her hands around his neck. "You're very good at this game, you know."

"What game?" he asked, trailing a finger over her lower lip. She realized he'd wiped away a smudge of peanut butter just as he sucked his finger into his mouth.

His action made her go a little weak at the knees.

"This game we're playing. The one where we pretend that we're not trying to get into each other's pants," she said, dropping a tiny kiss on the pulse point of his neck.

Joseph inhaled sharply, and she leaned back with a shark smile.

Then he turned the tables by stepping forward so his body touched hers in all the right places. "I thought that was subtle foreplay. If you're done with that, we can get on with the obvious foreplay. Wait, do you have some nongirly soap? I have to go in to work later, and I don't want to smell like a field of flowers."

She lifted onto her toes because he was tall. Pressing her lips against his lightly, she whispered, "So smell like me."

He may have growled or something equally hungry sounding, but she didn't have time to think about that because he was all over her, his mouth taking hers, hands on her ass pulling her to him, and it felt incredible. The man knew his way around a kiss and a woman's body. He was very competent with his pat down, too. If she were prone to wearing weapons, he'd have found them right off the bat.

Tennyson was so wrapped up in Joseph taking her breath away that she didn't comprehend the phone ringing until it started a second round.

"Joseph," she murmured against his hair. "I have to get that."

"Mm?" he groaned against the sensitive flesh of her neck. One hand had already dipped into her shorts and cupped her bare backside, while the other had crept around to invade the tight elastic of her sports bra. Her nipples were hard, her panties wet, and she hadn't felt this good in a year. Maybe two years. Could be three.

"The phone. It's my mom's ringtone, and I have to answer."

He lifted his head, his blue eyes heavy with desire. "Seriously?"

"Like, yes. Just let me grab my phone, make sure she's okay, and we can take this to my really big shower with the dual heads." She kissed his chin and untangled his hands from her body.

Her mother was on her way to spend the weekend with her and attend the bridal shower. Bronte was also coming up to join them that evening, and that night they were having a girls' night in, watching old movies and drinking wine. Loretta O'Rourke was perfectly capable of driving in from Texas by herself even though Tennyson had tried to buy her a plane ticket. In the words of her mother, it was "too much money and too much of a hassle," but her mother was also a terrible driver and prone to getting lost. And she never called two times in a row.

Tennyson scooped up her phone and went back into the kitchen. She hoped Joseph wouldn't change his mind. He stood with his back to her, staring out the window over her sink. Her abandoned waffle teetered on the edge of the counter.

"Mom?" she said when Loretta answered.

"Oh, hey, I can't remember if I'm supposed to wear a dress. Because I didn't pack one. I just drove through Tyler and remembered a cute little store I once shopped at, and it reminded me to ask you. But it's probably too late because I won't have time to go shopping. Well, maybe your sister could take me if you're otherwise engaged."

"You don't need a dress. But you're okay, right? I mean, you never call me twice in a row."

Joseph turned to her, his mouth curving into a sexy little smile. Maybe he was waiting to see why she'd pulled away and answered the phone. Maybe now he understood why she had to answer. She was a good daughter, and maybe that was somewhat sexy, too? Or maybe just responsible enough to show Joseph she wasn't a selfish rich bitch looking for a boy toy.

Because she wasn't.

Well, maybe she was looking for a boy toy.

Her mother made a contrite sound. "I didn't mean to scare you, but it felt very important for a few minutes because I don't want to disappoint Emma and Andrew. And I suppose I'm a bit bored. This is such a long trip. What are you doing?" Loretta asked. Tennyson could hear Air Supply singing in the background.

Should she say *I'm doing Officer Rhett*?

Probably not.

Her mother was devoutly Catholic and not approving of casual sex. Committed sex she had no problem with. In fact, Loretta was a big proponent of experimentation. She'd once sent Tennyson some really strange sex toys from an "intimate" party she'd attended with her friends. Tennyson hadn't known whether to send a thank-you note or check on her father.

"Um, I'm cooking breakfast," she said, gasping a little when Joseph's lips grazed the back of her neck.

"Mm, you taste salty," he whispered in her ear.

A little shiver ran down her spine as he slid his hands under her top, crossing over her stomach and bringing her back against his front.

"You don't cook," her mother said in her other ear.

"Um, well, I am boiling water," she managed, closing her eyes as his fingers started delicious slow circles working up to her sports bra. His mouth was doing wonderful things to her neck.

"For what?" her mother asked, sounding genuinely intrigued.

"Uh, just some, uh, tea," Tennyson said as Joseph slid his hands beneath her bra and palmed her breasts. She hadn't been super into guys messing with her breasts since she'd had the boob job, but the way he plucked her nipples and made little noises against her neck was driving her crazy. She couldn't think straight. She couldn't even think curvy.

"You drink tea?" her mother asked. "I never knew you liked tea."

Joseph ground his hips against her ass, and her knees went a *lot* weak. His soft laugh against her skin made her smile.

"I don't. Mom, I'm just going to be straight with you. You don't need a dress, and I have to go because there is a policeman here who has to interrogate me."

"Body search in progress," he growled into her ear as he spun her around. Tennyson grinned at him. The spark in his eyes made her happy. Very happy. Because she was almost certain that Officer Joseph Rhett was about to make her day. In a non–Clint Eastwood way.

"Oh my stars, are you in trouble?" her mother asked, her voice going all high and panicked.

"I hope so," Tennyson said, laughter escaping her. "I hope he realizes what a bad girl I've been and maybe even uses his handcuffs on me."

"Tennyson Marie O'Rourke, you better be joking with me," her mother said.

Joseph was now working his way down her neck to her chest. His hands were busy, too, and she may have sighed as he did something that wasn't a standard pat down.

"I am. Truly. I have to go, Mom."

"Are you sure? You sound weird, like you're all out of breath and . . . oh. Oh." Her mother went silent.

Tennyson started laughing. "I'll see you soon, Mom."

"Dear Lord, Teeny. You're going to be the death of me. Bye." She hung up.

Tennyson tossed the phone onto the counter. "My mom is good. Let's shower."

Joseph lifted his head, picked her up, and set her legs around his waist. He briefly ground his hard parts into her soft ones, using the counter for leverage.

"Is that your nightstick, Officer?" she joked, biting his earlobe.

"You're about to find out," he said with a laugh, palming her ass as he walked toward the hallway that led to her bedroom. "Good thing I know where your bedroom is."

Tennyson covered his mouth with hers, giving him the most passionate kiss she could manage while being bounced toward her bedroom. "I'm so thankful for raccoons right now. They're, like, the best animal in the whole animal kingdom."

When they reached the bathroom, he lowered her onto the double vanity and kissed her with a heat that made her toes curl against the smooth, white cabinets.

"Yeah, I'm now a huge fan of raccoons. About that shower," he said, looking at her large walk-in shower. "We probably don't want to get our clothes wet."

∽

An hour later, Tennyson rolled over and blinked at Joseph, who was lying on his back on her king-size bed, looking quite similar to the fat raccoon they'd shooed out over a month ago. Sated, pleased, and perhaps a little dangerous.

Okay, dangerous in the sheets.

The man had skills. Who would have thought Mr. Buttoned Up would be a total animal in the shower, against the wall, and on the soft goose down duvet?

Score.

"Shower is the theme of the weekend. I'm going to be squeaky clean come Sunday," she said, making a loopy-loop in his chest hair with her index finger.

"Huh?"

"Tomorrow is the bridal shower for my son's fiancée. I'm doing an Italian theme, and the planner will be here in thirty minutes."

"Are you booting me out?" he asked with a sleepy smile.

Tennyson sat up and covered her breasts with her hands. "No. Well, yes. Sorta."

"Don't do that," he said, tugging her hands from her breasts. "They're too magnificent to cover."

He pulled her to him, bestowing a kiss on each tip. Immediately she felt like straddling him again. Both their breathing kicked up a notch. She could probably go another round, but Marc would be prompt. She knew this because he'd essentially told them that he was never late, timing was everything, and he expected reciprocation from them on this *very* important element of their client-planner relationship.

So she pulled back and looked down at her breasts. "Yeah, they're good work. I had them done after I nursed Andrew. Kids are hell on the body."

"And the pocketbook. Especially girls. Mine are still young, and it's already started with the certain brands of shoes and clothes. Boys are easier, right?" he asked.

"Until they get to be teenagers and want pickup trucks, sound systems, and Nike high-tops. Oh, and you have to go to the grocery store three times a week in order to have anything in the pantry for yourself. Or in my case, order groceries. I'll miss that about Manhattan."

"Um, I think they have delivery here. We're not totally backward. Just halfway," he said, sitting up and looking around for his clothes.

"Still in the bathroom," she said, pulling the soft angora throw from the foot of her bed and wrapping it around her breasts and the rest of her body. He made a sad face. "You can come by tomorrow night. My sister is taking my mother to her place in Natchitoches for a few days, and I will have lots of fancy Italian food left over. Tiramisu and brandy-soaked cakes."

He pulled on his boxers, and she noted in the light of the bathroom how spectacular his ass really was. Hard, curved stone, like a model's ass. She made her own "don't put that away" sad face.

Which made him smile.

"Cake doesn't persuade me," he said, tugging on his shirt and running a hand through his hair. He didn't have to smooth his hair. It was so short, it hadn't gotten mussed by her hands in it. But he seemed very particular about looking "right."

"Okay, well, then I'll have Italian beer—Peroni and Ghisa—and plenty of fun cocktails."

He pulled on his shorts, doing the automatic tuck thing, which made her smile. "Um, I don't drink, so . . ."

"You don't? Are you a saint? Or wait, are you a Puritan?" she joked.

"Are Puritans still around?" he asked, sticking his head out the bathroom door.

She giggled. "I don't know, but if you don't drink, how do you get through life?"

"Actually, I don't drink because I see how it stops life. I've been sober for five years," he said, snagging a sock and looking for the other one. She pointed to the wastebasket where it lay draped over the edge. He grabbed it and pulled it on.

Then he smiled at her.

There was power in that smile. Damn, how had she become so smitten with Officer Rhett in such a short amount of time? He was so adorable with his ramrod posture, military cut, and tucked-in T-shirt. Oh, and his rock-hard ass and abs weren't bad, either. Not to mention those gorgeous baby blues. And his insightful texts. She didn't want to totally objectify him, after all.

"So if you don't want dessert or a cold one, how about me?" she asked, unwrapping the blanket and leaning back into her best bomb-shell calendar pose, thrusting her breasts upward, arching her back, and curving her legs back to tuck under her.

Joseph stopped tying his shoes and looked his fill. "Now that's something I wouldn't mind extra helpings of."

Tennyson smiled. "Then I'll see you tomorrow night?"

"Let me check my schedule."

She made a pouty face, letting the blanket drop and cupping her breasts.

"I'll just do that now," he said, picking up the phone he'd taken out of his pocket earlier. "Um, yep, it says here that I have to ensure public safety on Fairlane Boulevard. So I guess I better come on by."

Tennyson laughed and wrapped the blanket around herself. "Good. I expect to be protected and served. Maybe served several times."

Joseph came back into the bedroom and swept her into his arms, giving her a hard kiss. "If you don't want to be served right now and embarrass your fancy party planner, you will stop showing me what I'm going to be missing for the next twenty-four hours."

Tennyson dotted kisses along his jaw before pushing back. "This is crazy, you know."

"What? Having a good time?"

That was exactly what she'd been thinking, but having him say that it was something just fun made her feel a bit . . . sad? Which was weird because she'd already failed at so many relationships that she'd decreed she would live out the rest of her days as a single woman. She liked being by herself for the most part, and dating the field was fun. Sure, there were some bad apples, but they usually made for good stories when she was with her friends. So, yeah, she wanted to keep it casual with Joseph. After all, they had nothing in common. Not really.

Okay, the sex had been amazing, and she liked him. Or thought she did. She really didn't know him beyond the four or so times she'd met him and the inane texts they'd shared over the past few weeks. So why would she feel slightly miffed that he wanted to keep her at arm's length? That was what she wanted. Right?

"Yeah, you're right. It just happened fast. I'm not usually one for hopping right into bed with a guy. I require at least three dates and a nice bottle of wine."

Joseph gave her another hard kiss. "You didn't hop into bed. You hopped into the shower."

"You know what I mean," she said.

He headed toward the bedroom door just as the doorbell rang. "You better get dressed. Though I have to say you look fantastic with messy hair and no clothes."

Tennyson stood and let the blanket drop again. "Think I can answer the door this way?"

"Seriously, woman, you're killing me. Put on some clothes already before I'm forced to detain you and search your gorgeous body for another hour or two," he said, giving her another wolfish grin before opening the door. "I'll let your planner inside before I go."

"Guess I better put on some clothes and some lipstick. My mom will be here soon, too. She's southern, which means lipstick is as essential as a good pair of pearls, a nice set of stationery, and a framed picture of Elvis Presley."

Joseph started shutting the door, but before it closed, he called back, "We're going to have some fun this summer, Tennyson."

A whole summer? It might take that long to get the hot cop out of her system. He was awfully good in bed, if not a brilliant conversationalist. But really, who needed someone clattering off facts, details, and observations all the time? There was value in solitude, in a man knowing he didn't need to fill the air with aimless or even relevant conversation. Sometimes she appreciated a respite. She felt like Joseph was the kind of guy to give her room to breathe, time to sink into herself, and an opportunity to not worry about anything other than just being. He was also good at taking her breath away, so there was that.

She rose and padded into the bathroom, taking a left into her large walk-in closet. She rifled through the lingerie drawer, pulling on a lacy thong and matching bra that would remind her of hot sex with Joseph. She probably needed to shower, but she could smell him on her skin and wasn't ready to let go of that. She found a simple A-line cotton dress, grabbed a pair of thong sandals, and wound her hair up into a messy bun. A quick dash of powder, mascara for her lashes, and a swipe of Dior lipstick called Insolent, and she was out the door.

And then back for a slight misting of Baccarat Rouge 540.

Because she wanted the smell of Joseph to be hers alone.

When she entered the living room, Marc was sitting on her sofa, balancing a cup of tea on the knee of his natty trousers, and Hot Cop was sitting opposite him, reading *Town & Country*. His still being there surprised her, but then she realized he hadn't wanted to leave her there alone with another man while she was getting dressed. Something about that made her feel warm and gooey.

Joseph looked up. "This purse costs five grand."

A smile flirted around Marc's lips. "It's a Fendi."

"It's a vacation," Joseph said, shutting the magazine. "Well, I'm out. Great having lunch with you, Tennyson."

Marc waggled his eyebrows. "Nothing better than a good *lunch*."

Joseph shot Marc a sharp look before walking into the kitchen to grab the keys he'd set on her kitchen island. Marc watched him go.

"Nice," Marc murmured, turning back to her and setting the teacup on the glass coffee table.

"Thank you," she said in a low voice as Joseph retraced his steps toward the front door. He tossed her one last hungry glance before disappearing. The click of the door made her long to run to it, fling it open, and get one more taste of Officer Rhett.

But she had work to do.

"Well, I see you've had your fun. Now it's time to put our noses to the grindstone, my dear," Marc said, uncrossing his legs and rising. "First, I want to inspect the gardens to see if we need to bring in any last-minute greenery. I have ten lighted trees ready to line the pool. The gondola will be delivered in three hours, and we need to make sure it is absolutely stable. Cesar is a temperamental artist, but the best operatic tenor in the South. And since his booking is a huge favor from his agent to me, we can't have him falling into your pool. Tents will be erected as soon as we get the trees and gondola secured. A pair of peacocks will be wandering the grounds as you requested, but I do think we should have guests sign a waiver when they arrive. Never know with peacocks. Oh, and I've arranged with the bartender to have the signature cocktails handed out at the door."

"You found a valet company?"

"Done. The gilded chargers, table linens, five hundred lemons, and miles of lace and tapestry are all in the crates that have been delivered. My team will arrive in the morning bright and early for setup. You've approved fabrics and arrangements, so don't worry. I promise you all is well."

Tennyson sucked in a deep breath and exhaled. "Good. Let's head out back and go over everything, including table placements. I'll have my attorney send the waivers because Lord knows I don't want anyone to sue me over a peacock attack. Do peacocks normally attack people?"

Marc shrugged. "I haven't a clue. We're renting the pair from a family in Texas. Maybe they can tell me."

She and Marc walked out back and toured the new gardens. The roses brought in were in full bloom and, though recently planted, looked as if they'd been there for years. The newly constructed retaining wall made the backyard look less unplanned and more tailored. A team had cleaned the pool and fountain, and the new patio furniture looked sleek and inviting.

"The three-piece ensemble will be just inside your house, playing while guests arrive." Marc pointed toward olive tree topiaries decorated with kumquats and lemons that flanked her French doors. "I have torches and lanterns to light the path from the driveway, and a lovely flowered trellis will welcome guests at the entrance. It's all very natural, very chic, and very expensive."

Tennyson tried to envision what the shower would look like, but since Marc was vehemently opposed to Pinterest (her favorite!) she couldn't quite catch on to his vision. So she'd have to trust that what she was paying him would net her the shower of her dreams.

Emma's shower. She had to remind herself.

Okay, sure. She hated that she never had a bridal shower. Or a traditional wedding. She and Stephen were married by a justice of the peace when she was a whopping nine months pregnant with Andrew. She'd married her third husband, Robert, in Hawaii with only his business partners as witnesses, and the ill-fated, short-lived mistake in the middle of the two had taken place in Italy surrounded by number two's leeches, ahem, family. So she'd never had a rehearsal dinner, wedding shower, or her father to walk her down the aisle. In fact, her family hadn't been to a single one of her weddings. So she knew she was living her own dreams through this shower. That was why everything had to be perfect.

"The Murano glass ornaments are all wrapped and ready to be given to guests. Where are we putting those?" Tennyson asked.

"I thought you were giving away puppies?" Marc joked.

"I seriously considered inviting a local shelter to come and bring their adoptable puppies, but after the engagement party, dogs aren't welcome at any of the events," Tennyson said with a smile.

"Word gets around. Janie Thackery wore half that cake, as I understand it," Marc said, stifling a chuckle.

"At least. Let's keep it at majestic peacocks wandering the grounds. Prada will be staying in my laundry room in her kennel. I don't want anyone slipping in puppy pee."

They walked back toward the house. "Your landscape designer did a nice job. I think we're good on greenery. I have written out a schedule. It includes Andrew's arrival, toasts, Cesar's solo, and the fireworks."

"Perfect. Do you think the fireworks will be okay? The shower is from six to eight thirty. It won't be totally dark."

"They will be perfect against the darkening sky. Everything will be perfect. I promise." Marc crossed his arms and looked emphatic.

"It better be," Tennyson said, tempering her words with a smile.

CHAPTER FIFTEEN

Melanie stopped in the center of the pathway that opened into Emma's bridal shower, uh, make that *extravaganza*, and blinked a good three or four times before the craziness in front of her truly registered.

"Whoa, is this for real?" her friend Sandy breathed. The cofounding member of their book club stood beside her, mouth open, eyes wide as she swiveled her head from side to side.

"Eh, I think it's *Tennyson's* reality, which is to say, no, it's not real for most people," Melanie said, moving forward so the people behind her could come into Tennyson's backyard, which did not resemble a backyard. It was more like Disney crashed into Las Vegas while dancing the cha-cha and . . . wait, was someone singing opera?

Melanie tugged a gawking Sandy along the well-lit path. Large urns of flowers spilled out between each oversize lantern lining both sides of the path. Above them, crisscrossed strings of lighted bulbs lent their merriment to the entrance. When they finally stepped onto the patio, a tuxedoed waiter handed them a fluted glass.

"Aperol spritz, madam," he said with a nod.

"Thank you," Melanie managed before sidestepping a peacock.

Yep, Kit had been right. Peacocks, for heaven's sake.

Sandy grabbed her arm, stepping back and almost knocking her Aperol spritz from her hand. "Is that a peacock? Dear lord."

"Sister, you know your birds," Melanie murmured, unable to believe her eyes herself. Around her were jugglers, mimes, and an organ grinder? And in the center of Tennyson's backyard, standing in a gondola that was anchored incredibly in the center of the pool, was a man wearing a tuxedo belting out an aria. She blinked and realized who it was. "Dear Lord, that's Cesar Santos. I saw him with the Dallas philharmonic last year."

"Cesar who? She paid an opera singer to stand in that boat?" Sandy asked, giving Melanie the side-eye. Sandy stood six feet in flats and had layered red hair and green eyes that reminded her of her old tomcat Jimbo. Her friend taught French at a local elementary school, and they'd been in the same book club—the Reading Krewe—for ten years. Sandy was as close as she got to "ride or die." And that wasn't that close. Not really.

Huge, clear tents soared overhead, and a line of fruit-bedecked, lighted trees flanked the pool. On one end of the rectangular pool was a cascading waterfall with colored LED lights that changed from violet to blue to green. Waiters circulated with hors d'oeuvres, and two large bars anchored each side of the yard. The large oak trees flaunted large, lit Japanese-style lanterns, and tables hunkered beneath the widespread branches, covered in white linens, elegant tapestry, and large crystal hurricane lanterns full of lemons and flowers.

Sandy kept sliding glances to her. Glances that said *are you kidding me?*

But her expression was one that many wore. Several guests were milling about with wide eyes and whispers.

"Mom!"

Melanie turned to find her daughter, clothed in a simple red sheath and strappy sandals, coming toward her with outstretched arms. "Can you believe all this?"

She grabbed her daughter's hands and shook her head. "I would say no, but I've known Tennyson for a long time. I know she likes to dazzle."

Emma laughed. "Well, mission waaaay accomplished."

Emma said hello to Sandy and then looked over at Andrew, who was in a conversation with a group of people Melanie didn't know. "I wish Daddy were here."

She did, too.

Melanie had left Kit that morning after one of the best evenings they'd had in forever. After having drinks on the patio back in Destin, she and Kit had returned to their room and had naughty sex against the mirrored closet. Kit had been super into her whole "bad girl with a cigarette" vibe. They'd showered and gone down to meet Charlotte—eye roll from her every time Kit mentioned that woman's name—only to find out that the girl wonder had a migraine. Or maybe Charlotte knew when she was beat? Whichever. Didn't matter because Melanie had gotten to have an intimate dinner with her husband. They'd laughed, and everything had felt like old times, like she was back to being the Melanie he loved. After hurrying through key lime pie, they'd rushed upstairs, kissing passionately in the elevator, and again against the wall outside their room, before tumbling back inside and indulging in amazing sex. Like ah-mazing.

So when she'd woken that morning, she'd felt like a new woman, a woman who had made some definite steps in the right direction with her husband.

Thank God.

Kit had gotten dressed and slipped out to go to his meeting, and she'd ordered room service, indulging in waffles because she'd burned a lot of calories with Kit the night before. She lay in bed, singing some of her favorite Broadway tunes, slurping up syrupy waffles, and essentially loving life. But all that came crashing down when she'd rolled her suitcase downstairs and looked for Kit's meeting room so she could tell him goodbye. When she finally found the boardroom, she opened the door to the sight of Charlotte resting her head on Kit's shoulder. They were sitting in the back, and he was holding a can of ginger ale and looking very worried.

Melanie narrowed her eyes and caught his attention.

Both he and Charlotte rose and joined her in the hallway.

"What's up?" Kit asked, looking a bit like he did when he filched the cookies she'd made for the PTA bake sale. He took Charlotte's elbow and set her against the wall.

"I'm about to leave and wanted to say goodbye. Is she okay?"

"The migraine she had last night is hanging on and making her feel sick," Kit said, looking back with concern at Charlotte, who did, in fact, look wan.

"I'll be okay, Kit," Charlotte said with a wave of her manicured hand.

"Does she need to fly back with me?" Melanie asked, half hoping the answer was no because she didn't want to deal with a sick person on her flight back to Shreveport. Especially since it wasn't a nonstop flight. And half hoping the answer would be yes, so she wouldn't have to leave her husband alone with a heifer who had designs on him.

"No," Charlotte said, shaking her head and wincing. "I have to be here. We have our presentation, Kit."

Kit nodded. "Yeah. She thinks she'll be okay. She took some medicine and said it's starting to work."

"Okay, my car will be here in a few minutes, so I need to get to the lobby. I will miss you." Melanie rose on her toes and kissed his cheek. "It was really nice being here with you, Kit."

Kit smiled and gave her a squeeze. "I'm glad you came."

Charlotte tried on a smile. "Safe travels, Melanie."

"Thanks. And I hope you feel better."

Charlotte straightened, throwing back her shoulders. "I'll be fine. After all, I have a good partner who will take care of me." She placed a possessive hand on Kit's arm.

Melanie tried not to growl. Because Kit had just spent the entire night kissing every inch of her body and telling her things that would make a, well, not a whore, but a woman with really loose morals blush. So Melanie should feel good about waltzing out the door and leaving her husband behind. But Charlotte made that hard to do.

Kit smiled at Charlotte and patted her shoulder. "I'm happy to be here for you."

Charlotte smiled at him. And then she smiled at Melanie with all her beautiful straight, white teeth. The spark in the woman's eyes said all that needed to be said. "And I'll take care of Kit for you, Melanie. Don't worry."

Melanie swallowed and thought about ripping Charlotte's hair out and then maybe beating her head against the tasteful gray wallpaper behind them. Really give her an effing headache. "I'm sure you would like to, but Kit's pretty good at taking care of himself. So just focus on yourself, honey."

Melanie jerked Kit's head down to hers and kissed him. Hard. Like a warning.

He seemed to understand.

"Okay, tell Emma I love her, and I'm very, very sorry to miss the shower. Also, try to behave. I have heard rumors of tents and peacocks," Kit said, stepping away from both women and putting his hand on the door to the conference room.

"Peacocks?" Melanie repeated.

"You know Teeny."

Melanie had nodded and strolled away, leaving a now flushed Charlotte moving to catch up with her husband. She longed to turn around, remind Kit of his vows, to suggest he think hard about replacing Charlotte before she ruined their marriage, but she didn't. Because ultimately Kit had to decide what he wanted in his life. He had a wife who loved him, who wanted to make things work, who got a blipping bikini wax and shaved her legs on back-to-back days in order to look like she cared. She'd let him do things to her she'd only read about. They had two children, a beautiful life, and a dog who occasionally chewed up their shoes. And if he wanted to toss that for a younger piece of ass, he'd do it with or without her reminding him what he'd be destroying.

She couldn't spend her life running around trying to stop her husband from cheating.

"Hello, everyone," Tennyson said, jarring Melanie back to the carnival in which she now stood. Her nemesis, who was starting to feel less nemesis-y, glided up to them with a martini in hand and Marc Mallow on her heels. Tennyson wore the electric-green dress she'd bought in Dallas with a pair of sky-high heels that allowed her to tower over everyone around her. Her hair had been piled upon her head in a manner designed to look haphazard but was likely secured within an inch of its life. Blingy earrings swished at her earlobes. She looked rich, attractive, and utterly interesting.

"Tennyson, this is so incredible and so are you," Melanie said, because it was true. She'd never attended anything remotely similar to this party. Not even close.

The opera singing grew louder, and Tennyson winced and looked annoyed. "Thanks. Is he singing louder? It seems like he's singing louder."

They all turned to the man gesturing wildly and singing passionately as if the gondola was about to go down and his life was at stake. Everyone else seemed to be watching the performance, too.

"I had to pay him extra to get in the gondola. He was very miffed I wanted him to pretend to be a gondolier," Tennyson yelled over the soaring notes Cesar amplified as he approached the high C note.

"He's really going for it," Melanie murmured as the opera singer spread his hands and drew them together as his voice rose so high she half expected a gang of cats to join in. Finally, he peaked, his body sagging as he fell forward, almost pitching into the bow. The whole performance was rather astounding, if not totally odd to be occurring in the middle of a bridal shower.

People around her clapped.

Cesar smiled, nodding his thanks, before extending his hand to his assistant, who had pulled the gondola to the side of the pool. Cesar swayed only slightly before stepping from the vessel onto the pavers. He was a rather large man, so the boat wobbled under duress before he thankfully righted himself by grabbing one of the potted, lit trees. Several kumquats plopped off and fell into the pool. The celebrated tenor headed straight for Tennyson. "I quit."

Tennyson's eyes bugged as he brushed past her. "You can't quit. I paid for you for the entire evening."

Cesar didn't stop. He kept trucking toward the triple pairs of French doors that led into Tennyson's house, one of which was open so guests could presumably use the facilities. The three-piece ensemble just inside stopped setting up and watched open-mouthed as the opera singer stomped by. Before Cesar disappeared, he turned and shouted, "I, madam, am not for sale. I am *no* common hired singer. A gondola! Who sings Franchetti or Puccini in a swimming pool? It's madness."

Another man, presumably Cesar's assistant or manager, threw Tennyson an apologetic look before he followed his meal ticket out the door. Many guests stood wide-eyed, paused in their imbibing and gossiping, as all this took place.

"When they say opera singers are temperamental, they aren't lying. Oh well, he was a bit too uppity anyhow," Tennyson said, throwing Marc an irritated look. "What are we going to do for music?"

"Don't worry, Tennyson. I'll pull the three-piece ensemble out onto the veranda. And we'll have the Amazon Echo play something Italian inside the house," Marc said, moving toward the house. The guests seemed to sense the drama was over and went back to the Aperol spritzes.

Andrew strolled over. "What was that all about? Did Marc just call our patio a veranda? Do we have a veranda?" Her daughter's fiancé was all smiles and good humor in spite of the scene with the opera singer. Maybe the cake throwing had prepared him for the ups and downs of doing a wedding with his mother and her sworn enemy. Melanie rather liked his ability to defuse situations.

"Temperamental artists," Tennyson said with a wave of her hand. "Now, where were we? Oh, yes, I was saying hello to you and . . . ?"

"Tennyson, this is my friend Sandy Vines. She's in my book club. Her son went to preschool with Emma," Melanie said, glad Tennyson had decided to let Cesar go and not stubbornly demand he come back. After all, the man had a point. She *had* put one of the premier tenor singers in a swimming pool.

"Nice to meet you," Sandy said, extending her hand. "I've heard a lot about you."

"It's all true, I'm afraid." Tennyson laughed, sipping her martini and sounding blasé. Yeah, many people in Shreveport had heard what Tennyson had done, but it wasn't something Tennyson should sound braggy about. There had been catastrophic ramifications, and to have Tennyson treat it all so cavalierly dragged back the resentment Melanie felt. Why did Tennyson have to be so . . . Tennyson? As her daughter would say—Tennyson was so extra.

Sandy made a confused face and turned toward the buffet sitting beneath the covered patio. "I'm starving, so I think I'll grab a plate. You coming, Melanie?"

"Go ahead. I'll be there in a moment." She wanted to give Emma the bracelet in her bag. She and Kit had picked it out last week after their cathartic appointment with the therapist. Bearing a tiny row of sapphires, which was Emma's birthstone, and a matching row of peridots, Andrew's birthstone, the bracelet would work perfectly as the something blue and something new for the bride to wear on her wedding day. The twined length of gold chain also symbolized her full acceptance of this marriage. Or at least she hoped it would show that to her daughter. "I have a little something for you, Emma."

Tennyson perked up. "Are you giving a gift to her now? I thought we would open gifts before the toast and fireworks."

"Fireworks?" Melanie repeated.

"Yes, just hold on to her gift for another hour or so. Mix and mingle, get a plate, and for heaven's sake, have a drink or two, Melanie." Tennyson pulled Emma and Andrew away. "Come on, you two. I have some friends who flew in from New York who want to meet the girl who caught Andrew."

Melanie was left standing in the middle of the party, her hand in her purse clasping the wrapped present. What had she expected? For Tennyson to let her have that moment with her daughter?

This was Tennyson she was dealing with.

The girl who had upstaged every principal actor in every production in high school. The girl who wore her uniform skirts rolled at the waist so the hem was midthigh, and always wore a hot-pink lace bra under her white T-shirt. Tennyson never shared the spotlight.

Melanie sighed, released the gift back into her bag, and went to find Sandy, who had somehow managed to locate Melanie's mother. Her friend held two plates of food and was steering Anne toward a forgotten table on the opposite side of the patio.

"Hello, Mother," Melanie said, dropping a kiss on her mother's dry cheek. Anne wore a black dress that covered her from neck to knee. The pearls her father had given her before he died sat at her throat like gris-gris against bad taste.

"This is the tackiest event I have ever attended. Just look how half these people are dressed." She eyed three women wearing tiny halter tops and sequined hot pants. At that moment another peacock strolled by, its feathers brushing their feet. Melanie's mother looked aghast, stepping back and hissing at the impertinent bird.

Melanie would have laughed, but she knew her mother wouldn't appreciate it.

"Where's Hilly?" Melanie asked.

"Don't use that ridiculous name for your sister," her mother said, sipping a glass of water with a lemon wedge teetering on the rim.

"Sorry. Where is *Hillary*?" Melanie asked, looking around, hoping to spy her sister ideally holding a plate of food. Hillary had promised she'd come, even going as far as sending Melanie pictures of three different dresses she was deciding among. Melanie had told her she would come by and pick her up, but Hillary said she'd escort their mom since the party was at Tennyson's and Anne needed some moral support to show up at the home of someone who she often and vocally proclaimed had ruined their lives. Melanie agreed it would be good to have Hillary with their mother so she hadn't pressed the issue and had instead offered Sandy a ride so she wouldn't have to arrive alone.

"Hillary isn't here." Anne inhaled and blew out a breath. "*She* has good sense."

"But she said she would come. That she wanted to be here for you. And Emma," Melanie said, feeling sharp hurt her sister had yet again refused to show, but that was followed immediately by anger. How selfish did a person have to be? Yeah, Hilly was thin and embarrassed about her appearance, but shouldn't her love for her niece—for her own sister—be enough to drag her from bed for a few measly hours?

"I didn't need Hillary to accompany me here. I will stay until Emma opens my gift, and then I will leave. Your sister didn't feel well, so I suggested she stay home."

"She never feels well."

"She is fine, but tonight felt ill." Anne arched an eyebrow as if daring her to say differently.

Sandy lifted the plates and jerked her head toward the still-empty table. Melanie gave her an affirming nod, and her friend quietly exited stage right.

Melanie returned her focus to her mother. Anne stood like a soldier ready to defend the fortress, one hand fisted at her side, her knuckles white on the sweating glass. Her fierce expression the same it always was when they battled about Hillary. Anne hid the shame and pretended nothing was truly wrong with her sister beyond a nervous disposition. Her mother's refusal to yield to weakness, to allow her concern to come up for air, was what had crippled Hillary for far too long. Her mother being who she thought she should be—polite, private, and prideful—caused more harm than good. Anne's ridiculous ego and refusal to address the ugly beneath pretty veneers had been part of what killed Melanie's father.

Anne liked to blame Tennyson for what happened to their family. But she had played her own role in Albert's suicide.

"Hillary has been 'ill'"—Melanie crooked her fingers in the air—"most of her life, but she can't get better if she uses that as an excuse . . . if you let her use that as an excuse. This is Emma's wedding shower. Hillary should have come even if it were for only a little while."

Anne gave her a hard look. "It's better for your sister to remain home."

"So everyone doesn't have to see what she's done to herself? So she doesn't embarrass the family?"

Melanie didn't want to feel so hurt by her sister, so angry at her mother for enabling Hillary, but she did. Both Hillary and Anne used Hillary's "condition" to get her out of familial obligations. Though she knew her sister loved her, Hillary's actions made her feel so unloved, so not important. Couldn't her mother see this wasn't about Hillary showing up, but more about Hillary making a flipping sacrifice to show she loved Emma and Melanie?

Damn, she was tired of always taking a back seat. In everything. This wedding. Her family. Her marriage. People didn't see her anymore. They were too caught up in their own issues. Same song and dance she'd sat through for years.

"I refuse to have this conversation here of all places," Melanie's mother said, her face tight from the plastic surgery and bitterness she carried around like a badge of honor. The proud widow and beleaguered mother who refused to show one iota of vulnerability.

"Wouldn't matter where it was. You try to pretend issues away. Sometimes you have to acknowledge that other people are weak. That they make mistakes. You have to recognize—"

Anne turned in the middle of Melanie's tirade and walked off.

Melanie snapped her mouth shut and glared at her mother's back.

"Right," Melanie said, sucking in a breath and releasing it.

"What's wrong?" Tennyson said, appearing at her elbow. Tennyson was like a weed, popping up where she was not needed. But even as she had that thought, even as Tennyson bugged the crap out of her, she was glad someone who understood how infuriating her mother was stood right beside her.

"Hillary. And Mother."

"I heard Hilly wasn't doing well," Tennyson said, her hand grazing Melanie's back before Tennyson seemed to think better of it. "Um, that she still battled bulimia. I thought I would try to go visit her. You know I always loved Hilly. She's the best."

"She is," Melanie said, her voice softening. Tennyson had always loved Hillary. When they were younger, Tennyson always sought Hillary out to fix her hair, check that her eyeliner was straight, or just gossip about the older girls Hillary knew. Her concern was sincere.

"Is she well enough to see me?"

"I don't know. My mother hides so much." As soon as she said the words, she wished she hadn't. Because it was like taking the gauze off a wound before one should, making blood pulse out and splatter the grounds. Reminding her of what was once hidden and how Tennyson had unearthed the secret and then used it against Melanie. Reminding her about the hurt that still sat in their family, fat and oozing, with her mother refusing to acknowledge that it was still there and needed to be dealt with.

"Everyone hides things," Tennyson said, her voice . . . regretful.

"I guess."

"All I'm saying is that everyone here has things they don't want others to know. Everyone here has regrets, wrinkles, and crazy uncles. Everyone has a closet with a skeleton." Gone was the cocky, brash woman, and in her stead was a woman who perhaps had weathered her own battles, who understood that things hidden away could corrode a person, leaving her a shell. What things had Tennyson hidden? What hurts had she borne? Melanie had never considered that the invincible Tennyson might have deep scars or places still unhealed. She'd been too busy hating her to see her as an actual person.

This woman didn't feel like the one who barged into her house with sunglasses, stilettos, and a dog in her purse. This woman was her old friend. If Melanie squinted enough, she could see the freckles Tennyson hated and the scar from a bike wreck nestled in her eyebrow.

"Well, my mother has always been the warden of our vault of secrets."

For a moment they were both silent. The world whirled around them in unbelievable fashion, people laughing, clinking glasses, jugglers performing, an empty gondola floating like a forgotten centerpiece. But for one small moment, she and Tennyson were suspended in something deeper than they should be flirting with. Something laced with regret and hemmed with uncertainty on how to proceed with who they now were. It was like standing on a cliff, deciding whether to jump into the water and embrace the danger and exhilaration . . . or turning around and climbing back down, deciding the fall could break a person apart.

Tennyson snapped out of her sudden reverie and smiled brightly. "My mother and Bronte are here. They wanted to say hello to you. I mean, if you want to say hello."

"I will. Let me get a drink," Melanie said, grabbing another Aperol spritz off a passing waiter and nodding toward the open tent where Tennyson's family had to be sitting.

Fifteen minutes later, while Bronte was laugh-snorting her way through a story about Tennyson and Melanie trying to learn how to drive Heathcliff's old Mustang, Marc Mallow stepped to the front of the tent and struck his fork against his glass, demanding attention.

"Hello, everyone. Welcome to Emma and Andrew's wedding shower. I hope you all have been enjoying the food, drinks, and entertainment." Marc did a weird jazz hand circle with one hand, a bit of razzmatazz. The people gathering around him nodded because who didn't enjoy stuffed jumbo shrimp and crawfish étouffée pistolettes? And free top-shelf liquor? And mimes? Well, there were plenty of people who didn't like mimes, Melanie being one. She didn't nod for that reason alone.

"As you know, Tennyson has so lovingly thrown this party in celebration of her only child's forthcoming nuptials in August, and she has a special gift she'd like to bestow on the happy couple," he said, motioning Emma and Andrew forward.

The betrothed couple clasped hands and looked slightly embarrassed by all the attention. Emma's ears had turned scarlet, a true indication of her nerves, but she smiled and looked adoringly at Andrew, who kept looking down at her like she was the second coming.

Had Kit ever looked at Melanie that way? She couldn't remember that much warmth, that much pure adoration ever shining in those blue eyes. Maybe she'd just forgotten to remember.

Tennyson tugged Melanie's arm. "Come on. Bring your gift."

Melanie pulled away. She didn't want everyone to watch Emma open her gift, and since it was for Emma only, it seemed wrong to have her open it here. She hadn't thought to get something for Andrew. The bracelet would have been better on the wedding day or at the rehearsal dinner. "No, I'll give mine later. You go ahead."

She couldn't imagine what Tennyson had gotten Emma and Andrew that could top the elaborate shower. The flowers had to have set the woman back at least ten grand, and Melanie could only guess what the catering bill would be. But maybe Tennyson would get some money back on Cesar since he'd bailed.

Tennyson stepped toward the couple, her smile almost crocodilian. Melanie knew Tennyson's stage presence was perfectly in place. "I couldn't even begin to put into words how much I love this boy. That he would find the perfect girl for him has always been my fervent prayer. I'm not going to lie, at first, I wondered how this could work."

The crowd issued a little chuckle because some of them had been at Melanie's wedding and knew the discord between Tennyson and Melanie. Some laughed because everyone else had, and they had no clue why Emma and Andrew marrying was . . . well, nuts.

"But"—Tennyson turned to Emma and tucked a glossy strand of hair behind Melanie's daughter's ear. It was a tender demonstration of her approval of Emma. Melanie tried not to roll her eyes at the affectation. "I can't think of a more fitting wife for Andrew. In less than two months, I will gain a daughter, and my heart is very full."

So over the top. So Teeny. But at the same time, it *was* sort of sweet to see Tennyson care about Emma that much.

"Emma will be starting medical school in a few weeks. She knows how to cut it close," Tennyson said with a laugh, giving Emma an indulgent smile. "And Andrew has a new job, so a true honeymoon is impossible at present. Still, everyone deserves a few weeks of alone time when they're newly married. Since fall break comes at the most beautiful time off the coast of Amalfi, I thought a trip to Italy would be the perfect belated honeymoon."

Emma's mouth fell open, and Andrew laughed. "Seriously?"

All the gathered guests oohed and aahed, then broke into applause. Melanie finally closed her agape mouth.

A trip to Italy?

Motherfu . . . ugh. Of course Tennyson had bought them an Italian honeymoon.

Melanie could never measure up to Tennyson. The woman would always outdo her. From the wedding to grandchildren to her funeral, Tennyson would always have the best ideas, presents, vacations, and casket. Melanie would never be able to compete.

And she never had. Tennyson had always commanded the attention of the room, she'd always turned heads, she'd always won whatever she'd set out to win, whether it was the library's summer reading contest or head cheerleader. Now it was evident as her former friend stood in the middle of the most ridiculous bridal shower in the history of Shreveport, looking ten years younger than Melanie, splashing thousands upon thousands of dollars around, that Melanie would always be the dark horse.

Sometimes the dark horse won.

And sometimes they broke their leg on the track.

Tennyson took the envelope from Marc and handed it to Andrew. "Congratulations, sugar. I hope you make the best memories in Italy."

Emma and Andrew beamed at each other as they opened the envelope, gasping over the first-class flight to Rome and the five-star accommodations. Melanie was happy for her daughter for receiving a honeymoon of a lifetime. She wasn't that petty. But still. The gift was meant to show off what Tennyson could and would do.

It was at that moment that Melanie's mother appeared beside her. "Melanie, we must go."

"Wow, when you said you would leave after Emma opened presents, you weren't kidding," Melanie said, turning to her mother. Sandy was with her, her cute sequined clutch in hand. Both their expressions alarmed her. "What? What's wrong?"

"We have to go to the hospital." Anne's mouth flatlined with annoyance.

"Someone called your mother from University Health. They just brought your sister there by ambulance," Sandy said, putting a comforting hand on Melanie's mother's shoulder.

Anne brushed off Sandy's hand and started toward the lit path. "I told you she was ill."

"Did they say why? Who called?" Melanie asked, looking around for Emma so she could explain. At that moment, fireworks erupted overhead, exploding brilliance against the darkening sky, scaring the hell out of Melanie. She clasped her chest and sucked in a deep breath. "Oh, good gracious."

Sandy gave her a light squeeze. "I'm not sure who called your mother. Go find Emma. I'll call for the car."

"Thank you," Melanie said, glancing up at the bursts of light followed by heart-stopping booms that rattled the hurricane glass on the tables. Of course there were fireworks. Because that, too, was so Tennyson.

Jesus.

"Prosecco to toast the happy couple?" a waiter asked as she pushed through the crowd staring up at the show above them.

"No, thanks," she said, looking at where she'd last seen Emma.

Tennyson intercepted her, her smile fading when she read Melanie's body language. "What's wrong, Melly?"

"Where's Emma?"

"She and Andrew went to take pictures out by the oak with the Japanese lanterns. I thought with the fireworks behind them . . . wait, what's wrong?"

Melanie passed a hand over her face. "They've taken Hillary to the hospital. I don't know what's wrong. Someone called Mother, and we have to go to University and see what's going on."

"Oh no," Tennyson said, taking Melanie's elbow and turning her toward the exit. "Don't worry. Just go see about Hillary. I'll let Emma know where you've gone. She can come to the hospital once the party's over."

Melanie nodded. "Thank you."

Tennyson halted. "Is it serious?"

Melanie felt fear rise inside her. "It's always serious when it comes to Hillary."

"Then go to her."

And so Melanie left without toasting the future happy couple.

CHAPTER SIXTEEN

Tennyson's feet felt as if she'd put them through a meat grinder, and her lower back ached, but she couldn't stop the smile on her face when Officer Joseph Rhett appeared poolside, wading through the staff scurrying around as they broke down the tables and chairs.

"Hello, handsome," she said, her heels hooked in one hand, a glass of prosecco in the other. "I would offer you a drink, but you wouldn't take it."

"I didn't come for a drink," he said, his expression intense, his gaze dropping to her breasts. She remembered how fond he was of Anna and Elsa, the nicknames he'd given to her breasts. Obviously, the man had watched a lot of *Frozen* with his daughters.

"Yeah? Good thing I have what you came for," she teased.

"Leftovers?" He crooked a sexy eyebrow.

That made Tennyson laugh. "I got those, too."

Joseph leaned down and kissed her right in front of God and everybody. Okay, just the cleanup crew, but it still made her feel vulnerable. To kiss a man in public sent a message that they were together. And they weren't together. Just having good sex.

But even as she had that anticipatory thought, another graver one niggled its way into her conscience.

Hillary.

Melanie's older sister had been the sister that Tennyson had always wanted. Slightly chubby, endearingly kind, and attentive to her younger sister and her best friend, Hillary was the kind of person everyone wanted to have beside them when life got tough. A gentle spirit with calm hands that braided their hair, ready laughter when she and Melanie dressed up and sang karaoke, and whimsical input on the plays Tennyson would write for the girls to perform on long summer nights in the Brevard playroom. It never occurred to Tennyson that the reason why Bronte wanted nothing to do with her and Melanie was because Bronte had a horde of gal pals. Hillary had none, so she was happy to be with the younger girls. When Hillary was in high school, she lost a bunch of weight. After six months, Hillary was thin and pretty, prettier than Bronte even. Suddenly, Hillary had boys coming around, a group of friends who wanted to smoke joints out by the pool and throw weekend parties with Everclear and ecstasy.

Still, even as Hillary became popular, she always treated Melanie and Tennyson with kindness, sometimes looking as if she would rather go back to being their talent show judge and doing makeovers rather than "partying" with her newfound friends.

When Hillary went to college and lost even more weight, it became evident there was a problem. After only a year, she had to drop out, go to a program for people with eating disorders, and enter weekly therapy. Hillary eventually gained some weight and started apprenticing in a salon. After two years, she struck out for Baton Rouge and a partnership in a new salon. She got married, got divorced, and at some point, reclaimed her lifelong struggle with anorexia and bulimia.

After Tennyson and Melanie's friendship ended, Tennyson tried to keep up with Hillary, but that was before social media was relevant. She hadn't seen Hillary in many years.

Joseph cradled her face, leveling her gaze to his. "What's wrong? I thought you wanted me to come by after the party?"

"I did. I do. It's just I have some things on my mind," she said.

"Maybe I could distract you?" he asked, his lips at her ear.

The words were meant as seduction, and Tennyson could easily let herself go where her wakening body wanted to go, but there was also part of her that needed to do *something*. It was this part of herself that she sometimes wished she could ignore, but once a stirring latched on to her thoughts, it became a bit bulldoggish and would give her no peace until she complied. Which was how she'd ended up back in Shreveport in the first place.

Stepping back from Joseph, she met his eyes. "Can you do me a favor?"

Joseph narrowed his eyes. "Why do I sense this favor won't lead me to that really soft bed you have?"

Tennyson smiled. "Maybe later?"

"Definitely later," he said, looping his arms about her waist. "What do you need, Tennyson?"

Loaded question indeed. She needed a shower. Pajamas. Multiple orgasms. Another martini. A man who would stay beside her and not be distracted by other women, more money, and her net worth. She settled on, "A ride to the hospital?"

"The hospital? Is there something I should know?" he asked, now looking concerned.

"I have a . . ." She couldn't say *friend* because she and Melanie weren't friends any longer. And Lord knew Anne Brevard would love to see her eviscerated and hanged by her own entrails, so it wasn't like she was going to be welcomed by the family. Still, something about the way Melanie looked when she told her they had taken Hillary to the hospital made the hair on the back of Tennyson's neck stand at attention. Something felt really wrong about the whole situation, and some intangible, weird impulse drove her to check on Melanie. "There's just someone I need to be there for. I've had a few martinis, so I can't drive. Would you?"

He released her. "Of course."

"Let me settle things with Marc, and then we can go," she said, rising on the aching balls of her feet and giving his cheek a light kiss. "You really are a good guy. You protect, serve, and give a gal a ride to the hospital."

She felt him watch her as she walked toward the event planner, who was sitting with his bow tie untied, his top button undone, and his knees akimbo. That was about as disheveled as she'd ever seen the dapper Marc Mallow.

He looked up from his phone when she stopped in front of him. "We did good, Tennyson. Well, outside of the whole Cesar thing, but really, the man is a queen bee. If he would have stayed, he would have been screeching at us all night. *Look at me. Hear me. Adore me.* Better that he left. Don't worry, I will demand he return half the fees paid to him, or I will write a scathing review on my blog and share it all over creation."

Tennyson wanted to laugh at his antics, but she felt too sad to do so.

Marc gestured to the chair beside him. "Sit, darling. Unless you have better things to do? Like that handsome man wearing the absolute worst trousers I've ever seen. Where do you suppose he bought them? Sam's Club?"

"He looks good in them." Tennyson sat, eyeing Joseph, who had pulled his phone out and was no doubt checking baseball scores. She knew this because he'd checked the scores after the second time they'd had sex. He'd suggested it was his version of an after-sex cigarette. She hadn't fallen for that one.

Marc smiled. "True."

"I have to go. A friend needs me. Can you please oversee the cleanup? And let Prada out to potty?" Tennyson gave him her best "pretty please" face.

"How much will you pay me?" Marc asked.

Tennyson leveled an exasperated look at him. "I have a blog, too, you know."

"Really? What's it called?"

"Event Planners Who Hire Opera Singers Who Don't Complete Their Gig."

"Never heard of it, but I'm sure it would give *MarshMallow Thoughts* a run for its money. And I will let Prada out. No charge."

Tennyson patted his knee and rose. "I'm putting on flats, and Hot Cop is giving me a ride. The bridal shower was good, Marc. Thanks for all you did to make it so nice for the kids."

His mouth curved into something less sarcastic and more sincere. "That's my job."

Ten minutes later she wore a T-shirt dress that had seen better days and a pair of gingham Tretorns she'd bought on impulse and kept only because they were like wearing velvet clouds. Of course, that could be because she normally wore heels. Heels made her legs look long and her ass firm. A woman had to make sacrifices. But tonight she needed to be comfortable because her presence wouldn't be appreciated.

Or maybe it would. Sometimes just showing up said all that needed to be said. Or sometimes words needed to be said, but the timing was off. She wasn't certain why she hadn't said the words she needed to say by now. They just wouldn't come, but maybe it was time they did.

"Ready?" Joseph looked up from his phone when she stuck her head out the back door. She caught sight of the baseball logos set against a scoreboard on his screen and realized, though she hadn't known him for long, she already knew him well. How had he become so familiar to her? They had nothing in common. Like baseball. Tennyson *had* attended a few of Andrew's baseball games, but the other mothers had made her feel silly for wearing a sundress and heels to the ballpark. Hey, she'd made sure to wear team colors. But in hindsight, maybe it had been that she'd elected to bring sushi instead of eating the corn dogs and cheese fries offered by the ballpark concession stand.

She liked sushi. Sue her.

"As I'll ever be," she said as he fell into step beside her, shoving his phone into the back pocket of his khaki jeans. Together they walked through the house, ignoring Prada's yipping. She liked the way it felt having Joseph with her. Far less lonely. Far more comforting.

By the time they arrived at the hospital, Tennyson had fallen asleep and drooled onto her dress, which was pretty embarrassing, even though she wasn't sure Joseph had actually noticed.

"Here we are, sleepyhead," Joseph said, putting the 4Runner into park and opening the door.

Tennyson hurriedly wiped her chin with the back of her hand. Gak. She probably looked like death warmed up, and her mouth tasted like blue-cheese olives. She found a tin of mints in her purse, popped one, swiped gloss over her lips, and fluffed her hair all by the time Joseph jogged around to open her door. Hot *and* polite. She'd hit a pair of aces with this guy.

"You're coming with me?" she asked.

"Um, yes. I wouldn't let the toughest motorcycle cop walk this street by himself."

Tennyson wrinkled her nose. "Because not many people like cops?"

"No, because it's a dangerous area . . . and maybe a few people don't like law enforcement. But that comes with the territory," he said, closing the door and pressing the key fob so his light flashed and the car made a toot-toot to assure them the vehicle was locked.

They made their way to the entrance, where they encountered a squat, frowning woman at the information desk. Her hair seemed to stand on end, and it was obvious her eyes had seen too much.

"I'm not sure they'll tell me anything. I'm not family," Tennyson whispered to Joseph.

He dug in his pocket and pulled out his badge. "Hello, Raylene. I need to locate . . ."

"Hillary Brevard," Tennyson finished.

"Well, Officer Rhett. How you been doin'?" Raylene asked as she tapped, tapped, tapped on the computer in front of her. She shot Hot Cop a winsome smile. She may have even batted her false eyelashes at him.

"Can't complain," Joseph said.

"Brevard? I don't see her in the system." Raylene tapped a bit more and shook her head.

"They just brought her by ambulance. Um, about an hour and a half ago," Tennyson said, trying to peer at the screen. Raylene frowned and shot her an accusing look, moving the screen away from Tennyson.

"Okay, yeah, I see right here she came through ER. Y'all go right on down there and tell Stacey that I sent you, Joseph," she said, ignoring Tennyson completely.

"Thanks, Raylene. I still remember that pumpkin bread you made me. I'm going to be needing some more come fall. It's worth the extra weight," he said, rubbing his flat belly and giving the desk clerk a charming smile that made Tennyson want to pinch him. Those smiles were for her.

"Oh, you. You ain't got an inch of flab on you, sugar," Raylene said with a wave of her hand.

Tennyson and Joseph pushed through a heavy swinging door that would take them into the bowels of the hospital. She looked over at him. "Laying it on thick, weren't you?"

"Sometimes you got to use what the good Lord gave you to get what you need."

Tennyson issued a chuckle. "Always been my motto."

"I knew you'd understand."

They ended up in a bustling ER where another nurse who also seemed to know Joseph, this one with a bigger chest and biceps that rippled, sent them upstairs to the intensive care unit. The halls were mostly empty after the hectic speed of the ER, and when the elevator opened and they started walking toward the ICU waiting room, it felt as if they were entering a tomb. A pall hung over this entire part of the hospital floor, and it was so thick it felt like Tennyson needed to wipe it from her skin.

She stopped in the doorway of the ICU waiting room and spied Melanie sitting alone on a couch, staring into the vacuum of space before her. Her hair, once bouncy, now hung on either side of her face as if defeated. She clasped her hands in her lap, turning them over each other in a kneading motion. Tennyson had never seen Melanie look so lost before.

The motion at the entrance drew Melanie's attention. "Tennyson?"

"I'm going to grab some coffee, 'kay?" Joseph said in her ear, his tone implying he understood she needed privacy.

Melanie stood, still looking confused. "What are you doing here? Who's that guy?"

Tennyson moved into the room. "I thought I should come check on you. And that's Joseph. He's . . . uh, a friend."

"Oh well," Melanie said, plucking at the dress she still wore. The conservative crepe dress with a floral pattern was now crumpled against Melanie's newly beach-burnished skin. Her face, however, looked like curdled custard it was so pale and tired. "I, uh, I'm waiting to meet the doctor."

"Where is everyone else?"

"Mother is in the chapel with her friend Margaret Ellison. Do you remember her? Big teeth? And Emma went home to get Noah. Kit's still in Florida. Um, they don't think . . . they . . ." Melanie started panting, her big brown eyes filling with tears. "What are you *doing* here? You . . . didn't . . . you aren't . . ."

"Why don't we sit down. Okay? I think you should." Tennyson gently took her arm.

"I can't just sit. I need to do something," she said, fidgeting her hands and staring at the opening to the waiting area. Tennyson glanced around the room. A woman sat with what looked to be her teenaged son, a blanket wrapped around her, weariness radiating from her eyes as she glanced their way and then turned her head. The stack of used coffee cups and worn books indicated the two had been here awhile.

"I know you do, but there's nothing to do right now. Why don't we sit and talk? Come on," Tennyson said, leading Melanie to the far side of the room, which was still visible from the doorway but also away from the other occupants.

Melanie allowed Tennyson to lead her to a set of chairs.

For a few minutes they sat side by side. Then Melanie turned to Tennyson. "Why are you here?"

"I told you. I just felt like I should"—Tennyson turned over the palms resting on her knees—"check on you."

Melanie looked at her strangely. It was as if she were studying her with the eye of a fashion photographer, deciding what light would be best, what position she should take. Finally, Melanie released a pent-up breath. "She's going to die."

"No. You don't know that," Tennyson said, her heart filling with anguish at the thought the world would lose Hillary. Sweet Hillary with her twinkling eyes and bouncing hair. Hillary with her uninhibited laugh and need to save baby birds and worms crossing hot pavement. It wasn't fair. At all. "You don't."

"I could tell. You can see it in the doctor's eyes."

"What happened?"

Melanie sucked in a breath and exhaled. "Hilly knew something was wrong and called for Martha. Mother had the foresight to ask her to come stay with Hilly when she said she wasn't feeling well. The doctor said it was cardiac arrest." Melanie closed her eyes and pressed her gathered fingers against them.

"At least the ambulance got there fast. Maybe it was enough time," Tennyson said, reaching over and pulling one of Melanie's hands away. "Come on. Be positive."

"Hilly's not strong enough, Teeny. Her body just isn't. It's been through too many years of abuse. I've read everything there is to read about eating disorders. Cardiac arrest is a leading cause of death. They just deny and deny and deny their bodies nutrients, and then those bodies don't work anymore. God, her body just doesn't work." Melanie wrapped her arms around her stomach and fell forward. Her face twisted in anguish, and bright blood appeared on her bottom lip. She'd chewed it until it bled.

Tennyson didn't know what to do. Why had everyone left Melanie alone, assuming she could handle this situation by herself? Why did she have to be the one to talk to the doctor? Why did everyone else get a pass to deal with their own feelings but Melanie didn't?

The thought pissed Tennyson off. Ever since she'd been back, she'd watched Melanie handle everything for everyone else.

Slowly, she began to rub Melanie's back, the same way she'd done with Andrew when he'd been sick as a child. "It's okay, Melly. It's okay to be scared."

Under her hand, Melanie stilled, her silent sobs abating. After a few more seconds, Melanie sat up and wiped her face. "Oh God. I *am* scared."

Tennyson looked at her. "I am, too. All the time."

"You're not scared. You never have been."

"Wrong. I . . . well, you know me, Melanie. I have to play it off. I have to put on a front."

Melanie smiled at her then, a tremulous, wobbly smile. "You want to know a secret?"

She didn't respond because she was fairly certain that secrets were the reason she and Melanie were no longer friends. That, and the fact that Tennyson had purposefully, albeit drunkenly, spilled the biggest secret of the Brevard family in front of hundreds of wedding guests. So that Melanie would offer up something using the word *secret* made her wary.

"I missed who I am with you," Melanie whispered.

Tennyson felt something weird break apart in her chest at that confession. "Yeah? You miss getting detention and punished for sneaking out late?"

A tear slipped from Melanie's brown eyes. "Yeah. We got in trouble a lot, but the thing is, I don't like who I am much anymore. I'm older, fatter, and take more crap from people than I used to. I settle all the time and allow myself to be used, underappreciated, or whatever just so someone will pay attention to me. I am the doormat they walk across and wipe their crap on. I don't have any true friends. Okay, a couple. But no one asks me to have cocktails or go on girls' trips or be their ride or die. You know what I mean?"

"Ride or die? Or the doormat thing?"

Melanie made a confused face. "Both?"

Tennyson realized she didn't have many friends, either. Oh sure, she'd had friends who invited her for cocktails and even took a few trips to her place in Colorado or the place husband number three had in Cabo, but she didn't have ones who knew who she truly was. She had faux friends, people who looked the part, but never held her hand when she cried, never showed up with Oreos or ice cream when she had a crap day, never cared about the real Tennyson. None of them saw through her crap and held her accountable. No one told her no. That she was acting stupid. Or ridiculous. She hadn't had a friend like that since . . . Melanie.

And Tennyson had thrown that friendship away over a damned man. Because she couldn't accept Kit choosing Melanie over her, even when she didn't truly want him anymore. She had always been jealous of what Melanie had—the big house, the fancy cars, the damned country club membership. She hadn't wanted her to have Kit, too.

So she'd done what she thought she had to in order to steal Melanie's "perfect" world. She was a shitty person.

"I know what you mean, but you don't have to be everything to everybody, Melly. You know? You get to choose yourself sometimes," she said, mostly because she couldn't seem to admit that to herself, much less Melanie. Or maybe this was a new revelation—that she truly missed Melanie. How could she say she made the biggest mistakes of her life when she was twenty-three years old? And that she'd spent too many years regretting those mistakes, atoning for one with money, pretending the other one didn't matter to her anymore? She'd spent too many years chasing happiness that she would never catch. Because she thought who she'd been couldn't be good enough. She'd hated being powerless, so she'd ensured she never felt that way by buying a lifestyle.

Melanie nodded. "You're right. I know I should stand up to my family, but I can't seem to do it."

Tennyson pulled a few tissues from the box beside her. "Here."

Melanie took them, blew her nose with one, and wiped her eyes with the other. "Thank you. You always seem to be doing that."

"There's been a lot of emotion going on, and you're welcome."

"I mean it. Thank you for coming. You didn't have to, but you did."

"What is she doing here?"

The accusation rang out across the room, and Tennyson felt her stomach sink when she saw Anne Brevard standing in the opening to the waiting room next to a horse-faced woman who did indeed have big teeth. Anne's face reflected absolute outrage.

"Mother, Tennyson came to check on us," Melanie said, rising and holding her hands up in a motion that suggested the older woman calm down.

"And now she can leave," Anne said, her voice the temperature of an arctic storm.

Joseph came in right behind the two women, holding a cardboard carrier of domed cups. "I have coffee. Figured everyone could use a cup about now."

He slid by the frigid Asian woman, giving her a soft smile before heading toward Tennyson and Melanie. Anne stalked into the room behind him, her eyes now flashing anger. "I don't know who this man is or why he's here, but you need to leave. You are not welcome here."

Anne had been pointing her finger at Tennyson, and now she stopped in front of her, wearing the black dress she'd worn to the bridal shower, looking pristine and marbled, unlike her rumpled daughter. She waited one second, two, even a third, before arching her perfectly drawn eyebrows in a supercilious manner.

"I'm not here for you, Mrs. Brevard. I'm here for Melanie," Tennyson said, suddenly very grateful that Joseph had stayed with her. He stood next to her, and she could feel his wariness as he read the situation.

"Melanie doesn't need you, either. Leave. Now," Anne said.

"Ma'am"—Joseph held up a hand—"Tennyson doesn't have to go anywhere. This is a public space."

Anne turned toward Joseph, looking like a weapon repositioning and focusing its red target light onto his forehead. "That may be, but this woman is not welcome to converse with any of us. Come with me, Melanie."

Melanie stopped moving toward her mother. "What? No."

Anne turned to her daughter and gave her a look. It was one that said *excuse me, missy?* It was a look Tennyson had seen many times, and it always caused Melanie to fall in line. "I beg your pardon?"

"I mean it. I've had enough of all this . . ." Melanie waved her hand around. "It's time to stop."

"There will never be a time for this to *stop*," Anne said, turning on her heel. "Never."

"It has to be, Mother. I'm done with the hate and discord. Tennyson came when others didn't. I'm not asking her to leave."

Her mother tossed Tennyson a frosty glare over her shoulder. "Fine. You do whatever you wish, daughter. You always have." And then her mother walked away.

Melanie looked at Tennyson and shrugged. Then Melanie sat down. To wait. On the word if her sister was alive or dead. That her mother was leaving, her regard for her own ego more important than the feelings of her daughter, made it all the more tragic. It also made Tennyson feel something she hadn't felt for Melanie in a while—a sense of loyalty she had forgotten.

The horse-faced woman shot Melanie an apologetic look and followed Anne from the waiting room.

Joseph extended the cardboard carrier toward Tennyson. She shook her head. The last thing she could do was drink coffee. Melanie reached over and grabbed one, taking a swig. Then her former BFF looked up at the hot cop. "I'm Melanie, by the way."

He picked up a creamer container and held it up, waggling it. Melanie took it. "I'm Joseph. Tennyson's friend." Then he gave Melanie one of his pretty smiles.

"Good. She probably needs someone like you. We all probably need someone like you," Melanie said.

Tennyson looked at Joseph. His eyes met hers, and he conveyed a look that said *I'm in over my head here*. She could only mouth *thank you* to the man who had not only walked her in but had fetched coffee. This was the kind of man she'd never had in her life, outside of her father. Melanie hadn't been wrong. Tennyson had needed someone like Joseph for a while.

"Melanie and I have a complicated history," Tennyson finally said.

"I gathered as much," Joseph said.

Melanie poured the cream into her coffee, then took a stirrer from the cardboard carrier. "So it started with college. Tennyson went to NYC to be famous, and Kit and I went to LSU.".

Tennyson figured it was going to be a long wait, so she grabbed the other coffee. "And Kit and Melanie fell in love."

Joseph nodded. "So who is Kit?"

Tennyson glanced over at Melanie before looking at her hot cop. "He's Melanie's husband. But before he was hers, he was mine. And that's where it all started . . . and ended."

CHAPTER SEVENTEEN

Kit and Melanie's Wedding Day, 1996

Melanie rubbed her lips together, adjusted her veil, and gave a final glance into the mirror of the church's bridal suite. She looked about as perfect as she could get, mostly thanks to her sister, who had curled her hair, worked to make her both "glamorous and natural," and tried not to cry while she was doing it. Hillary was nothing if not sentimental.

"You look so darn pretty, Melanie," Carrie Carlisle said, blending her own lipstick behind her. "I swear Kit's tongue's going to loll out like an ol' coon dog when he sees you coming down the aisle."

Melanie smiled at her sorority sister and bridesmaid. Carrie was from nearby Minden and loved to use country euphemisms like she had grown up on a farm. Everyone knew Carrie had been raised in a large, historic house on Main Street, had a trust fund, and a new dress for cotillion. "I'm not sure my mother would like that."

"Oh, pish," Carrie said, waving away Melanie's comment with a hand. "Who cares what Mama thinks when you got a man like that waiting at the altar?"

She did, indeed, have a hunk waiting for her to say "I do," and sometimes she couldn't believe that Kit was finally going to be hers. She couldn't count the number of times she pinched herself when she remembered he would be her husband. "You have a point, Carrie."

"Darn tootin'." Carrie turned to the other bridesmaids. "Y'all ready, girls? Who's holding my bouquet? Who has Melanie's?"

The hustle and bustle fell away as Melanie rose and tried to concentrate on everything she was supposed to remember. Her daddy would be on her right side. She had to walk slowly because people needed to enjoy seeing the bride. Hillary had the ring tied to her bouquet. All Melanie had to do was remember how to breathe, wait for the pastor to cue her, and say her vows loud enough so everyone could hear her.

She turned to watch her sister and her bridesmaids make last-minute adjustments to their makeup and hair. Hilly looked so much better these days, her cheeks glowing, and the weight from the pregnancy making her finally look more herself. Hillary had been married for just over a year and had recently found out she and Kyle were expecting a little one at the beginning of next year. Her daddy was so excited to be a grandfather. He'd been carrying around cigars and passing them out to everyone ever since Hillary and Kyle had told the family they were pregnant.

Everything felt surreal but right. The only thing that felt wrong was Tennyson not being at her wedding. They'd both planned their weddings when they were ten years old, with each promising to be the other's maid of honor. Melanie could remember poring over bridal magazines, clipping pictures of dresses and four-tiered wedding cakes, dreaming about the groom waiting for them at the altar. They'd taken Melanie's lacy slips out of the drawers and pulled them on their heads to be makeshift veils, with the hairbrush alternating as both the bouquet and the microphone for when they launched into "Hopelessly Devoted to You" off the *Grease* soundtrack. Somehow it seemed such a travesty that Tennyson wouldn't be standing beside Melanie when she became someone's wife.

But that was because of who that *someone* was.

Tennyson had been so furious at her and Kit. She wouldn't even take Melanie's calls, and the letters she'd written and sent to New York City had come back with an angry "refused" scrawled across the front. The postal service's red Return to Sender stamped atop validated that Tennyson didn't want her apology. Even Kit had tried to talk some sense into Tennyson when she last visited Shreveport, but she'd slammed the door in his face. Melanie didn't understand why she was so mad at them. Tennyson and Kit had been broken up for years, and Tennyson knew they had been dating for a few years. It wasn't like she and Kit had cheated. Wasn't like they had planned on falling in love. It just sorta happened.

When Melanie and Kit had first told Tennyson they were together, she'd thrown a glass of water at them both. Then she stood in the middle of Strawn's and called Melanie the *c* word. She'd also accused her of always being in love with Kit and being jealous of her for years. After that little scene, she'd stormed out and not spoken to either of them since. Melanie had felt not only guilty because some of her words were true—she had been half in love with Kit for several years, even though she would have never interfered between Tennyson and Kit—but she'd also been angry at her friend for implying she'd been anything but a good friend to her.

Melanie had always stood in Tennyson's shadow, supporting her, encouraging her, letting her have all the things—first dibs on everything. And this was how her "friend" acted?

Yet even though she was upset with Tennyson, she understood. Because had their roles been reversed, she would have a hard time giving up Kit, too.

Everyone had told her she was insane, but she'd sent a wedding invitation to the last address she'd had for Tennyson in Manhattan and hoped time had softened her friend's heart. Because she wanted, no, needed Tennyson to forgive her and see that Melanie and Kit were meant to be. Surely, her friend could search her heart and find some generosity. Tennyson could be a pill, but she wouldn't miss Melanie's wedding.

Hillary moved so she was beside her. "Hey, you okay? You look upset."

Melanie smiled and ran a finger under her lashes. "I'm sad that Teeny isn't here. She should be here. We're . . . or rather, we were best friends. She promised we'd always be besties no matter what."

Hillary smiled. "I know, but you're kinda marrying her ex-boyfriend. That's hard for some girls. Especially girls like Tennyson."

"Why?"

"Because she doesn't have much confidence."

"Teeny?" Melanie turned to her sister, her mouth dropping open. "You've met her, right? She breathes fire and never sweats. I've seen her stare down a police officer who was going to give her a ticket, but somehow ended up apologizing to her for pulling her over. She can't possibly have more confidence than she has now."

"That's all bluster. Underneath all that bravado is someone who believes she's not good enough. She's a total fraud on many levels."

Melanie shook her head. "No."

"Yes." Hillary smiled, twisted one of the curls around Melanie's face, and tucked it into place. "I swear this hair doesn't want to behave today. But you look beautiful, anyway."

Hillary air-kissed her cheek and moved over to where their mother stood with the wedding planner. Anne Brevard, no doubt, was going over all the details one final time. Beyond the door, Melanie could hear the organ swelling and the muffled chatter of guests arriving. After listening to their mother for a few seconds, Hillary slipped outside the room.

Melanie tried to quell the butterflies rising in her stomach. Nerves? Yeah, but mostly she was excited. In thirty minutes she and Kit would climb into the back of the limo as man and wife. Then they would be whisked away to the country club to cut the three-tiered wedding cake and debut their practiced waltz for their first dance. They'd netted Betty Lewis & the Executives for the band, and Daddy had sprung for an open bar *and* a sit-down dinner. Their reception with their friends would be exactly as she planned—fun and memorable.

"She came," she heard her sister whisper to their mother.

"Who came?" Melanie asked.

"Teeny's here," Hillary said.

"She's here. She actually came to the wedding?" Melanie asked, moving toward the door.

Hillary stepped in front of her. "You're not going out there."

"I'm not. I wanted to peek. Is she standing in the foyer?" Melanie tried to sidestep her sister. She was so relieved Tennyson had come. Did this mean her friend had finally accepted Melanie and Kit together? Maybe they could get past this, laugh about it one day.

"No. She's already inside. She sat right behind Kit's mom and dad." Hillary shot a look toward their mother. "I really wish you hadn't invited her, Melly bean."

"I had to. It's Teeny. I mean, I know she's mad, but maybe this is a peace offering. Maybe she wants to—"

The entire time Hillary had been shaking her head, so Melanie stopped talking. Hillary made a strange face. "I don't think that's why she's here, Melly. She looks . . . well, she looks like trouble."

Melanie shook her head. "No. I know she's crazy dramatic, but Teeny has a big heart. Really. I've known her forever, and she's just upholding the promise we both made to each other—that we would both be there for each other for all the important things. She wasn't going to miss my wedding. She's loyal to a fault. And we pinkie swore on it."

Hillary didn't look so certain, but Melanie didn't have a chance to convince her sister because the planner started lining them up and going through a checklist to make sure all the wedding party remembered their marks, had her bouquet, and no one had lipstick on their teeth.

A minute later, Melanie was looping her arm through her father's and trying to keep her bouquet from shaking in her trembling fingers.

"You ready, dumplin'?" her father said, beaming down at her with twinkling hazel eyes. Albert Brevard was still such a handsome man with his dark hair, smooth skin, and cleft chin. His silver temples made him look distinguished, and he smelled like the peppermints he always had in his pocket right beside the soft handkerchief he was quick to pull out for bloody noses or sad movies.

"I guess I have to be," she said, giving him a smile.

"You're one of the best things I've ever done, Melly bean. If this fella gives you any problems, I keep my granddaddy's gun well oiled."

"Daddy," Melanie groaned.

He gave her a tender smile. "I'm not afraid to pull that trigger."

Then it was time. The doors swooshed open, and everyone in the church rose, staring at her in her Italian lace gown with the cathedral-length train. She wore a circlet of silk flowers in her hair with a veil that trailed past her fingertips, so her view of the groom and the church filled with their friends and family was absolutely unobstructed.

Her first thought was that Kit looked nervous and ready to bolt.

However, when she got halfway down the aisle, her future husband smiled so sweetly at her that her heart swelled, and tears threatened to mar the elaborate makeup Hillary had so painstakingly applied. That smile was like sun breaking through dark clouds, and all was right with her world.

But then she saw Tennyson.

Melanie actually stutter-stepped when she saw the tight black dress and hat with the black netting swathing half her face. Tennyson had painted her lips a dark red . . . and she wasn't smiling. The veil obscured her eyes, but Melanie could only imagine the fury in the glacial depths. The whole mourning ensemble was dramatic, ridiculous, and so very much what Tennyson would do that Melanie almost started laughing.

But she didn't because her mother would turn up her toes and die if she did something so irreverent in the middle of a holy sacrament.

Several hours later, after taking more pictures than anyone could fathom and enduring the best man's long-winded wedding toast, Melanie finally had a chance to take a breath. The country club ballroom had been turned into an elegant reception with sparkling crystal, white tablecloths, and vases of roses in shades of blush and bashful because she was a southern girl who had watched *Steel Magnolias* a good thirty or forty times and knew what her colors must be. She and Kit sat in the middle of the head table, and she felt like a queen next to her king. They drank Dom Pérignon from Waterford glasses and took quick bites in between the copious well wishes that came their way. She had just taken a bite of her coconut cream wedding cake when she noticed Tennyson.

The veil had vanished, but the tight dress displayed a good portion of her former friend. Unlike Melanie, Tennyson had a lot of goods. More than Melanie remembered, in fact. Her former friend held a half-filled martini glass and stared at them, taking little sips of the dirty martini, never letting her eyes stray. The table where she sat was empty, and Melanie could only imagine why.

Who wanted to sit with the ex-girlfriend of the groom . . . oh, who happened to be dressed to kill? Like, perhaps, literally to kill?

Obviously, no one.

But then one of Kit's fraternity brothers plonked down and whispered something in her ear. He grinned like a jackanapes.

She saw Tennyson's lips move.

The guy's smile ran away as he rose and left.

"What are you looking at?" Kit said, dropping a kiss on her neck. The move was romantic, designed to make the guests swoon at the love between the two. Any other time, she would have enjoyed it, but the affectionate gesture had made Tennyson's nostrils flare. Tennyson tossed back her drink and slammed the empty glass on the table.

Kit followed her line of vision. "I saw her earlier. We shouldn't have invited her, you know."

"I know that *now*. Lord, she's dressed for a funeral. Or a whorehouse. Both?" Melanie tried to joke, pulling her attention from Tennyson and putting it on Kit. "She's really angry. Do you think she'll cause a scene?"

Kit gave her a smile. And a kiss on the nose. So adorable. "Nah. You know Tennyson. She loves drama, and this 'statement' is something everyone will be talking about. Bet she's gone before the band strikes up."

But that didn't prove to be true. They had their first dance and then spent the next hour or so dancing with their college friends, Uncle James, and a few of the flower girls who seemed to enjoy the dance floor more than anyone else. In between it all, she caught glimpses of her former friend, always with a cocktail in hand and a frown affixed to her pretty face. Soon it was time for their send-off.

First, Melanie tossed her bouquet. Her second cousin Lydia caught it after shoving aside her own sister Deidre. Everyone laughed at the silly antics. Melanie noticed afterward that Tennyson hadn't stood with the single women. She'd been off to the side, looking aloof and bothered by something so trivial as the tossing of the bouquet.

Then someone fetched a chair for Kit and handed him the microphone.

"Okay, fellas. Gather round. You know what all this means, right? The guy that catches the garter gets laid tonight? Oh, no. Wait, that's me." He laughed and pulled Melanie onto his lap, angling her legs to the side. She rolled her eyes, laughing along with him. Her mother was going to be upset about Kit saying something so inappropriate in front of their friends. But, hey, it was accurate. He *was* getting laid that night.

Kit pulled up the hem of her dress, revealing her legs. He did an eyebrow waggle thing that elicited more laughter from the crowd. "Here, hold this, honey." He handed her the microphone as the band started playing something that sounded like a burlesque tune.

Her new husband played it up, snagging the satin garter and popping it against her thigh. He slowly started sliding it down, pretending to fan himself and wipe his brow. His fraternity brothers whistled catcalls, and Melanie turned the appropriate shade of vermillion. Kit leaned over and said into the microphone, "I'm a lucky, lucky man."

Finally, he slipped her satin heel off and pulled the garter free.

Melanie made a face and said into the microphone, "Finally, I almost took a nap."

Everyone hooted, and she thought at that very moment with her groom looking adoringly up at her and her friends and family radiating joy around them that she had never been happier in her entire life.

"Okay, off my lap, I gotta get this hot little number off my hands," Kit joked.

Melanie leaned down, kissed him, and then slid from his lap. It was at that moment she felt someone behind her.

She turned.

Tennyson pushed her backward and grabbed the microphone.

"Tenn—" Kit started to say, but Tennyson pressed him back down into the chair. Then she hiked up her dress, straddled him, and sat in his lap.

Angling his head, she kissed him.

Like she was punishing him.

Kit's arms flailed. Everyone around them gasped, and several people made to move toward them but stopped because they didn't really know what to do. Melanie understood because she stood beside them, stunned and . . . stunned.

After one second, two seconds, three, Tennyson broke the kiss and said, "I just wanted you to remember what you'll be missing tonight."

Then she stood, took the microphone, and said, "By the way, Melanie's dad is a gay porn star named Thorn Bighorn. You should check out his movies. I'd personally recommend *Cowboy Up*." Then she tossed the microphone into Kit's lap and stalked away.

Melanie felt like Tennyson had hit her in the head with a tire iron.

She told everyone. The secret Tennyson had pinkie sworn to never tell after they'd watched that video on that afternoon so long ago, the secret her father had guarded for more than twenty years, the shame her sweet-natured father had carried like a load of bricks, had just rolled off Tennyson's lips like it was nothing.

Melanie turned to the videographer, who was still filming. "Stop!"

Around her she could feel everyone's shock. She turned and watched Tennyson's backside disappear, and then she saw her daddy's face.

He looked as if he might actually vomit.

Melanie only knew about what her father had done because she and Tennyson had accidently discovered his secret career after opening a box she thought contained their stickers. She and Tennyson had watched the video because they couldn't not watch something that looked that titillating. What two children had seen that early September day had scarred them, and the two girls had both cried when they realized Melanie's father had been in the movie. They'd put the video back in the packaging, taped up the box, and placed it back on the porch. They'd sworn to never speak of it again.

Later, when Melanie was in college, her father had told her and Hillary what he'd done. He'd been destitute, having eaten the last of the bologna and saltines he'd bought from the deli down the street. With only thirty-six cents in his pocket, he'd decided to use his handsome face and runner's body to make enough money to live on and send to his family. His own father had left when he was a child, and his mother struggled to pay the mortgage on the farm and feed his brothers and sisters. He hadn't liked what he'd done, but he couldn't turn down the money. Once he'd become a successful surgeon and family man, he'd spent a lot of money and time tracking down and destroying the copies of the old seventies porn tapes. Thorn Bighorn, a.k.a. Albert Brevard, had done five movies, playing a Native American in campy western pornos, and while there were a few sites dedicated to vintage porn movies that still mentioned him, that desperate twenty-two-year-old was gone. Hardly anyone would recognize the long-haired, lanky youth as their distinguished surgeon.

It was their family secret, he'd said, but he'd wanted them to know once they were old enough. He never knew that Melanie already knew his secret.

But now . . . now . . . oh God.

Melanie covered her mouth as her father left the room. All the guests were looking at each other, voicing their shock and outrage at Tennyson's display of absolute lunacy. But also, in their eyes was a question.

Was it true?

Kit picked up the microphone, shoving the garter belt into his jacket pocket, and cued the band. They started playing a decade-old Chicago tune, and Melanie rushed over to her mother and sister.

Anne Brevard was the color of ash. She grabbed Melanie's arms and hissed, "How did *she* know?"

Melanie opened her mouth, then shut it. Hillary had tears in her eyes.

"Melanie?" her mother said, voice dripping with ice.

"She's known since we were kids. We opened a box we thought had the stickers we'd been waiting on, but instead inside we found a VHS tape. We were children. We didn't understand what it was, and then we watched it . . . Mother, I'm so sorry. Tennyson swore she would never tell. She promised."

Anne clutched her pearls and wove a bit as if she might pass out. Hillary took her arm, but Anne shrugged her off. "Don't touch me."

"Mother, I think—"

"We have to act as if it's not true," Anne whispered vehemently. "We must pull ourselves together and persevere. Someone find your father. He cannot disappear and look guilty."

Melanie could feel the eyes of the guests on them, so she issued a laugh and then hugged her sister. In her ear, she whispered, "Go find Daddy. Bring him back."

She felt Hillary nod, and then she walked back to Kit. So that everyone could hear, she said, "I knew she would cause trouble. Can you believe the lengths some people go to ruin other people's fun?"

Kit made a confused face as their friends gathered around, everyone looking concerned. "What was all that about? Gay porn?"

He truly had to ask in front of everyone? Couldn't he have sensed that it was something that should be ignored? Melanie rolled her eyes. "It's just crap Tennyson makes up. My father looks like some goofy porn star from the seventies. We found a tape when we were kids, and you know Tennyson. I think the car's here. We should probably say our goodbyes."

Kit nodded. "I'm sorry this happened, sweetheart."

Their friends joined in on the apologies, but Melanie knew everyone would be talking about what Tennyson did. Not to mention looking up Thorn Bighorn as soon as they got home to their computers. Some people would realize that what Tennyson had revealed was true. Some people would talk. Her father could be potentially ruined because Tennyson had to be Tennyson. Because she couldn't accept the one thing Melanie had that she didn't.

Her new husband took her hand, and she realized that the joy that had danced inside her had taken a seat. Dread filled her because everything had changed that night. When they thought of their wedding day, they would remember how Tennyson had taken something so precious and blown it up.

They would remember it as the day the Brevard family lost a piece of itself.

CHAPTER EIGHTEEN

When the doctor entered the ICU waiting room, Melanie didn't need to hear the words that would come from his mouth. She knew already.

Her sister was dead.

"Mrs. Layton?" the doctor queried softly from the door.

"Right here," she managed, closing her eyes and wishing she didn't have to go through what was coming next.

The doctor had kind eyes, and she knew by the way he knotted his dark hands at his sides that he dreaded walking into the waiting room and saying the thing he did not want to say. He glanced around at the mostly empty waiting room. "Is your mother available?"

Dr. Williams had met with both her mother and her several hours ago and given them a truthful account of what Hillary was up against—she was unstable, her organs failing. Her mother had asked for other doctors, men and women she'd known once upon a time when her husband had worked in this very hospital. Dr. Williams had endured her mother's rather rude queries, his dark eyes showing nothing but sympathy and weariness. He'd agreed to call one name he recognized, but so far, that had amounted to nothing.

"My mother stepped out. It's been a rather, um, emotional night. I can—"

"I'll look in the chapel," Joseph interrupted, passing the doctor.

Tennyson's friend didn't look like anyone Melanie would expect her former friend to be seeing. She was certain the guy's barber worked at Cheapcuts, he had no clue what Dolce & Gabbana was, and didn't know what a Lamborghini felt like beneath his really nice rump. Tennyson had always dated and wed men who were of a certain type, or so she'd heard through the grapevine. Joseph was a guy-next-door type who could probably fix a leak and change the filter in a lawn mower. He was exactly what Tennyson needed—a bit of grounding. And it didn't hurt that he was incredibly easy on the eyes.

"Would you like to sit?" Dr. Williams asked, gesturing to the chair beside Tennyson.

Melanie didn't want to sit. She wanted to run. Just leave and go as far as she could manage. On foot. In a car. On a plane.

She didn't want to be there without Kit. Without any member of her family.

It was hugely ironic that the only person sitting with her when she got the second worst news of her life was the person who she'd spent so much time hating for being part of her woes. But even so, something about Tennyson being there felt right. Like she needed someone in her corner, and her former friend might be that perfect person. Which sort of blew her mind.

Tennyson took her hand as if demonstrating that very point.

Melanie looked down at their linked hands. She'd painted her own nails a ladylike pink, and her manicurist had filed them short. She'd worn the plain gold band that Kit had given her on her wedding day to the bridal shower, leaving the big diamond in the safe almost to emphasize how sensible she was compared to Tennyson, whose nails were long and French tipped. Tennyson wore several rings, all of them big jewels with winking diamonds. At her thin wrist, a diamond tennis bracelet sparkled in the horrid fluorescent light.

So very different from one another.

"Mel," Tennyson said, her voice soft.

Melanie looked at her friend. Tennyson's blue-green eyes sparkled with tears, and her lips were bare for once. She hadn't seen Tennyson without makeup since they were preteens, and honestly, the woman didn't look bad without her war paint. In fact, she looked softer, more approachable, more the girl she'd once been. How could this Tennyson be the same one who did such a horrible thing?

Melanie sank onto the hard cushion of the waiting room chair.

The doctor hooked a chair with his foot and pulled it to him. He sat, knees spread, elbows sitting atop, face earnest . . . and sad.

Joseph appeared in the doorway, shook his head, and then shrugged before inching back to the wall, where he stood as if he were guarding the doorway.

Her mother was MIA.

"I don't believe my mother will be joining us for this conversation, Dr. Williams. Just go ahead and tell me," Melanie managed around a tongue that suddenly felt too big for her mouth. Her heart knocked against her ribs, a steady, hard thump that sounded in her ears. She was nearly certain a hooded executioner had poked a hook through her stomach and now scrambled her insides like a skillet of eggs.

Dr. Williams nodded. Gravely. "Your sister's heart was pretty weak, and her organs had long since been compromised."

Was. Had.

Tennyson hadn't let go of her hand, and now Melanie clutched it like she was dangling over a cliff and that was her only hope to survive.

"Mrs. Layton, I'm sorry to say your sister wasn't able to survive the cardiac arrest. We tried all we could to give her a chance, but nevertheless, she succumbed."

He made it sound almost pretty. *Succumbed* didn't sound as bad as *bit the dust* or *turned up her toes* or just plain ol' *died*. It sounded like a good alternative to fighting. Much easier.

"I'm very sorry." His expression was genuine, and she could see that he *was* sorry.

And like that, even though she knew what he'd been going to tell her, the bottom of her world dropped out, and she fell.

Tears slid down her cheeks. She had no way to stop them. In a small voice, she said, "Thank you for trying to save her."

He reached out and took her other hand in his big, warm, soft hands and rubbed it. A kind gesture that only served to break her heart more. But sitting right beside her heartbreak, awaiting its turn, was anger. Deep, disturbing, crackling anger.

Because she sat here as Hillary's only family.

Their bitch of a mother had walked away because of Tennyson. And, yeah, she understood why. Tennyson had outed her dad in front of everyone, but Tennyson hadn't been the one to do the porn movie. Anne had pretended that night away and never let them speak of it. She'd made Albert lie to the hospital board, she'd suppressed every truth, all so everyone would think that none of the Brevards made mistakes. And it hadn't stopped with her father.

She'd done the same with Hillary, helping her sister hide her sickness, never allowing Hillary to talk about her disease, never letting her have power over the bulimia and anorexia. Hillary agreed to therapy, but their mother never wanted it spoken of, like her sister was an embarrassment and her illness wasn't a result of the incessant pressure put upon her to be perfect. No one could know that Anne was letting her oldest daughter kill herself. They also couldn't know what a screwup Melanie could be. Her mother felt obligated to keep a close watch on her every move, scrutinizing every dress, every action, every mistake, as if Melanie was her last hope to prove the Brevards were above everyone else.

So, yeah, something seethed inside her.

Not to mention, Kit was still at the beach with Charlotte.

And her kids were probably stopping for effing Starbucks before coming to the hospital.

And here she sat, hearing about her sister's death with Tennyson and a man she didn't know. How wrong was that? How had she deserved to be the one to bear all the initial heartbreak?

Melanie pulled her hands away from both Tennyson and Dr. Williams. She sucked in a deep breath and exhaled noisily. She stood. "Okay, I'm fine. What do I need to do next?"

The doctor hadn't expected her to rebound so quickly. He blinked. "Uh, I will, uh, talk to—"

"Mel," Tennyson interrupted, rising beside her and demanding her attention. Of course. That's what Tennyson had always done best, right? But when she looked at her old friend, Melanie softened. Tears streamed down Tennyson's cheeks, and her nose was ruby red. She looked unsteady and not like a woman who stormed mile-high walls without a blink. "Are you sure you're okay?"

Melanie swiped at her damp face as if she could erase any evidence of her weakness. "Sure. I'm fine. I just need to make some calls." To prove it, Melanie stalked toward the window that gave her a view of inky darkness and a mostly empty parking lot.

She spoke to her lonely reflection. "I guess I need to call Hillary's ex-husband, Kyle. Though I don't know why. He's a proven asshole. Then I need to call Osborn Funeral Home and see about arrangements. Is there a death certificate? I think someone has to sign that, right? I can do it. Since I'm obviously the only person here."

On the edge. She was right on the edge of tipping over into madness. Into something she couldn't stop. Into a rage. A hissy fit. A place she didn't want to touch, like floating above in the water, refusing to feel a muddy lake bottom. She couldn't let her toes sink into the muck. She had to stay afloat, treading the water, shoving all the feelings aside, because if she let herself go there, she'd be stuck.

"Uh, I can check on that for you, Mrs. Layton."

Melanie watched in the reflection as Dr. Williams rose and looked at Tennyson as if she might tell him what to do. Surely, this doctor had seen every reaction there was to grief? Or maybe he didn't know what to do with a dysfunctional, repressed forty-six-year-old woman whose only defense was to be efficient and refuse to crumble? Maybe they hadn't taught him that in medical school.

Tennyson ran a finger under her eyelashes and sniffed. "I'll stay here with her."

He nodded. "Again, I'm so sorry, Mrs. Layton."

Melanie gave a nod. "Thank you. I'm sorry, too. Very, very sorry."

He walked out, and for a moment Tennyson stood, staring at her back as she looked out the window.

Finally, Melanie turned around. "What?"

"Nothing."

"You can go, you know. I've got everything here under control."

Tennyson gave her a soft smile. "I'm sure you think you do."

"No. I do. I've been through much worse. When Daddy shot himself, I had to deal with all that. Horrible business. Replacing carpet, dealing with the coroner's office, and an ensuing investigation. This will be a piece of cake. I mean, yeah, they both killed themselves, but this will be easier, don't you think? So, by all means, take your cute guy and go on home."

"Yeah, but I don't think I will."

"He's really good looking, by the way," Melanie said.

"Yeah, he is. But I'm not concerned about him. He's a tough guy and used to waiting." So Tennyson was staying because of her. She probably thought Melanie was going to lose her shit or something. Didn't she know that Melanie didn't have that luxury? A ladylike tear or two? Yes. Breaking down? Not acceptable.

Tennyson stepped toward her and just stood there. Like she didn't know what to do.

"Suit yourself," Melanie said, pulling her phone out and calling her mother. The phone rang. And rang. And went to voice mail. When she clicked end, she saw that Emma had indeed gone to Starbucks and wanted to know if she wanted a skinny vanilla latte. She typed no thanks and put the phone into her pocket. "You don't want Starbucks, do you? Because Emma is there now."

"No."

Melanie could feel something inside her rising like magma. Was that what that red stuff was called? Yeah, it became lava when it erupted. She felt like melted rock churned in her gut, threatening to gush forth and spew everywhere. She sucked in a breath. And another. And one more for good measure. *Push it all down, Melanie. Don't let it up.* "I'm good. I'm good."

Tennyson narrowed her eyes. "Come on."

"What?"

"Come on. Let's go."

Melanie pulled away and looked around the waiting room, remembering she was still in a public space. The mother and son huddling in the corner stared at her with abject sorrow on their faces. They knew the score—doctors went in and out of this horrible room all day and night, consulting families, holding fate in their hands. If she were a betting woman, she'd wager these two had seen a few "we're so sorry for your loss" faces before. Something about those two watching her, the coffee stain in the shape of an amoeba on the green floor, and the horrible landscapes on the wall beside plants that looked like many of the patients beyond the double doors—barely hanging in there—made her livid. Made her feel like someone needed to wipe everything away. Just toss out the worn furniture, tear out the plants, throw the ugly paintings across the room. Just destroy it all. She thought about being the one who did that. The image of her stomping around and Godzillaing everything in her path made her giggle. She used the toe of her tasteful sandal to tap the stain. "What do you think this shape looks like?"

Tennyson looked down. "I don't know. Jesus?"

Melanie started laughing harder. "You don't know what Jesus looks like."

"And you do?" Tennyson asked, arching an eyebrow. Wow. Her brows were pretty. Who had pretty eyebrows, anyway?

"I'm closer to God than you are."

"Because you go to church? Okay. Whatever." But Tennyson smiled through her tears. Then she moved closer to her. "You want a smoke?"

"Here?" Melanie looked at the **NO SMOKING** sign by the open double doors leading to the hallway. She absolutely wanted a cigarette. Like, desperately.

"No. Back at my place." She moved closer and lowered her voice. "I have a few joints."

"Tennyson," Melanie said, knowing her eyes were about to pop.

"Don't tell the cop. I actually got Marc to get them. I was going to take them to Hillary. Weed makes you crazy hungry, and I thought . . . you know." Tennyson looked totally earnest.

"You were going to take Hillary marijuana?" she whispered.

Tennyson shrugged.

Melanie started laughing. "You're crazy. I mean, truly bonkers, but I sort of love that about you. I'm not sure I know anyone who would procure illegal drugs to give my sister but you."

"So? You wanna?"

"I can't leave. My sister just died. I have to—"

Tennyson held up a hand. "Whoa, hey, this is exactly the best time to do this. Like, I think Hillary would approve. I think she'd tell everyone waiting on you to do everything responsible, dutiful, tactful, and appropriate to fuck off."

"Hillary would never say *fuck*."

Tennyson rolled her eyes. "She'd hold up her three fingers and say *read between the lines*."

Exactly.

Melanie stood for a moment, glancing around at the nearly empty space around them. At the handsome police officer leaning against the wall in the hallway. Then she looked back at Tennyson, who wore the same kind of T-shirt dress she'd always loved in high school. And Tretorns. She didn't know they still made those. This woman didn't look like the Tennyson with the Birkin purse who had sashayed back into her life and busted it open. This woman looked like the friend she'd once loved like a sister.

Her sister.

Hilly was dead.

"Let's go," Melanie said.

CHAPTER NINETEEN

It had been a long time since Tennyson had smoked a joint.

She forgot how weird marijuana made her feel. Like her skin was slippy and she could meld herself into the couch and live there forever. It also made her want cereal. Not the fiber kind, either. The big honey-comb ones filled with sugar that her mother used to buy her as a prize at the grocery store. She hadn't had a big bowl of that particular sin in many years.

"We should order some cereal," Tennyson said, taking another hit and passing it to Melanie, who wore an old T-shirt of Andrew's and a pair of workout pants. Melanie's dress sat folded neatly over her evening handbag, which sat on the Eames chair in the corner.

Melanie took a toke, fanning the air. "I don't think you can order cereal like you can order pizza."

"So why is that not a thing?"

Melanie shrugged. "Are you that high?"

"I don't think so. I mean, maybe? It's been a while since I've done drugs," Tennyson said.

Melanie sat up and looked at her, wide eyed. "Have you done other drugs? Like real drugs?"

Tennyson made a face. "I did a lot of things I don't want to talk about."

"Why not?"

Because she was ashamed of much of what she'd done. Not ridiculously ashamed like Melanie's father had obviously been, but ashamed enough to not want to admit to doing lines of coke in a club bathroom, a threesome with a B-list actor and his girlfriend, or the one summer she became a dominatrix so she could pay rent. Her memory was scarred by that particular summer, which had concluded with the affair with Rolfe. Seeing those two lines on a pregnancy test for the second time in her life had been enough to bring her crashing back to reality. She'd just turned twenty-three years old and knew that she had to get her shit together if she were going to be a mom.

At first, she hadn't been sure if she could actually raise a child. Her world was unstable. Rolfe had refused to leave his wife and had gotten heavily into the drug scene. Tennyson had not been able to afford to stay in school, even with the dominatrix stint, and had taken a job as a singing waitress at a Times Square tourist spot. She had no real prospects with her career and was days away from packing it in and moving back to Shreveport. At that point, she hadn't known what she was going to do about the pregnancy. And then she'd received the wedding invitation.

In some ways, her horrible actions on Melanie's wedding night had driven her into the marriage with Stephen. She'd been so ashamed of herself for having gotten drunk while she was pregnant and then doing what she'd done, that it had made saying yes to Stephen and falling into a version of a life she had never wanted attractive. She'd be doing something good—giving Stephen the chance to be a father and husband. She told herself she wouldn't miss her old life with auditions, postshow drinks with the cast, or the search for true love. Kit now belonged to Melanie, so that chapter was closed, Rolfe had bailed, and her bank account was nonexistent.

So she said yes.

Suddenly, she had a housekeeper, a limitless credit card, and a husband who didn't love her. And though Stephen was the kindest of men, who loved Andrew wholly and unconditionally, the man was gay and wasn't going to love her as a husband should. But he'd showed her what it was to be respected and to enjoy a certain lifestyle. Stephen had taught her how to be an adult, make sacrifices, and enjoy the best life had to offer. She'd never had reason to do drugs again. She'd been hooked on Chanel, private jets, and her son's drooling smile.

In the end, she'd had zero regrets about marrying Stephen Abernathy.

"I may have done a few drugs back in college," she said, rising from the sofa. "I definitely have the munchies, though. Let's see if I have something to snack on that isn't diet or healthy."

Melanie stubbed out the joint in the makeshift ashtray—an empty rinsed-out container for caviar the caterers had left—and followed her to the kitchen. "I never smoked weed before. It's very smelly."

Tennyson laughed. "Yeah, there's that. You didn't smoke in college?"

"Cigarettes, but only in secret. I didn't want people to think I was that kind of girl," she said, opening the jar of salsa Tennyson set on the cabinet.

"And what kind of girl is that?" Tennyson said, ripping open the tortilla chips with her teeth. Lord, her veneers had cost a small fortune. She didn't need to break one and have to go to the dentist. She'd rather go to the gynecologist than the dentist. She didn't have to look up her ob-gyn's nose—just observe his bald spot.

"I don't even know. That's so stupid to even say something like that." Melanie made a face.

"No, you're just saying what you think you should say to someone like your mother. She made you super conscious of everything you did . . . and do."

Melanie nodded her head slowly. "Maybe. I never thought about it that way."

"You just like everyone to get along, and so you say the things to make that happen. It's a defense mechanism." Tennyson snagged a chip and went to town with the salsa. "Dang, this is good salsa. Awesome Annie's."

"I've had it before, and honestly, store-bought salsa from a jar would taste like heaven right now. I've been on a diet for the past six weeks. Ever since I saw how incredible you looked." Melanie dug a chip into the container and made a face. "And then there's Charlotte with her size 4 bikini. Ugh."

"Is that the cow who tried to mount Kit at the engagement party?"

Melanie sighed. "Yeah. She works with him. It seems she's brilliant, climbs mountains, and laughs at everything he says. He professes she's 'just a coworker,' but it doesn't feel that way. I think she's after more than a promotion."

"First, don't sell yourself short, Melanie. You're an incredibly attractive woman, even more so because you're very unaware of it. You're a natural beauty who doesn't need the artifice of plastic surgery or fillers. Second, have you talked to Kit about how she makes you feel?"

"We're in therapy."

Tennyson ate five more chips, brushing the crumbs from her chin. "That's good. So what does he say about your concerns?"

"Nothing. He essentially implies that I'm crazy."

Well, that figured. She was nearly certain that was the exact thing Robert said when they were in therapy. Anytime she remarked on being concerned about the time he spent at work and that he could be tempted by the ambitious junior partners, he'd say, "You're imagining things, Tennyson."

But she hadn't been. And to prove her suspicions, she set up a sting. She found his daily planner, noted when he was "advising JL," and hired a private eye who, using the building across the street, managed to get incriminating photographic evidence. Robert was dumb enough to schedule his "mentoring sessions" at the same time several times a week. Which made it easy for Tennyson to barge past the administrative assistant who kept shouting, "He's in a private meeting," at her back and catch the man who said she was imagining things with his head between Julie Littman's slender thighs.

"You're not crazy." Tennyson walked over to the fridge and pulled out a crisp sauvignon blanc.

"I'm not?" Melanie's tone suggested she already knew this.

"No, a woman's intuition is a strong thing." Tennyson rooted through the pantry, looking for the travel bag of goodies Andrew had stashed on a shelf. She was certain he had put peanut M&M's inside. She found the bag, grabbed the family-size bag of candy, and reemerged. "You need to put an end to that shit, Melly."

Melanie scooped up more salsa with a chip and popped it into her mouth. She chewed for a few minutes, making thinking faces. "Yeah, but I can't. If Kit wants to cheat, he will. I can't follow him around or guilt him into not doing it if he's *going* to do it."

"No, no." Tennyson wagged her finger, grabbing two goblets and a bottle of sauvignon blanc. "I mean, yeah, technically you can't stop him, but you don't let him stay in the situation he's in. It's like leaving a hungry woman in a room full of donuts. Eventually, she's going to eat a donut."

Melanie's face flashed with pain.

"Damn it, Mel. I'm sorry. I shouldn't have . . . that was a stupid analogy." For a good half an hour, she'd forgotten what had happened that night. She'd forgotten about Hillary's death and Melanie's near breakdown. About how horrible she felt watching Melanie floundering around, looking for someone to throw her a rope. She hadn't planned on bringing the woman back to her house, but she knew Melanie had needed someone to help her.

And there had been no one else there to do it but Tennyson.

Melanie schooled her features. "I know you didn't mean anything by it. You don't intentionally hurt . . ." Melanie didn't finish her sentence. Instead she shook her head and ate another chip.

Tennyson poured the wine into the goblets and handed one to Melanie.

"I should go. I've avoided dealing with my mother and family for long enough. My mother may be a queen bitch, but she's still my mother. She's just lost her daughter, and that's no easy thing, especially as it leaves her completely alone. Anne is a hard woman, but beneath, she's not really as tough as she likes people to believe. I saw that with my father's death."

Tennyson's stomach twisted. Albert Brevard had been a good man, never shouting at the girls when they rooted through his office looking for a stapler and willingly leaving his work behind to take them for ICEEs on hot summer evenings. He had been a gifted surgeon, very dedicated to his patients, but when she and Melanie had been around, he'd given them his total attention. Tennyson had been so angry, so bent on vengeance that she'd dragged that man down in order to hurt Melanie. When she'd uttered those fateful words into the microphone that night, she hadn't punished Melanie as she intended; she'd punished the entire Brevard family.

As she'd walked away, dropping the microphone in Kit's lap, she'd felt the absolute satisfaction of making her old friend pay for stealing her man, but then she'd caught sight of Albert's face. At that moment, the horror of what she'd actually done had rolled over her. The full implication hit her in the parking lot, and she'd vomited behind the oleanders on the fifteenth hole.

Everyone in the Brevard family had blamed her for ruining Albert Brevard's career . . . and some had declared her responsible for the man's suicide years later.

Maybe that was true to some degree, but she also knew that eventually Albert's short-lived career in porn films would have been discovered.

Those sorts of secrets always found the light of day, especially once AOL dragged everyone into a whole new online world with databases and a massive porn network. Vintage porn was fairly collectible, and collectors loved the vampy, campy late sixties and seventies porn, which was exactly what Albert had done with titles like *Barebackin* and *Bronco Willy*.

Still, she'd played a part and couldn't make amends for the promise she'd broken in a snit of outrage. Her words, so angrily declared, had been like the old adage about gossip. Pluck a chicken at the top of a mountain, and then try to gather all the scattered feathers.

Impossible.

"About that," Tennyson said, running her nail along the veined marble. "I've never actually apologized for breaking my promise."

"What?" Melanie looked confused.

"When we found that tape, I pinkie swore that I wouldn't tell. That I would forget what we'd seen. I broke that promise."

"In spectacular fashion," Melanie murmured.

Regret prickled up her spine. "I was angry."

Melanie snorted. "I actually figured that out."

"You invited me to the wedding to rub my nose in the fact you'd won Kit," Tennyson said, still refusing to look at her old friend. "I couldn't believe you would do something so cruel, and I wanted to . . . hurt you."

"But I didn't invite you to rub your nose in anything. I invited you because I couldn't stand the rift between us. We'd been best friends, and the thought of you not being there with me when I got married broke my heart. In hindsight, I guess it may have looked that way, like I wanted to hurt you, but surely you knew me well enough to know I wouldn't do something so mean spirited. I just missed you, Teeny, and hoped you'd realized Kit and I loved each other. I thought maybe you'd get over it and want to be there." Melanie's voice had grown small.

Tennyson looked up. "You invited me because you *missed* me?"

Melanie lifted a shoulder. "Yeah. I thought if you came, you would see that Kit and I were . . . I just never expected you to be so cruel. That's not you. You're a lot of things, but you were never a mean girl."

The thought that Melanie had sent the invitation because she missed their friendship had never crossed Tennyson's mind. Maybe because she couldn't fathom doing something like that. When she'd opened that envelope, she was three days off finding out she was pregnant. *Panic* wasn't even the word for where she was in figuring out her life. She'd spent too many years hanging around a different kind of crowd—spoiled heiresses with spoons up their nose and dislike in their eyes and guys who hustled and thought nothing of stepping on people in their climb to the top. Tennyson had grown accustomed to people who had motives for everything they did. Reading that elegant script inviting her to the marriage of Melanie Elizabeth to Christopher Douglas Layton, she'd burned with fury. Then she'd crumpled into grief over losing the man she thought would be hers. She'd felt betrayed and angry enough to do something rash and uncaring.

And she'd done just that.

"It never occurred to me that you truly wanted me there. I don't know why I didn't see that. It was a hard year for me. No excuse for what I did, but maybe I could give you a little background on where I was in my life. You asked me about drugs. I was into that scene. Participating in that irresponsible selfishness led me to getting pregnant with Andrew. His biological father was a small-time director who had a coke problem and a wife. I had been booted off a low-budget horror film for coming in drunk. I didn't have money, a man, or a clue about what to do about the baby. I just knew I wasn't going to have an abortion or pretend my mistake away. I had already done that once before. So, yeah, it wasn't good for me the day I got the invitation. But you didn't deserve what I did. Nothing really justifies what I did. I can't take it back, but I can say I'm sorry, Melly. I've been sorry for a long time."

A few seconds ticked by, and Tennyson hoped that her old friend might offer her the forgiveness she never knew she craved so much. But Melanie didn't. Instead she looked down at her fingernails. "I should go. I'm sure people have been texting and calling asking where I am and if I'm okay. It was super irresponsible to leave everyone. It was selfish."

Tennyson shook her head. "Don't do that. You needed a moment to deal. They are not the only people dealing with a loss, Melly. It's okay to need some time, to be a little selfish."

Melanie shrugged. "Maybe so. I probably shouldn't have smoked a joint, though."

"I don't think it hurt."

"It's illegal." As Melanie said those words her eyes widened a little as if she truly realized that she'd not only been a little selfish, but she'd also broken the law.

"Not in some states."

"But here it is."

Tennyson smiled. "You can get it medically. I think."

"I don't have glaucoma, Teeny," Melanie said, her mouth tightening back into that now familiar disapproving line.

"But you have Anne for a mother."

Melanie stared at the refrigerator for a few seconds and said, "Well, that's true."

The sound of the front door opening made both of them turn. Andrew called out. "Hey, anyone home?"

"In the kitchen," Tennyson shouted.

Her son appeared in the doorway, still wearing his suit sans the tie and the tucked-in shirt. His hair stuck up in a few places, and his mouth looked tight. His gaze landed on Melanie, his eyes widened, and then his shoulders sagged in what she could only guess was relief. "Oh, here you are. Emma's been calling you for the last half hour."

"My phone's in the living room," Melanie said. She looked away, guilt reflected in the brown depths of her eyes.

"They're all at the hospital and—" He stopped and made a face. Then he inhaled. "Has someone been smoking weed?"

Tennyson wasn't sure how to answer that.

Melanie brushed the crumbs from the counter, sweeping them into her hand. She tossed them into the sink. Looking at Andrew, she lifted one shoulder. "We may have."

"You *may* have?" He looked at Tennyson with a gobsmacked expression that was both endearing and irritating. "I don't know what you two have been doing at a critical time for this family, but we really need to get back to the hospital. Everyone is really upset."

"Melanie needed a few minutes away," Tennyson said. Melanie remained quiet, studying her fingernails.

"Do you even know what has happened while y'all were here drinking and doing illegal drugs?" Andrew sounded very much like a parent.

"I *know* what happened," Melanie said, straightening and heading toward the living area where she'd left her clothes and purse. "I was there by myself when my sister died. None of my family was there. My husband's in Florida, my mother is more concerned about being right than present, and my children are obviously more concerned with lattes, so don't lecture me or your mother on where I should have been."

Andrew stared at her wide eyed as she passed by him. Then he looked at Tennyson. "What's happening here?"

"I think your soon-to-be mother-in-law is telling you to get your head out of your ass. Does anyone *ever* think about her? She does so much for that family, and they just take and take."

Andrew tilted his head. "I thought you two didn't like each other?"

Melanie breezed back in. "We don't. I went with her because she had weed."

Her reply was so saucy that Tennyson turned around to hide her smile. Then she schooled her features into something more suiting the situation and turned back to her son. "Take Melanie back to the hospital. You're right. It's time she was with her family."

Melanie had her dress over her arm, but the only shoes she had were a pair of pumps, which looked ridiculous with the workout pants and T-shirt.

"Hold on," Tennyson said, jogging toward her bedroom. She entered her enormous closet and flipped the custom shoe cabinet back to reveal her sandal and flip-flop collection. She snagged a pair of flat Tory Burch thongs she'd never worn and went back to the kitchen. "Here's a bag for your clothes and a pair of sandals. You can't go out in those heels."

Melanie gave her a small smile. "That's nice of you."

"I can be nice. Every full moon or so, once I make a sacrificial offering."

"It's not a full moon," Melanie said, tugging off the pumps and sliding the thongs on.

"Eh, the weed made me do it," she said, eyeing Andrew on the phone, most likely with Emma.

Melanie shoved the dress inside. "Thank you."

"You're welcome. And if you need anything, call someone else," she joked, feeling suddenly vulnerable in front of the woman she'd once known better than anyone.

"Yeah," Melanie said.

Then Melanie reached out and gave her a quick squeeze. It was the first time she'd voluntarily touched Tennyson, outside of zipping her up in the dressing room weeks ago. Tennyson closed her eyes briefly against the wave of emotion that engulfed her.

Then her old friend released her and walked out of the kitchen, leaving Tennyson with a full bottle of wine, half a bag of Tostitos, and a small sprig of hope uncurling in her heart.

CHAPTER TWENTY

Almost nine weeks later

Melanie studied the basil planted in the galvanized bucket and tried to remember if Hillary had said to pinch off the blooms or let it go ahead and seed. Hillary had always helped her plant the herbs in her kitchen garden every early March. Her sister had been brilliant when it came to gardening and using herbs in cooking. She always knew what a pinch of rosemary or a dash of oregano could do for a dish. Sad thing was, her sister hadn't been able to overcome her own roadblocks to use the homegrown tomatoes for a savory red sauce or batter the eggplants for crispy chips. And now her sister was dead. And had been for eight weeks, five days, fourteen hours, and a few minutes. Not that she was keeping track.

"Mom?" Emma called from the kitchen.

Melanie shoved the trowel into the rich loam and made sure her pack of cigarettes was tucked into Jerry the frog's butt. She wasn't sure why she was still hiding her habit other than she didn't want to deal with exposing it days before the wedding. Besides, she didn't light one up often. She usually smoked maybe a single pack in three or four months. Of course, since Hillary died, she'd smoked a pack every two weeks. The only time she felt peace come was when she sat alone in the garden, taking a drag on a cigarette, pretending everything would be okay.

Of course, relying on something that gave people cancer to feel better was dangerous, ridiculous, and selfish on her part. Her sister had died because she'd refused to deal with her feelings. Hillary ate them and then vomited them up. Melanie knew she, too, was using something unhealthy as a coping mechanism. She should join Pure Barre with Emma. Or do Jazzercise or Zumba. Those activities should be her coping mechanisms, not sucking in tar, nicotine, and whatever else they used to make the addictive little devils these days.

"Out here," she called to her daughter, spraying a little bug spray into the air.

"Hey," Emma said from the open door. "Wow, it's hot out here. Why are you gardening in the heat of the day?"

"I guess it's not the best time, but I saw the blooms on this basil and couldn't remember if Hillary told me to wait and let it seed or pinch it off and dry it. I just couldn't remember."

Emma gave her a soft smile. "Why don't you leave it? We can look up how best to regrow basil on the internet. Besides, I have some things to go over with you if you have the time."

Melanie brushed her hands on her old shorts and walked into the blessedly cool kitchen. "I need to get ready for the lingerie shower, though I'm not sure if I will ever be ready for that."

Emma chuckled. "Um, I'm not sure I will be, either. My friends have promised to keep it rated R and not rated X. I reminded Julianna that you and Tennyson would be there. Of course, who knows what Tennyson might bring. She's very big on sexual empowerment. Those were her exact words, so I'm a bit frightened to open her gift."

Melanie had bought her daughter some soft PJ Harlow camisoles and matching satin boxers. They were pretty and functional. She was certain that Emma would love them because she'd been wanting some since she'd spied them at a local boutique. Melanie knew people would think her gift was boring, but sometimes a girl needed a bit of practicality. "I heard her saying something about a dildo collection, so . . ."

Emma nearly dropped her teacup. "Oh my God. You're not serious?"

"Just kidding."

"Mom," Emma said, her eyes all googly. "You *didn't* just make that joke."

Melanie started to apologize, but then realized she didn't need to. She had a freaking sense of humor, and her daughter was an adult. "I did. Is Tennyson still dating that cop? She seems extraordinarily, well, happy. Maybe because she no longer has to use her collection."

"My ears are bleeding," Emma joked, her blue eyes sparkling. Melanie hadn't seen her truly look light and happy in weeks. Losing one's aunt and making a million decisions all the while balancing medical school wasn't exactly a breeze. "Yeah, she's still seeing him, though Tennyson balked at calling it *dating*. Still, he's over at the house a lot. And I don't think it's all sexy times. He grilled some steaks for us the other night, and it was fun seeing her rendered speechless by him. Joseph's a really nice guy, and he totally calls her out on her bullshit. Uh, pardon my language."

"Good. She needs a guy like that, and I'm happy she's happy." Melanie couldn't believe she felt that way about Tennyson, but she did. For the last seven weeks, the wedding preparations had taken a back seat to Melanie's grief. Suddenly besting Tennyson didn't seem so important. Honestly, not many of the decisions they'd been making—a deep lilac or a periwinkle for the ribbon on the groom's boutonniere?—seemed super important. Who the hell would even remember? Who really cared?

When one's sister died, superfluous things like deciding between tuberoses or calla lilies don't seem so life-altering. Not that Emma truly understood this. She still cared very much about the preparations and all the little details that took a wedding from "ho-hum to fabulous." Out of the mouth of Marc Mallow, no doubt.

"Yeah, she's been a little bit easier to deal with here lately. I guess with Aunt Hilly and everything, Tennyson decided to lay off being the supreme diva she is," Emma said, unwrapping a tea bag and plopping it into the cup. She set the kettle to boiling and pulled a stool up to the counter. "How are you doing? You seemed a little lost in the kitchen garden. You do that a lot lately."

Did her daughter suspect about the smoking? No, she was super careful to hide the evidence and spray Deep Woods bug spray around the area after she smoked. "It's been hard to concentrate. I miss Hillary. We talked almost every day, and she was . . . well, you know things between me and your Gee Ma aren't the best."

"Gee Ma loves you, Mom."

"I know she does, but our relationship has always been . . . difficult. I guess sometimes it's like that between mothers and daughters. Not us, I hope."

Emma smiled. "You've always been such a good mother to me."

Melanie had tried so hard to be a good mother, mostly because her own hadn't been there for her when she was growing up. Anne had worked as a partner in a law firm specializing in taxes and bankruptcy. Her mother had been very diligent in her work, spending long hours at the office and bringing even more work home. She'd never bought a minivan so she could run carpool or brought snacks to any of Melanie's softball practices. Vacation had been a week in a Mediterranean resort with someone to mind Hillary and Melanie while she and Albert relaxed on the beach. *Hands-on* had never been a descriptor for Anne Brevard.

So Melanie had busted her ass to be the opposite, minivan and all.

"Thanks. I tried."

The back door opened, and Kit came in, his head pinning his cell phone to his shoulder as he muttered, "Yeah, yeah, okay, sounds good."

He plopped his briefcase down on the counter and clicked off his phone. "Whew, what a day."

"Hey, Daddy."

"Hello, pumpkin. You aren't here for more money, are you?" Kit asked.

Emma laughed. "No, but if you've got extra, I'm not opposed."

"So what are you two doing?" he asked, snagging a banana from the top of the fruit basket, knocking an apple off the counter. It hit the floor and lob-rolled to Melanie's feet. She picked it up, noting the damage, and walked it to the trash can.

"Just finished class and about to go over my list. One last time. Marc is frantically trying to get everything confirmed before the rehearsal tomorrow. Mom and I just need to record final numbers on everything, and we should be set. I still can't believe I'll be a married woman in a few days. So weird, but exciting." Emma pulled the chirping teapot off the stove and poured the water into her cup. A fragrant curl of steam escaped. Chai.

"I'm not sure either your mother or I are ready to let you grow up. Can't you play Barbies or something instead?" Kit joked.

"If you build me a Barbie DreamHouse," Emma said, taking a sip.

Kit smiled before glancing toward the stained-glass turtle Emma made in the third grade that hung in the kitchen window. Her husband looked a little . . . something. *Disturbed* would be the closest description. Or maybe more like off-kilter. "Tennyson brought by a check today. She was downtown for something and came by with it."

"A check? For what? I told her we would pay for our daughter's wedding," Melanie said, feeling aggravation rear its head. Why did the woman have to have her hand in everything? Just because she had lots of money didn't mean everyone else depended on her to pay their way. The woman was too much. The floral spray Tennyson sent for Hillary's funeral had to be carried in by two people. The monstrosity had loomed over all the other arrangements, asserting Tennyson even in the somber occasion. The woman needed someone to dial her down a few notches on all levels. "She's just ridicu—"

"We paid the deposit on the bistro where we're having the rehearsal, remember? She's reimbursing you and Dad," Emma interrupted.

"Oh. Well. Okay." Melanie felt bad for jumping to conclusions. She was good at that. Or so Kit liked to imply.

Kit strolled out of the kitchen, leaving his banana peel on the counter. His phone and briefcase also cluttered the space she'd cleaned before going into the garden.

Melanie tried not to be irritated, because her husband had been so patient and kind with her over the past weeks. He seemed to feel guilty for having stayed in Florida for his presentation before driving back with Charlotte and arriving a full twenty-four hours after her sister had died. Melanie couldn't deny that his failure to be there for her had been disappointing. Yeah, his presentation had been important to him, but was it more important than being with his wife, who'd just lost her sister?

She wasn't really buying that it was.

Once Melanie had left Tennyson's house, she'd been engulfed in duty—signing the death certificate, making arrangements, picking out Hillary's favorite dress to wear even though her mother had elected to have a private viewing for the family and closed casket for the general public. She'd made too many pots of coffee, selected the flowers for the casket spray, contacted the pastor, and every other detail that went with the passing of someone as young as Hillary, all the while trying to cope with the waves of intense grief that washed over her. Once Kit had arrived, he'd patted her back, offered her a shoulder, and made himself a bit more useful around the house.

Still, his messiness aggravated her.

For the next thirty minutes, she and Emma went over the checklist Marc had sent. Mostly it consisted of confirming numbers for everything from the number of honorary cake and punch servers to those who checked a vegan/gluten-free option. She and Emma chuckled over her uncle John making his own box on the RSVP titled "meat and flour" lover. Of course he'd spelled *flour* as *flower*, which made it that much more amusing, so she'd handwritten *flower lover* under his name on the place card.

After they'd emailed the list to Marc, Emma carried herself off to get ready for her shower and bachelorette party. Instead of a traditional bachelorette party, her friends were throwing her a cocktail lingerie shower, and then they would take limos to drag queen bingo at a local bar and grill. The theme for the evening was Getting Married's Not a Drag.

Melanie figured Tennyson would be in her element with all the sequins, glitter, and fake boobs.

She headed toward the bedroom, intent on starting the shower so she could wash her hair. She'd asked her stylist to give her layers and highlights that made her look younger. The mission had been accomplished, but it required a good ten minutes more of style time. But the end result took years off her face. Not to mention, the upside to grieving was weight loss. She'd dropped another ten pounds and found a muted blue mother-of-the-bride dress that had a little sparkle, a plunging back, and a cute, small mermaid-ish swoosh just below her knees. And, bonus, it was a size 8. She was rather proud of how good she looked in it. She couldn't wait for Kit to see her on Saturday. Their therapy had been going really well. It was as if her sister's death had allowed her to open up and reveal some of the issues she'd been so quick to hide from her husband. Even though her heart still hurt over Hillary's death, she felt like her marriage was finally on the right track.

Kit sat on the bed, still clad in his work clothes, staring at the framed picture of the family in Turks and Caicos. Something about his expression made her feel itchy.

"What? Thinking about going back? We could go for our anniversary," she said, stopping and studying him.

"I need to talk to you," he said.

Something in his tone made her stomach drop down to her recently manicured toenails. He sounded so serious. And sad. "What's wrong?"

He sucked in a deep breath. "Look, I know things are really, really stressful for you these days. With the wedding and Hillary's death, you've had more than you can handle."

She walked over to the bed and sank down beside him. Taking his hand, she looked up at him with a small smile. "It's been very stressful, but we're getting through it. After this weekend, things will go back to normal. Hopefully."

He gave her hand a squeeze and then released it. He set the frame on the bedside table. "So maybe I haven't been completely honest with you in therapy. You've been through a lot, especially with Hillary, so I didn't want to put any other burdens on you. You needed time to heal, and I think you're getting there. But I have been struggling myself here lately. Work has been difficult. You know how tough it is getting the permits and lining up all the vendors. I'm up to my eyeballs."

"I hope you haven't avoided being honest with me because you wanted to protect me. Just because I'm grieving my sister doesn't mean you have to hide your feelings. If work is stressing you out, you should say so."

Kit shrugged. "Yeah, work has been tough, that and some other things. Tennyson came by today."

Melanie rose and padded into the bathroom, her stomach still fluttering with a weird premonition. It was as if she'd seen this scenario played out before. Maybe in a dream or a movie. Something ominous. She opened the shower door and twisted the knobs to the perfect temperature combination. "You told me she came by. To repay the rehearsal venue deposit."

Kit followed her into the large bathroom, sinking onto the upholstered ottoman in the center. She could see his toenail clippings on the oriental rug beneath the linen skirt. She'd asked him fifteen million times to collect his stupid clippings. He never did.

Her husband sat with knees spread and hands clasped. "Yeah, she brought the check."

Melanie wanted to strip out of the sweaty T-shirt and old gym shorts, but something about the vibe in the bathroom kept her in her clothes. She and Kit hadn't had sex since Destin. Her hopes of resuming a closer, intimate relationship afterward had flown out the window with her sister's death. Just getting through the day and the incessant wedding preparations had been hard enough. Each night she stayed up while Kit went to bed, watching the Hallmark channel, working on crocheting the scarf she'd started for Hillary and never finished. For some reason, it seemed really important to complete the colorful accessory her sister would never wear, and weirdly enough she found great comfort in the characters on television getting their nauseating happily ever after. She did not, however, go to bed and take solace in the arms of her husband. Maybe that was what this was about.

Kit liked sex. And he'd initiated it several times over the past week or so only to have her start crying. She'd felt bad about that, but she couldn't seem to want to be physical. It made her feel too alive, which made her feel guilty. And sad.

"So . . . ?" Melanie finally asked when he'd stared at his hands long enough.

"I think we need to consider a separation," Kit said.

Melanie blinked. "What?"

"Just a trial separation. You know?"

At that moment, Melanie knew exactly how Wile E. Coyote felt when the wrecking ball came out of nowhere and smashed him into a cliffside. "You want to file for separation? Like, as in the first step of dissolving our marriage?"

Kit pressed his hands toward her. "No, that's not what I said. I said a trial. We don't need to do anything rash. Just see how we feel being apart for a little while. Things have been very tense, and I'm struggling to feel any sort of joy in life, Melanie."

She wanted to shout *join the effing crowd* but could find no words.

Kit continued. "I just don't know what I want anymore. I thought I knew, but I'm nearly fifty years old. I keep wondering: Is this it? Is this all there is? And I'm sure you feel the same way."

Melanie opened her mouth, but, again, no words came out. Her husband wondered if their marriage, their two children, their business they'd built from the ground up, the life they'd so carefully constructed into something they both desired was "all there was"?

Wasn't the very "it" he spoke of the American dream?

What the ever-loving hell?

Kit stood and started pacing, shoving his hand into his hair. "I mean, you have to be having the same questions. Look at your sister. That was it for her. She's done, and what did she have to show for it? Honestly, I'm not sure I want to die tomorrow having my whole life just be *this*." He spread his hands and twirled around.

"What's wrong with this?"

"Oh, come on, Mel. Think about all the things you've never done. 'Cause that's all I can think about—the scuba lessons I've never taken, the motorcycle you wouldn't let me buy, the mountains I've never climbed. Life is zipping past us, and we're worrying about the brakes on the truck, the exterminator using dangerous chemicals, and the returns we're getting on our stocks. I mean, who cares? We're frittering our lives away on endless details that don't matter. I'm done with all that. I want more."

She didn't know what to say. Her mouth felt like someone had crammed that crinkly stuff thoughtless people used in gift baskets, the stuff that required getting out the vacuum once you'd taken all the goodies out. If she said something, all that crinkly stuffing would come out, zipping and zagging all over the place, leaving papery pieces of herself everywhere. She wasn't sure if there was a broom or vacuum big enough to clean up that sort of mess. So she said nothing. Just stared at her pacing husband with his exquisitely tortured face, as if he were the one wounded by the thought of their marriage being broken apart.

"Say something," he demanded, stopping in front of her.

Melanie couldn't. Her clogged throat, thick with unshed tears and stinging anger, remained closed. She shook her head, trying not to cry. Trying not to fall apart.

His expression softened. "Hey, I know you didn't expect this, and my timing is, well, pretty bad, but what Tennyson said made such sense. Some things require decisiveness. You either shit or get off the pot."

Tennyson?

Melanie turned her head and caught her reflection in the bathroom mirror. Her frizzy, layered hair looked ridiculous, the self-tanner too ruddy, her face too pasty. Her clothes were baggy and stained. This was what she looked like when her husband declared their marriage over. Because trial separation meant divorce. She could count on one hand the number of friends who separated and had their marriages survive. In fact, she'd have to make a fist. "What exactly did Tennyson say?"

Kit stopped and looked at her. "It wasn't so much what she said. Or maybe it was. Essentially she moved me to a place that made me examine what I really want in life."

"And that is?"

"Fulfillment."

Melanie bit her lip and thought about that. "So Tennyson told you that you should be seeking fulfillment? And you think fulfillment is climbing a mountain? Would that be with Charlotte beside you? And would that be before or after you've had sex with her?"

"Here you go again," Kit said, waving a hand and dropping it to his side with a slap. "You're obsessed with Charlotte. I'm not having an affair with her. Yeah, I admire her. She's independent and seizes life by the horns. She's not afraid to go after what she wants."

"And I am afraid?"

Kit rolled his eyes. Rolled. His. Eyes. "Come on, it's like what we tell the kids. Just because I'm complimenting one doesn't mean I'm dissing the other. Of course I admire you. You're a terrific mother."

Yes. Terrific mother. That's what everyone said. She'd spent the last twenty-odd years assuring that no one could ever look askance at her parenting skills. She volunteered, hand-sanitized, and organic-snacked her way into the Motherhood Hall of Fame. Yet her sister was dead, her mother was a raging bitch, and now her husband was leaving her because he wasn't fulfilled. But she was a good mother, by golly. There *was* that.

"Well, thank you, Kit. I really appreciate that. You can leave now."

He made a face. "I know you're upset."

She angled her eyes to the corner of the bathroom as if she were in contemplation, and then she looked at him and shrugged. "Um, no. I'm not upset. In fact, I think it's an excellent idea. You go. I don't want you to have to worry about the obligations of this house. I wish you well. Enjoy an apartment and the swimming pool. Hey, some even have a fitness center. Living away from all *this* will be awesome."

"That's not what I meant."

"No, no. Feel free to have some fun while you're on your trial separation. You know, seize the day and all that. I hear the singles scene in Shreveport is dead, but a guy like you—almost fifty years old with a great one-bedroom apartment—ought to be just the thing. I hope you get fulfilled. I hope you get fulfilled hard, buddy."

"Mel, come on. Think of this as another form of therapy. Let's just give each other some space, you know? It's a trial. Not permanent." Kit came to her and put his hands on her shoulders.

"Take your hands off me," she said, shrugging him off.

He did as she asked, looking a little hurt that she'd been so firm with him.

She exhaled and inhaled a few times. "I'm not stupid. I know why you want a 'trial' separation. Because it gives you permission to 'fulfill' yourself, and if I agree that it's some form of therapy, your divorce attorney will call it mutually agreed upon. Like it was both our idea, right? But here's the thing, Kit. I know you won't really divorce me, because I have the money and an ironclad prenup."

"Oh, come on," Kit said, his hurt fading, irritation taking its place. "The whole prenup thing? You said we didn't have to worry about that. Remember? I signed it only to satisfy your father."

It was then that Melanie smiled. "Well, you also said vows you're willing to toss aside. I suppose I said some things I didn't mean, either. The prenup stands. Thank goodness for my daddy."

Kit's features tightened.

Melanie crossed her arms. "You're not stupid, Kit. You're not willing to give away half the company and almost all the assets we've built just to schlep around with Miss Independent Size 4. Have you told her that you're only worth about twenty percent without me?"

"Mel, come on."

"I bet you haven't. I bet she's talking about all the fun she'll have when y'all get married. But she just doesn't know, does she? All that delicious money belongs to the Brevards."

"I have money," Kit said, like a kid who'd been told no dessert until he cleaned his plate. Now he was the one in a snit.

"You do have some. In fact, I actually used *your* account to pay for the wedding. Now, don't let the door hit you on the ass when you leave." Melanie opened the door and made a grand goodbye sweep of her arm.

"Mel," he cajoled.

"Oh, and before you leave, pick your fucking toenail clippings up off my bathroom floor, you disgusting pig."

CHAPTER TWENTY-ONE

Something was wrong with Melanie. That much Tennyson knew.

Of course, it wasn't like drag queens and booze were her former friend's favorite things to begin with, being that she was horribly repressed and superconcerned about what everyone thought about her, but the woman had been somber as a mortician throughout most of the night. Not even the edible panties and the penis mixer had drawn a smile.

And Melanie was dressed like a ninja—black pants, black shirt, and no statement piece to break it up. Just plain black.

Bella, the six-foot-five drag queen with gorgeous skin and glitter eyelashes, sauntered by. "Still no bingos at this table? Lord, you people need to step it up. Ain't one of my tables yelled bingo yet."

Tennyson pointed to her card. "I think I got a dud. Can you rig it so I can win?"

Bella grinned, her teeth white and straight . . . and big. Like a vampire's. "How much money you got, sugar?"

"I'm sure she'll show you all her bank statements if you ask nice," Melanie muttered, looking up at the screen where Ginger and Candy, each clad in a sequin ball gown and tiara, ran the bingo board. Melanie narrowed her eyes and looked back at her card.

"Uncalled for," Tennyson said in a singsong voice, motioning the waitress over so she could order another cosmo.

She and Melanie had been stuck at a table in the back because there was no room at the reserved table. Two of Emma's friends who hadn't thought they would make the festivities arrived at the last minute, so she and Melanie had agreed to sit at the back table with Milford Mann, a retired mail carrier who'd known Tennyson's father; Justin and Jolie Green, a middle-aged couple from Plain Dealing; and Frank Something or Other, a rough-around-the-edges farmer who kept looking at Bella like she was a fillet and he'd just tied a bib around his neck.

"Bite me," Melanie said, looking directly at Tennyson.

"What's with you tonight?" Tennyson made a face.

Melanie gave her a withering look and turned her head.

"Looks like your friend is in a huff over not winning that last round. A toaster is a nice prize, and she was so close," Milford said, happily stamping N-32 after one of the emcees pulled it from the hopper.

"Very true," Tennyson said, stamping her own N-32 and ignoring Melanie's sour face.

"You have a daughter getting married, huh?" Jolie asked Tennyson.

"Son. It's Melanie's daughter, Emma, he's marrying on Saturday," Tennyson said, straining to hear the next number. She was one away, and if she bingo'd, she would win a case of Pepsi and free chicken wings at the Old Port Diner for a whole year.

Come on, O-69.

Ginger pulled another number from the hopper and made an O with her mouth. Then she fanned her overexposed cleavage. "Oh, lovies, you won't believe it, but it's my absolute favorite number. Oh, yes, it is."

Tennyson stamped her card.

"O-69, y'all!" Ginger called out.

"Bingo!" Tennyson shouted, leaping up and giving a fist pump. She then did a little dance, and Emma's table broke out in applause. "Woo-hoo!"

Bella, grin as big as a gator's, came over and eyeballed her card, then she pulled out one of those confetti poppers and pulled the string. Streamers and glitter caught in Tennyson's hair, and Bella gave her a kiss on the cheek, no doubt leaving a hot-pink imprint. The rest of the room, sans Emma's table and her own, groaned in defeat.

"Chicken wings," Frank said with a gleam in his eye. "They have really good ones. You're a lucky woman to get them free for a whole year."

Tennyson laughed. "I don't really care for wings. Why don't you have the prize, Frank? I don't mind."

"Naw, I couldn't take your prize," he said, blushing when Bella walked by and lightly raked her long nails over the back of his neck.

"I want you to have it. I'm not going to use it, anyway," Tennyson said, giving him a smile. Something about his embarrassment and longing for Bella made her heart warm. She knew how it felt to be tempted by someone who didn't seem to make a good deal of sense. Of course, she'd gotten her hot cop. And the chase had been such fun.

"Okay, then. I'll gladly take those wings off your hands, little lady," Frank said, his cheeks still heated.

For the past two months, Tennyson had found herself growing more and more attached to the police officer who showed up several times a week to check things out around her house. His favorite place to check for trouble was the bedroom. He was always so thorough in his search.

So odd to think how much she had been enjoying her pared-down life. With Emma and Andrew steps away and a pseudoboyfriend sprawled on her couch watching *SportsCenter*, she was living a life close to what her parents had led—mundane, somewhat boring, but also comforting. Her former life had been one most only dreamed of—box tickets at the Met, private planes to Paris, personal shoppers, and a complete house staff—but over the past few months she'd discovered she didn't miss her old life one bit. Something about squabbling over who should get the last bite of Halo Top ice cream, deciding who got to choose the next movie, and cleaning her own oven felt fulfilling. She didn't want to put a label on what she had with Joseph because she didn't want to rock the boat, but so far, she felt like she'd found a place to belong.

Not only had Joseph given her a sense of contentment, but he'd turned out to be a great listener, offering sage advice when she grappled with relationships or a sense of purpose. Just last week he'd made a suggestion that had sort of blown her boat out of the water. They'd been talking about her failure to get her degree and what her upcoming year might look like once the wedding was over. Tennyson had admitted that she didn't have a direction.

"Why don't you go back to school? You could go to LSUS or even Centenary. What is it you studied?" he'd asked, looking up from the steak he was pulling from the marinade. He'd started growing a beard, which was hot as hell. Maybe they should let those fillets marinate a bit longer while they played house in her king-size bed.

"Yeah, I majored in theatre. I'm not sure they have a degree program in that at LSUS."

"Maybe not, but there are movie studios that come into Shreveport and film. They've done a lot of films here. My cousin does extra work. Or if that doesn't do it for you, you could use some of your theatre experience in other ways. Or you could always go into something like counseling or being a drama teacher. I think you'd be terrific as a teacher." He capped the bottle of olive oil and placed it back into her pantry, carefully wiping away any drips on the marble counter. Joseph was very conscientious. She liked that about him.

"Me? Oh, I couldn't teach kids these days. They're animals. Don't you watch YouTube?"

Joseph laughed. "Um, I'm pretty sure those are isolated incidences. How about working in counseling? You said you had a lot of regrets in your past. The counselors who have lived the life and walked the walk are the ones who are most effective because they've been there. I mean, I don't know what experiences you've had, but you might rely upon the mistakes you've made to clear a path for the future. Unless you like just floating around in the pool and worrying about what series you'll watch next on Amazon?"

"Are you implying that I have no purpose?" she asked, her pride taking a punch with his words. It wasn't as if she were useless. She did stuff. But then Melanie's words from the bridal gown shopping trip came back to her. *Have you even had a job? Or was your career merely marrying wealthy men and spending their money? Or maybe it's marathon champagne drinking?* Is that what people thought about her? That she had no purpose beyond handing over her credit card or getting her nails done?

"No. I'm not saying that at all. I'm just trying to challenge you because I think you need that in your life. You were made to be of use. I see that in everything you do or touch. You enjoy the process. So this isn't me dragging you down, it's me lifting you up so you can see that you have a lot of talents that could be put to use."

Tennyson had bitten her lip and thought about his words. They'd stayed with her all through dinner, through reruns of *Seinfeld* (because Joseph had never seen the series), and after they lay sated in her sheets, breathing hard, coming down from another amazing bout of soul-stirring, toe-curling sex. And even still, after she pulled on his T-shirt and snuggled under the coverlet, his words pricked at her.

To be of use. To have purpose. To apply her talents.

The next day she'd called City Hub Volunteers and signed up to serve as a mentor. She'd gone to an orientation and made an immediate connection with the director of the counseling center, Annette Grafton. Tennyson had even revealed to Annette her deepest, darkest, guilt-ridden sin—the abortion she'd had her freshman year of college. Annette had held her as she cried, told her that she had been brave and strong, and given her something no one had given her before—absolution.

Tennyson had never gone to confession about what she'd done, even though she'd been a "good" Catholic girl. She couldn't seem to utter the words, not even to ask for forgiveness. She'd been too afraid to tell her parents, especially since she didn't know if the baby was Kit's or one of the other two boys she'd hooked up with when she returned from Christmas break her freshman year. When she got back, she'd been so hurt by Kit, she'd been determined to rinse the taste of him from her mouth. So she'd partied, slept with a few fellow students, and done her first line of cocaine. A month later, she'd tossed her cookies while painting backdrops. She continued vomiting every morning for five days straight. She stopped believing it was bad Chinese food and took a home pregnancy test.

It had been positive.

She'd been nineteen, up for a part in the university spring show, and living on student loans. Fear had turned her spit to ash and taken her to a clinic, where she made an appointment. Two weeks later she'd had the procedure that had erased her bad decision. When the director had given her a pamphlet about counseling and mental health after pregnancy termination, Tennyson had trashed it. She would be fine.

Except she started having nightmares and days when she could think of nothing but the unborn child and who he or she might have been. That guilt led to more bad decisions—she tried to drown the pain with drugs and booze. Tennyson went off the rails and lost herself for many years.

When she'd finally gotten her shit together, married Stephen, and felt the wee kicks of baby Andrew, she'd started writing the checks to the centers to help women who hadn't been able to deal with the loss of pregnancy, whether intentional or not. It was the only way she could sleep a full night. If she could help someone else, she could somehow make her own mistake less.

She blinked as someone passed her a new bingo card.

Wow, those memories had dragged her away a bit too easily. Maybe it was easier to go to that place in her heart now because Annette had given her a space to be honest. The director had talked about her own abortions, about how she used the sadness and anxiety of her past to help others. Tennyson didn't feel so alone after confessing her hurt. Joseph had been right—being counseled by someone who had walked the same journey was far more effective than sharing with someone who hadn't felt the same emotions.

"Melly and Teeny, we're going to do one more round," Emma called back to their table. Andrew's intended had the high flush of happiness and a sparkle of excitement in her eyes. Tennyson acknowledged her with a wave and a smile.

Melanie sighed. "I really wish they would move on to the club or wherever they're going so I can go home."

That was the longest sentence Melanie had used all night—and it was a grumpy one. Tennyson knew the woman was still grieving Hillary, so she hadn't pushed her earlier at the cocktail party and lingerie shower when she sat like a bump on a frog's ass. She'd thought maybe Melanie would be in a better mood, especially after the conversation Tennyson had yesterday with Kit. She'd gone by his office to drop the reimbursement check for the deposit on MK Bistro, the venue for the rehearsal dinner.

Kit's assistant had looked surprised when she strolled into the office. Of course, she'd dropped in unannounced, so that could be the reason, but the woman's reaction gave her a funny feeling.

"Can I help you?" the woman said, lifting the mouthpiece thingy so she could speak.

"Is Kit in?" Tennyson asked, repositioning her new Percy sunglasses atop her head. She wore the LALAoUNIS chandelier earrings that husband number two had bought her (with her own money) while they vacationed in Athens, along with a new floral Erdem dress with a black lace overlay. She knew she looked chic, confident, and a bit off-putting since she was carrying her red crocodile Birkin bag. Not that the receptionist would even know it was an Hermès and cost about the same as a car.

"Uh, I think he's in a meeting." The receptionist cast a nervous glance at the double doors leading into Kit's inner sanctum.

Déjà vu. She'd been here and done this before.

"Don't worry, I'll announce myself," she said, breezing by the desk and opening the office door. It wasn't even locked.

Amateur.

When she walked in, she saw Kit and the heifer on the couch together. Whatever her name was had her shoes off and her feet curled beneath her tight skirt. Her forearm was on Kit's shoulder as she leaned in, looking at whatever was on the iPad in his hand. When they heard the door open, they leaped apart, the woman tucking her hair behind her ear and uncurling her legs.

"Oh, Tennyson, you scared the bejesus out of me," Kit said, setting the iPad on the coffee table and rising, pulling his jacket aright.

"Look at you talking about Jesus," Tennyson drawled, looking pointedly at the woman, who was searching for her pumps with her feet.

Kit made a confused face before donning his normal grin. "What brings you here?"

"Money."

He looked even more confused as he moved behind his desk and sank onto the plush leather. "Money?"

She withdrew the check from her bag. "I owe you for the deposit on MK Bistro."

"Oh yeah. Thanks." Kit tucked the check into a drawer. Then he looked at her as if he expected her to leave. But Tennyson didn't want to. Not without a private word with the man she'd once declared her soul mate. She'd been wrong about that. But then again, she'd been wrong a lot in her life, so this revelation came as no big surprise.

Tennyson turned to Charlotte, who had pulled herself together and now stood at the back of the office, hands clasped. "I need a word with your boss. If you don't mind . . ."

Charlotte's eyes slid to Tennyson's bag. "Oh sure. I'm Charlotte, by the way."

"I remember," Tennyson said, offering no reciprocal greeting to the smiling opportunist, who obviously recognized Hermès.

Charlotte squared her shoulders. "Right. Kit, we can pick up where we left off later this afternoon. I have a few calls to make, anyway."

He nodded. "Sure."

Once the door closed, Tennyson turned to Kit. "What in the hell do you think you're doing?"

"I beg your pardon?"

Tennyson parked her hip on the overstuffed chair across the desk from Kit. "You've got a worm in your apple, Christopher."

"Are you implying something? Because it sounds like you think you know something you don't know." He leaned back, looking very confident, clasping his hands over his flat stomach. His smug manner irked her. This was quintessential Kit, deflecting with his arrogance and adding that Cheshire cat smile that essentially said *you truly don't believe that of me, do you? Not little ol' me.* Kit was slick as owl shit.

"You know, Kit, for years I pined for you, building up this fantastical image in my mind of this golden boy with his beguiling smile and carefree attitude. We had so many good times together—you made me laugh, cry, want to hit you, and want to kiss you. You were the whole enchilada. Girls do that, you know. They romanticize their first loves.

But more and more, I'm realizing just how little substance there is to you, Kit."

He frowned. "So let me get this straight—not only are you accusing me of doing something despicable, but you're also shitting on me? Thanks, Teeny. That's just what I wanted—a side of insult with my accusation of adultery. Which is *not* true, by the way."

Tennyson looked back at the couch and then back at him, arching an eyebrow.

Kit threw up his hands. "Oh please, we were going over some bids. Her feet were hurting. She's my associate, not my lover."

"So you say."

Kit sat up, the chair snapping back to its original position. "Just because you're trying to make up with Melanie doesn't mean you get to poke your nose into our business. Nothing is going on here. I'm tired of people implying that Charlotte and I are being inappropriate."

"Well, if it looks like a dog, smells like a dog, and barks like a dog . . ."

"Tennyson, this is ridiculous. I haven't had an affair." He sucked in a deep breath and exhaled.

She was a good judge of character and had been lied to enough in her life that she was good at spotting the tells. Kit seemed to be telling the truth; however, that didn't mean he wasn't on the precipice. He said he hadn't, not that he wasn't going to. That cozy little scenario she'd barged into was cause for concern. Kit might not have dipped his stick in the water, but the water was lapping at his toes. And this particular water was aggressive, slender, and had a really annoying laugh. Like a braying donkey. "Okay, maybe so, and I'm not trying to make up for what I did to Melanie. Whether any of us like it or not, we're about to be intertwined through marriage, and I don't want your bad decisions pulling down the rest of us. So all I'm saying is you might want to consider cutting that worm out and saving the rest of your apple."

Kit just looked at her, his hands now tented on his desk.

"Unless you don't like apples," she said.

"So you think I should *fire* Charlotte?" Kit asked. He sounded like he thought she was crazy.

"I think you need to think about the life you have. It's a good one, right? And you're holding that life in the center of your palm, like a beautiful, ripe apple . . . that has a worm. Do you want to keep the apple? Because if you let the worm keep eating away, it won't be an apple anymore. You'll be starting all over with new fruit, and you don't know what you'll get."

Kit folded his hands and looked at her. "So you're saying I need to think about what really matters most to me." It was a statement.

"That's exactly what I'm saying. We're not getting any younger, right? I mean, in a few years, we could actually be *grandparents*. And if you want to know the honest-to-God truth—I have to use readers to see the menu at restaurants. So, yes, I'm saying you need to think about who you want to be. Give your life some thought. You have a lot riding on what you decide."

"A lot of what you've said makes sense. I've been struggling these past months. There's been a lot going on, business-wise and on a personal level, so I have been . . . *confused* isn't the exact right word. Maybe *complacent* is a better word, but actually, you're right. I have to think about what I want the next years of my life to be like, and I have to consider my family while also being true to myself." Kit leaned back in the chair and glanced out the window that overlooked Texas Street. "Sometimes I feel like I don't even know the man I've become."

Tennyson hadn't expected to feel such a sense of accomplishment. This small intervention told her all she needed to know about how good she'd be volunteering at the counseling center. Joseph was right—she had a knack for understanding people and helping them see what was most important in their lives. "Everyone gets a bit lost sometimes, and we all have to stop and readjust. Look, I have to run. We have the lingerie shower and drag queen bingo tonight. See you tomorrow at the church."

Kit stood when she rose. "Hey, sometimes it takes someone else looking in on one's life to show them what they've been doing. I'm still a bit insulted that you think I'm a no-good cheater, but I do appreciate you being brave enough to say something. I've always admired that about you, Teeny. You charge in with guns blazing."

She lifted a shoulder. "Sometimes you have to make an entrance."

Tennyson had left his office feeling like she'd done at least one good thing for Melanie, not that she was truly making restitution for her bad behavior. But it still felt good. Now Kit could see putting his marriage and family ahead of selfish desires and his ego was the right choice.

So why was Melanie being such a grinch tonight? They were playing drag queen bingo, for heaven's sake. What was there to not like about that?

She looked at Melanie, who was sipping a Diet Coke and frowning at her bingo card. The others at their table cast wary looks at her as if she were a stray cat who could lash out and claw them at any moment.

"It's just one more round, Melly," Tennyson said, trying to sound encouraging.

"I told you not to call me that," Melanie said, not bothering to look up at her.

"God, what is your freaking problem, *Melanie*?"

Her head snapped up, her brown eyes crackling with something dangerous. Tennyson glanced around like perhaps she'd dropped down into a movie set and something alien might come bursting out of Melanie's torso. The woman looked blazing-eyes possessed.

"You want to know what my problem is? You *really* want to know?" Melanie hissed, narrowing her eyes. "It's you. You're my problem, Teeny."

Everyone at the table played at being statues, their eyes wide.

"What?" Tennyson asked, making a confused face. "What now?"

"What now? You. You've always been my problem. Wherever you go, bad things follow. You're like a fucking plague that kills everything in its path. It's been like that from the very beginning. You destroy everything with your big ideas, your grand plans, your over-the-top ridiculous-ass exploits. Everything you touch falls apart." Melanie had stopped with the low, hissing modulation. Her voice had risen to a full roar, and everyone in the place stopped talking and stared at their table.

"What are you talking about?"

Melanie uncurled her hands from the table, her mouth drawing back to reveal her clenched teeth. She picked up the red bingo dauber and launched it at Tennyson's head.

Tennyson threw up her hands at the last minute, deflecting the marker. She may have squealed. "Stop it! What is wrong with you?"

"Think I wouldn't find out about what you told my husband, you stupid, meddling whore?" Melanie shouted, coming around the table.

People gasped at the language, but Tennyson didn't have time to catch the shock on their faces because suddenly Melanie's hands were wrapped around her throat. She felt the chair tilt, and they both pitched backward, slamming to the floor. For a brief moment, she was free. She started scrabbling back, but Melanie was quicker than she looked. She shoved Tennyson down and straddled her.

"Why did you tell him to leave me? Haven't you done enough to me?" Melanie was screaming now, wrestling against Tennyson's hands, trying to get to her face. Tennyson pulled her arms up to ward off further attack while twisting her body, trying to free herself.

"Stop," Tennyson yelled, turning her head.

"Why do you hate me so much?" Melanie yelled.

Tennyson paused at that, withdrawing her arms to look at Melanie. Her old friend took advantage and slugged her. Melanie landed a good one on Tennyson's cheekbone before Tennyson turned away, bucking her hips in an effort to get Melanie off her.

"I didn't do anything. Mel, stop. You're acting crazy."

With that, Melanie fell off and rolled into a ball, sobbing. "He's leaving me. He's leaving. You told him to do it."

Bella reached beneath Tennyson's armpits and lifted her. Tennyson slapped at the drag queen's hand. "No. Let me go. I'm fine."

"Sugar, I've seen a lot of drama in my life, but this beats it all," Bella said, steadying her.

Tennyson pressed a hand against her cheek and looked down at the woman curled into a ball issuing big body-racking sobs. A keening wail came from Melanie, a sound that was almost feral but heartbreaking at the same time.

Dropping to her knees, she placed a hand on Melanie's shoulder. "Mel. Come on. Stop."

Jolie looked at her husband. "Call 911. That was totally an assault."

Emma skidded onto the scene, her mouth open and obviously at a loss. Tennyson held up a hand to Jolie. "No. No police. It's just a misunderstanding."

Ginger clacked over with a *tat-tat-tat* of her platform shoes. "What in the hell is going on? We don't allow this kind of bullshit up in here."

Tennyson looked up from where she kneeled. "I'm sorry. Uh, she's not feeling well. A death in the family and a lot of stress with the wedding. We're going now. If there are any damages, send me the bill. I gave Bella my information earlier."

Ginger flipped her wig over her bronzed shoulder. "Don't think I won't do that. 'Cause I will. That chair is broken. Broken. Now y'all get on and take this woman out of here."

"Mel," Tennyson said, jiggling Melanie's arm. The woman had curled into the fetal position and hadn't stopped sobbing during the whole conversation. "Come on. We have to go."

Melanie sat up and pushed Tennyson's hands away. "Don't touch me. I hate you. I fucking hate you."

Tennyson drew back, not understanding what had just happened. Her cheek throbbed, and everyone still stared at them. She stood, moving backward away from Melanie and the absolute hatred in her old friend's eyes. Melanie had said Kit left her. That couldn't be true. He'd said that . . . he'd essentially said that he understood what he needed to do.

Oh. God.

Surely, he hadn't thought Tennyson meant . . .

But maybe he'd taken it that way. Maybe Kit had taken her apple analogy and punted.

Emma managed to get her mother up and out the door, the bridal party trailing behind her, all looking worried and completely bamboozled about what had just occurred. Tennyson kept stepping backward, her hands shaking, her body joining in on that chorus.

Kit had left Melanie?

And he'd obviously told her it was Tennyson's idea.

"Well, shoot, I guess I ain't gonna get those chicken wings after all," Frank said, completely unaware that Tennyson was still in the room. He slapped Jason on the back, and they moved back to the table and their forgotten bingo cards. The drag queens started up the music and assumed their vampy positions. The world started turning again.

Tennyson bumped up against a jukebox and reached out a steadying hand so she didn't buckle under the emotion swamping her.

Tennyson never cried because she was too tough to cry.

But at that moment, everything she'd claimed to be left her, and all that was left were the saltiest of tears.

CHAPTER
TWENTY-TWO

Melanie lay in bed and stared up at the ceiling. She'd painted it last February, a clean white that reflected too much light. The muted gray had been a better choice, but she'd been obsessed with "a bright, clean white" because she felt like that would project what her life was—streamlined, pure, and full of light.

She was obviously a dumb ass, because right now she'd have to paint that ceiling black. Or at least a dark charcoal.

"Mom?" Noah stood in the doorway of her bedroom.

Melanie glanced at her bedside clock, which read 1:32 a.m. "Hey, honey, what are you doing up?"

The Xanax she'd taken had made her woozy, but she still couldn't sleep. The images of the day kept circling through her mind. It had started fine—she'd had the bump of sadness and two cigarettes in the kitchen garden—but she'd been looking forward to the evening. She'd never been to a drag queen show before and thought the idea Emma's girlfriends had come up with was fun. Plus, they had the rehearsal and wedding to look forward to. Marc had done an amazing job with the little time he'd been given, and he hadn't gone too far over budget. Even better.

Emma was happy, glowing with excitement. Andrew had proved suitably protective, making sure his bride was resting and eating as she started medical school. Noah had done well with summer baseball, and Kit had been more attentive, a firm rock to lean on when she missed Hillary. Even her mother seemed to have lessened the severity of her criticism.

So how had the day gone so wrong?

Tennyson.

That woman had turned up like a bad penny, urging Kit to make a concrete choice about his life. Obviously, her words had made him doubt what he'd chosen all those years ago, and Melanie wouldn't put it past Tennyson to have planned on destroying their marriage all along. Maybe that was why she'd moved back. More revenge. After all, Kit had been a source of contention between them from the moment he'd strolled into their high school. Tennyson had never been able to accept defeat.

So why had Tennyson been so nice to her, talking her into buying a dress, coming to the hospital, giving her a joint?

What was that old saying? Keep your friends close but your enemies closer?

That rule had been made for her and Tennyson.

Noah shuffled his feet as he hung on to the doorframe. "I'm just checking on you."

Melanie sat up, and the room rocked a little. "I'm okay, honey."

"Are you going to have to go to a hospital or something? Hunter Alack's mom had a breakdown and had to go to Forest Grove for a month."

Melanie patted the bed beside her, and Noah dutifully trucked the length of her bedroom and sank down, looking awkward. "I'm fine. I guess I haven't really comprehended the loss of Aunt Hilly, and the stress has been, like, a lot. Your daddy and I had an argument this afternoon, and I think it all just culminated into . . . an episode. I'm fine now."

He twisted his hands. This child had always been the more sensitive of her two, and he was prone to anxiety and worry. "I'm just worried. Dad's not even here. Where is he?"

"I think he's staying in a hotel tonight," she said, electing for the truth. Part of her wanted to smooth it all over and make it not what it was, but she also wouldn't protect Kit's bad behavior. Or lie to her child.

"Are y'all going to get a divorce?" Noah asked, his voice almost a whisper, with worry nattering at the edges of the query.

She brushed back his hair. "You know, I don't really know."

He whipped his head around. "Seriously?"

Melanie moved her hand down and rubbed his back. "Your dad and I are both going through a rocky time. It doesn't mean that we will choose to divorce, but I'm not going to tell you there's not a possibility. I think I should be truthful with you because you're old enough to understand that sometimes things don't work between people."

"Yeah. I guess."

"Honestly, being an adult really sucks, Noah."

"Yeah, I think I want to be one until something like this happens. Then I'm pretty good just staying a kid who doesn't have to make all the decisions. That's probably lame to admit. I'm kinda nervous about college and being so far away."

"Everyone gets nervous about college. That's just a given but remember there are colleges that are close by. You don't have to go far away." Part of her wanted him to stay. For her to have one person here with her, as selfish as that thought was. Because she felt so alone and lost at present. Just having Noah here, leaving his water bottles scattered around the house and the television on, would feel normal. She needed some normal in her life right now.

Noah shrugged and flopped back on the bed. "Yeah. Maybe."

"But we have time to think about that. The thing is, I don't want you to worry about me. I'm fine." As she said the words, she knew she was lying to him, doing the thing she said she wouldn't do. But at the same time, she knew that one day she *would* be fine. Because, though her husband was sleeping at the Marriott, her daughter wasn't talking to her, and she'd pretty much assaulted her soon-to-be in-law, she would be okay. Maybe because she had that much of her mother inside her. She wasn't going to give up or go down just because it would be the easiest thing to do.

She stroked Noah's head, loving the feel of his silky brown hair beneath her fingers and that waft of teen boy that was somewhere between salty heat and wet dog, with an Axe body spray finish. He closed his eyes and fell asleep half on, half off her bed. She scooted over to Kit's side, punched the pillow, and then let the calming drug do its thing.

The next morning when she woke to the sun streaming in her window, she had two thoughts—tomorrow her daughter would marry Tennyson's son, and she wasn't sure how she would handle everyone knowing that Kit had left her.

Noah had disappeared at some point in the night, likely slinking back to his own room, and she could hear Poppy barking to be let out of the laundry room. Glancing at the clock, she was surprised to find that it was close to 10:00 a.m. She hadn't slept that late since she'd given birth to Noah and Kit's mother had come to stay with them.

She climbed out of bed, brushed her teeth, and tugged on her robe, the first of many mornings that would be different. By the time she let Poppy outside and filled her kibble bowl, she was more than ready for her morning coffee. When she padded into the kitchen, she was surprised to find her other child standing in front of the espresso machine, spooning eggs onto two plates.

"Emma?"

"Morning, Mom," Emma said. Her voice sounded funny, but not irritated as it had been last night when she virtually dumped Melanie into her bedroom, rifled through the bathroom cabinet where Melanie kept their family's medications, and forced her to take the anxiety drug.

"Morning. What are you doing here?" Melanie sank onto a stool, the thought of coffee long gone as she faced her daughter. This wasn't going to be as easy as dealing with Noah.

"Making sure you're not bouncing off the walls or trying to drown yourself in the bathtub." Emma fetched a cup from the cupboard and filled it with fragrant coffee. She added a splash of creamer and handed it to Melanie. She also set down a plate of eggs covered in cheese.

"I know you're upset," Melanie said, accepting the cup and taking a long sip. The brew was perfect—something Emma prided herself on. She eyed the coffee mug they'd bought at Disney World ten years ago. It had been such a fun vacation, full of pigtails, sunscreen, character autograph books, and Dole pineapple whips. A lifetime ago. Another world.

"I am, but I'm also worried about you. What you did last night . . . well, Tennyson could have had you arrested. You tried to choke her. And you gave her a black eye."

"I did? I mean, I know I sort of lost it. But a black eye?" Lord, Tennyson would be incensed having a black eye for her son's wedding. She almost smiled, and Emma caught her.

"Oh no. Don't you dare think anything about this is funny. You acted like a maniac and ruined my bachelorette party. We got kicked out of drag queen bingo. *Drag queens* found us obnoxious enough to kick out."

"Well, at least it was memorable," Melanie said, taking another draw on her coffee.

Emma pulled up a stool, plonked down her own plate, and set her cup of tea next to it. "Too soon, Mom."

"Sorry."

For a few seconds they sat, neither one saying anything. Just drinking their respective morning beverages, noodling around with the eggs, and trying to, no doubt, figure out how to repair what Melanie had done the night before.

Finally, Emma cleared her throat. "Is it true? Did Daddy leave?"

Melanie swallowed, studying a chip in the polish on her pinkie. "I don't know. I guess."

"Why?"

Well, that was the loaded question, wasn't it? Melanie wasn't sure what to say. Should she tell Emma that Kit likely wanted to have a more "intimate" relationship with Charlotte? Or maybe she should tell her daughter it could be because Melanie didn't want to have sex with him every other night? Maybe it was more than sex. Maybe it was something else. Maybe it was because Melanie was boring or repressed or not as young and pretty as she once was. Or maybe she herself had no clue what she'd done to drive Kit from the life they'd built together and loved until . . . well, until they both hadn't loved it anymore. How did a woman tell her daughter that she may have fallen out of love with her father, but she wasn't sure because she'd been too busy grieving her sister, planning a wedding, and hating Tennyson to worry as much about her husband? So Melanie went with, "It's complicated."

"Yeah, well, that's not an actual answer, Mom."

"No, but it's all I have at this point. I'm not sure why your father left. Things have been difficult."

"Does this mean a divorce?" Same question Noah asked. Melanie could remember asking this one herself when her father's secret had been spilled and her own mother had been furious at Albert, coldly eviscerating him for his flaws and then ignoring him. She'd even moved to the guest bedroom for several months. Even then, Melanie had been afraid that her parents might split. It was probably every child's worst nightmare, losing that one stable element in their life.

"I don't know. Your dad is asking for some room. I'm not sure what that means."

Probably meant he was gently cupping Charlotte's head as he plowed her against the hotel room headboard. For men, *space* meant permission to sample the single life, and Kit had a willing whore at hand just waiting to give him what his wife wasn't.

"So why did you attack Tennyson? I thought things were better between you two? Over the past month or so you were almost friendly, and then—" She snapped her fingers.

"It's between me and Tennyson."

"Horseshit."

"Em," Melanie chided, wishing she had a cigarette. This might mean she had a full-fledged addiction to nicotine. Time to toss the Newports and go cold turkey. She couldn't use the upheaval in her life to justify doing something that could kill her. Hillary had taught her that much. "I'm serious. It's between us."

"Well, I pretty much already know. Everyone at the bingo game knows. You think she told Dad to leave you."

Okay, Melanie had probably been a bit louder than she intended when she yelled whatever she'd yelled at Tennyson. She didn't remember exactly what that was, but it was damned sure some accusation. All she knew was that she'd spent the whole evening trying to pretend she was fine, but she was so *not* fine that eventually she became a powder keg of emotion. Having Tennyson constantly pecking at her with "what's your problem" all night hadn't helped. Instead it had felt like the woman had tossed gasoline in her face each time Tennyson looked at her like she was a wet blanket. "Tennyson did what Tennyson does best—she stirred the ant mound with a stick."

"Because she told Dad to fire Charlotte?" Emma asked.

Melanie set the coffee down a little too hard. A plop of hot coffee landed on her hand. "Wait. What? Fire Charlotte?"

"This is the second time this morning that I've made coffee, you know." Emma arched her brows expectantly. Lord, the child was good at making Melanie feel squirmy. She'd make a great mother someday.

"You've already spoken to Tennyson?"

Emma nodded. "We accidently left her at the grill last night, so she had to Uber home. I felt horrible about that, especially since my own mother assaulted her. I went to check on her this morning. The black eye is legit, but good makeup will hide it."

This time the thought of Tennyson with a black eye wasn't amusing. The woman told Emma that she'd told Kit to cut Charlotte loose. Melanie could actually see Tennyson doing that. She was never good at staying out of everyone's business. But Kit had made no reference to Tennyson suggesting such a thing. He made it sound like Tennyson had issued a warning to live his best life . . . one without Melanie.

"Is Dad having an affair with Charlotte?" Emma asked.

"I don't think so, but I don't know."

Emma nodded. "But Charlotte wants Dad."

"Yeah. Probably," Melanie said, looking down at the droplets of coffee against the marbled white counter. "What exactly did Tennyson tell you?"

"That she had gone to his office to drop off a check and had a talk with Dad. She suspected something and confronted him, reminding him that he had a good life and he was putting that in jeopardy. She said she never told him to do anything like what you accused her of saying. She said she thought she was helping you."

"I don't need her to help me."

Emma looked at her, studying her. Melanie smoothed a hand through her hair and looked away. She didn't want that wriggling guilt squirming inside her. She'd jumped to conclusions about Tennyson. But still, the woman had no business sticking her nose into her and Kit's business. Her good intentions had done irreparable damage.

"Mom, I'm pregnant," Emma said.

Melanie literally almost fell off the stool. She'd been shifting her weight with one foot on the foot rest, and at Emma's words, her foot had slipped. She grabbed the counter edge and righted herself. "What?"

"I'm almost eighteen weeks along. I found out right before graduation, right after Andrew proposed to me. That's why we needed to get married this summer," Emma said, cradling the coffee cup that held . . . tea.

Of course. Tea, the refusal to drink alcohol, the glow. So many indications she'd missed. How had she missed all that? So much now made sense. Dear Lord, her daughter was *pregnant*.

"Why didn't you tell me?"

Emma gave her an apologetic look. "Andrew and I decided to wait until I was past the first trimester. Lots of women have miscarriages. We weren't actually planning on getting married during my first year of school, but once we found out that we were pregnant, we knew that was the right thing to do. We also didn't want people thinking that was the sole reason we were getting married. I don't mind people knowing once the wedding is over, but having people think we're only doing it because of the baby sort of dampens the whole experience. We wanted our wedding to be about our commitment. We had planned to tell y'all tomorrow. You probably noticed I've been wearing tunic dresses and baggier clothes. That's why I wanted a wedding dress that wasn't a mermaid style. No hiding a little baby bump in one of those suckers." Her smile was soft as she cupped the little bump revealed when she pressed her hand against her T-shirt.

"A baby?" Melanie whispered, tears gathering in her eyes. She pressed a hand against her mouth. "You're having a baby?"

Emma looked up, her own eyes glistening with emotion. "End of January."

"Oh my God," Melanie said, wiping away the tears splashing on her cheeks. "Do you know if it's a boy or girl yet?"

Emma shook her head. "Not yet. We can find out next month."

Melanie reached out a hand and laid it on her daughter's stomach. Emma was still so thin, but there was a definite bump. "Who else knows?"

"You and Andrew. And my doctor, of course."

"You told me first?" Melanie asked.

"You're my mama."

"I can't believe this. I'm going to be a grandmother. Oh my God." She laughed.

"I know you're a little young for it, but you'll be a terrific one." Emma reached over and grabbed a napkin from the lazy Susan holding the spices and handed it to Melanie.

She swiped at her face, still trying to come to terms with this new surprise. There were almost too many changes to comprehend. But . . . a baby.

Lord.

"So, Mom, that's one of the reasons I really hoped you and Tennyson would, I don't know, figure out a way to coexist, because it's not just about me and Andrew. It's about this baby. You both will be the grandmothers, and, I'm sorry, but we can't have you two throwing cake at one another or trying to strangle each other. You have bad blood between you, but you need to find a way to take this new blood"—Emma cupped her stomach—"and let it heal you."

Melanie picked up her coffee with trembling hands. "I don't know if I can truly forgive her for what she did to me . . . to my family."

Emma rose, scooting the stool back. She wrapped her arms around Melanie and gave her a squeeze. "I guess that's up to you, Mama. You have the power to forgive and to make amends so that we can build a new, better future for this baby. Tennyson wasn't trying to hurt you, and, yeah, I get it—she's a pill sometimes, but she's not all bad. You want to know what I really think?"

Melanie pulled back and looked up at her daughter. "I have a feeling you're going to tell me."

"I think Tennyson misses you. And I think she's trying really hard to make amends. I also think you want to forgive her, because there are these flashes where I can see you are better versions of yourselves when you're together. That probably sounds crazy, but I would swear that you fit each other."

Melanie made a face. "Fit each other?"

"Like a balancing scale. You give her a place to land, but she gives you wings." Emma walked to the sink and dumped the remainder of her tea. "I have to go. I have a lot to do today. I'll see you at the church tonight."

Melanie sat staring at her cup, thinking over her daughter's last words. They reminded her of other images—pinkie swears, matching sweatshirts, an old necklace she should have thrown away years ago. Fitting together.

Emma kissed her on the head. "Bye, Mama."

Then she was gone, leaving Melanie without many words but with a great deal to think about.

CHAPTER
TWENTY-THREE

Tennyson stared at her phone and the message Melanie had sent her ten minutes before.

Code Hot Pink.

What did that mean?

Back in the day, it meant an emergency. Come right away with no delay. But these days it could mean that Melanie wanted to whale on her some more. Tennyson already sported a nice shiner on her left cheekbone. Thank God she had booked an appointment with a hairstylist and makeup artist for both the rehearsal and the wedding. She'd need a lot of concealer and luminescent highlighter to disguise the dark circle beneath her eye. Her family had been arriving in waves, thankfully, all wanting to catch up with old friends that day rather than pester Tennyson with lots of questions and demands, so she hadn't had to address the shiner. Yet.

Code Hot Pink.

Well, she had exactly two hours until she had to be at the salon. This would have to be dealt with.

She tapped back, What time?

Now?

Give me ten minutes.

She hurried to her room, pulling on a pair of flat sandals. She would have to drive to her old neighborhood and allot for time to figure out how to get back to their meeting spot. Thankfully, she wore a button-down shirt so she could go directly from their meeting spot to the salon if she needed to. She picked up her purse, and then as she passed her dresser, she paused.

When they were young, they always had worn their best-friends necklace when a Code Hot Pink was called. When they arrived, they would press the two halves of the heart together, like they were the Wonder Twins and the uniting of the heart gave them superpowers. It was hokey, stupid, and . . . Tennyson opened her jewelry box and reached past the Cartier Love Bracelets, David Yurman pieces, and baubles from Tiffany to the oxidized pendant coiled beneath. She pulled out the old necklace, wincing as it blackened her hands.

Would Melanie bring hers?

Probably not. She'd probably thrown the cheap necklace out long ago. Because why would she keep it?

Gone was that whimsical girl who made monkeys of clouds and mud pies from the clay bank. In her place was a logical, responsible, somewhat boring woman. Once upon a time, Melanie had been interesting, full of dreams, and now . . . well, now she was someone Tennyson didn't know and really didn't want to rediscover. Still, there were glimpses. Like when Melanie had thrown the cake and then laughed when Tennyson had smashed another piece in her face. Or in the dressing room. Or smoking the joint and scarfing down Tostitos. At those moments, Tennyson had felt hope.

She slipped the necklace into the pocket of her shorts.

Ten minutes later she pulled up in front of her old house. The place had gone downhill, the paint faded and peeling, a shutter missing, and the yard her father had once taken such pride in had gone to weed. The window boxes were full of dead petunias, and the driveway had cracked. She shut off the engine and climbed out. There was a power company access three houses down. She should have parked there and walked back, but her car had a mind of its own, obviously.

She walked down the sidewalk, trying to recall her former neighbors' names. The Taylors lived in the blue house. They had two girls who were younger than she was. The Hendersons were in the redbrick ranch with the big picture window. Her brother had hit a baseball through that window once. She cut back through the path the energy company kept trimmed so the transformers could be reached and walked along the edge of the culvert. They'd done some drainage work, but in the distance she could see the old weeping willow tree. Beneath it was a bench. Sitting on that bench was Melanie.

Tennyson stopped a few feet from the bench.

Melanie wore an old T-shirt and capri leggings, and her hair was in a ponytail. Her old friend looked tired, even defeated. Melanie bit her lip and looked up. "Thanks for coming."

"Sure. So what's the deal?"

"You want to sit down?" Melanie asked, moving over to make room for Tennyson.

She wasn't sure if she wanted to sit down. Melanie wasn't showing much emotion, and while she was fairly sure the woman wasn't going to bodily assault her again, she wasn't sure how close she wanted to be to her former friend.

After a few seconds' hesitation, Melanie patted the space. "I won't bite. Or hit. Or try to choke you. Promise."

Tennyson shrugged and sank onto the warm bench. The sun was hot, making sweat trickle between her shoulder blades, and there wasn't much of a breeze between the two worlds the culvert separated. Felt like August, which meant it felt like waiting in line for a ticket into hell.

"Where'd you park?" Tennyson asked.

"In front of my old house. Thank goodness the Hamiltons still live next door. I told Mr. Marvin that I needed to take a picture because I wanted to paint the willow tree. He seemed a bit suspicious, but he let me go through his backyard."

"I parked in front of my old house, too. Looks shitty. People just don't care these days. My dad would be so upset to see his grass."

Melanie's mouth curved. "That man loved his lawn. Remember how he would sit out in his lawn chair and water the bare spots?"

"He was a bit nuts."

For a few seconds they sat, looking at the August-dry culvert and the dead grass lining it.

"When did they put a bench here?" Tennyson asked, only because she felt more and more awkward sitting beside Melanie. Was the woman going to say something? Apologize for the attempted manslaughter the night before? Suggest a good cover-up for the bruise? Finish what she had started?

Melanie shifted to reveal the placard on the back of the bench. **MARCUS JAMES (1968-1977)**. "I think it was the boy who drowned when there was that flash flood."

"I remember," Tennyson said, nodding. "My mom was always so afraid for me to come back here after it rained. I had to promise a million times I wouldn't go near it."

"Yeah, and then we did. Our parents were stupid to trust us. One time you fell in. Trying to get—"

"That cookie cutter," Tennyson finished for her. "We were making animal cookies from the mud."

Melanie chuckled. "Yeah."

"Mel, why did you Code Hot Pink me?"

Melanie swallowed and then stared out at the scraggly grass gathered around a telephone pole. "You remember when we were little, and we would talk about our kids. I was going to have twin girls—Molly and Megan. You were going to have just one—good job on that goal, by the way—and her name was going to be Sunrise."

"Yeah, I wasn't so great at the name game. My mom obviously instilled the bad-name-choice gene in me."

"Andrew's a good name."

"Stephen picked it," Tennyson said.

"Well, anyway, back then we would have loved to be where we are now. You know, our two kids marrying each other." Melanie stopped and looked down at her hands, which she'd been twisting in her lap. "I've made a mess of this."

Tennyson wanted to deny it, but she couldn't. They'd both made a lot of mistakes, but what happened yesterday wasn't something Tennyson could claim. She may have unintentionally had a hand in it, but the rest was all Melanie.

Finally, Melanie looked up at her. "I'm sorry, Tennyson. For what I did to you last night. It was . . . I have no excuse. I am really bad at jumping to conclusions and making assumptions. Emma came by this morning. She told me the truth. That you had been trying to help me."

"Okay, sure. I accept your apology." Suddenly she felt nervous. Like Melanie was about to take her somewhere she wasn't sure she wanted to go. Tennyson had been waiting for weeks for Melanie to broach the subject of their past and the mistakes they'd both made, but now she wasn't sure she wanted to wade in. Their past was like walking into a house so old a stiff wind could knock it down. Inside were spiderwebs, broken windows, and weak spots that could send her plummeting.

Better to accept the apology and return to a safe place. "You have a helluva right hook."

"Oh God. Don't remind me of how horribly I behaved."

"You know everyone behaves badly sometimes. Some of us more than others."

Melanie looked away, her face twisted with regret . . . pain. "I assumed you wanted to cause trouble between me and Kit, but the problem is, I've been the person causing the trouble. I've been looking to place blame for my rocky marriage on everyone but myself."

"Bullshit. Did Kit tell you that?"

Tears had gathered in her eyes and silently leaked out. "No. But I . . . I don't know. Things have been so difficult. And, no offense, but my daughter marrying the son of my former best friend turned enemy has been hard to deal with, especially on top of Hillary, my mother, and my husband's business partner trying to climb his leg. Our marriage hasn't been solid in a while. We've been disconnected from each other for so long that I don't know if we can find our way back. For someone everyone says 'has it together,' my life is falling spectacularly apart. You were an easy target."

Tennyson smiled. "I make myself an easy target."

"You didn't deserve what I did."

"Yeah, I did. That's why I didn't fight back. I could have, but somehow I couldn't because I knew that wasn't just about Kit. It was about the senior party, your grandmother's ashes, the broken baton, the calling 'dibs' first every time, and for essentially ruining your wedding and your father's career. I deserved this," she said, tapping her cheek.

Melanie looked over at her, the tears still coming, but questions were in her brown eyes.

Tennyson reached out and took Melanie's hand. "I was never an easy friend."

"But you were always a friend."

"Until I took that away. That was on me, Melanie. You tried to change that, and I couldn't accept you and Kit. You know me—I want all the toys." Tennyson paused and looked out at the spot where they had acted out little-girl fantasies. Back then, they'd been fierce friends, joined at the hip, invincible. "I wasn't sure why I came back to Shreveport. I mean, it was a weird choice."

"Andrew's here," Melanie said.

"Yeah, but still. It's not like I couldn't fly in to see him on occasion, and he's going to be busy making his own life. He has about twenty minutes a day, if that, for his old mom. No, the more I thought about it, the more I realized that subconsciously I couldn't move on, couldn't be happy, until I fixed what I did. But the thing is, that's impossible. It's like asking someone to empty an ocean one bucketful at a time. I can't undo what I did to your family."

Melanie turned her hand over, clasping Tennyson's. "True, but I'm tired of the past. Tired of being angry about it. Anger does no good. Just festers. Maybe that's why I'm where I am now. I didn't say anything to Hillary. Never fought back against my mother. And even with Kit, I pussyfooted around the truth. I'm my own worst enemy."

"We all are." Tennyson wiped her face, which was a mixture of flop sweat and a few stealth tears that had found their way to the party. "So what do we do about us?"

Melanie reached into the hidden pocket of her athletic capris and pulled something out. When she uncurled her hand, the best friends locket lay in her hand. Tennyson felt something stick in her throat. She knew it was more tears. Maybe a sob. Something that needed to come out.

"You remember this? You bought it when you went to Silver Dollar City," Melanie said.

Tennyson pulled her own locket out and held it up.

She could tell Melanie was surprised she had hers. Melanie's mouth curved into a smile as she took the jagged half heart between her thumb and finger and offered it to Tennyson. Tennyson did the same, fitting her piece into Melanie's. They held them connected for several seconds, both of them with tears sliding down their faces.

Tennyson finally pulled hers away and swiped at her face. "You used to say magical things happened when we put our hearts together."

Melanie smiled. "Because it's true."

Tennyson laughed. "Well, our children are getting married tomorrow. That's pretty magical. And we're sitting here together. Again."

Melanie nodded. "I can do you one better—Emma's pregnant."

Tennyson blinked. "Wait, what? Pregnant?"

"Yeah, we're going to be grandmothers. How's that for magic?" Melanie laughed, not even bothering to wipe the tears from her face.

Tennyson wasn't sure if it was the heat or Melanie's words, but suddenly she felt faint. She couldn't be a grandmother. Grandmothers were old. Joseph would dump her. No man his age slept with a grandmother. Oh God.

Melanie took the necklace and dropped it over her head. It fell onto her T-shirt, a high school homecoming shirt for a reunion Tennyson hadn't attended. "Emma said something to me this morning that was profound. I mean, the baby thing was a shock, no doubt, but it was something about me and you."

Tennyson waited a few moments, still grappling with the thought of Emma and Andrew being parents. They weren't old enough to get married, much less have a baby. It was all too much. "What did she say?"

"She said that when we are together, she can see how we once were better versions of ourselves. She said that I gave you a place to land and you gave me wings." Melanie paused and swallowed, the tears welling in her eyes again. "I felt that, you know. There were times over the month that I forgot I was supposed to hate you. There were times I felt like you needed me, and I needed you. Like there was this hole just waiting and yearning to be filled."

"You missed me." Tennyson looked down at her own necklace still in her hand.

"Yeah. I think I'm better when you're around. I feel like I'm more who I'm supposed to be, Teeny. You do that to me."

Those words were like pouring a ribbon of caramel, pooling and then filling that empty place with the sweetest emotion known to man. "That sounds crazy, you know. I mean, with everything between us."

Melanie issued a laugh. "Weird, huh? But I started to realize what you do for me. You make me bold. You make me expect more from my life. You push me—quite aggravatingly, I might add—to break out of my comfort zone. You don't let rules dictate your actions. You karate kick the rules, Tennyson. I didn't realize it, but I need you to remind me that my life is . . . well, a bit too vanilla."

"I've never been a fan of vanilla," Tennyson said, the necklace still wrapped in her hand.

Melanie laughed again. "I know you aren't. Everyone knows you aren't."

"So, um, I will admit that I need someone to kick my ass every now and then. Not literally. I don't like messing this up," Tennyson said, waving her hands down her body. "But I'm ridiculous, self-centered, overconfident, annoying, and often miss what is truly important in life because I worry too much about the stupid things. You don't do that. You hold me accountable, and you know the real me. Maybe you do give me a place to rest. Maybe that's what I've needed all along. 'Cause I'm tired of being . . . who I was."

This time, Tennyson reached over and took Melanie's hand. "I missed you, too, Melanie. There were so many times I needed your comfort, your faith in me, and your shoulder to cry on. I pretend a lot of shit, Mel. But you always gave me the real stuff, the stuff that really matters."

Tennyson dropped Melanie's hand, fell forward, and buried her face in her palms. Melanie's arms came around her, and she turned and clutched this woman who she once had vowed to hate for all eternity, but just never really did. "I'm sorry I hurt you, Melly."

"And I'm sorry I hurt you, Teeny," Melanie said, patting and rubbing her back.

After several seconds of sweating and crying on each other, they pulled away, each snuffling and drying her eyes. Tennyson looked over at Melanie, whose red, swollen face likely reflected her own. "So can we start over?"

Melanie picked up her necklace, the tarnished *be fri* barely visible. "I think we should try."

Tennyson slipped the necklace over her head, letting it fall on her sweaty chest. "Okay, then. We're going to do better, not just because of Emma and Andrew. Or the baby. But because *we* deserve a second chance."

"Yeah. I think that's exactly what we deserve." Melanie rose, tugging her shirt down. "Hey, don't bring the dog tonight."

"I'm not. Prada has a spa day planned at the doggy day care center. I felt guilty leaving her shut up all day," Tennyson said, rising and falling in beside her friend.

Her friend.

Could they ever get back what they had once had? Probably not. They were two different people. Still, Emma had seen what they couldn't—each needed the other in some way.

"I'll see you tonight," Melanie said, starting toward the bridge that traversed the culvert. "Oh, and I call dibs on my grandmother name."

Tennyson rolled her eyes. "Okay, fine. Whatever."

The grass tickled her shins as she swished back toward her old neighborhood. Then she stopped and turned around. "Wait, can't we just be Teeny and Melly?"

Melanie turned around and stood for a few seconds. Then she smiled. "That sounds . . . pretty perfect."

CHAPTER TWENTY-FOUR

Melanie sat at the head table beside Kit, cutting through succulent chicken and drinking the Italian wine Tennyson had flown in for the reception. Years and years before, she and Kit had been the bride and groom, and now she wasn't sure what they were. Parents of the bride. That was a safe moniker, one that had been used all day long.

"Mama of the bride, we need you here. Father of the bride, stand right here." Marc Mallow had uttered those words so many times that he probably had them tattooed across his forehead.

Around them, family and friends laughed, danced, and drank signature cocktails. The rooftop was open with twinkling lights strung like tiny fireflies against the dark sky, and she had to admit that for a three-month planning period, the wedding and reception had been spectacularly done.

The actual wedding had been so beautiful, reverent, gorgeous . . . just all the words. She would forever remember the way Andrew had looked when he saw Emma coming down the aisle toward him. That face, which reminded her so much of Tennyson when she was happy, had looked utterly in love with her daughter. Emma had been calm, but tears had glistened in her blue eyes. Melanie was certain that there hadn't been a dry eye in the church. Except maybe Marc's. He just looked like a cat who'd lapped up all the cream. Very knowing, that man.

Emma leaned over, holding her glass of sparkling cider. "Did you tell Daddy about the baby?"

"No, sugar. That is yours to tell."

"But you told Tennyson."

Melanie glanced down the table to where Tennyson sat next to her handsome cop. Her friend looked flushed, slightly tipsy, and a bit like a woman in love as she laughed at something Joseph said. "You told me to make peace with Teeny. I needed some ammunition."

Emma followed her gaze. "I knew something had changed because you both behaved for two days in a row."

"Do I get a gold star?" Melanie asked.

"Maybe," Emma quipped, adding a smile. "I'm happy. I mean, obviously. I'm just glad you and Tennyson could find middle ground."

That was what the meeting spot had always been about. Two girls from separate worlds finding a way to bridge, connect, and forge a friendship that hadn't been so easy to toss away. When she'd met Tennyson the day before, she'd finally examined who she was, where she came from, and what she'd settled for. She'd spent almost half a century content to be in the shadows, taking what she was given, and supremely satisfied that she'd won Kit. What kind of woman claimed nabbing her husband as her greatest achievement?

And that was a huge problem. There had been an imbalance between her and Kit from the beginning. She'd taken a back seat to him, bowing to his wishes and visions, and being grateful for what she had instead of wanting more for herself.

Then Tennyson had landed like a pack of firecrackers on the Fourth of July and proceeded to blow apart her tidy, ungratifying world, causing it to explode in a dizzying array of color and noise. Yesterday, she'd realized that she'd needed that in her life more than she could ever have known. Emma was right. They fit each other.

Marc Mallow appeared at the microphone as the band wound down "Mustang Sally." He wore an impeccably tailored navy-blue suit with a lime-green-and-lilac bow tie. His glasses were a shocking crimson. In other words, he looked perfect. "Folks, folks, it's time the groom and bride cut their cake. I'm warning you now that their mothers are a bit dangerous around cake. Janie Thackery, sugar, you make sure you stand in the back or something."

Everyone gave amused chuckles. Tennyson leaned over, looked at Melanie, and rolled her eyes.

Marc turned to the band. "Let's have a song or two while the gorgeous bride and her lovestruck groom make their way to the cake."

There was the scrabbling of chairs as people rose.

Kit leaned over. "What's he talking about?"

"Tennyson and I got into a cake fight at the tasting."

Her husband's eyes widened. "Seriously?"

"Yeah. It was actually kind of fun. I stopped hating her when she smashed praline buttercream in my face."

"Are you drunk?" Kit asked, sounding like he was joking.

"No, but I'm trying," she said, draining the last of her champagne. "Are you coming to get the rest of your things?"

He stiffened. "I'm not sure. I really don't know what to do about us."

"Yeah, it's not easy, is it? But I have found it's not so bad sleeping by myself. I thought it would be. That I would be lonely, but . . . no."

Kit stilled before his forehead crinkled in thought. "So what are you saying?"

"That I think you should come pack up your things and find something more permanent than the Marriott." Until she said the words, she hadn't been sure. But more and more, she realized that she wasn't taking Kit back just because he wanted it. What she wanted mattered, too, and she wasn't so certain that she wanted the marriage she'd had with him. If they reconciled, it would include her terms. It would need to be a different marriage. She was done with letting her husband and everyone else walk all over her and tell her the sky was blue when she knew it wasn't.

She lifted her eyes to his. In those blue depths, she saw the surprise . . . and the hurt.

Good.

He needed to feel what she'd been feeling for the last few months. It would be good for Kit to feel a bit unwanted.

"You're not really serious, are you?" he asked, setting his highball glass on the table and turning to her. "I mean, I've been doing some thinking, and I'm not sure I should have left. I was confused, but after today, after watching our daughter make those vows, I remembered ours. We've had a good life together."

"We have, but you're right—we needed some space. I've been suffocating here lately, and I'm tired of feeling like I can't move. I'm not saying we're over, Kit, but we need some work. More work than I thought. So, yeah, I think we better move to weekly therapy and start examining who we each want to be as our world changes. Noah will be leaving, Emma is starting her own family, and I'm considering finding some other purpose than sweeping up dust motes, ordering A/C filters, and picking up your vitamins."

"But you can't," he said, shaking his head. "I didn't do anything wrong."

"You left. You started this. Don't look to me to fix it for you," she said, rising as the band launched into "We Are Family."

Something in her heart tore a bit when she thought about this song and the way Hillary had always sung it when they did karaoke, but then she felt a tug on her hand.

"Wanna dance, pretty lady?" Tennyson asked, angling her toward the dance floor.

Tennyson wore a tight violet dress with a huge bow above her rounded backside. There was no back in the thing, and her boobs were fluffy meringue atop the glittering bodice. There was a good chance if she shimmied a bit too hard, her girls were going to make an encore performance.

Hell, that could be the reason Tennyson wanted to dance. She was extraordinarily proud of those breasts. Obviously.

Melanie nodded. "All right, let's shake a leg and show Shreveport that we—"

"Are family?" Tennyson finished.

Melanie laughed. "Well, heck, I guess it's true now."

They made their way to the dance floor, stopping to give a hug here or there to friends and family who wanted to say how beautiful the wedding was, how gorgeous (and glowing) Emma looked, and who did the flowers, by the way? The whole time they wove through the guests, Melanie could feel her mother's gaze on her. Anne still hadn't spoken to Tennyson and had endured the wedding party pictures with a stoic expression that resembled a smile only when they did the pictures of Anne and Emma by themselves. Melanie cast a look at her mother right before she and Tennyson reached the dance floor. Her mother narrowed her eyes and frowned.

Melanie waved and gave her a big smile.

Tennyson lifted her hands and started gyrating, her old slinky-snake standby, and Melanie started her shoulder shake. The lights around the stage flashed pink, purple, and blue, and everyone was laughing and shaking it to the surprisingly good band Andrew had found through a friend.

Melanie looked at Tennyson, who sang along, pointing her finger at Melanie when she got to the "I got all my sisters and me," and felt tears prick at her eyes. This was the way it was supposed to be—her and Teeny laughing with each other again. She was grateful. Lord, she was grateful that they had found each other again.

Because life was fun when Teeny was in it.

Then Emma and Andrew showed up, dancing with them, delight in their eyes. The bracelet Melanie had given her the night before glinted in the flashing lights, representing the newly united family.

The traditional first dances had been sedate and sentimental. This was altogether different. This was a celebration. As if sensing the same, the band rolled right into "Celebration."

Melanie giggled when Tennyson grabbed her hand and twirled her beneath her arm. She returned the favor, much as she'd done when they were eleven years old, dancing to Kool and the Gang when the song was new. Joseph appeared, looking very much the hot cop that Tennyson had dubbed him, in his tuxedo with the purple tie that she bet Tennyson had paid too much for. He grabbed Tennyson around the waist and grooved with her.

Kit joined them, too, looking less joyous but determined that the wedding reception would be one to remember for Emma and Andrew. He caught her eye, and she smiled at him.

Maybe.

She wasn't sure if she and Kit would make it. Oh, she still loved him, but sometimes love wasn't enough. Not if it erased one of the people.

Kit took her hand and pulled her to him. "You look gorgeous tonight, Mel. Even prettier than the day I married you. Thank you for giving me the world."

Melanie smiled. "You're welcome."

Then she let his hand go and grabbed Tennyson's. Her friend rocked and rolled, her feet bare because no one could dance in the things she'd worn for the wedding.

"I have something for you," Melanie yelled over the music.

"You do?" Tennyson asked, dipping low.

"Your boobs are about to fall out," Melanie called down to her.

Tennyson's eyes lit with amusement. "That's why I'm taped up."

The song ended, and everyone moved over to the table with the cake, where Marc stood looking perturbed that the band had gone rogue and gotten him off schedule. The confection was gorgeous with beautiful flowers that mimicked the ballet-pink ones on Emma's dress. Melanie's daughter and new son-in-law stood behind the cake and thanked everyone for coming. A photographer swarmed like a yellow jacket, snapping pictures, buzzing this way and that. He turned and snapped one of her and Tennyson when they were unprepared.

"Lord, I'm all sweaty," Melanie said.

"Me too, but who cares? We just burned a crap ton of calories. I'm eating a big piece of cake. Now what did you want to give me?"

Melanie held up her wrist and unclasped one of the bracelets she wore. She took Tennyson's arm and fastened the bracelet there. Tennyson watched with a bemused look on her face. After Melanie released her hand, Tennyson brought her arm up and caught hold of the gold circlet with the small medallion that read **4EVER**.

"That's what we forgot," Melanie said.

"What?"

"You bought us the best friends necklace. We should have added the *4ever*. That's been the problem. We forgot the *4ever*."

Tennyson's eyes sheened with tears. "Well, of course. How stupid of us."

"Yep. And I have one, too. To remind me that some things should be forever." Melanie held her own arm up and wriggled it so the bracelet flashed in the dim lighting. It was her apology, her promise to her friend.

Together they turned as Andrew smashed a piece of cake all over Emma's face.

"He totally takes after his mother." Melanie laughed.

Emma retaliated by pouring champagne on Andrew's head. The two young newlyweds then dissolved into laughter, kissing one another and licking the icing off their fingers. Everyone around them smiled and clapped.

"How come no one clapped when we did that?" Tennyson asked.

"Because we were displaying 'bad behavior,'" Melanie said, hooking her fingers in the air and grinning.

"Well, my dear, that's the absolute best kind," Tennyson said, wiping away the moisture glistening in her eyes.

Melanie smiled as the band struck up "Brick House." "They're playing our song."

Tennyson nodded. "Let's go."

Melanie had a sneaking suspicion that she would be hearing those words often in the next few years. And that was perfectly fine with her.

Time to fly.

ACKNOWLEDGMENTS

I'm often asked how I come up with story ideas. It's easy—all you must do is have an active imagination and friends who love the absurd. This book came about on a walk with my writer friends Phylis Caskey and Jennifer Moorhead. As we often do, we were chatting about our lives, and at one point I said, "Oh my goodness. Can you imagine those two women having to do a wedding together?" And then I immediately said, "That would make a good book. I might write that book." They both said, "You absolutely should."

And so I did.

Tennyson came to me very easily, as did Melanie. They blossomed into real people, and I felt as if I had known them all my life. Their story was a joy to write . . . and all that goodness originated in laughter with friends. Maybe the best stories come from laughing with friends.

So I would like to acknowledge Phylis and Jennifer for their contributions, creativity, and humor. I would also like to acknowledge my editor, Alison Dasho, who has steadfastly believed in me, and my agent, Michelle Grajkowski, who is my biggest cheerleader (other than my mother). Special thanks to Selina Mclemore for her editing skills and the entire team at Montlake and Amazon Publishing, who have always been helpful. Special thank-you to Kayla Southard of Moonlight and Lace Weddings for her insights into planning a wedding. A special shout-out to my Fiction from the Heart sisters Tracy Brogan, Jamie

Beck, Sonali Dev, K. M. Jackson, Virginia Kantra, Donna Kauffman, Sally Kilpatrick, Falguni Kothari, Priscilla Oliveras, Hope Ramsay, and Barbara Samuels. They give me wings.

And as always, my love to my family. My mother and father come to all my signings, rain or shine. My husband is great at carrying boxes and quietly cheering for my successes. And my boys are good at saying, "Cool, Mom," when I tell them fun things about writing.

Finally, I acknowledge all of you who buy my books and thus become part of my life. Without readers, there is no reason to write. It's a contract between me and you and fulfilled when you close the last page. My sincere thank-you for spending this time with me.

DISCUSSION QUESTIONS

1. Wedding planning can be a huge stressor on families. What is the benefit of spending so much time, energy, and money on an event like this? How does planning a wedding help bring mothers, daughters, or other family members closer together? How can it help blend two families into one?

2. Melanie and Tennyson complement one another well. Do you relate more strongly to one or the other of them? Would you like a friend (or do you have a friend) like Mel or Teeny?

3. Melanie's mother, Anne, prioritizes keeping up appearances over all things. What does this cost her, in terms of her relationships? Do you think she understands the things she's lost, or do you think she believes she's been right to always focus on how things appear to those outside the family?

4. Put yourself in Melanie's shoes. Could you ever forgive Tennyson for the way she acted at the wedding?

5. Was Melanie's father's suicide due entirely to Tennyson's revelations at the wedding? What other hints does the author give us about his character and his frame of mind? Do you think he might have committed suicide one day even if Tennyson had not revealed his secret so publicly?

6. How do Tennyson and Melanie use their wealth to hide or cover up their emotions?

7. Who was your favorite character in the novel? Who did you dislike the most, and why?

8. What do you think the future holds for Melanie and Kit? Will they reconcile? Should they, in your opinion?

9. What about Tennyson and Hot Cop? Do they seem to have a relationship that will endure, or will she wind up alone again?

10. How valuable are female friendships in today's world? What can a close friend give you that a spouse may not provide?

ABOUT THE AUTHOR

Photo © 2017 Courtney Hartness

A finalist for both the Romance Writers of America's prestigious Golden Heart and RITA Awards, Liz Talley is the author of *Room to Breathe*, *Come Home to Me*, and *Charmingly Yours* and *Perfectly Charming* in the Morning Glory series, among many more novels. Finding a home writing heartwarming contemporary romance, the author sets her stories in the South, where the tea is sweet, the summers are hot, and the porches are wide. Liz lives in North Louisiana with her childhood sweetheart, two handsome children, three dogs, and a naughty kitty. Readers can visit Liz at www.liztalleybooks.com to learn more about her upcoming novels.